D1474982

CHILDREN'S CLASSICS
EVERYMAN'S LIBRARY

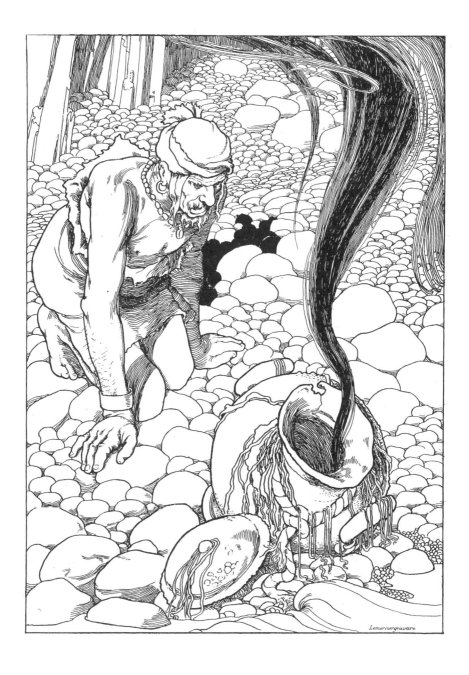

Aladdin

and other Tales from the Arabian Nights

With Illustrations by W. Heath Robinson and others

EVERYMAN'S LIBRARY
CHILDREN'S CLASSICS
Alfred A. Knopf New York London Toronto

THIS IS A BORZOI BOOK
PUBLISHED BY ALFRED A. KNOPF

First included in Everyman's Library Children's Classics 1993
Design and typography © 1993 by Everyman's Library
Book design by Barbara de Wilde, Carol Devine Carson
and Peter B. Willberg

Sixth printing (US)

Five of Ernest H. Shepard's illustrations from *Dream Days* by
Kenneth Grahame are reprinted on the endpapers by permission of
The Bodley Head, London. The sixth illustration is by S. C. Hulme Beaman.

US website: www.randomhouse.com/everymans

ISBN 978-0-679-42533-5 (US)
LC92-55071
978-1-85715-912-7 (UK)

A CIP catalogue record for this book is available from the British Library

Printed and bound in Germany by GGP Media GmbH, Pössneck

CONTENTS

THE STORY OF ALADDIN;
OR, THE WONDERFUL LAMP

PART I

I N the capital of one of the large and rich provinces of the king-dom of China there lived a tailor, whose name was Mustapha, so poor, that he could hardly, by his daily labour, maintain himself and his family, which consisted of a wife and son.

His son, who was called Aladdin, had been brought up after a very careless and idle manner, and by that means had contracted many vicious habits. He was wicked, obstinate, and disobedient to his father and mother, who, when he grew up, could not keep him within doors, but he would go out early in the morning, and stay out all day, playing in the streets and public places with little vagabonds of his own age.

When he was old enough to learn a trade, his father, not being able to put him out to any other, took him into his own shop, and showed him how to use his needle; but neither good words nor the fear of chastisement were capable of fixing his attention. All that his father could do to keep him at home to mind his work was in vain; for no sooner was his back turned than Aladdin was gone for that day. Mustapha chastised him, but

Aladdin was incorrigible; and his father, to his great grief, was forced to abandon him to his own devices; and was so much troubled at not being able to reclaim him, that he fell into an illness, of which he died in a few months.

The mother of Aladdin, finding that her son would not follow his father's business, shut up the shop, sold off the implements of the trade, and with the money she got for them, and what she could get by spinning cotton, hoped to maintain herself and her son.

Aladdin, who was now no longer restrained by the fear of a father, and who cared so little for his mother that, whenever she chid him, he would fly in her face, gave himself entirely over to dissipation, and was never out of the streets from his companions. This course he followed till he was fifteen years old, without giving his mind to any thing whatever, or the least reflection on what would become of him. Things being thus, as he was one day playing, according to custom, in the street, with his vagabond troop, a stranger passing by stood still to observe him.

This stranger was a famous magician, called the African Magician, as he was a native of Africa, and had been but two days come from thence.

The African magician had observed in Aladdin's countenance something which was absolutely necessary for the execution of the plan he came about; he enquired artfully about his family, who he was, and what was his disposition; and when he had learned all he desired to know, he went up to him, and taking him aside from his comrades, said to him, "Child, was not your father called Mustapha the tailor?"

"Yes, sir," answered Aladdin, "but he has been dead a long time."

At these words the African magician threw his arms about Aladdin's neck, and kissed him several times with tears in his eyes. "Alas! my son," cried the African magician with a sigh, "how can I forbear? I am your uncle; your good father was my own brother. I have been a great many years abroad travelling, and now that I am come home in the hope of seeing him, you tell me he is dead. It is a great grief to me to be deprived of the comfort I expected. But it is some relief that, so far as I can remember him, you are so like him." Then he asked Aladdin, putting his hand into his purse, where his mother lived; and as soon as Aladdin had informed him, he gave him a handful of small money, saying "Go, my son, to your mother, give my love to her, and tell her that I will come and see her to-morrow, if I have time, that I may have the satisfaction of seeing where my good brother lived so long, and ended his days."

As soon as the African magician left his newly-adopted nephew, Aladdin ran to his mother, overjoyed at the money his uncle had given him. "Mother," said he, "have I an uncle?"

"No, child," replied his mother, "you have no uncle on your father's side, or mine."

"I have just now come," answered Aladdin, "from a man who says he is my uncle on my father's side, assuring me that he is his brother. He cried and kissed me when I told him my father was dead; and to show you that what I tell you is the truth," added he, pulling out the money, "see what he has given me; he charged me to give his love to you, and to tell you, if he has any time to-morrow, he will come and pay you a visit, that he may see the house my father lived and died in."

"Indeed, child," replied his mother, "your father had a brother, but he has been dead a long time, and I never heard of another."

The mother and son talked no more then of the African magician; but the next day Aladdin's uncle found him playing in another part of the town with other children, and embracing him as before, put two pieces of gold into his hand, and said to him, "Carry this, child, to your mother, and tell her that I will come and see her to-night, and bid her get us something for supper; but first show me the house where you live."

After Aladdin had showed the African magician the house, he carried the two pieces of gold to his mother, and when he had told her of his uncle's intentions, she went out and bought provisions. She spent the whole day in preparing the supper; and at night, when it was ready, she said to Aladdin, "Perhaps your uncle knows not how to find our house; go and see, and bring him if you meet with him."

Though Aladdin had showed the magician the house, he was very ready to go, when somebody knocked at the door, which Aladdin immediately opened; and the magician came in loaded with wine, and all sorts of fruit, which he had brought for dessert.

After the African magician had given what he brought into Aladdin's hands, he saluted his mother, and desired her to show him the place where his brother

Mustapha used to sit on the sofa; and when she had so done, he presently fell down and kissed it several times, crying out, with tears in his eyes, "My poor brother! how unhappy am I, not to have come soon enough to give you one last embrace!" Aladdin's mother desired him to sit down in the same place, but he would not. "No," said he, "I shall take care how I do that; but give me leave to sit here over against it, that if I am deprived of seeing the master of a family so dear to me, I may at least have the pleasure of seeing the place where he used to sit." Aladdin's mother pressed him no farther, but left him at liberty to sit where he pleased.

When the magician had sat down, he began to enter into conversation with Aladdin's mother: "My good sister," said he, "do not be surprised at your never having seen me all the time you were married to my brother Mustapha, of happy memory. I have been forty years absent from this country, which is my native place, as well as my late brother's; and during that time have travelled into the Indies, Persia, Arabia, Syria, and Egypt, and have resided in the finest towns of those countries; and afterwards crossed over into Africa, where I made a longer stay. At last, as it is natural for a man, how distant soever it may be, to remember his native country, relations, and acquaintances, I was very desirous to see mine again, and to embrace my dear brother; and finding I had strength and courage enough to undertake so long a journey, I immediately made the necessary preparations, and set out. I will not tell you the time it took me, all the obstacles I met with, what fatigues I have endured, to come hither; but nothing ever mortified and afflicted me so much as hearing of my brother's death, for whom I always had a brotherly love and friendship. I observed his features in the face of my nephew, your son, and distinguished him from among a number of children with whom he was at play; he can tell you how I received the most melancholy news that ever reached my ears. But it is a comfort to me to find him again in a son who has his most remarkable features."

The African magician, perceiving that Aladdin's mother began to weep at the remembrance of her husband, changed the conversation, and turning towards Aladdin, asked him his name.

"I am called Aladdin," said he.

"Well, Aladdin," replied the magician, "what business do you follow? Are you of any trade?"

At this question Aladdin hung down his head, and was not a little abashed when his mother made answer, "Aladdin is an idle fellow; his father, when alive, strove all he could to teach him his trade, but could not succeed; and since his death, notwithstanding all I can say to him, he does nothing but idle away his time in the streets, as you saw him, without considering that he is no longer a child; and if you do not make him ashamed of it, and make him leave it off, I despair of his ever coming to any good. He knows that his father left him no fortune, and sees me endeavour to get bread by spinning cotton every day; for my part, I am resolved one of these days to turn him out of doors, and let him provide for himself."

After these words, Aladdin's mother burst into tears; and the magician said, "This is not well, nephew; you must think of helping yourself, and getting your livelihood. There are a great many sorts of trades; consider if you have not a liking for some of them; perhaps you did not like your father's trade, and would prefer another: come, do not disguise your feelings from me; I will endeavour to help you." But finding that Aladdin returned no answer, "If you have no mind," continued he, "to learn any trade and prove an honest man, I will take a shop for you, and furnish it with all sorts of fine stuffs and linens, and set you to trade with them; and the money you make of them lay out in fresh goods, and then you will live in an honourable way. Tell me freely what you think of it: you shall always find me ready to keep my word."

This proposal greatly flattered Aladdin, who mortally hated work, and had sense enough to know that such shops were very much esteemed and frequented, and the owners honoured and respected. He told the magician he had a greater liking for that business than for any other, and that he should be very much obliged to him all his life for his kindness. "Since this profession is agreeable to you," said the African magician, "I will take you with me to-morrow, and clothe you as richly and handsomely as the best merchants in the city, and after that we will think of opening such a shop as I mean."

Aladdin's mother, who never till then could believe that the magician was her husband's brother, no longer doubted it after his promises of kindness to her son. She thanked him for his good intentions; and after having exhorted Aladdin to render him worthy of his uncle's favour by his good behaviour, served up supper, at which they talked of several indifferent matters; and then the magician, who saw that the night was pretty far advanced, took his leave of the mother and son, and retired.

He came again the next day, as he promised, and took Aladdin with him to a great merchant, who sold all sorts of clothes for different ages and ranks, ready made, and a variety of fine stuffs. He asked to see some that suited Aladdin in size; and after choosing a suit which he liked best, and rejecting others which he did not think handsome enough, he bid Aladdin choose those he preferred. Aladdin, charmed with the liberality of his new uncle, made choice of one, and the magician immediately bought it, and all things necessary, and paid for it without haggling.

When Aladdin found himself so handsomely equipped from top to toe, he returned his uncle all imaginable thanks: who, on the other hand, promised never to forsake him, but always to take him with him; which he did to the most frequented places in the city, and particularly to where the chief merchants kept their shops. When he brought him into the street where they sold the richest stuffs and finest linens, he said to Aladdin, "As you are soon to be a merchant as well as these, it is proper you should frequent these shops, and be acquainted with them." Then he showed him the largest and finest mosques, and took him to the khans or inns where the merchants and travellers lodged, and afterwards to the sultan's palace, where he had free access; and at last he took him to his own khan, where, meeting with some merchants he had got acquainted with since his arrival, he treated them, to make them and his pretended nephew acquainted.

This treat lasted till night, when Aladdin would have taken his leave of his uncle to go home; but the magician would not let him go by himself, but conducted him safe to his mother, who, as soon as she saw him so finely dressed, was transported with joy, and bestowed a thousand blessings upon the magician, for being at so great an expense for her child. "Generous relation!" said she, "I know not how to thank you for your liberality! I know that my son is not deserving of your favours; and was he never so grateful, he would be unworthy of them. For my part," added she, "I thank you with all my soul, and hope you may live long enough to be a witness of my son's gratitude, which he cannot better show than by regulating his conduct by your good advice."

"Aladdin," replied the magician, "is a good boy, and minds well enough, and I believe we shall do very well; but I am sorry for one thing, which is, that I cannot perform to-morrow what I promised, because it is Friday, and the shops will be shut up, and therefore we cannot hire or furnish one, but must leave it till Saturday. But I will call on him to-morrow, and take him to walk in the gardens, where the most fashionable people generally walk. Perhaps he has never seen these amusements, he has only been hitherto among children; but now he must see men." Then the African magician took his leave of the mother and son, and retired. Aladdin, who was overjoyed to be so well clothed, looked forward to the pleasure of walking in the gardens which lay about the town. He had never been out of the town, nor seen the environs, which were very beautiful and pleasant.

Aladdin rose early the next morning, and dressed himself, to be ready when his uncle called on him; and after he had waited some time, he began to be impatient, and stood watching for him at the door; but as soon as he perceived him coming, he told his mother, took leave of her, and ran to meet him.

The magician caressed Aladdin when he came to him. "Come along, my dear child," said he, "and I will show you fine things." Then he led him out at one of the gates of the city, to some large fine houses, or rather palaces, with beautiful gardens, into which anybody might go. At every house he came to, he asked Aladdin if he did not think it fine; and Aladdin was ready to answer, "Here is a finer house, uncle, than any we have seen yet." By this artifice, the cunning magician got Aladdin a good long way into the country; and, pretending to be tired, the better to rest Aladdin, he took the opportunity to sit down in one of the gardens by a fountain of clear water, which fell from a lion's mouth of

bronze into a great basin. "Come, nephew," said he, "you must be weary as well as I; let us rest ourselves, and we shall be better able to walk."

After they had sat down, the magician pulled from his girdle a handkerchief with cakes and fruit, which he had provided on purpose, and laid them on the edge of the basin. He broke a cake in two, gave one half to Aladdin, and ate the other himself. During this short repast, he exhorted his nephew to leave off keeping company with children, and to seek that of wise and prudent men, to improve by their conversation; "for," said he, "you will soon be at man's estate, and you cannot too early begin to imitate them." When they had eaten as much as they liked, they got up, and pursued their walk through the gardens, which were separated from one another only by small ditches, which marked out the limits without interrupting the communication: so great was the confidence the inhabitants reposed in each other. By this means, the African magician drew Aladdin insensibly beyond the gardens, and crossed the country, till they almost came to the mountains.

Aladdin, who had never been so far in his life before, began to feel much tired with so long a walk, and said to the magician, "Where are we going, uncle? We have left the gardens a great way behind us, and I see nothing but mountains; if we go much further, I do not know whether I shall be able to reach the town again."

"Never fear, nephew," said the false uncle; "I will show you another garden which surpasses all we have yet seen; it is not far off, it is but a little step; and when we come there, you will say that you would have been sorry to be so near it, and not to have seen it." Aladdin was soon persuaded; and the magician, to make the way seem shorter and less fatiguing, told him a great many stories.

At last they came between two mountains of moderate height and equal size, divided by a narrow valley, which was the place where the magician intended to bring Aladdin, to put into execution a design that had brought him from Africa to China. "We will go no further, now," said he to Aladdin: "I will show you here some very extraordinary things, such as nobody ever saw before; when you have seen them, you will thank me; but while I strike fire, do you gather up all the loose dry sticks you can see, to kindle a fire with."

Aladdin found there so many dried sticks that, before the magician had lighted a match, he had gathered up a great heap. The magician presently set them on fire, and when they were all in a blaze, the magician threw in some incense he had about him, which raised a great cloud of smoke. This he dispersed on each side, by pronouncing several magical words which Aladdin did not understand.

At the same time the earth trembled a little, and opened just before the magician and Aladdin, and showed a stone about half a yard square, laid horizontally, with a brass ring fixed into the middle of it, to raise it up by. Aladdin was so frightened at what he saw, that he would have run away; but he was to be useful to the magician, who caught hold of him, scolded him, and gave him such a box on the ear that he knocked him down, and nearly beat his teeth down his throat. Poor Aladdin got up again trembling, and, with tears in his eyes, said to the magician, "What have I done, uncle, to be treated in this severe manner?"

"I have my reasons for it," replied the magician: "I am your uncle, and supply the place of your father, and you ought to make no reply. But, child," added he, softening, "do not be afraid of anything; for I shall not ask anything of you, except that you should obey me punctually, if you would reap the advantages which I intended you should." These fair promises calmed Aladdin's fears and resentment; and when the magician saw that he was come to himself, he said to him: "You see what I have done by virtue of my

incense, and the words I pronounced. Know, then, that under this
stone there is hidden a treasure, which is destined to be yours,
and which will make you richer than the greatest monarch in the
world: this is so true, that no other person but yourself is permitted to touch this stone, and to pull it up and go in; for I am forbidden ever to touch it, or to set foot in this treasure when it is

opened; so you must without fail execute what I tell you, for it is a matter of great consequence both to you and to me."

Aladdin, amazed at all he saw and heard the magician say of the treasure, which was to make him happy for ever, forgot what was past, and rising up, said to the magician: "Well, uncle, what is to be done? Command me; I am ready to obey you."

"I am overjoyed, child," said the African magician, embracing him, "to see you make the resolution: come, take hold of the ring, and lift up that stone."

"Indeed, uncle," replied Aladdin, "I am not strong enough to lift it; you must help me."

"You have no occasion for my assistance," answered the magician; "if I help you, we shall not be able to do anything; you must lift it up yourself; take hold of the ring, only pronounce the names of your father and grandfather, then lift it up, and you will find it will come easily." Aladdin did as the magician bade him, and raised the stone with a great deal of ease, and laid it on one side.

When the stone was pulled up, there appeared a cavity about three or four feet deep, with a little door, and steps to go down lower.

"Observe, my son," said the African magician, "what I am going to say to you: go down into that cave, and when you are at the bottom of those steps you will find a door open, which will lead you into a large vaulted place, divided into three great halls, in each of which you will see four large brass vessels placed on each side, full of gold and silver; but take care you do not meddle with them. Before you go into the first hall, be sure to tuck up your gown, and wrap it well about you, and then go through the second into the third without stopping. Above all take care that you do not touch the walls, so much as with your clothes; for if you do, you will die instantly. At the end of the third hall, you will find a door which leads to a garden planted with fine trees loaded with fruit; walk direct across the garden by a path which will lead you to five steps that will bring you upon a terrace, where you will see a niche before you, and in that niche a lighted lamp. Take the lamp down, and put it out; when you have thrown away the wick, and poured out the liquor, put it in your breast and bring it to me. Do not be afraid that the liquor will spoil your clothes, for it is not oil; and the lamp will be dry as soon as it is thrown out. If you have a mind for any of the fruit in the garden, you may gather as much as you please."

After these words, the magician drew a ring off his finger, and put it upon one of Aladdin's, telling him that it was a charm against all evil, so long as he observed what he had prescribed to him. After these instructions he said, "Go down boldly, child, and we shall both be rich all our lives."

Aladdin jumped into the cave, went down the steps, and found the three halls just as the African magician had described them. He went through them with all the precaution the fear of death could inspire; crossed the garden without stopping, took down the lamp from the niche, threw out the wick and the liquor, and, as the magician told him, put it in his bosom. But as he came down from the terrace, he stopped in the garden to observe the fruit, which he had only had a glimpse of in crossing it. All the trees were loaded with extraordinary fruit, of different colours on each tree. Some bore fruit entirely white, and some clear and transparent as crystal; some pale red, and others deeper; some green, blue, and purple, and others yellow: in short there were fruits of all colours. The white were pearls; the clear and transparent, diamonds; the deep red, rubies; the paler, ballas rubies; the green, emeralds; the blue, turquoises; the purple, amethysts; and those that were of yellow cast, sapphires; and so on with the rest. All these fruits were so large and beautiful that nothing was ever seen like them. Aladdin was altogether ignorant of their value, and would have preferred figs and grapes, or any other fruits instead. And though he took them only for coloured glass of little value, yet he was so pleased with the colours and the beauty and extraordinary size of the fruit, that he gathered some of every sort; and accordingly filled his two pockets, and the two new purses his uncle had bought for him with the clothes; and as he could not put them in his pockets, he fastened them to his girdle. Some he wrapped up in the skirts of his gown, which was of silk, large and wrapping, and crammed his breast as full as it could hold.

Having thus loaded himself with riches he knew not the value of, Aladdin returned through the three halls with the same precaution, and made all the haste he could, that he might not make his uncle wait, and soon arrived at the mouth of the cave, where the African magician awaited him with the utmost impatience. As soon as Aladdin saw him, he cried out, "Pray, uncle, lend me your hand, to help me out."

"Give me the lamp first," replied the magician, "it will be troublesome to you."

"Indeed, uncle," answered Aladdin, "I cannot now; it is not troublesome to me: but I will as soon as I am up."

The African magician was so obstinate, that he would have the lamp before he would help him up; and Aladdin, who had encumbered himself so much with his fruit that he could not well get at it, refused to give it to him till he was out of the cave. The African magician, provoked at this obstinate refusal of the lad, flew into a terrible passion, and threw a little of his incense into the fire, which he had taken care to keep in, and no sooner had he

pronounced two magical words than the stone which had closed
the mouth of the cave moved into its place, with the earth over it,
in the same manner as it had been at the arrival of the magician
and Aladdin.

This action of the African magician plainly showed him to be
neither Aladdin's uncle, nor Mustapha the tailor's brother; but a
true African. For as Africa is a country whose inhabitants delight
more in magic than those of any other part of the whole world, he
had applied himself to it from his youth; and after about forty
years' experience in enchantments, fumigations, and reading of
magic books, he had found out that there was in the world a wonderful lamp, the possession of which, if he could obtain it, would
render him more powerful than any monarch in the world; and by
a recent operation he found out that this lamp lay concealed in a
subterranean place in the midst of China. Fully persuaded of the
truth of this discovery, he set out from the furthest part of Africa;
and after a long and fatiguing journey, he came to the town nearest
to this treasure. But though he had a certain knowledge of the
place where the lamp was, he was not permitted to take it himself,
nor to enter the subterranean place where it was, but must receive
it from the hands of another person. For this reason he addressed
himself to Aladdin, whom he looked upon as a young lad of no consequence, and fit to serve his purpose, resolving, as soon as he got
the lamp into his hands, to sacrifice poor Aladdin to his avarice and
wickedness by making the fumigation mentioned before, and saying those two magical words, the effect of which was to remove
the stone into its place again, that he might have no witness of
what he had done.

The blow he gave Aladdin, and the authority he assumed over
him, were only to accustom him to fear him, and to make him obey
the more readily, and give him the lamp as soon as he asked for it.
But his too great hurry in executing his wicked intention on poor

Aladdin, and his fear lest somebody should come that way during their dispute and discover what he wished to keep secret, produced an effect quite contrary to what he proposed.

When the African magician saw that all his great hopes were frustrated for ever, he started that same day for Africa; but went quite round the town, and at some distance from it, for fear lest any persons who had seen him walk out with the boy should see him come back without him, entertain suspicions, and stop him.

According to all appearances there was no prospect of Aladdin being heard of any more. But when the magician plotted his death, he had forgotten the ring he put on his finger, which preserved him, though he knew not its virtue; and it is amazing that the loss of that, together with the lamp, did not drive the magician to despair; but magicians are so much used to misfortunes that they do not lay them to heart, but still feed themselves, all their lives, with unsubstantial notions.

As for Aladdin, who never suspected this bad usage from his pretended uncle, after all his caresses and what he had done for him, his surprise is more easily imagined than described. When he found himself buried alive, he cried, and called out to his uncle, to tell him he was ready to give him the lamp; but all in vain, since his cries could not be heard, and he remained in this dark abode. At last, when he had quite tired himself out with crying, he went to the bottom of the steps, to get into the garden, where it was light; but the door, which was opened before by enchantment, was now shut by the same means. Then he redoubled his cries and tears, and sat down on the steps, without any hope of ever seeing the light again, and in a melancholy certainty of passing from the present darkness into a speedy death.

Aladdin remained in this state for two days, without eating or drinking, and on the third day looked upon death as inevitable. Clasping his hands with entire resignation, he said, "There is no

strength or power but in the great and high God." In joining his
hands he rubbed the ring which the magician had put on his
finger, and of which he knew not yet the virtue, and immediately a
genie of enormous size and frightful look rose out of the earth, his
head reaching the vault, and said to him, "What wouldst thou?
I am ready to obey thee as thy slave, and the slave of all who

have the ring on thy finger; I and the other slaves of that ring."

At another time, Aladdin, who had not been used to such visions, would have been so frightened, that he would not have been able to speak; but the danger he was in made him answer without hesitation, "Whoever thou art, deliver me from this place, if thou art able." He had no sooner made an end of these words, than the earth opened, and he found himself on the very spot where the magician had first brought him.

It was some time before Aladdin's eyes could bear the light, after having been so long in total darkness: but after he had endeavoured by degrees to look about him, he was very much surprised not to find the earth open, and could not comprehend how he had got so soon out of it. There was nothing to be seen but the place where the fire had been, by which he could nearly judge whereabouts the cave was. Then turning towards the town, he perceived it in the midst of the gardens that surrounded it, and knew the way back by which the magician had brought him; then, returning God thanks to see himself once more in the world, where he had never expected to be, he made the best of his way home. When he got to his mother's door, his joy at seeing her, and his faintness for want of food for three days, made him swoon, and he remained for a long time as dead. His mother, who had given him over for lost or dead, seeing him in this condition, omitted nothing to bring him to himself again. As soon as he recovered, the first words he spake, were, "Pray, mother, give me something to eat, for I have not put a morsel of anything into my mouth these three days."

His mother brought what she had, and set it before him. "My son," said she, "be not too eager, for it is dangerous; eat but a little at a time, and take care of yourself. Besides, I would not have you talk; you will have time enough to tell me what has happened to you, when you have recovered. It is a great comfort to me to see you again, after the grief I have been in since Friday, and the pains I have taken to learn what had become of you, ever since night came, and you had not returned."

Aladdin took his mother's advice, and ate and drank moderately. When he had done, "Mother," said he, "you believed he was my uncle, as well as I; and what other thoughts could we entertain of a man who was so kind to me? But I must tell you, mother, he is a rogue and a cheat, and only did what he did, and made me all those promises, to accomplish my death; but for what reason neither you nor I can guess. For my part, I can assure you I never gave him any cause to deserve the least ill treatment from him. You shall judge of it yourself, when you have heard all that passed from the time I left you, till he came to the execution of his wicked plan."

Then Aladdin began to tell his mother all that had happened to him from the Friday, when the magician took him to see the palaces and gardens about the town, and what happened on the way, till they came to the place between the two mountains, where the strange deeds were performed; how, with incense which the magician threw into the fire, and some magical words which he pronounced, the earth opened, and discovered a cave, which led to an inestimable treasure. He did not forget the blow the magician gave him, and in what manner he softened again, and got him by great promises, putting a ring on his finger, to go down into the cave. He did not omit the least item of what he saw in crossing the three halls and the garden, and in taking the wonderful lamp, which he showed to his mother, as well as the transparent fruit of different colours, which he had gathered in the garden as he returned. But, though these fruits were precious stones, brilliant as the sun, she was as ignorant of their worth as her son, and cared nothing for them. She had been brought up in a middling rank of life, and her husband's poverty prevented his being possessed of such things, nor had she, or her relations or neighbours, ever seen them; so that we must not wonder that she looked on them as things of no value, and only pleasing to the eye by the variety of their colours.

Aladdin put them behind one of the cushions of the sofa he sat upon, and continued his story. When he came to the end, he said to his mother, "I need say no more; you know the rest. This is my adventure, and the danger I have been exposed to since you saw me."

Aladdin's mother heard, with patience, this surprising and wonderful story, though it caused no small affliction to a mother who loved her son tenderly; but yet in the part which disclosed the perfidy of the African magician, she could not help showing, by the greatest indignation, how much she detested him; and when Aladdin had finished his story, she broke out into a thousand reproaches against that vile impostor. She called him perfidious traitor, barbarian, assassin, deceiver, magician, and an enemy and destroyer of mankind. "Without doubt, child," added she, "he is a magician, and they are plagues to the world, and by their enchantments and sorceries have commerce with the Evil One. Bless God for preserving you from his wicked designs; for your death would have been inevitable, if you had not called upon Him, and implored His assistance." She said a great deal more against the magician's treachery; but finding that whilst she talked her son Aladdin began to nod, she put him to bed.

Aladdin, who had not had one wink of sleep while he was in the subterranean abode, slept very heartily all that night, and never waked till late the next morning; when the first thing he said to his mother was, he wanted something to eat. "Alas! child," said she, "I have not a bit of bread to give you; you ate up all the provisions I had in the house yesterday; but have a little patience, and it shall not be long before I will bring you some: I have a little cotton, which I have spun; I will go and sell it, and buy bread, and something for our dinner."

"Mother," replied Aladdin, "keep your cotton for another time, and give me the lamp I brought home with me yesterday; I will go and sell that, and the money I shall get for it will serve both for breakfast and dinner, and perhaps supper too."

Aladdin's mother took the lamp, and said to her son, "Here it is, but it is very dirty; if it was a little cleaner I believe it would fetch something more." She took a little fine sand and water to clean it; but no sooner had she begun to rub it than a hideous genie of gigantic size appeared before her, and said in a voice like

thunder, "What wouldst thou have? I am ready to obey thee as thy slave, and the slave of all those who have that lamp in their hands; I, and the other slaves of the lamp."

Aladdin's mother was not able to speak at the sight of this frightful genie, but fainted away; when Aladdin, who had seen such a genie in the cavern, without losing time on reflection, snatched the lamp out of his mother's hands, and said to the genie boldly, "I am hungry; bring me something to eat." The genie disappeared immediately, and in an instant returned with a large silver basin on his head, and twelve covered plates of the same metal, which contained excellent meats; six large white loaves on two other plates, two bottles of wine, and two silver cups in his hands. All these things he placed upon a table, and disappeared; and all this was done before Aladdin's mother came out of her swoon.

Aladdin went and fetched some water, and threw it on her face, to recover her. Whether that or the smell of the meats the genie procured brought her to life again, it was not long before she came to herself. "Mother," said Aladdin, "do not mind this; it is nothing at all; get up, and come and eat; do not let such fine meat get cold, but fall to."

His mother was very much surprised to see the great basin, twelve plates, six loaves, and the two bottles and cups, and to smell the delicious odour which exhaled from the plates. "Child," said she to Aladdin, "to whom are we indebted for this great plenty? Has the sultan been made acquainted with our poverty, and had compassion on us?"

"It is no matter, mother," said Aladdin; "let us sit down and eat; for you are in almost as much need of a good breakfast as myself; when we have done, I will tell you." Accordingly both mother and son sat down, and ate with first-rate appetites. But all the time Aladdin's mother could not forbear looking at and admiring the basin and plates, though she could not well tell whether they were silver or any other metal, so little accustomed were she and her son to see such things.

In short, the mother and son sat at breakfast till it was dinnertime, and then they thought it would be best to put the two meals together; yet after this they found they should have enough left for supper, and two meals for the next day.

When Aladdin's mother had taken away and set by what was left, she went and sat down by her son on the sofa. "Aladdin," said she, "I expect now that you should tell me exactly what passed between the genie and you while I was in a swoon;" which he at once complied with.

She was in as great amazement at what her son told her as at the appearance of the genie; and said to him, "But, son, what have we to do with genies? I never in my life heard that any of my acquaintance had ever seen one. How came that vile genie to address himself to me, and not to you, to whom he had appeared before in the cave?"

"Mother," answered Aladdin, "the genie you saw is not the same who appeared to me, though he resembles him in size; no, they had quite a different appearance and habits; they belong to different masters. If you remember, he that I first saw called himself the slave of the ring on my finger; and this one you saw called himself the slave of the lamp you had in your hand: but you did not hear him, for I think you fainted away as soon he began to speak."

"What!" cried his mother, "was your lamp the occasion of that

cursed genie's addressing himself to me rather than to you. Ah! my son, take it out of my sight, and put it where you please. I will never touch it. I had rather you would sell it than run the risk of being frightened to death again by touching it: and if you would take my advice, you would part also with the ring, and not have anything to do with genies, who, as our prophet has told us, are only devils."

"With your leave, mother," replied Aladdin, "I shall take care how I sell a lamp which may be so serviceable both to you and me. Have you not seen what it has procured us? It shall still continue to furnish us with subsistence. My false and wicked uncle would not have taken so much pains, and undertaken so long and tedious a journey, if it had not been to get into his possession this wonderful lamp, which he preferred before all the gold and silver which he knew was in the halls, and which I have seen with my own eyes. He knew too well the merit and worth of this lamp; and since chance has shown the virtue of it to us, let us make a profitable use of it, without making any great stir, and drawing the envy and jealousy of our neighbours upon us. However, since the genies frighten you so much, I will take it out of your sight, and put it where I may find it when I want it. As for the ring, I cannot resolve to part with that either, for without that you would never have seen me again; and though I am alive now, perhaps, if it was gone, I might not be so some moments hence; therefore I hope you will give me leave to keep that, and to wear it always on my finger. Who knows what dangers you and I may be exposed to, which neither of us can foresee, and from which it may deliver us?"

As Aladdin's arguments were just, and had great weight, his mother had nothing to say against them; but only replied, that he might do what he pleased, but for her part she would have nothing to do with genies, but would wash her hands of them, and never say anything more about them.

By the next day they had eaten all the provisions the genie had brought; and the next day Aladdin, who could not bear the thought of hunger, took one of the silver plates under his coat and went out early to sell it, and addressing himself to a man whom he met in the streets, took him aside, and pulling out the plate, asked him if he would buy it. The cunning man took the plate and examined it, and no sooner found that it was good silver than he asked Aladdin at how much he valued it. Aladdin, who knew

not the value of it, and never had been used to such traffic, told him he would trust to his judgment and honour. The man was somewhat taken aback at this plain dealing; and, doubting whether Aladdin understood the material or the full value of what he offered him, he took a piece of gold out of his purse and gave it him, though it was but the sixtieth part of the worth of the plate. Aladdin took the money very eagerly, and as soon as he got it in his pocket, retired with so much haste, that the man, not content with his exorbitant profit, was vexed he had not penetrated into Aladdin's ignorance, and was going to run after him to get some change out of the piece of gold; but Aladdin ran so fast, and had got so far, that it would have been impossible to overtake him.

Before Aladdin went home to his mother, he called at a baker's, bought a loaf, changed his money, and went home, and gave the rest to his mother, who went and bought provisions enough to last them some time. After this manner they lived, till Aladdin had sold the twelve plates, one at a time, to the man, for the same money; who, after the first time, durst not offer him less, for fear of losing so good a customer. When he had sold the last plate, he had recourse to the basin, which weighed ten times as much as the plate, and would have carried it to his old purchaser, except that it was too large and cumbersome; therefore he was obliged to bring him home with him to his mother's, where, after the man had examined the weight of the basin, he laid down ten pieces of gold, with which Aladdin was very well satisfied.

They lived on these ten pieces in a frugal manner a good while; and Aladdin, though formerly used to an idle life, had left off playing with young lads of his own age ever since his adventure with the African magician. He spent his time in walking about, and talking with people with whom he had got acquainted. Sometimes he would stop at the best merchants' shops, where people of distinction met, and listen to their talk, by which he gained some little knowledge of the world.

When all the money was spent, Aladdin had recourse again to the lamp. He took it in his hand, looked for the place where his mother had rubbed it with the sand, and rubbed it also, and the genie immediately appeared, and said, "What wouldst thou have? I am ready to obey thee as thy slave and the slave of those who have that lamp in their hands; I, and the other slaves of the lamp."

"I am hungry," said Aladdin; "bring me something to eat."

The genie disappeared, and presently returned with a basin, and the same number of covered plates, etc., and set them down on a table, and vanished again.

Aladdin's mother, knowing what her son was going to do, went out at that time about some business, on purpose to avoid being in the way when the genie came; and when she returned, which was not long afterwards, and found the table and sideboard so furnished a second time, she was almost as much surprised as before at the prodigious effect of the lamp. However she sat down with her son, and when they had eaten as much as they wanted, she set enough by to last them two or three days.

As soon as Aladdin found that their provisions and money were spent, he took one of these plates, and went to look for the man again; but as he passed by the shop of a goldsmith, who had the character of a very fair and honest man, the goldsmith called to him, and said, "My lad, I have often observed you go by, loaded as you are at present, and talk with a certain merchant, and then come back again empty-handed. I imagine that you carry something to sell to him; but perhaps you do not know what a rogue he is; he is the greatest rogue among all the merchants, and is so well known that nobody will have anything to do with him. What I tell you is for your own good. If you will show me what you now carry, and if it is to be sold, I will give you the full value of it; or I will direct you to other merchants who will not cheat you."

The hope of getting more money for this plate induced Aladdin to pull it from under his coat and show it to the goldsmith. The old man, who at first sight saw that it was made of the finest silver, asked him if he had sold any such as that to the merchant, and Aladdin told him plainly that he had sold him twelve such for a piece of gold each.

"What a villain!" cried the goldsmith; "but," added he, "my son, what is past cannot be recalled. By showing you the value of this plate, which is of the finest silver we use in our shops, I will let you see how much the merchant has cheated you."

The goldsmith took a pair of scales, weighed the plate, and after he had told Aladdin how much an ounce of fine silver was worth, he showed him that his plate was worth by weight sixty pieces of gold, which he paid him down immediately. "If you dispute my honesty," said he, "you may go to any other of our trade, and if he gives you any more, I will forfeit twice as much."

Aladdin thanked him for his good advice, so greatly to his advantage, and never after went to any other person, but sold him all his plates and the basin, and had as much for them as the weight came to.

Though Aladdin and this mother had an inexhaustible treasure of money in their lamp, and might have had whatever they had a mind to, yet they lived with the same frugality as before, except that Aladdin went more neat; as for his mother, she wore no clothes but what she earned by spinning cotton. Hence the money for which Aladdin had sold the plates and basin was sufficient to maintain them some time. They went on for many years by the help of the produce that Aladdin, from time to time, made of his lamp.

During this time Aladdin frequented the shops of the principal merchants, where they sold cloth of gold and silver, and linens, silk stuffs and jewellery, and oftentimes joining in their conversation, acquired a complete knowledge of the world, and assumed its manners. From his acquaintance with the jewellers, he came to know that the fine fruit which he had gathered, when he took the lamp, was not coloured glass, but stones of extraordinary value. For as he had seen all sorts of jewels bought and sold in the shops, but none so beautiful or so large as his, he found that instead of coloured glass he possessed an inestimable treasure; but he had the prudence not to say anything of it to any one.

One day, as Aladdin was walking about the town, he chanced to see the Princess Badroulboudour, the sultan's daughter, attended by a great crowd of ladies, slaves, and attendants, just at a moment when she unveiled her face. Aladdin had never seen any woman unveiled except his mother, and the princess was so beautiful that he was filled with amazement, and could think of nothing else for several days and nights. At last his mother inquired why he was so silent and absent-minded. "Mother," said Aladdin, "I cannot live without the beautiful and amiable Princess Badroulboudour, and I am firmly resolved to ask her in marriage from her father."

Aladdin's mother listened with attention to what her son told her; but when he talked of asking the Princess Badroulboudour in marriage of the sultan, she could not help bursting out into a loud laugh. Aladdin would have gone on, but she interrupted him: "Alas! child," said she, "what are you thinking of? you must be mad to talk so."

"I assure you, mother," replied Aladdin, "that I am not mad, but in my right senses: I foresaw that you would reproach me for folly and extravagance; but I must tell you once more, that I am resolved to demand the Princess Badroulboudour of the sultan in marriage, and your remonstrances shall not prevent me."

"Indeed, son," replied his mother, seriously, "I cannot help telling you that you have quite forgotten yourself; and I do not see who you can get to venture to propose it for you."

"You, yourself," replied he immediately.

"I go to the sultan!" answered his mother, amazed and surprised. "I shall take good care how I engage in such an affair. Why, who are you, son," continued she, "that you can have the assurance to think of your sultan's daughter? Have you forgotten that your father was one of the poorest tailors in the capital, and that I am of no better extraction; and do not you know that sultans never marry their daughters but to princes, sons of sultans like themselves?"

"Mother," answered Aladdin, "I have already told you that I foresaw all that you have said, or can say: and tell you again that neither your discourse nor your remonstrances shall make me change my mind. I have told you that you must ask the Princess Badroulboudour in marriage for me: it is a favour I request with all the respect I owe you; and I beg of you not to refuse me, unless you would rather see me in my grave, than by so doing give me new life."

The good old woman was very much embarrassed, when she found Aladdin so obstinately persisting in so foolish a design. "My son," said she again, "I am your mother, and there is nothing reasonable that I would not readily do for you. If I were to go and treat about your marriage with some neighbour's daughter, whose circumstances were equal to yours, I would do it with all my heart; and even then they would expect you to have some little estate or fortune, or be of some trade. When such poor folks as we are to marry, the first thing they ought to think of is how to live. But without reflecting on your lowly birth, and the little merit and fortune you have to recommend you, you aim at the highest; you demand in marriage the daughter of your sovereign, who with one single word can crush you to pieces. How could so extraordinary a thought come into your head, as that I should go to the sultan, and make a proposal to him to give his daughter in marriage to you? Suppose I had, not to say the boldness, but the impudence to present myself before the sultan and make so extravagant a request, to whom should I address myself to be introduced to his majesty? Do you not think the first person I should speak to would take me for a mad woman, and chastise me as I should deserve? Of course, I know there is no difficulty to those who go to ask justice, which he distributes equally among his subjects; I know too that to those who ask some favour he grants it with pleasure when he sees that it is deserved, and the persons are worthy of it. But is that your case? And do you think you have deserved the favour you would have me ask for you? Are you worthy of it? What have you done, either for your prince or country? How have you distinguished yourself? If you have done nothing to merit so great a favour, nor are worthy of it, with what face shall I ask it? How can I open my mouth to make such a proposal to the sultan? His majestic presence and the splendour of his court would immediately silence me. There is another reason, my son, which you do not think of; nobody ever goes to ask a favour of the sultan without a present. But what presents have you to make? And if you had any that was worthy of the least attention of so great a monarch, what proportion could it bear to the favour you would ask? Therefore, reflect well on what you are about, and consider that you aspire to a thing which it is impossible for you to obtain."

Aladdin heard very calmly all that his mother could say to dissuade him from his design, and made answer: "I own, mother, it is great rashness in me to presume so far; and a great want of consideration to ask you with so much suddenness to go and make the proposal of my marriage to the sultan, without first taking proper measures to procure a favourable reception; I therefore beg your pardon. But be not surprised that I did not at first sight see everything that it was necessary to do to procure me the happiness I seek after. I love the Princess Badroulboudour beyond everything you can imagine; and shall always persevere in my design of marrying her, which is a thing I have determined and resolved on. I am much obliged to you for the hint you have given me, and look upon it as the first step I ought to take.

"You say it is not customary to go to the sultan without a present, and that I have nothing worthy of his acceptance. As to what you say about the present, do you not think, mother, that what I brought home with me the day on which I was delivered from certain death, may be an agreeable present? I mean those things you and I both took for coloured glass; they are jewels of inestimable value, and fit for the greatest monarch. I know the worth of them through frequenting the jewellers' shops; and you may take my word for it, all the jewels that I have seen in the best jewellers' shops were not to be compared to those we have, either for size or beauty. Neither you nor I know the value of ours; but I am persuaded that they will be received very favourably by the sultan; you have a large porcelain dish fit to hold them; fetch it, and let us see how they will look, when we have arranged them according to their different colours."

Aladdin's mother fetched the china dish, and he took the jewels out of the two purses in which he had kept them, and placed them in the dish. But the brightness and lustre they had in the daytime, and the variety of the colours, so dazzled the eyes of both mother and son that they were astonished beyond measure; for they had only seen them by the light of a lamp; and though Aladdin had seen them hang on the trees like fruit, beautiful to the eye, yet as he was then but a boy, he did not take much notice of them.

After they had admired the beauty of this present some time, Aladdin said to his mother, "Now you cannot excuse yourself from going to the sultan, under the pretext of not having a present to make him, since here is one which will gain you a favourable reception."

Though Aladdin's mother did not believe it to be so valuable as her son esteemed it, she thought it might nevertheless be agreeable to the sultan, and found that she had not anything to say against it, but kept thinking of the request Aladdin wanted her to make to the sultan. "My son," said she, "I cannot conceive that your present will have its desired effect, and that the sultan will message of yours, I shall have no power to open my mouth; and, therefore, I shall not only lose my labour, but the present, which you say is so extraordinarily valuable, and shall return home again in confusion. I have told you the consequences, and you ought to believe me; but," added she, "I will do my best to please you; though certainly he will either laugh at me, or send me back like a fool, or be in so great a rage as to make us both the victims of his fury."

She used a great many more arguments to make him change his mind; but Aladdin persisted, and his mother, as much out of tenderness as for fear he should be guilty of some worse piece of extravagance, consented.

As it was now late, and the time for going to the sultan's palace
was past, it was put off till the next day. The mother and son
talked of different matters the remaining part of the day; and
Aladdin took a great deal of pains to encourage his mother in
the task she had undertaken; while she, notwithstanding all
his arguments, could not persuade herself that she could ever
succeed; and it must be confessed she had reason enough
to doubt. "Child," said she to Aladdin, "if the sultan should
receive me as favourably as I wish for your sake, and hear my
proposal with calmness, and after this kind reception should
think of asking me where lie your riches and your estate (for he
will sooner enquire after these than your person), if, I say, he
should ask me the question, what answer would you have me give
him?"

"Let us not be uneasy, mother," replied Aladdin, "about what
may never happen. First, let us see how the sultan receives you,
and what answer he gives. If it should so happen that he desires to
be informed of all that you mention, I have thought of an answer,
and am confident that the lamp, which has assisted us so long, will
not fail me in time of need."

Aladdin's mother could not say anything against what her son
then proposed; but reflected that the lamp might be capable of
doing greater wonders than merely providing food for them. This
satisfied her, and at the same time removed all the difficulties
which might have prevented her from undertaking the service she
had promised her son; when Aladdin, who penetrated into his
mother's thoughts, said to her, "Above all things, mother, be sure
to keep the secret, for thereon depends the success;" and after
this caution, Aladdin and his mother parted to go to bed. Aladdin
rose at daybreak, and went and awakened his mother, begging her
to get dressed to go to the sultan's palace, and to get in first, as the
grand vizier, the other viziers, and all the great officers of state

went in to take their seats in the divan, where the sultan always presided in person.

Aladdin's mother did all that her son desired. She took the china dish, in which they had put the jewels the day before, tied up in two napkins, one finer than the other, and set out for the sultan's palace, to the great satisfaction of Aladdin. When she came to the gates, the grand vizier, and the other viziers and most distinguished lords of the court, were just gone in; and, notwithstanding the crowd of people who had business there, which was extraordinarily great, she got into the divan, which was a large spacious hall. She placed herself just before the sultan, the grand vizier, and the great lords, who sat in that council, on his right and left hand. Several cases were called, according to their order, and pleaded and adjudged, until the time the divan generally broke up, when the sultan rising, dismissed the council, and returned to his apartment, attended by the grand vizier; the other viziers and ministers of state returned, as also did all those whose business called them thither; some pleased with gaining their cases, others dissatisfied at the sentences pronounced against them, and some in expectation of theirs being heard at the next sitting.

Aladdin's mother, seeing the sultan rise and retire, and all the people go away, rightly judged that he would not come again that day, and resolved to go home. When Aladdin saw her return with the present, he knew not at first what to think, and from the fear he was in lest she should bring him some bad news, he had not courage enough to ask her any questions, till his mother, who had never set foot in the sultan's palace before, and knew not what was done there every day, freed him from his embarrassment, and said, "Son, I have seen the sultan, and am very well persuaded he has seen me too; for I placed myself just before him, and nothing could hinder him from seeing me; but he was so much taken up with all those who talked on all sides of him, that I pitied him, and wondered at his patience to hear them. At last I believe he was heartily tired, for he rose up suddenly, and would not hear a great many who were prepared to speak to him, but went away, at which I was very well pleased, for indeed I began to lose all patience, and was extremely tired with staying so long. But there is no harm done; I will go again to-morrow; perhaps the sultan may not be so busy."

Though Aladdin was very violent, he was forced to be satisfied with this, and to fortify himself with patience. He had at least the satisfaction of finding that his mother had got over the greatest difficulty, which was to procure access to the sultan, and hoped that the example of those whom she saw speak to him would embolden her to acquit herself better when a favourable opportunity offered.

The next morning she went to the sultan's palace with the present, as early as the day before, but when she came there, she found the gates of the divan shut, and understood that the council only sat every other day, and that therefore she must come again the next. This news she carried to her son, whose only relief was patience. She went six times afterwards on the days appointed, placed herself always directly before the sultan, but with as little success as on the first time, and might have perhaps come a thousand times to as little purpose, if the sultan himself had not taken particular notice of her.

At last, after the council had broken up, and when the sultan returned to his own apartment, he said to his grand vizier, "I have for some time observed a certain woman, who comes constantly every day that I go into council, and has something wrapped up in a napkin: she always stands up from the beginning of the breaking up of the council, and places herself just before me. Do you know what she wants?"

"Sir," replied the grand vizier, who knew no more than the sultan, but did not like to seem uninformed, "perhaps this woman has come to complain to your majesty that somebody has sold her some bad flour, or some such trifling matter." The sultan was not satisfied with this answer, but replied, "If this woman comes again next council-day, do not fail to call her, that I may hear what she has to say." The grand vizier made answer by kissing his hand, and lifting it up above his head, signifying his willingness to lose it if he failed.

By this time, Aladdin's mother was so much accustomed to go to the council, and stand before the sultan, that she did not think it any trouble, if she could but satisfy her son that she neglected nothing that lay in her power: so the next council-day she went to the divan, and placed herself before the sultan as usual; and before the grand vizier had made his report of business, the sultan perceived her, and compassionating her for having waited so long, he said to the vizier, "Before you enter upon any business, remember the woman I spoke to you about: bid her come near, and let us hear and despatch her business first." The grand vizier immediately called the chief of the officers; and pointing to her, bade him go to the woman, and tell her to come before the sultan.

The chief of the officers went to Aladdin's mother, and at a sign she followed him to the foot of the sultan's throne, where he left her, and retired to his place by the grand vizier. Aladdin's mother, following the example of a great many others whom she saw salute the sultan, bowed her head down to the carpet, which covered the steps of the throne, and remained in that posture till the sultan bade her rise, which she had no sooner done than the sultan said to her, "Good woman, I have observed you a long time; what business brings you here?"

At these words, Aladdin's mother prostrated herself a second time; and when she got up again, said, "Monarch of monarchs, before I tell your majesty the extraordinary and almost incredible business which brings me before your high throne, I beg of you to pardon the boldness or rather impudence of the demand I am going to make, which is so uncommon that I tremble, and am ashamed to propose it to my sultan." In order to give her the more freedom to explain herself, the sultan ordered everybody to go out of the divan but the grand vizier, and then told her she might speak without restraint.

Aladdin's mother, notwithstanding this favour of the sultan's to save her the trouble and confusion of speaking before so many people, was not a little apprehensive; therefore, she said, "I beg your majesty, if you should think my demand the least injurious or offensive, to assure me first of your pardon and forgiveness."

"Well," replied the sultan, "I will forgive you, be it what it will, and no hurt shall come to you: speak boldly."

When Aladdin's mother had taken all these precautions, for fear of the sultan's anger, she told him faithfully how Aladdin had seen the Princess Badroulboudour, and had fallen in love with her, the declaration he had made to her when he came home, and what she had said to dissuade him, "But," continued she, "my son, instead of taking my advice and reflecting on his boldness, was so obstinate as to threaten me with some desperate act if I refused to come and ask the princess in marriage of your majesty; and it was not till after doing violence to my feelings that I was forced to come, for which I beg your majesty once more to pardon not only me, but Aladdin my son for entertaining such a rash thought."

The sultan hearkened mildly, without showing the least anger; but before he gave her any answer, he asked her what she had brought tied up in that napkin. She took the china dish, which she had set down at the foot of the throne, before she prostrated herself before him; she untied it, and presented it to the sultan.

The sultan's amazement and surprise were inexpressible, when he saw so many large, beautiful, and valuable jewels collected in one dish. He remained for some time motionless with admiration. At last, when he had recovered himself, he received the present from Aladdin's mother's hand, crying out in a transport of joy, "How rich and how beautiful!" After he had admired and handled all the jewels, one after another, he turned about to his grand vizier, and showing him the dish, said, "Look here, and confess that your eyes never beheld anything so rich and beautiful before." The vizier was charmed. "Well," continued the sultan, "what sayest thou to such a present? Is it not worthy of the princess my daughter? And ought I not to bestow her on one who values her at so great a price?"

These words put the grand vizier into a great fright. The sultan had some time before signified to him his intention of bestowing the princess his daughter on a son of his; therefore he was afraid, and not without grounds, that the sultan might change his mind. Thereupon, going up to him, and whispering he said, "Sir, I cannot but own that the present is worthy of the princess; but I beg of your majesty to grant me three months before you come to a decision. I hope before that time that my son, on whom you have had the goodness to look with a favourable eye, will be able to make a nobler present than Aladdin, who is an entire stranger to your majesty."

Though the sultan was very sure that it was not possible for the vizier to provide so considerable a present for his son to make, he hearkened to him, and granted the favour. So turning to Aladdin's mother, he said to her, "Good woman, go home, and tell your son that I agree to the proposal you have made me; but I cannot marry the princess my daughter till some furniture I intend for her be got ready, which cannot be finished for three months; but at the end of that time come again."

Aladdin's mother returned home much more overjoyed than she could have imagined, and told Aladdin all that had happened.

Aladdin thought himself the most happy of all men at hearing this news, and thanked his mother for all the pains she had taken. When two of the three months were past, his mother one evening went to light the lamp, and finding no oil in the house, went out to buy some, and when she came into the city, found a general rejoicing. The shops, instead of being shut up, were open. The streets were crowded with officers in robes of ceremony, mounted on horses richly caparisoned, each attended by a great many footmen. Aladdin's mother asked the oil-merchant what was the meaning of all these doings. "Whence come you, good woman," said he, "that you don't know that the grand vizier's son is to marry the Princess Badroulboudour, the sultan's daughter, to-night? These officers that you see are to assist at the procession to the palace, where the ceremony is to be solemnised."

This was news enough for Aladdin's mother. She ran till she was quite out of breath home to her son, who little suspected any such thing. "Child," cried she, "you are undone! you depend upon the sultan's fine promises, but they will come to nothing." Aladdin was terribly alarmed at these words. "Mother," replied he, "how do you know the sultan has been guilty of breaking his promise?"

"This night," answered his mother, "the grand vizier's son is to marry the Princess Badroulboudour." She then related how she had heard it; so that he had no reason to doubt the truth of what she said.

At this Aladdin was thunderstruck. Any other man would have sunk under the shock; but soon he bethought himself of the lamp, which had till then been so useful to him; and without venting his rage in empty words against the sultan, the vizier, or his son, he only said, "Perhaps, mother, the vizier's son may not be so happy to-night as he thinks: while I go into my room, do you go and get supper ready." She accordingly went about it, and guessed that her son was going to make use of the lamp, to prevent the marriage if possible.

When Aladdin had got into his room, he took the lamp, and rubbed it in the same place as before, and immediately the genie appeared, and said to him, "What wouldst thou have? I am ready to obey thee as thy slave, and the slave of all those who have that lamp in their hands; I and the other slaves of the lamp."

"Hear me," said Aladdin; "thou hast hitherto brought me whatever I wanted as to provisions; but now I have business of the greatest importance for thee to execute. I have demanded

the Princess Badroulboudour in marriage of the sultan her father;
he promised her to me, but only asked three months' time; and
instead of keeping that promise, he has planned to marry her to
the grand vizier's son. I have just heard this, and have no doubt
of it. What I ask of you is, that you bring them both hither to me."

"Master," replied the genie, "I will obey you. Have you any
other commands?"

"None at present," answered Aladdin; and then the genie disappeared.

Aladdin went downstairs to his mother, with the same tranquillity of mind as usual; and after supper talked of the princess's
marriage as of an affair wherein he had not the least concern; and
afterwards sat up till the genie had executed his orders.

In the mean time, everything was prepared with the greatest
magnificence in the sultan's palace to celebrate the princess's
wedding; and the evening was spent with all the usual ceremonies
and great rejoicings.

Suddenly the genie, as the faithful slave of the lamp, to the
great amazement of bride and bridegroom, took them up, and
transported them in an instant to Aladdin's house, where he set
them down.

Aladdin had waited impatiently for this moment. "Take this
man," said he to the genie, "and shut him up, and come again to-
morrow." The genie took the vizier's son and carried him away;
and after he had breathed upon him, which prevented his stirring,
he left him.

Great as was Aladdin's love for the Princess Badroulboudour, he
did not talk much to her, but only said, "Fear nothing, adorable
princess; you are in safety. If I have been forced to come to this
extremity, it is not with any intention of affronting you, but to prevent an unjust rival's marrying you contrary to the sultan your
father's promise to me."

The princess, who knew nothing of these particulars, gave very little attention to what Aladdin said. The fright and amazement of so surprising and unexpected an adventure had put her into such a condition that he could not get one word from her.

Next morning the genie came at the hour appointed, and said to him, "I am here, master; what are your commands?"

"Go," said Aladdin, "fetch the vizier's son out of the place where you left him, and then take them back to the sultan's palace." The genie presently returned with the vizier's son, and in an instant they were transported into the palace. But we must observe, that all this time the genie never appeared to either the princess or the grand vizier's son. His hideous form would have made them die with fear. Neither did they hear anything of the discourse between Aladdin and him; they only perceived the motion, and their transportation from one place to another; which we may well imagine was enough to frighten them.

Next day the princess was very melancholy and alarmed, and the sultan and his wife thought she must either be mad, or else have had a bad dream.

The rejoicings lasted all that day in the palace, and the sultaness, who never left the princess, did all she could to divert her.

But the princess continued so gloomy and ill-tempered that the sultan, provoked with his daughter, said to her in a rage, with his sabre in his hand, "Daughter, tell me what is the matter, or I will cut off your head immediately."

The princess, more frightened at the menaces and tone of the enraged sultan than at the sight of the drawn sabre, at last broke silence, and said, with tears in her eyes, "My dear father the sultan, I ask your majesty's pardon if I have offended you, and hope you will have compassion on me when I have told you what a dreadful thing has happened." Then she told him all.

The sultan felt extreme uneasiness at so surprising an adventure. "Daughter," said he, "efface all these troublesome ideas out of your memory; I will take care and give orders that you shall have no more such disagreeable and insupportable adventures."

As soon as the sultan got back to his own apartment, he sent for the grand vizier. "Vizier," said he, "have you seen your son, and has he told you anything?"

The vizier replied, "No."

Then the sultan related all that the Princess Badroulboudour had told him, and said, "I do not doubt that my daughter has told me the truth; but nevertheless I should be glad to have it confirmed by your son; therefore go and ask him."

The grand vizier went immediately to his son, and communicated what the sultan had told him, and enjoined him to conceal nothing, but to tell him the whole truth.

"I will disguise nothing from you, father," replied the son, "for indeed all that the princess says is true. All this ill-usage does not the least lessen the respect and gratitude I entertain for the princess, and of which she is so deserving; but I must confess that, notwithstanding all the honour and splendour that attends my marrying my sovereign's daughter, I would much rather die than marry her if I must undergo again what I have already endured. I do not doubt but that the princess entertains the same sentiments, and that she will readily agree to part, which is so necessary both for her repose and mine. Therefore, father, I beg you to get the sultan's consent that our marriage may be broken off."

Notwithstanding the grand vizier's ambition to have his son allied to the sultan, the firm resolution which he saw he had formed to be separated from the princess made him go and give the sultan an account of what he had told him, assuring him that all was but too true, and begging him to give his son leave to retire from the palace, alleging, for an excuse, that it was not just that the princess should be a moment longer exposed to so terrible a persecution upon his son's account.

The grand vizier found no great difficulty in obtaining what he asked. From that instant the sultan, who had determined upon it already, gave orders to put a stop to all rejoicings in the palace and town, and sent post-haste to all parts of his dominions to countermand his first orders; and in a short time all rejoicings ceased.

This sudden and unexpected change gave rise, in both the city and kingdom, to various speculations and inquiries; but no other account could be given of it except that both the vizier and his son went out of the palace very much dejected. Nobody but Aladdin knew the secret. He rejoiced over the happy success procured for him by his lamp. But neither the sultan nor the grand vizier, who had forgotten Aladdin and his request, had the least thought that he had any hand in the enchantment which caused the marriage to be broken off.

Nevertheless, Aladdin waited till the three months were completed, which the sultan had appointed for the marriage between the Princess Badroulboudour and himself; but the next day sent his mother to the palace, to remind the sultan of his promise.

Aladdin's mother went to the palace, as her son had bidden her, and stood before the divan in the same place as before. The sultan no sooner cast his eyes upon her than he knew her again, and remembered her business, and how long he had put her off: therefore when the grand vizier was beginning to make his report, the sultan interrupted him, and said, "Vizier, I see the good woman who made me the present some months ago; forbear your

report till I have heard what she has to say." The vizier presently perceived Aladdin's mother, and sent the chief of the officers for her.

Aladdin's mother came to the foot of the throne, and prostrated herself as usual, and when she rose up again, the sultan asked her what she wanted. "Sir," said she, "I come to represent to your majesty, in the name of my son Aladdin, that the three months, at the end of which you ordered me to come again, are expired; and to beg you to remember your promise."

The sultan had little thought of hearing any more of a marriage which he imagined would be very disagreeable to the princess, when he considered only the meanness and poverty of Aladdin's mother, and this summons for him to be as good as his word was somewhat embarrassing to him; he declined giving an answer till he had consulted his vizier.

The grand vizier freely told the sultan his thoughts on the matter, and said to him, "In my opinion, sir, there is one certain way for your majesty to avoid so unequal a match without giving Aladdin any cause of complaint; which is, to set so high a value upon the princess, that were he never so rich, he could not come up to it. This is the only way to make him desist from so bold, not to say rash, an undertaking."

The sultan, approving of the grand vizier's advice, turned about to Aladdin's mother, and after some reflection, said to her, "Good woman, it is true sultans ought to be as good as their word, and I am ready to keep mine, by making your son happy by his marriage with the princess my daughter. But as I cannot marry her without some valuable present from your son, you may tell him, I will fulfil my promise as soon as he shall send me forty basins of massy gold, brim-full of the same things you have already made me a present of, and carried by the like number of black slaves, who shall be led by as many young and handsome white slaves, all dressed magnificently. On these conditions I am ready to bestow the princess my daughter on him; therefore, good woman, go and tell him so, and I will wait till you bring me his answer."

Aladdin's mother prostrated herself a second time before the sultan's throne, and retired. On her way home she laughed to herself at her son's foolish imagination. "Where," said she, "can he get so many large gold basins, and enough of that coloured glass to fill them? Must he go again to that subterranean abode, the entrance into which is stopped up, and gather them off the trees? But where will he get so many slaves such as the sultan requires? It is altogether out of his power, and I believe he will not be so well satisfied with my embassy this time." When she came home, full of these thoughts, she said to her son, "Indeed, child, I would not have you think any further of your marriage with the Princess Badroulboudour. The sultan received me very kindly, and I believe he was well disposed to you; but if I am not very much deceived, the grand vizier has made him change his mind." Then she gave her son an exact account of what the sultan said to her, and the conditions on which he consented to the match. Afterwards she said to him, "The sultan expects your answer immediately; but," continued she, laughing, "I believe he may wait long enough."

"Not so long, mother, as you imagine," replied Aladdin; "the sultan is mistaken if he thinks by this exorbitant demand to prevent my entertaining thoughts of the princess; his demand is but a trifle to what I could have done for her. But go and get us something for dinner, and leave the rest to me."

As soon as Aladdin's mother was gone out to the market, Aladdin took the lamp, and rubbed it; the genie appeared, and offered his services as usual. "The sultan," said Aladdin to him, "demands forty large basins of massy gold, brim-full of the fruits of the garden from whence I took this lamp you are slave to; and these he expects to have carried by as many black slaves, each preceded by a young, handsome, well-made white slave, richly clothed. Go and fetch me this present as soon as possible, that I may send it to him before the divan breaks up." The genie told him his command should be immediately obeyed, and disappeared.

A little while afterwards the genie returned with forty black slaves, each bearing on his head a basin of massy gold of twenty marks' weight, full of pearls, diamonds, rubies, and emeralds, all larger and more beautiful than those presented to the sultan before. Each basin was covered with a silver stuff, embroidered with flowers of gold: all these, and the white slaves, quite filled the house, which was but a small one, and the little court before it, and a little garden behind. The genie asked Aladdin if he had any other commands. Aladdin told him that he wanted nothing further then, and the genie disappeared.

When Aladdin's mother came back from the market, she was greatly surprised to see so many people and such vast riches. As soon as she had laid down her provisions, Aladdin said, "Mother, let us lose no time; before the sultan and the divan rise, I would have you return to the palace, and go with this present as the dowry he asked for the Princess Badroulboudour, that he may judge by my diligence and exactness how anxious I am to procure the honour of this alliance." Without waiting for his mother's reply, Aladdin opened the street-door, and made the slaves walk out; a white slave followed always by a black one with a basin on his head. When they were all out, the mother followed the last black slave, and he shut the door, full of hope that the sultan, after this present, which was such as he required, would at length receive him as his son-in-law.

The first white slave that went out of the house made all the people, who were going by and saw him, stop; and before they were all out of the house, the streets were crowded with spectators, who ran to see so extraordinary and noble a sight. The dress of each slave was so rich, both from the stuff and the jewels, that those who were dealers in them valued each at no less than a million of money. Besides the neatness and propriety of the dress, the good grace, noble air, and beauty of each slave was unparalleled; their grave walk at an equal distance from each other, the lustre of the jewels, which were large, and curiously set in their girdles of massy gold, and the precious stones in their  hats, put the crowds of spectators into such great admiration that they could not weary of gazing at them, and following them with their eyes as far as possible; but the streets were so crowded with people, that none could move out of the spot they stood on. As the procession had to pass through a great many streets to get to the palace, a great part of the city had an opportunity of seeing them. As soon as the first of the slaves arrived at the palace-gate, the porters formed themselves into order, and took him for a king, and were going to kiss the hem of his garment; but the slave, who was instructed by the genie, prevented them, and said, "We are only slaves; our master will appear at the proper time."

Then this slave, followed by the rest, advanced into the second court, which was very spacious, and in which the sultan's household was ranged during the sitting of the divan. The magnificence of the officers, who stood at the head of the troops, was very much eclipsed by the slaves who bore Aladdin's present, of which they themselves made a part. Nothing was ever seen so beautiful and brilliant in the sultan's palace before; and all the lustre of the lords of his court was not to be compared to them.

As the sultan, who had been informed of their coming to the palace, had given orders for them to be admitted when they came, they met with no obstacle, but went into the divan in good order, one part filing to the right, and the other to the left. After they had all entered, and had formed a great semicircle before the sultan's throne, the black slaves laid the basins on the carpet, and all prostrated themselves, touching the carpet with their foreheads, and the white slaves did the same. When they all rose again, the black slaves uncovered the basins, and then all stood with their arms crossed over their breasts.

In the meantime Aladdin's mother advanced to the foot of the throne, and having paid her respects, said to the sultan, "Sir, my son Aladdin is aware that this present, which he has sent your majesty, is much below the Princess Badroulboudour's worth; but hopes, nevertheless, that your majesty will accept it."

The sultan was not able to give the least attention to this compliment of Aladdin's mother. The moment he cast his eyes on the forty basins, brim-full of the most precious, brilliant, and beautiful jewels he had ever seen, and the fourscore slaves, who looked, from the comeliness of their persons and the richness and magnificence of their dress, like so many kings, he was so struck that he could not recover from his admiration; but instead of answering the compliment of Aladdin's mother, addressed himself to the grand vizier, who could no more than the sultan comprehend from whence such a profusion of riches could come. "Well, vizier," said he aloud, "who do you think it can be that has sent me so extraordinary a present? Do you think him worthy of the Princess Badroulboudour, my daughter?"

The vizier, notwithstanding his envy and grief to see a stranger preferred to his son, dared not say so. Aladdin's present was more than sufficient, therefore he returned this answer: "I am so far, sir, from thinking that the person who has made your majesty so noble a present is unworthy of the honour you would do him, that I should be bold to say he deserved much more, if I was not persuaded that the greatest treasure in the world ought not to be put on a level with the princess your majesty's daughter." This advice was applauded by all the lords who were then in council.

The sultan no longer hesitated, nor thought whether Aladdin was endowed with the qualifications requisite in one who aspired to be his son-in-law. The sight alone of such immense riches, and Aladdin's diligence in satisfying his demand without the least difficulty, easily persuaded him that he lacked nothing to render him accomplished, and such as he desired. Therefore, to send Aladdin's mother back with all the satisfaction she could desire, he said to her, "Good woman, go and tell your son that I wait to receive him with open arms, and the more haste he makes to come and receive the princess my daughter from my hands, the greater pleasure he will do me."

As soon as Aladdin's mother retired, overjoyed to see her son raised beyond all expectation to such great honour, the sultan put an end to the audience for that day; and rising from his throne, ordered that the princess's servants should come and carry the basins into their mistress's apartment, whither he went himself to examine them with her at his leisure. The fourscore slaves were not forgotten, but were conducted into the palace; and some time after, the sultan, telling the Princess Badroulboudour of their magnificent appearance, ordered them to be brought before her apartment, that she might see them through the lattice.

In the meantime Aladdin's mother got home, and showed in her face the good news she brought her son. "My son," said she to him, "you have now all the reason in the world to be pleased. Not to keep you too long in suspense, the sultan, with the approbation of the whole court, has declared that you are worthy to marry the Princess Badroulboudour, and waits to embrace you, and arrange your marriage; therefore lose no time in going to him."

Aladdin, charmed with this news, made very little reply, but retired to his room. There, after he had rubbed his lamp, the obedient genie appeared. "Genie," said Aladdin, "I want to bathe immediately, and you must afterwards provide me the richest and most magnificent robe ever worn by a monarch." No sooner were the words out of his mouth, than the genie rendered him, as well as himself, invisible, and transported him into a bath of the finest marble of all sorts of colours; where he was undressed, without seeing by whom, in a neat and spacious hall. From the hall he was led to the bath, and there rubbed and washed with all sorts of scented water. After he had passed through several degrees of heat, he came out, quite a different man from what he was before. When he returned into the hall, he found, instead of his own clothes, a suit the magnificence of which very much surprised him. The genie helped him to dress, and when he had done, transported him back to his own room, where he asked him if he had any other commands. "Yes," answered Aladdin, "I expect you to bring me, as soon as possible, a horse that surpasses in beauty and goodness the best in the sultan's stables, with a saddle, bridle, and harness worth a million of money. I want also twenty slaves, as richly clothed as those who carried the present to the sultan, to walk by my side and follow me, and twenty more to go before me in two ranks. Besides these, bring my mother six women-slaves to wait on her, as richly dressed at least as any of the Princess Badroulboudour's, each loaded with a complete suit fit for any sultaness. I want also ten thousand pieces of gold in ten purses. Go, and make haste."

As soon as Aladdin had given these orders, the genie disappeared and presently returned with the horse, the forty slaves, ten of whom carried each a purse with one thousand pieces of gold, and six women-slaves, each carrying on her head a different dress for Aladdin's mother, wrapped up in a piece of silver stuff, and presented them all to Aladdin.

Of the ten purses Aladdin took but four, which he gave to his mother, telling her that those were to supply her with necessaries; the other six he left in the hands of the slaves who brought them, with an order to throw them by handfuls among the people as they went to the sultan's palace. The six slaves who carried the purses, he ordered likewise to march before him, three on the right hand and three on the left. Afterwards he presented the six women-slaves to his mother, telling her they were her slaves, and that the dresses they had brought were for her use.

When Aladdin had thus settled matters, he told the genie he would call for him when he wanted him, and thereupon the genie disappeared. Aladdin's thoughts now were only of answering, as soon as possible, the desire the sultan had shown to see him. He despatched one of the forty slaves to the palace, with an order to address himself to the chief of the officers, to know when he might have the honour to come and throw himself at the sultan's feet. The slave soon acquitted himself of his message, and brought for answer that the sultan waited for him with impatience.

Aladdin immediately mounted his horse, and began his march in the order we have already described; and though he never was on a horse's back before, he rode with such extraordinary grace that the most experienced horseman would not have taken him for a novice. The streets through which he was to pass were almost instantly filled with an enormous crowd of people, who made the air echo with their shouts, especially every time the six slaves who carried the purses threw handfuls of gold into the air on both sides. Those who knew him once when he played in the streets like a vagabond, did not know him again; those who had seen him but a little while before hardly knew him, so greatly were his features altered: such were the effects of the lamp.

Much more attention was paid to Aladdin than to the pomp and magnificence of his attendants, which had been taken notice of the day before, when the slaves walked in procession with the present to the sultan. Nevertheless the horse was very much admired by good judges, who knew how to discern his beauties without being dazzled with the jewels and richness of the harness: and when the report was everywhere spread about that the sultan was going to give the Princess Badroulboudour in marriage to him, nobody thought of his birth, nor envied his good fortune, so worthy he seemed of it.

When he arrived at the palace everything was prepared for his reception; and when he came to the second gate, he would have alighted off his horse, agreeable to the custom observed by the grand vizier, the generals of the armies, and governors of provinces of the first rank; but the chief of the officers who waited on him by the sultan's order prevented him, and attended him to the council-hall, where he helped him to dismount. The officers formed themselves into two ranks at the entrance of the hall. The chief put Aladdin on his right hand, and through the midst of them led him to the sultan's throne.

As soon as the sultan perceived Aladdin, he was surprised to see him more richly and magnificently clothed than ever he had been himself. Besides, he had a certain air of unexpected

grandeur, very dif-
ferent from the
poverty his mother
had appeared in.

But notwith-
standing, his sur-
prise did not hinder
him from rising off
his throne, and
descending two or
three steps, quick
enough to prevent
Aladdin's throwing himself at his feet. He embraced him with all
the demonstrations of friendship. After this, Aladdin would have
cast himself at his feet again; but the sultan held him fast by the
hand, and obliged him to sit between him and the grand vizier.

Then Aladdin said, "I receive, sir, the honour which your
majesty out of your great goodness is pleased to confer on me; but
permit me to tell you that I have not forgotten that I am your
slave; that I know the greatness of your power, and that I am not
unaware how much my birth is below the splendour and lustre of
the high rank to which I am raised. I ask your majesty's pardon for
my rashness, but I cannot dissemble that I should die with grief if
I should lose my hope of marrying the princess."

"My son," answered the sultan, embracing him a second time,
"you would wrong me to doubt my sincerity for a moment."

After these words the sultan gave a signal, and immediately the
air echoed with the sound of trumpets and hautboys, and other
musical instruments: and at the same time the sultan led Aladdin
into a magnificent hall, where there was prepared a noble feast.
The sultan and Aladdin ate by themselves; the grand vizier and
the great lords of the court, according to their dignity and rank,

waited all the time. The conversation turned on different subjects; but all the while the sultan hardly ever took his eyes off him; and throughout all their conversation Aladdin showed so much good sense, that it confirmed the sultan in the good opinion he had of him.

After the feast, the sultan sent for the chief judge of his capital, and ordered him to draw up immediately a contract of marriage between the Princess Badroulboudour, his daughter, and Aladdin.

When the judge had drawn up the contract in all the requisite forms, the sultan asked Aladdin if he would stay in the palace, and solemnise the ceremonies of marriage that day. To which he answered, "Sir, though great is my impatience, yet I beg of you to give me leave to defer it till I have built a palace fit to receive the princess in; I therefore desire you to grant me a convenient spot of ground near your palace, that I may come the more frequently to pay

my respects to you, and I will take care to have it finished with all diligence."

"Son," said the sultan, "take what ground you think proper; there is land enough before my palace." After these words he embraced Aladdin again, who took his leave with as much politeness as if he had always lived at court.

Aladdin mounted his horse again, and returned home in the order he came, with the acclamations of the people, who wished

him all happiness and prosperity. As soon as he
dismounted he retired to his own room, took the
lamp, and called the genie as before. "Genie,"
said Aladdin, "I have had all the reason in the
world to commend you hitherto, but now if you
have any regard for the lamp your mistress, you
must show, if possible, more zeal and diligence
than ever. I want you to build me, as soon as you
can, a palace at a proper distance from the sultan's, fit to receive my wife the Princess
Badroulboudour. I leave the choice of the materials to you, that is to say, porphyry, jasper, agate,

lapis lazuli, and the finest marble of the most varied colours; and
the style of the building. But in the highest storey of this palace
you shall build me a large hall with a dome and four equal fronts;
and instead of layers of bricks, the walls shall be made of massy
gold and silver, laid alternately; each front shall contain six windows, the lattices of all of which shall be so enriched with diamonds, rubies, and emeralds that they shall exceed everything of
the kind that has ever been seen in the world. I would have an
inner and outer court before this palace, and a garden, but above
all things take care that there be laid in a place, which you shall
point out to me, a treasure of gold and silver coin. This palace
must be well provided with kitchens and offices, store-houses,
and rooms in which to keep choice furniture for every season of
the year. I must have stables full of the finest horses, with their
equerries and grooms, and hunting equipage. There must be
officers to attend the kitchens and offices, and women-slaves to
wait on the princess. You understand what I mean, therefore go
about it, and come and tell me when all is finished."

By the time Aladdin had instructed the genie with his intentions respecting the building of his palace, the sun was set. The

next morning by break of day, Aladdin was no sooner up than the genie presented himself, and said, "Sir, your palace is finished; come and see how you like it." The genie transported him thither in an instant, and he found it so much ⌣⌣yond his expectation that he could not enough admire it. The genie led him through all the apartments, where he met with nothing but what was rich and magnificent, with officers and slaves, all dressed according to their rank and the services to which they were appointed. Then the genie showed him the treasury, which was opened by a treasurer, where Aladdin saw heaps of purses of different sizes, piled up to the top of the ceiling. The genie assured him of the treasurer's fidelity, and thence led him to the stables, where he showed him some of the finest horses in the world, and the grooms busy dressing them. From thence they went to the storehouses, which were filled with all necessary provisions, for both the food and ornament of the horses.

When Aladdin had examined the palace from top to bottom, and particularly the hall with the four-and-twenty windows, and found it much beyond whatever he could have imagined, he said to the genie, "Genie, no one can be better satisfied than I am, and indeed I should be very much to blame if I found any fault. There is only one thing wanting, which I forgot to mention. That is, to lay from the sultan's palace to the door of the apartment designed for the princess, a carpet of fine velvet for her to walk upon." The genie immediately disappeared, and Aladdin saw what he desired executed that minute. Then the genie returned, and carried Aladdin home before the gates of the sultan's palace were opened.

When the porters, who had always been used to an open view, came to open the gates, they were amazed to find it obstructed, and to see a carpet of velvet spread. They did not immediately see what it meant, but when they saw Aladdin's palace distinctly, their surprise was increased. The news of so extraordinary a wonder spread through the palace. The grand vizier, who came soon after the gates were open, was no less amazed than the others, but ran and told the sultan, and endeavoured to make him believe it to be all enchantment. "Vizier," replied the sultan, "why do you say it is enchantment? You know as well as I that it is Aladdin's palace, which I gave him leave to build to receive my daughter in. After the proof we have had of his riches, can we think it strange that he should build a palace in so short a time? He intends to surprise us, and let us see what wonders are to be done with ready money every day. Confess sincerely to me that that enchantment you talk of proceeds from a little envy."

When Aladdin had been conveyed home, and had dismissed the genie, he found his mother up, and dressing herself in one of the suits that were brought her. By the time the sultan came from the council, Aladdin had prepared his mother to go to the palace with her slaves, and desired her, if she saw the sultan, to tell him she came to do herself the honour of attending the princess towards evening to her palace. Accordingly she went, but though she and the women-slaves who followed her were all dressed like sultanesses, yet the crowd was nothing like so great, because they were all veiled. As for Aladdin, he mounted his horse, and took leave of his paternal house for ever, taking care not to forget his wonderful lamp, and went to the palace with the same pomp as the day before.

As soon as the porters of the sultan's palace saw Aladdin's mother, they went and informed the sultan, who presently ordered the bands of trumpets, cymbals, drums, fifes and hautboys, placed in different parts of the palace, to play and beat, so that the air resounded with sounds which inspired the whole city with joy; the merchants began to adorn their shops and houses with fine carpets and cushions, and bedeck them with boughs, and prepare illuminations for the night. The artists of all sorts left their work, and the people all repaired to the great space between the sultan's and Aladdin's palaces; which last drew all their attention, not only because it was new to them, but because there was no comparison between the two buildings. But they could not imagine by what unheard-of miracle so magnificent a palace could be so soon built, it being apparent to all that there were no prepared materials, or any foundations laid the day before.

Aladdin's mother was received in the palace with honour, and introduced into the Princess Badroulboudour's apartment. As soon as the princess saw her, she went and saluted her, and desired her to sit down on her sofa: and while her women finished dressing her, and adorning her with the jewels with which Aladdin had presented her, a collation was served up. At the same time the sultan, who wanted to be as much with his daughter as possible

before he parted with her, came and paid her great respect. The sultan, who had always seen Aladdin's mother dressed very meanly, not to say poorly, was surprised to find her as richly and magnificently clothed as the princess his daughter. This made him think Aladdin equally prudent and wise in whatever he undertook.

When it was night, the princess took leave of the sultan her father, and set out for Aladdin's palace, with his mother on her left hand, followed by a hundred women-slaves, dressed with surprising magnificence. All the bands of music, which played from the time Aladdin's mother arrived, joined together and led the procession. Four hundred of the sultan's young pages carried torches on each side, which, together with the illuminations of the sultan's and Aladdin's palaces, made it as light as day.

At length the princess arrived at the new palace. Aladdin ran with all imaginable joy to receive her at the entrance. His mother had taken care to point him out to the princess, in the midst of the officers that surrounded him, and she was charmed as soon as she saw him. "Adorable princess," said Aladdin to her, saluting her respectfully, "if I have displeased you by my boldness in aspiring to so lovely a princess, and my sultan's daughter, I must tell you that you ought to blame yourself, not me."

"Prince (as I may now call you)," answered the princess, "I am obedient to the will of my father; and it is enough for me to have seen you, to tell you that I obey without reluctance."

Aladdin, charmed with so agreeable and satisfactory an answer, would not keep the princess standing after she had walked so far, but took her by the hand, which he kissed with joy, and led her into a large hall, illuminated with an infinite number of wax candles, where, by the care of the genie, a noble feast was served up. The plates were of massy gold. The vases, basins, and goblets, with which the sideboard was furnished, were gold also, and of exquisite workmanship. The princess, dazzled to see so much riches collected in one place, said to Aladdin, "I thought, Prince, that nothing in the world was so beautiful as the sultan my father's palace; but the sight of this hall alone is enough to show that I was deceived."

Then Aladdin led the princess to the place appointed for her, and as soon as she and his mother were sat down, a band of the most harmonious instruments, accompanied with the voices of beautiful ladies, began a concert, which lasted without intermission to the end of the repast. The princess was so charmed that she declared she never heard anything like it in the sultan her father's court; but she knew not that these musicians were fairies chosen by the genie, slaves of the lamp.

When the supper was ended, and the table taken away, there entered a company of dancers. At length, Aladdin, according to the custom of that time in China, rose up and presented his hand to the Princess Badroulboudour to dance with her, and to finish the ceremonies. They danced with so good a grace that they were the admiration of all the company. Thus ended the ceremonies and rejoicings at the marriage of Aladdin with the Princess Badroulboudour.

THE STORY OF ALADDIN

PART II

ALADDIN and his wife had lived happily after this manner for several years, when the African magician, who undesignedly had been the means of raising him to such good fortune, bethought himself of him in Africa, whither, after his expedition, he had returned. And though he was almost persuaded that Aladdin had died miserably in the subterranean abode where he left him, he had the curiosity to learn about his end with certainty. As he was a great magician, he took out of a cupboard a square covered box, which he made use of in his observations; then sat himself down on his sofa, set it before him, and uncovered it. After he had prepared and levelled the sand which was in it, to discover whether or no Aladdin died in the subterranean abode, he cast the points, drew the figures, and formed a horoscope, by which, when he came to examine it, he found that Aladdin, instead of dying in the cave, had escaped out of it, lived splendidly, was very rich, had married a princess, and was very much honoured and respected.

The magician no sooner understood by the rules of his diaboli-
cal art that Aladdin had arrived at that height of good fortune,
than a colour came into his face, and he cried out in a rage, "This
poor sorry tailor's son has discovered the secret and virtue of the
lamp! I believed his death to be certain, but find too plainly he
enjoys the fruit of my labour and study! But I will prevent his
enjoying it long, or perish in the attempt." The next morning the
magician mounted a horse which was in his stable, set out, and
stopped only to refresh himself and horse till he arrived at the capital of China. He alighted, took up his lodging in a khan, and
stayed there the remainder of the day and the night, to rest after
so long a journey.

The next day his first object was to inquire what people said of
Aladdin; and, taking a walk through the town, he went to the most
public and frequented places, where people of the highest distinction met to drink a certain warm liquor, which he had drunk
often when he was there before. As soon as he sat down he was
given a glass of it, which he took; but listening at the same time to
the discourse of the company on each side of him, he heard them
talking of Aladdin's palace. When he had drunk off his glass, he
joined them, and taking the opportunity, asked them what palace
it was they spoke so well of. "From whence come you?" said the
person to whom he addressed himself; "you must certainly be a
stranger not to have seen or heard talk of Prince Aladdin's palace
(for he was called so after his marriage with the Princess
Badroulboudour). I do not say," continued the man, "that it is one
of the wonders of the world, but that it is the only wonder of the
world; since nothing so grand, rich, and magnificent was ever
seen. Certainly you must have come from a great distance, not to
have heard of it; it must have been talked of all over the world. Go
and see it, and then judge whether I have told you more than the
truth."

"Forgive my ignorance," replied the African magician; "I arrived here but yesterday, and came from the furthest part of Africa, where the fame of this palace had not reached when I came away. For the affair which brought me hither was so urgent, that my sole object was to get here as soon as I could, without stopping anywhere, or making any acquaintance. But I will not fail to go and see it; I will go immediately and satisfy my curiosity, if you will do me the favour to show me the way."

The person to whom the African magician addressed himself was pleased to show him the way to Aladdin's palace. When he came to the palace, and had examined it on all sides, he doubted not that Aladdin had made use of the lamp to build it; for he knew that none but the genies, the slaves of the lamp, could have performed such wonders; and piqued to the quick at Aladdin's happiness and greatness, he returned to the khan where he lodged.

The next thing was to learn where the lamp was; if Aladdin carried it about with him, or where he kept it; and this he was able to discover by an operation of magic. As soon as he entered his lodging, he took his square box of sand, which he always carried with him when he travelled, and after he had performed some operations, he knew that the lamp was in Aladdin's palace, and so great was his joy at the discovery that he could hardly contain himself. "Well," said he, "I shall have the lamp, and I defy Aladdin to prevent my carrying it off and making him sink to his original meanness, from which he has taken so high a flight."

It was Aladdin's misfortune at that time to have gone hunting for eight days, of which only three were past. After the magician had performed the operation which gave him so much joy, he went to the master of the khan, entered into talk with him on indifferent matters, and among the rest, told him he had been to see Aladdin's palace; and added, "and I shall not be easy till I have seen the person to whom this wonderful edifice belongs."

"That will be no difficult matter," replied the master of the khan; "there is not a day passes but he gives an opportunity when he is in town, but at present he is not at home, and has been gone these three days on a hunting-match, which will last eight."

The magician wanted to know no more: he took leave of the master of the khan, and returning to his own chamber, said to himself, "This is an opportunity I ought by no means to let slip." For this purpose he went to a maker and seller of lamps, and asked for a dozen copper lamps: the master of the shop told him he had not so many by him, but if he would have patience till the next day, he would get them for him. The magician appointed this time, and bade him take care that they should be handsome and well polished. After promising to pay him well, he returned to his inn.

The next day the magician called for the twelve lamps, paid the man his full price for them, put them into a basket which he bought on purpose, and with the basket hanging on his arm, went straight to Aladdin's palace; and when he came near it he began crying, "Who will change old lamps for new ones?" As he went along, he gathered a crowd of children about him, who hooted at him, and thought him, as did all who chanced to be passing by, mad or a fool, to offer to change new lamps for old ones.

The African magician never minded all their scoffs and hootings, but still continued crying, "Who will change old lamps for new ones?" He repeated this so often, walking backwards and forwards about the Princess Badroulboudour's palace, that the princess, who was then in the hall with the four-and-twenty windows, hearing a man cry something, and not being able to distinguish his words, by reason of the hooting of the children and increasing mob about him, sent one of her women-slaves down to know what he cried.

It was not long before the slave returned, and ran into the hall, laughing heartily. "Well, giggler," said the princess, "will you tell me what are you laughing at?"

"Madam," answered the slave, laughing still, "who can help laughing to see a fool with a basket on his arm, full of fine new lamps, ask to change them for old ones; the children and mob, crowding about him so that he can hardly stir, make all the noise they can by deriding him."

Another woman-slave, hearing this, said, "Now you speak of lamps, I know not whether the princess has observed it, but there is an old one on the shelf, and whoever owns it will not be sorry to find a new one in its stead. If the princess has a mind she may have the pleasure of trying if this fool is so silly as to give a new lamp for an old one without taking anything for the exchange."

The lamp this slave spoke of was Aladdin's wonderful lamp, which he, for fear of losing, had laid on the shelf before he went hunting, which precaution he had taken several times before, but neither the princess, the slaves, nor the attendants had ever taken any notice of it. At all other times he carried it about with him, and then indeed he might have locked it up, but other people have been guilty of oversights as great, and will be so to the end of time.

The Princess Badroulboudour, who knew not the value of this lamp, and the importance for Aladdin, not to mention herself, of keeping it safe from everybody else, entered into the joke, and bade an attendant take it, and go and make the exchange. The attendant obeyed, went out of the hall, and no sooner got to the palace gates than he saw the African magician, called to him, and showing him the old lamp, said to him, "Give me a new lamp for this."

The magician never doubted but this was the lamp he wanted. There could be no other like it in this palace, where all was gold or silver. He snatched it eagerly out of the man's hand, and thrusting it as far as he could into his breast, offered him his basket, and bade him choose which he liked best. The man picked out one, and carried it to the Princess Badroulboudour, but the exchange was no sooner made than the place rang with the shouts of the children, deriding the magician's folly.

The African magician gave everybody leave to laugh as much as they pleased. He stayed not long about Aladdin's palace, but made the best of his way back without crying any longer "New lamps for old ones." His end was answered, and by his silence he got rid of the children and the mob.

As soon as he got out of the square between the two palaces he skulked down the streets which were the least frequented, and having no more need for his lamps or basket, set them all down in the midst of a street where nobody saw him; then scouring another street or two, he walked till he came to one of the city gates, and pursuing his way through the suburbs, which were very long, he bought some provisions before he left the city, got into the fields, and turned into a road which led to a lonely remote place, where he stopped for a time to execute the design he came about, never thinking about his horse, which he had left at the khan, but considering himself perfectly compensated by the treasure he had acquired.

In this place the African magician passed the remainder of the day, till the darkest time of night, when he pulled the lamp out of

his breast and rubbed it. At that summons the genie appeared, and said, "What wouldst thou have? I am ready to obey thee as thy slave, and the slave of all those who have that lamp in their hands, both I and the other slaves of the lamp."

"I command thee," replied the magician, "to transport me immediately and the palace which thou and the other slaves of the lamp have built in this town, just as it is, with all the people in it, to a place in Africa." The genie made no reply, but with the assistance of the other genies, the slaves of the lamp, transported him and the palace entire immediately to Africa, where we will leave the magician, palace, and the Princess Badroulboudour, to speak of the surprise of the sultan.

As soon as the sultan rose the next morning, according to custom, he looked out of the window to have the pleasure of contemplating and admiring Aladdin's palace. But when he first looked that way, and instead of a palace saw an empty space such as it had been before the palace was built, he thought he was mistaken, and rubbed his eyes. He looked again, and saw nothing more the second time than the first, though the weather was fine, the sky clear, and the daybreak had made all objects very distinct. He looked through the two openings on the right and left, and saw nothing more than he had formerly been used to see out of them.

His amazement was so great that he stood for some time turning his eyes to the spot where the palace had stood, but where it was no longer to be seen. He could not comprehend how so large a palace as Aladdin's, which he saw plainly every day, and but the day before, should vanish so soon and not leave the least trace behind. "Certainly," said he, to himself, "I am not mistaken. It stood there. If it had tumbled down, the materials would have lain in heaps, and if it had been swallowed up by an earthquake there would be some mark left." Though he was convinced that no palace stood there, he could not help staying there some time, to see whether he might not be mistaken. At last he retired to his apartment, not without looking behind him before he quitted the spot, and ordered the grand vizier to be fetched in all haste, and in the meantime sat down, his mind agitated by many different thoughts.

The grand vizier did not make the sultan wait long for him, but came with so much haste that neither he nor his attendants as they passed by missed Aladdin's palace; neither did the porters, when they opened the palace gates, observe any alteration.

When he came into the sultan's presence, he said to him, "Sir, the haste with which your majesty has sent for me makes me believe something very extraordinary has happened, since you know this is council-day, and I should not fail to attend you there very soon."

"Indeed," said the sultan, "it *is* something very extraordinary, as you say, and you will allow it to be so. Tell me what has become of Aladdin's palace."

"Aladdin's palace!" replied the grand vizier, in great amazement. "I thought, as I passed by, that it stood in its usual place; such substantial buildings are not so easily removed."

"Go to my window," said the sultan, "and tell me if you can see it."

The grand vizier went to the window, where he was struck with no less amazement than the sultan had been. When he was well assured that there was not the least appearance of this palace, he returned to the sultan. "Well," said the sultan, "have you seen Aladdin's palace?"

"Sir," answered the vizier, "your majesty may remember that I had the honour to tell you that that palace, which was the subject of your admiration, with all its immense riches, was only the work of magic and a magician, but your majesty would not pay the least attention to what I said."

The sultan, who could not deny what the grand vizier had represented to him, flew into a great passion. "Where is that impostor, that wicked wretch," said he, "that I may have his head cut off immediately?"

"Sir," replied the grand vizier, "it is some days since he came to take his leave of your majesty; he ought to be sent to to know what is become of his palace, since he cannot be ignorant of what has been done."

"That is too great a favour," replied the sultan: "go and order a detachment of thirty horse, to bring him to me loaded with chains." The grand vizier went and gave orders for a detachment of thirty horse, and instructed the officer who commanded them how they were to act, that Aladdin might not escape them. The detachment pursued their orders; and about five or six leagues from the town met him returning from hunting. The officer went up to him, and told him that the sultan was so impatient to see him, that he had sent them to accompany him home.

Aladdin had not the least suspicion of the true reason of their meeting him, but pursued his way hunting; but when he came within half a league of the city, the detachment surrounded him, and the officer addressed himself to him, and said, "Prince Aladdin, it is with great regret that I declare to you the sultan's order to arrest you, and to carry you before him as a criminal; I beg of you not to take it ill that we acquit ourselves of our duty, and to forgive us."

Aladdin, who felt himself innocent, was very much surprised at this declaration, and asked the officer if he knew what crime he was accused of; who replied he did not. Then Aladdin, finding that his retinue was much smaller than this detachment, alighted off his horse, and said to the officer, "Execute your orders; I am not conscious that I have committed any crime against the sultan's person or government." A large long chain was immediately put about his neck, and fastened round his body, so that both his arms were pinioned down; then the officer put himself at the head of the detachment, and one of the troopers took hold of the end of the chain, and proceeding after the officer, led Aladdin, who was obliged to follow him on foot, into the town.

When this detachment entered the suburbs, the people who saw Aladdin thus led as a state criminal, never doubted but that his head was to be cut off; and as he was generally beloved, some took sabres and other arms; and those who had none, gathered stones, and followed the detachment. The last five of the detachment faced about to disperse them; but their number presently increased so much that the detachment began to think that it would be well if they could get into the sultan's palace before Aladdin was rescued; to prevent which, according to the different extent of the streets, they took care to cover the ground by extending or closing. In this manner they arrived at the palace square, and there drew up in a line, and faced about till their officer and the troopers that led Aladdin had got within the gates, which were immediately shut.

Aladdin was carried before the sultan, who waited for him attended by the grand vizier on a balcony; and as soon as he saw him, he ordered the executioner, who waited there on purpose, to cut off his head, without hearing him, or giving him leave to clear himself.

As soon as the executioner had taken off the chain that was fastened about Aladdin's neck and body, and laid down a skin stained with the blood of the many criminals he had executed, he made Aladdin kneel down, and tied a bandage over his eyes. Then drawing his sabre, he prepared to strike the blow by flourishing it three times in the air, waiting for the sultan's signal to separate his head from his body.

At that instant the grand vizier, perceiving that the populace had forced the guard of horse, and crowded the great square before the palace, and were scaling the walls in several places and beginning to pull them down to force their way in, said to the sultan, before he gave the signal, "I beg of your majesty to consider what you are going to do, since you will risk your palace being forced; and who knows what fatal consequences may attend it?"

"My palace forced!" replied the sultan; "who can have such boldness?"

"Sir," answered the grand vizier, "if your majesty will but cast your eyes towards the great square, and on the palace walls, you will know the truth of what I say."

The sultan was so frightened when he saw so great a crowd, and perceived how enraged they were, that he ordered the executioner to put his sabre in the scabbard immediately, and to unbind Aladdin; and at the same time bade the officers declare to the people that the sultan had pardoned him and they might retire.

Then all those who had already got upon the walls and were witnesses of what had passed, got quickly down, overjoyed that they had saved the life of a man they dearly loved, and published the news among the rest, which was presently confirmed by the officers from the top of the terraces. The justice which the sultan had done to Aladdin soon disarmed the populace of their rage; the tumult abated, and the mob dispersed.

When Aladdin found himself at liberty, he turned towards the balcony, and perceiving the sultan, raised his voice, and said to him in a moving manner, "I beg of your majesty to add one favour more to that which I have already received, which is, to let me know my crime."

"Your crime!" answered the sultan: "perfidious wretch! do you not know it? Come up hither, and I will show you."

Aladdin went up, and presented himself to the sultan, who walked in front, without looking at him, saying, "Follow me;" and then led him into his room. When he came to the door, he said, "Go in; you ought to know whereabouts your palace stood; look round, and tell me what has become of it."

Aladdin looked round, but saw nothing. He perceived very well the spot of ground his palace had stood on; but not being able to divine how it had disappeared, this extraordinary and surprising event threw him into such great confusion and amazement that he could not answer one word.

The sultan growing impatient, said to him again, "Where is your palace, and what has become of my daughter?"

Then Aladdin, breaking silence, said to him, "Sir, I see very well, and own that the palace which I have built is not in the place where it was, but is vanished; neither can I tell your majesty where it may be, but I can assure you I have had no hand in it."

"I am not so much concerned about your palace," replied the sultan; "I value my daughter ten thousand times before it, and would have you find her out, otherwise I will cause your head to be struck off, and no consideration shall prevent it."

"I beg your majesty," answered Aladdin, "to grant me forty days to make my inquiries; and if in that time I have not the success I wish for, I will come again and offer my head at the foot of your throne, to be disposed of at your pleasure."

"I give you the forty days you ask for," said the sultan; "but think not to abuse the favour I show you by imagining you shall escape my resentment; for I will find you out in whatsoever part of the world you are."

Aladdin went out of the sultan's presence with great humiliation, and in a condition worthy of pity. He crossed the courts of the palace, hanging down his head, and in such great confusion that he dared not lift up his eyes. The principal officers of the court, who had all professed themselves his friends, and whom he had never disobliged, instead of going up to comfort him, and offer him a refuge in their houses, turned their backs on him to avoid seeing him, lest he should know them. But had they accosted him with a word of comfort or offer of service, they would not have known Aladdin. He did not know himself, and was no longer in his senses, as plainly appeared by his asking everybody he met, at every house, if they had seen his palace, or could tell him any news of it.

These questions made everybody believe that Aladdin was mad. Some laughed at him, but people of sense and humanity, particularly those who had had any connection of business or  friendship with him, really pitied him. For three days he rambled about the city after this manner, without coming to any decision, or eating anything, but what some good people forced him to take out of charity.

At last, as he could no longer, in his unhappy condition, stay in a city where he had formerly made so fine a figure, he quitted it, and took the road to the country; and after he had traversed several fields in frightful uncertainty, at the approach of night he came to a river-side. There, possessed by his despair, he said to himself, "Where shall I seek my palace? In what province, country, or part of the world, shall I find that and my dear princess? I shall never succeed; I had better free myself at once from so much fruitless fatigue and such bitter grief." He was just going to throw himself into the river, but, as a good Mussulman, true to his religion, he thought he could not do it without first saying his prayers. Going to prepare himself, he went first to the river-side to wash his hands and face, according to custom. But that place being steep and slippery, owing to the water's beating against it, he slid down, and would certainly have fallen into the river, but for a little rock which projected about two feet out of the earth. Happily also for him, he still had on the ring which the African magician put on his finger before he went down into the subterranean abode to fetch the precious lamp. In slipping down the bank he rubbed the ring so hard, by holding on the rock, that immediately the genie appeared whom he saw in the cave where the magician left him. "What wouldst thou have?" said the genie. "I am ready to obey thee as thy slave, and the slave of all those that have that ring on their finger; both I and the other slaves of the ring."

Aladdin, agreeably surprised at an apparition he so little expected, replied, "Save my life, genie, a second time, either by showing me to the place where the palace I have caused to be built now stands, or by immediately transporting it back to where it first stood."

"What you command me," answered the genie, "is not in my power; I am only the slave of the ring; you must address yourself to the slave of the lamp."

"If it be so," replied Aladdin, "I command thee, by the power of the ring, to transport me to the place where my palace stands, in what part of the world soever it is, and to set me down under the Princess Badroulboudour's window." These words were no sooner out of his mouth than the genie transported him into Africa, to the midst of a large meadow, where his palace stood, a small distance from a great city, and set him exactly under the windows of the princess's apartment, and then left him. All this was done almost in an instant.

Aladdin, notwithstanding the darkness of the night, knew his palace and the Princess Badroulboudour's apartment again very well; but as the night was far advanced, and all was quiet in the palace, he retired to some distance, and sat down at the foot of a large tree. As he had not slept for five or six days, he was not able to resist the drowsiness which came upon him, but fell fast asleep where he was.

The next morning, as soon as the dawn appeared, Aladdin was agreeably awakened not only by the singing of the birds which had roosted in the tree under which he had passed the night, but of all those which perched in the thick trees of the palace garden. When he cast his eyes on that wonderful building, he felt an inexpressible joy to think he should soon be master of it again, and once more see his dear Princess Badroulboudour. Pleased with these hopes, he immediately got up, went towards the princess's apartment, and walked under her window, in expectation of her rising, that he might see her. Meanwhile, he began to consider with himself from whence his misfortune proceeded; and after mature reflection, he no longer doubted that it was owing to his having put his lamp out of his sight. He accused himself of negligence, and the little care he took of it, to let it be a moment away from him. But what puzzled him most was that he could not imagine who had been so jealous of his happiness. He would soon have guessed this, if he had known that both he and his palace were in Africa, the very name of which would soon have made him remem-

ber the magician, his declared enemy; but the genie, the slave of
the ring, had not made the least mention of the name of the place,
nor had Aladdin asked him.

The Princess Badroulboudour rose earlier that morning than
she had done since her transportation into Africa by the magician,
whose presence she was forced to endure once a day, because he
was master of the palace; but she had always treated him so
harshly that he dared not reside in it. As she was dressing, one

of the women
looking through
the window per-
ceived Aladdin,
and ran and told
her mistress. The
princess, who
could not believe
the news, went
herself to the win-
dow, and seeing
Aladdin, immedi-

ately opened it. The noise the princess made in opening the window made Aladdin turn his head that way, and, knowing the
princess, he saluted her with an air that expressed his joy. "To lose
no time," said she to him, "I have sent to have the private door
opened for you; enter, and come up." She then shut the window.

The private door, which was just under the princess's apartment, was soon opened, and Aladdin was conducted up into the
princess's room. It is impossible to express their joy at seeing each
other after a separation which they both thought was for ever.
They embraced several times, and these embracings over, they sat
down, shedding tears of joy, and Aladdin said, "I beg you, Princess,
before we talk of anything else, to tell me, both for your own sake,

the sultan your father's, and mine, what is become of an old lamp which I left upon the shelf in the hall of the four-and-twenty windows, before I went hunting?"

"Alas! dear husband," answered the princess, "I am afraid our misfortune is owing to that lamp: and what grieves me most is that I have been the cause of it."

"Princess," replied Aladdin, "do not blame yourself, since it was entirely my fault, and I ought to have taken more care of it. But let us now think only of repairing the loss; tell me what has happened, and into whose hands it has fallen."

Then the Princess Badroulboudour gave Aladdin an account of how she changed the old lamp for a new one, which she ordered to be fetched, that he might see it, and how the next morning she found herself in the unknown country they were then in, which she was told was Africa by the traitor who had transported her thither by his magic art.

"Princess," said Aladdin, interrupting her, "you have informed me who the traitor is, by telling me we are in Africa. He is the most perfidious of all men; but this is neither the time nor the place to give you a full account of his villainies. I desire you only to tell me what he has done with the lamp, and where he has put it."

"He carries it carefully wrapt up in his bosom," said the princess: "and this I can assure you, because he pulled it out before me, and showed it to me in triumph."

"Princess," said Aladdin, "do not be displeased that I trouble you with so many questions, since they are equally important both to you and me. But tell me, I implore you, how so wicked and perfidious a man treats you."

"Since I have been here," replied the princess, "he comes once a day to see me; and I am persuaded that the little satisfaction he receives from his visits makes him come no oftener. All his discourse tends to persuade me to break that faith I have pledged to you, and to take him for a husband; giving me to understand that I ought not to entertain any hope of ever seeing you again, for that you were dead, and had had your head struck off by the sultan my father's order. He added, to justify himself, that you were an ungrateful wretch; that your good fortune was owing to him, and a great many other things which I forbear to repeat: but, as he received no other answer from me but grievous complaints and tears, he was always forced to retire with as little satisfaction as he came. I doubt not his intention is to allow me time to vanquish my grief, in the hope that I may change my mind; and if I persevere in an obstinate refusal, to use violence. But my dear husband's presence removes all my disquiet."

"I think," replied Aladdin, "I have found means to deliver you from your enemy and mine: to execute this design, it is necessary for me to go to the town. I shall return by noon, and will then communicate my plan to you, and tell you what you must do to ensure success. But that you may not be surprised, I think it proper to tell you that I shall change my apparel, and beg you to give orders that I may not wait long at the private door, but that it may be opened at the first knock," all of which the princess promised to observe.

When Aladdin had got out of the palace by that door, he looked round about him on all sides, and perceiving a peasant going into the country, he hastened after him; and when he had overtaken him, made a proposal to him to change clothes, which the man agreed to. They made the exchange; the countryman went about his business, and Aladdin to the city. After traversing several streets, he came to that part of the town where all sorts of merchants and artisans had their particular streets, according to their trades. He went into that of the druggists; and going into one of the largest and best shops, asked the druggist if he had a certain powder which he named.

The druggist regarding Aladdin from his clothes as very poor, told him he had it, but that it was very dear; upon which Aladdin, penetrating into his thoughts, pulled out his purse, and showing him some gold, asked for half a drachm of the powder, which the druggist weighed, and wrapped up in a piece of paper, and gave him, telling him the price was a piece of gold. Aladdin put the money into his hand, and staying no longer in the town, except just to get a little refreshment, returned to the palace, where he waited not long at the private door. When he came into the princess's apartment, he said to her, "Princess, perhaps the aversion you tell me you have for the magician may hinder your doing what I am going to propose; but give me leave to tell you, it is proper that you should dissemble a little, and do violence to your feelings, if you would deliver yourself from him, and give the sultan your father the satisfaction of seeing you again.

"If you will take my advice," continued he, "dress yourself this moment in one of your richest robes, and when the African magician comes, give him the best reception; receive him with an open countenance, without constraint. From your conversation, let him suppose that you strive to forget me. Invite him to sup with you, and give him to understand you should be glad to taste of some of the best wines of his country. He will go and fetch you some. During his absence, put this powder into one of the cups, and setting it by, charge the slave who attends you to bring you that cup at a signal you shall agree on with her. When the magician and you have eaten and drunk as much as you choose, let her bring you the cup, and change cups with him. He will take it as so great a favour that he will not refuse you, and will drain the cup; but no sooner will he have drunk it off than you will see him fall backwards."

When Aladdin had finished, "I own," answered the princess, "I shall do myself great violence in consenting to make the magician such advances as I see are absolutely necessary for me to make;

but what cannot one resolve to do against a cruel enemy? I will therefore follow your advice." After the princess had agreed to the measures proposed by Aladdin, he took his leave of her, and went and spent the rest of the day in the neighbourhood of the palace till it was night, when he might safely return to the private door.

The Princess Badroulboudour, who was inconsolable at being separated not only from her dear husband, but also from the sultan her father, had, ever since that cruel separation, lived in great neglect of her person. She had almost forgotten to keep herself neat, particularly after the first time the magician paid her a visit; for she learned from some of the women, who knew him again, that it was he who took the old lamp in exchange for a new one, which notorious cheat rendered the sight of him more abhorrent. However, the opportunity of punishing him as he deserved made her resolve to gratify Aladdin. As soon, therefore, as he was gone, she sat down at her toilet, and was dressed by her women to the best advantage, in the richest robes. Her girdle was of the finest and largest diamonds set in gold, which she matched with a necklace of pearls, six on a side, so well setting off the one in the middle, which was the largest and most valuable, that the greatest sultanesses and queens would have been proud to be adorned with only two of the smallest. Her bracelets were of diamonds and rubies intermixed.

When the Princess Badroulboudour was completely dressed, she consulted her glass and her women as to how she looked, and when she found she would easily be able to flatter the foolish magician, she sat down on a sofa, awaiting his arrival.

The magician came at the usual hour, and as soon as he entered the great hall, where the princess waited to receive him, she rose up and pointed with her hand to the most honourable place, waiting till he sat down, that she might sit at the same time, which was a piece of civility she had never shown him before.

The African magician was very much surprised. The majestic and graceful air with which she received him, so opposed to her former behaviour, quite bewildered him.

When he had sat down, the princess, to free him from his embarrassment, broke silence first, and said, "You are doubtless amazed to find me so much altered to-day from what I used to be; but your surprise will not be so great when I tell you that I am naturally of a disposition so opposed to melancholy and grief, sorrow and uneasiness, that I always strive to put them as far away as possible when I find the reason of them is past. I have reflected on what you told me of Aladdin's fate, and know the sultan my father's temper so well that I am persuaded that Aladdin could not escape the terrible effects of his rage; therefore, should I continue to lament him all my life, my tears cannot recall him. To begin to cast off all melancholy, I am resolved to banish it entirely; and, persuaded you will bear me company to-night, I have ordered a supper to be prepared; but as I have no wines except those of China, I have a great desire to taste the African wine, and doubt not you will get some of the best."

The African magician, who had looked upon the happiness of coming so soon and so easily into the Princess Badroulboudour's good graces as impossible, could not think of words enough to express his gratitude: but to put an end the sooner to a conversation which would have embarrassed him, he turned it upon the wines of Africa, and said, "Of all the advantages Africa can boast, that of producing the most excellent wines is one of the principal. I have a vessel of seven years old, which has never been broached; and it is indeed not praising it too much to say that it is the finest wine in the world. If my princess," added he, "will give me leave, I will go and fetch two bottles, and return again immediately."

"I should be sorry to give you that trouble," replied the princess; "you had better send for them."

"It is necessary I should go myself," answered the African magician; "for nobody but myself knows where the key of the cellar is laid, or has the secret to unlock the door."

"If it be so," said the princess, "make haste back again; for the longer you stay, the greater will be my impatience, and we shall sit down to supper as soon as you come back."

The African magician, full of hope, flew rather than ran, and returned quickly with the wine. The princess, not doubting in the least but that he would make haste, put with her own hand the powder Aladdin gave her into the cup that was set apart for that purpose. They sat down at the table opposite to each other, the magician's back towards the sideboard. The princess presented him with the best on the table, and said to him, "If it pleases you, I will entertain you with a concert of vocal and instrumental music; but, as we are only two, I think conversation may be more agreeable." This the magician took as a new favour.

After they had eaten some time, the princess called for some wine, and drank the magician's health; and afterwards said to him, "Indeed you were right to commend your wine, since I never tasted any so delicious in my life."

"Charming princess," said he, holding in his hand the cup which had been presented to him, "my wine becomes more exquisite by your approbation of it."

"Then drink my health," replied the princess; "you will find I understand wines." He drank the princess's health, and returning the cup, said, "I think myself happy, princess, that I reserved this wine for so good an occasion; and I own I never before drank any so excellent in every respect."

Presently, the princess, who had completely charmed the African magician by her civility and obliging behaviour, gave the signal to the slave who served them with wine, bidding her bring the cup which had been filled for herself, and at the same time bring the magician a full cup. When they both had their cups in their hands, she presented to him the cup which was in her hand, and held out her hand to receive his. He for his part hastened to make the exchange with the greater pleasure because he looked upon this favour as the most certain token of an entire conquest over the princess, which raised his happiness to its height. Before he drank, he said to her, with the cup in his hand, "Indeed, I shall never, lovely princess, forget my recovering, by drinking out of your cup, that life which your cruelty, had it continued, would have made me despair of."

The Princess Badroulboudour, who began to be tired of this barefaced foolishness of the African magician, interrupted him, and said, "Let us drink first, and then say what you will after-wards;" and at the same time set the cup to her lips, while the African magician, who was eager to get his wine off first, drank up the very last drop. Then he fell backwards lifeless.

The princess had no occasion to order the back-door to be opened to Aladdin; for her women were so arranged from the great hall to the foot of the staircase, that the word was no sooner given that the African magician was fallen backwards than the door was opened that instant.

As soon as Aladdin entered the hall, he saw the magician stretched backwards on the sofa. The Princess Badroulboudour rose from her seat, and ran overjoyed to embrace him; but he stopped her, and said, "Princess, it is not yet time; oblige me by retiring to your apartment, and let me be left alone a moment, while I endeavour to transport you back to China as quickly as you were brought from thence."

When the princess, her women and attendants, had gone out of the hall, Aladdin shut the door, and going to the dead body of the magician, opened his vest, and took out the lamp carefully wrapt up; and on his unfolding and rubbing it, the genie immediately appeared. "Genie," said Aladdin, "I command thee, on the part of thy good mistress this lamp, to transport this palace directly into China." The genie bowed his head in token of obedience, and disappeared. Immediately the palace was transported into China, and its removal was only felt by two little shocks, the one when it was lifted up, the other when it was set down, and both in a very short interval of time.

Aladdin went down to the princess's apartment, and embracing her, said, "I can assure you, princess, that your joy and mine will be complete to-morrow morning." The princess, who had not quite finished supper, guessed that Aladdin might be hungry, and ordered the meats that were served up in the great hall, and were scarcely touched, to be brought down. The princess and Aladdin ate as much as they thought fit, and drank in like manner of the African magician's old wine; then they retired to rest.

From the time of the transportation of Aladdin's palace, and of the Princess Badroulboudour in it, the sultan, that princess's father, was inconsolable. He hardly slept night or day, and instead of taking measures to avoid everything that could keep up his affliction, he indulged it; he went now many times in the day to renew his tears, and plunged himself into the deepest melancholy.

The very morning of the return of Aladdin's palace, the sultan went, at break of day, into his room to indulge his sorrows. Centred in himself, and in a pensive mood, he cast his eyes in a melancholy manner towards the place where he remembered the palace once stood, expecting only to see an open space. Perceiving that vacancy filled up, he at first imagined it to be the effect of a fog; but looking more attentively, he was convinced beyond the power of doubt that it was his son-in-law's palace. Then joy and gladness succeeded to sorrow and grief. He immediately ordered a horse to be saddled, which he mounted that instant, thinking he could not make haste enough to get to Aladdin's palace.

Aladdin, who foresaw what would happen, rose that morning by daybreak, put on one of the most magnificent robes his wardrobe afforded, and went up into the hall of twenty-four windows, from whence he perceived the sultan coming, and got down soon enough to receive him at the foot of the great staircase, and to help him to dismount. "Aladdin," said the sultan, "I cannot speak to you till I have seen and embraced my daughter."

He led the sultan into the Princess Badroulboudour's apartment. She had been told by him when he rose that she was no longer in Africa, but in China, and in the capital of the sultan her father. The sultan embraced her with his face bathed in tears of joy.

At last the sultan broke silence, and said, "You have undergone a great deal; for a large palace cannot be so suddenly transported, as yours has been, without great fright and terrible anguish. Tell me all that has happened, and conceal nothing from me."

The princess, who took great pleasure in complying, gave the sultan a full account of how the African magician disguised himself like a seller of lamps, and offered to change new lamps for old ones; and how she amused herself in making that exchange, being entirely ignorant of the secret and importance of the lamp; how the palace and herself were carried away and transported into Africa, with the African magician, who was recollected by two of her women when he had the boldness to pay her the first visit after the success of his audacious enterprise, to propose that she should marry him; how he persecuted her till Aladdin's arrival; how he and she concerted measures together to get the lamp again, which he carried about him, and the success they had; and how she had invited him to supper, and had given him the cup with the powder, prepared for him. "For the rest," added she, "I leave it to Aladdin to give you an account."

Aladdin had not much to tell the sultan, but only said, "When the private door was opened, I went into the great hall, where I found the magician lying dead on the sofa. As soon as I was alone, and had taken the lamp out of the magician's breast, I made use of the same secret as he had done to remove the palace, and carry off the princess; and by that means the palace was brought into the same place where it stood before; and I have the happiness to bring back the princess to your majesty, as you commanded me. But that your majesty may not think that I impose upon you, if you will go up into the hall, you shall see the magician, punished as he deserved."

The sultan, to be assured of the truth, rose up instantly, and went up into the hall, and when he saw the African magician dead, he embraced Aladdin with great tenderness, and said, "My son, be not displeased at my proceedings against you; they arose from my love for my daughter, and therefore you ought to forgive the excesses to which it hurried me."

"Sir," replied Aladdin, "I have not the least reason to complain of your majesty's conduct, since you did nothing but what your duty required of you. This infamous magician, the basest of men, was the sole cause of my misfortune. When your majesty has leisure, I will give you an account of another villainous action he was guilty of to me, which was no less black and base than this, from which I was preserved in a very strange manner."

"I will take an opportunity, and that very shortly," replied the sultan, "to hear it; but in the meantime let us think only of rejoicing, and the removal of this odious object."

Aladdin ordered the magician's dead carcass to be removed. In the meantime the sultan commanded the drums, trumpets, cymbals, and other instruments of music to sound, and a feast of ten days to be proclaimed for joy at the return of the Princess Badroulboudour, and Aladdin with his palace.

Thus Aladdin escaped a second time the danger of losing his life.

But the African magician had a younger brother, who was as great a necromancer, and even surpassed him in villainy and pernicious designs. As they did not live together, or in the same city, but oftentimes when one was in the east the other was in the west, they each failed not every year to discover by their art where the other was, and whether he stood in need of any assistance.

Some time after the African magician had failed in his enterprise against Aladdin's happiness, his younger brother, who had not heard any tidings of him for a year, and was not in Africa, but in a distant country, was anxious to know in what part of the world he was, how he did, and what he was doing; and as he, as well as his brother, always carried a geomantic square instrument about with him, he prepared the sand, cast the points, and drew the figures. On examining the "houses" he found that his brother was no longer living, that he had been poisoned, and died suddenly; that it had happened in the capital of the kingdom of China, and that the person who had poisoned him was of low birth, and married to a princess, a sultan's daughter.

When the magician had after this manner learned his brother's fate, he lost no time in useless regret, which could not restore him to life again, but resolving immediately to avenge his death, he took horse, and set out for China, where, after crossing plains, rivers, mountains, deserts, and a long tract of country, without stopping, he arrived after incredible fatigue.

When he came to the capital of China, which his knowledge of geomancy pointed out to him, he took a lodging. The next day he went out and walked through the town, not so much to observe its beauties, to which he was indifferent, as to take proper measures to execute his pernicious design. He went into the most frequented places, where he listened to everybody's conversation. In a place where people went to play at all sorts of games, he heard some persons talking of the virtue and piety of a woman called

Fatima, who had retired from the world, and of the miracles she performed. As he fancied that this woman might be serviceable to him for the project he had in his head, he took one of the company aside, and desired him to tell him more particularly who this holy woman was, and what sort of miracles she performed.

"What!" said the person whom he addressed, "have you never seen or heard of her? She is the admiration of the whole town, for her fasting, her austerities, and her exemplary life. Except on Mondays and Fridays, she never stirs out of her little cell; and the days on which she comes into the town she does an infinite deal of good; for there is not a person who has the headache who is not cured by her laying her hand upon him."

The magician wanted no further information. He only asked in what part of the town this holy woman's cell was. After he had been told, he determined on a detestable design; watched her steps the first day she went out after he had made this enquiry, and never lost sight of her till evening, when he saw her re-enter her cell. Then he went to one of those houses where they sell a certain hot liquor, and where any person may pass the night, particularly during the great heats, when the people of that country prefer lying on a mat to going to bed. About midnight, after the magician had paid the master of the house for what little he had called for, he went direct to the cell of Fatima, the holy woman. He had no difficulty in opening the door, which was only fastened with a latch, and he shut it again after he had got in, without any noise. When he entered the cell he perceived Fatima in the moonlight lying on a sofa covered only by an old mat, with her head leaning against the wall. He awakened her, and clapped a dagger to her breast.

Poor Fatima, opening her eyes, was very much surprised to see a man with a dagger at her breast ready to stab her. "If you cry out," he said, "or make the least noise, I will kill you; but get up and do as I bid you."

Fatima, who had lain down in her clothes, got up, trembling with fear. "Do not be so frightened," said the magician; "I only want your gown: give it me at once, and take mine." Accordingly Fatima and he changed clothes. Then he said, "Colour my face as yours is, that I may look like you;" but perceiving that the poor creature could not help trembling, he said, "I tell you again, you need not fear anything; I will not take away your life." Fatima lighted her lamp, and made him come into the cell; and taking a pencil, and dipping it in a certain liquor, she rubbed it over his face and assured him that the dye would not change, and that his face was of the same colour as her own; after which, she put her own head-dress on his head, with a veil, with which she showed him how to hide his face as he passed through the town. After this, about his neck she put a long string of beads, which hung down to his waist, and, giving him the stick she was accustomed to walk with, she brought him a looking-glass, and bade him see if he were not as like her as possible. The magician found himself as much disguised as he wished to be; but he did not keep the promise he so solemnly gave to the good Fatima, for he killed her at once.

The magician, thus disguised like the holy woman, spent the remainder of the night in the cell. The next morning, two hours after sunrise, though it was not the day the holy woman used to go out, he crept out of the cell, being well persuaded that nobody would ask him any question about it; or, if they should, he had an answer ready for them. As one of the first things he had done after his arrival was to find out Aladdin's palace, he went straight thither.

As soon as the people saw the holy woman, as they imagined him to be, they gathered about him in a great crowd. Some begged his blessing, others kissed his hand, and some, more reserved, only the hem of his garment; while others, if their heads ached, or they desired to be preserved against headache, stooped for him to lay his hands upon them; which he did, muttering some words in form of a prayer. In short, he counterfeited so well that everybody took him for the holy woman.

After stopping frequently to satisfy these people, who received neither good nor harm from his imposition of hands, he came at last to the square before Aladdin's palace. The crowd was so great that the eagerness to get at him increased in proportion. Those who were the most zealous and strong forced their way through the crowd to get near. There were such quarrels and so great a noise that the princess, who was in the hall of the four-and-twenty windows, heard it, and asked what was the matter; but nobody being able to give an account, she ordered them to go and see. One of her women looked out of a window, and told her that a great crowd of people was gathered about the holy woman, to be cured of the headache by the imposition of her hands.

The princess, who had for a long time heard a great deal of this holy woman, but had never seen her, felt great curiosity to have some conversation with her, and immediately sent four chamberlains for the pretended holy woman.

As soon as the crowd saw the chamberlains coming, they made way, and the magician advanced to meet them, overjoyed to find his plot work so well. "Holy woman," said one of the officers, "the princess wants to see you, and has sent us for you."

"The princess does me too great an honour," replied the false Fatima, "but I am ready to obey her command," and he followed the chamberlains into the palace.

When the magician, who under a holy garment disguised such a wicked heart, was introduced into the great hall, and perceived the princess, he began a prayer, which contained a long enumeration of vows and good wishes for the princess's health and prosperity, and that she might have everything she desired. Then he displayed all his deceitful, hypocritical rhetoric, to insinuate himself into the princess's favour under the cloak of piety, which it was no hard matter for him to do; for as the princess herself was naturally good, she was easily persuaded that all the world was like her, especially those who made profession of serving God in solitary retreat.

When the pretended Fatima had made an end of his long harangue, the princess said to him, "I thank you, good mother, for your prayers. Come and sit by me." The false Fatima sat down with affected modesty: then the princess said, "My good mother, I have one thing to ask you, which you must not refuse me; which is, to stay with me, that you may teach me your way of living, and that I may learn from your good example."

"Princess," said the counterfeit Fatima, "I beg of you not to ask what I cannot consent to, without neglecting my prayers and devotions."

"That shall be no hindrance to you," answered the princess. "I have a great many apartments unoccupied; you shall choose which you like best, and shall have as much liberty to perform your devotions as if you were in your own cell."

The magician, who wanted nothing better than to introduce himself into Aladdin's palace, where it would be a much easier matter for him to execute his pernicious design, under the favour and protection of the princess, than if he had been forced to come and go from the cell to the palace, did not urge much to excuse himself from accepting the obliging offer the princess made him. "Princess," said he, "whatever resolutions a poor wretched woman, such as I am, may have made to renounce the pomp and grandeur of this world, I dare not presume to oppose the will and command of so pious and charitable a princess."

Upon this the princess rose up and said, "Come along with me, I will show you what empty apartments I have, that you may make choice of those which you like best." The magician followed the Princess Badroulboudour, and made choice of that which was the most poorly furnished, saying, "It is too good for me; I only accept it to please you."

Then the princess wished to take him back again into the great hall to dine with her; but considering that then he would be obliged to show his face, which he had all the time taken care to hide, and fearing that the princess might find out that he was not Fatima, he begged her earnestly to dispense with him, telling her that he never ate anything but bread and dried fruits, and that he desired to eat a slight repast in his own room. This the princess granted him, saying, "You may be as free here, good mother, as if you were in your own cell. I will order you a dinner, but, remember, I shall expect you as soon as you have finished."

After the princess had dined, the false Fatima failed not to wait upon her. "My good mother," said the princess, "I am overjoyed to have the company of so holy a woman as yourself, who will confer a blessing upon this palace. But now that I am speaking of this palace, pray how do you like it? And before I show you the rest, tell me first what you think of this hall."

At this question the counterfeit Fatima, who, to act his part the better, pretended to hang down his head, without so much as ever once lifting it, at last looked up; and, surveying the hall from one end to the other, he said to the princess, "As far as such a solitary being as I can judge, this hall is truly admirable and most beautiful; it lacks but one thing."

"What is that, good mother?" answered the Princess Badroulboudour, "tell me, I implore you. For my part, I have always believed and have heard that it lacked nothing; but if it does, that want shall be supplied."

"Princess," said the false Fatima, with great dissimulation, "forgive me for the liberty I have taken; but if my opinion can be of any importance, it is that if a roc's egg were hung up in the middle of the dome, this hall would have no parallel in the four quarters of the world, and your palace would be the wonder of the universe."

"My good mother," said the princess, "what is a roc, and where could I get an egg?"

"Princess," replied the pretended Fatima, "it is a bird of prodigious size, which inhabits the top of Mount Caucasus; the architect who built your palace can get you one."

After the Princess Badroulboudour had thanked the false Fatima for what she believed her good advice, she conversed with her upon other matters, but she could not forget the roc's egg, of which she determined to tell Aladdin when he returned from hunting. He had been gone six days, which the magician knew, and therefore took advantage of his absence. But he returned that evening after the false Fatima had taken leave of the princess, and retired to his room. As soon as he arrived, Aladdin went straight up to the princess's apartment, and saluted and embraced her. She seemed to receive him coldly. "My princess," said he, "I think you are not so cheerful as usual. Has anything happened during my absence to give you any trouble or dissatisfaction? If so, do not conceal it from me. I will leave nothing undone that is in my power to please you."

"It is a trifling matter," replied the princess, "which gives me so little concern that I should not have thought you would perceive it in my countenance. But since you have unexpectedly discovered it, I will no longer disguise a matter of so little consequence from you.

"I always believed, as you did," continued the Princess Badroulboudour, "that our palace was the most superb, magnificent, and complete one in the world, but I will tell you now what I find fault with upon examining the hall of four-and-twenty windows. Do you not think, with me, that it would be better if a roc's egg were hung up in the midst of the dome?"

"Princess," replied Aladdin, "it is enough that you think it needs such a thing. You shall see by my diligence that there is nothing which I would not do for your sake."

Aladdin left the Princess Badroulboudour that very moment, and went up into the hall of four-and-twenty windows. Pulling out of his bosom the lamp, which, after the danger he had been exposed to, he always carried about with him, he rubbed it, upon which the genie immediately appeared. "Genie," said Aladdin, "there ought to be a roc's egg hung up in

the midst of the dome. I command thee, in the name of this lamp, to repair the deficiency."

Aladdin had no sooner pronounced these words than the genie gave so loud and terrible a cry that the hall shook, and Aladdin could scarcely stand upright. "What? wretch," said the genie, in a voice that would have made the most undaunted man tremble, "is it not enough that I and my companions have done everything for you, that you, with unheard-of ingratitude, must command me to bring my master, and hang him up in the midst of this dome? This attempt deserves that you, your wife, and your palace should be immediately reduced to ashes. You are fortunate, however, in not being the real author of this request. It does not come from yourself. Know, then, that the true author is the brother of the African magician, your enemy, whom you have destroyed as he deserved. He is now in your palace, disguised in the clothes of the holy woman Fatima, whom he has murdered, and it is he who has suggested to your wife to make this pernicious demand. His design is to kill you, therefore take care of yourself." After these words the genie disappeared.

Aladdin lost not a word of what the genie had said. He had heard of the holy woman Fatima, and how she could cure the headache. He returned to the princess's apartment, and without mentioning a word of what had happened, he sat down, and complained of a great pain which had suddenly seized his head. Upon this the princess immediately ordered the holy woman to be fetched, and then told Aladdin how she had come to the palace.

When the pretended Fatima came, Aladdin said, "Come hither, good mother; I am glad to see you here at so fortunate a time. I am tormented with a violent pain in my head, and request your assistance. I hope you will not refuse me that kindness which you have done to so many persons afflicted with the headache." So saying, he rose up, but held down his head.

The counterfeit Fatima advanced towards him, with his hand all the time on a dagger, concealed in his girdle under his gown. Aladdin saw this, and, seizing his hand, pierced him to the heart with his own dagger, and then threw him down on the floor dead.

"My dear husband, what have you done?" cried the princess in surprise. "You have killed the holy woman!"

"No, my princess," answered Aladdin, without emotion, "I have not killed Fatima, but a wicked wretch that would have assassinated me, if I had not prevented him. This wicked man," added he, uncovering his face, "has strangled Fatima, whom you accuse me of killing, and disguised himself in her clothes, to come and murder me. He is the brother of the African magician." Then Aladdin told her how he came to know these particulars, and afterwards ordered the dead body to be taken away.

Thus was Aladdin delivered from the persecution of the two magicians. Within a few years afterwards, the sultan died in a good old age, and the Princess Badroulboudour, as lawful heir of the crown, succeeded him. She shared her power with Aladdin, and they reigned together many years, and left a numerous and illustrious posterity behind them.

THE KING OF PERSIA AND THE
PRINCESS OF THE SEA

THERE was once a King of Persia, who at the beginning of his reign had distinguished himself by many glorious and successful conquests, and had afterwards enjoyed such profound peace and tranquillity as rendered him the happiest of monarchs. His only occasion for regret was that he had no heir to succeed him in the kingdom after his death. One day, according to the custom of his royal predecessors during their residence in the capital, he held an assembly of his courtiers, at which all the ambassadors and strangers of renown at his court were present. Among these there appeared a merchant from a far-distant country, who sent a message to the king craving an audience, as he wished to speak to him about a very important matter. The king gave orders for the merchant to be instantly admitted; and when the assembly was over, and all the rest of the company had retired, the king inquired what was the business which had brought him to the palace.

"Sire," replied the merchant, "I have with me, and beg your majesty to behold, the most beautiful and charming slave it would be possible to find if you searched every corner of the earth; if you will but see her, you will surely wish to make her your wife."

The fair slave was, by the king's commands, immediately brought in, and no sooner had the king beheld a lady whose beauty and grace surpassed anything he had ever imagined, than he fell passionately in love with her, and determined to marry her at once. This was done.

So the king caused the fair slave to be lodged in the next finest apartment to his own, and gave particular orders to the matrons

N .

and the women-slaves appointed to attend her, that they should
dress her in the richest robe they could find, and carry her the
finest pearl necklaces, the brightest diamonds, and the richest
precious stones, that she might choose those she liked best.

The King of Persia's capital was situated in an island; and his
palace, which was very magnificent, was built upon the seashore;

his window looked towards the sea; and the fair slave's, which was pretty near it, had also the same prospect, and it was the more pleasant on account of the sea's beating almost against the foot of the wall.

At the end of three days the fair slave, magnificently dressed, was alone in her chamber, sitting upon a sofa, and leaning against one of the windows that faced the sea, when the king, being informed that he might visit her, came in. The slave hearing somebody walk in the room, immediately turned her head to see who it was. She knew him to be the king; but without showing the least surprise, or so much as rising from her seat to salute or receive him, she turned back to the window again as if he had been the most insignificant person in the world.

The King of Persia was extremely surprised to see a slave of so beauteous a form so very ignorant of the world. He attributed this to the narrowness of her education, and the little care that had been taken to instruct her in the first rules of civility. He went to her at the window, where, notwithstanding the coldness and indifference with which she had just now received him, she suffered herself to be admired, kissed, and embraced as much as he pleased, but answered him not a word.

"My dearest life," said the king, "you neither answer, nor by any visible token give me the least reason to believe that you are listening to me. Why will you still keep to this obstinate silence, which chills me? Do you mourn for your country, your friends, or your relations? Alas! is not the King of Persia, who loves and adores you, capable of comforting, and making you amends for the loss of everything in the world?"

But the fair slave continued her astonishing reserve; and keeping her eyes still fixed upon the ground, would neither look at him nor utter a word; but after they had dined together in absolute silence, the king went to the women whom he had assigned to the fair slave as her attendants, and asked them if they had ever heard her speak.

One of them presently made answer, "Sire, we have neither seen her open her lips, nor heard her speak any more than your majesty has just now; we have rendered her our services; we have combed and dressed her hair, put on her clothes, and waited upon her in her chamber; but she has never opened her lips, so much as to say, That is well, or, I like this. We have often asked, Madam, do you want anything? Is there anything you wish for? Do but ask and command us: but we have never been able to draw a word from her. We cannot tell whether her silence proceeds from pride, sorrow, stupidity, or dumbness; and this is all we can inform your majesty."

The King of Persia was more astonished at hearing this than he was before: however, believing the slave might have some reason for sorrow, he endeavoured to divert and amuse her, but all in vain. For a whole year she never afforded him the pleasure of a single word.

At length, one day there were great rejoicings in the capital, because to the king and his silent slave-queen there was born a son and heir to the kingdom. Once more the king endeavoured to get a word from his wife. "My queen," he said, "I cannot divine what your thoughts are; but, for my own part, nothing would be wanting to complete my happiness and crown my joy but that you should speak to me one single word, for something within me tells me you are not dumb: and I beseech, I conjure you, to break through this long silence, and speak but one word to me; and after that I care not how soon I die."

At this discourse, the fair slave, who, according to her usual custom, had hearkened to the king with downcast eyes, and had given him cause to believe not only that she was dumb, but that she had never laughed in her life, began to smile a little. The King of Persia perceived it with a surprise that made him break forth into an exclamation of joy; and no longer doubting but that she was going to speak, he waited for that happy moment with an eagerness and attention that cannot easily be expressed.

At last the fair slave, breaking her long-kept silence, thus addressed herself to the king: "Sire," said she, "I have so many things to say to your majesty, that, having once broken silence, I know not where to begin. However, in the first place, I think myself in duty bound to thank you for all the favours and honours you have been pleased to confer upon me, and to implore Heaven to bless and prosper you, to prevent the wicked designs of your enemies, and not to suffer you to die after hearing me speak, but to grant you a long life. Had it never been my fortune to have borne a child, I was resolved (I beg your majesty to pardon the sincerity of my intention) never to have loved you, as well as to have kept an eternal silence; but now I love you as I ought to do."

The King of Persia, ravished to hear the fair slave speak, embraced her tenderly. "Shining light of my eyes," said he, "it is impossible for me to receive a greater joy than what you have now given me."

The King of Persia, in the transport of his joy, said no more to the fair slave. He left her, but in such a manner as made her perceive that his intention was speedily to return: and being willing that his joy should be made public, he sent in all haste for the grand vizier. As soon as he came, he ordered him to distribute a thousand pieces of gold among the holy men of his religion, who had made vows of poverty; as also among the hospitals and the poor, by way of returning thanks to Heaven: and his will was obeyed by the direction of that minister.

After the King of Persia had given this order, he returned to the fair slave again. "Madam," said he, "pardon me for leaving you so abruptly, but I hope you will indulge me with some conversation, since I am desirous to know several things of great consequence. Tell me, my dearest soul, what were the powerful reasons that induced you to persist in that obstinate silence for a whole year together, though you saw me, heard me talk to you, and ate and drank with me every day."

To satisfy the King of Persia's curiosity, "Think," replied the queen, "whether or no to be a slave, far from my own country, without any hopes of ever seeing it again, – to have a heart torn with grief at being separated for ever from my mother, my brother, my friends, and my acquaintance, – are not these sufficient reasons for my keeping a silence your majesty has thought so strange and unaccountable? The love of our native country is as natural to us as that of our parents; and the loss of liberty is insupportable to every one who is not wholly destitute of common sense, and knows how to set a value on it."

"Madam," replied the king, "I am convinced of the truth of what you say; but till this moment I was of opinion that a person beautiful like yourself, whom her evil destiny had condemned to be a slave, ought to think herself very happy in meeting with a king for her master."

"Sire," replied the fair slave, "whatever the slave is, there is no king on earth who can tyrannise over her will. But when this very slave is in nothing inferior to the king that bought her, your majesty shall then judge yourself of her misery, and her sorrow, and to what desperate attempts the anguish of despair may drive her."

The King of Persia, in great astonishment, said, "Madam, can it be possible that you are of royal blood? Explain the whole secret to me, I beseech you, and no longer increase my impatience. Let me instantly know who are your parents, your brothers, your sisters, and your relations; but, above all, what your name is."

"Sire," said the fair slave, "my name is Gulnare, Rose of the

Sea; and my father, who is now dead, was one of the most potent monarchs of the ocean. When he died, he left his kingdom to a brother of mine, named Saleh, and to the queen, my mother, who is also a princess, the daughter of another powerful monarch of the sea. We enjoyed a profound peace and tranquillity through the whole kingdom, till a neighbouring prince, envious of our happiness, invaded our dominions with a mighty army; and penetrating as far as our capital, made himself master of it; and we had but just time

enough to save ourselves in an impenetrable and inaccessible place, with a few trusty officers who did not forsake us in our distress.

"In this retreat my brother contrived all manner of ways to drive the unjust invader from our dominions. One day, 'Sister,' said he, 'I may fail in the attempt I intend to make to recover my kingdom; and I shall be less concerned for my own disgrace than for what may possibly happen to you. To prevent it, and to secure you from all accident, I would fain see you married first: but in the miserable condition of our affairs at present, I see no probability of matching you to any of the princes of the sea; and therefore I should be very glad if you would think of marrying some of the princes of the earth. I am ready to contribute all that lies in my power towards it; and I am certain there is not one of them, however powerful, but would be proud of sharing his crown with you.'

"At this discourse of my brother's, I fell into a violent passion. 'Brother,' said I, 'you know that I am descended, as well as you, by both father's and mother's side, from the kings and queens of the sea, without any mixture of alliance with those of the earth; therefore I do not intend to marry below myself, any more than they did. The condition to which we are reduced shall never oblige me to alter my resolution; and if you perish in the execution of your design, I am prepared to fall with you, rather than to follow the advice I so little expected from you.'

"My brother, who was still earnest for the marriage, however improper for me, endeavoured to make me believe that there were kings of the earth who were nowise inferior to those of the sea. This put me into a more violent passion, which occasioned him to say several bitter words that stung me to the quick. He left me as much dissatisfied with myself as he could possibly be with me; and in this peevish mood I gave a spring from the bottom of the sea up to the island of the moon.

"Notwithstanding the violent displeasure that made me cast myself upon that island, I lived content in retirement. But in spite of all my precautions, a person of distinction, attended by his servants, surprised me sleeping, and carried me to his own house, and wished me to marry him. When he saw that fair means would not prevail upon me, he attempted to make use of force; but I soon made him repent of his insolence. So at last he resolved to sell me; which he did to that very merchant who brought me hither and sold me to your majesty. This man was a very prudent,

courteous, humane person, and during the whole of the long journey, never gave me the least reason to complain.

"As for your majesty," continued Queen Gulnare, "if you had
not shown me all the respect you have hitherto paid, and given me
such undeniable marks of your affection that I could no longer
doubt of it, I hesitate not to tell you plainly that I should not have
remained with you. I would have thrown myself into the sea out of
this very window, and I would have gone in search of my mother,
my brother, and the rest of my relations; and, therefore, I hope you
will no longer look upon me as a slave, but as a princess worthy of
your alliance."

After this manner Queen Gulnare discovered herself to the
King of Persia, and finished her story. "My charming, my adorable
queen," cried he, "what wonders have I heard! I must ask a thousand questions concerning those strange and unheard-of things
which you have related to me. I beseech you to tell me more about
the kingdom and people of the sea, who are altogether unknown
to me. I have heard much talk, indeed, of the inhabitants of the
sea, but I always looked upon it as nothing but a tale or fable; but,
by what you have told me, I am convinced there is nothing more
true; and I have a very good proof of it in your own person, who are
one of them, and are pleased to condescend to be my wife; which
is an honour no other inhabitant on the earth can boast of besides
myself. There is one thing yet which puzzles me; therefore I must
beg the favour of you to explain it; that is, I cannot comprehend
how it is possible for you to live or move in the water without
being drowned. There are very few amongst us who have the art of
staying under water; and they would surely perish, if, after a certain time, they did not come up again."

"Sire," replied Queen Gulnare, "I shall with pleasure satisfy
the King of Persia. We can walk at the bottom of the sea with as
much ease as you can upon land; and we can breathe in the water

as you do in the air; so that instead of suffocating us, as it does you, it absolutely contributes to the preservation of our lives. What is yet more remarkable is, that it never wets our clothes; so that when we have a mind to visit the earth, we have no occasion to dry them. Our common language is the same as that of the writing engraved upon the seal of the great prophet Solomon, the son of David.

"I must not forget to tell you, further, that the water does not in the least hinder us from seeing in the sea; for we can open our eyes without any inconvenience; and as we have quick, piercing sight, we can discern any object as clearly in the deepest part of the sea as upon land. We have also there a succession of day and night; the moon affords us her light, and even the planets and the stars appear visible to us. I have already spoken of our kingdoms; but as the sea is much more spacious than the earth, so there are a greater number of them, and of greater extent. They are divided into provinces; and in each province there are several great cities, well peopled. In short, there are an infinite number of nations, differing in manners and customs, just as upon the earth.

"The palaces of the kings and princes are very sumptuous and magnificent. Some of them are of marble of various colours; others of rock-crystal, with which the sea abounds, mother-of-pearl, coral, and of other materials more valuable; gold, silver, and all sorts of precious stones are more plentiful there than on earth. I say nothing of the pearls, since the largest that ever were seen upon earth would not be valued amongst us; and none but the very lowest rank of citizens would wear them.

"As we can transport ourselves whither we please in the twinkling of an eye, we have no occasion for any carriages or riding-horses; not but what the king has his stables, and his stud of sea-horses; but they are seldom made use of, except upon public feasts or rejoicing days. Some, after they have trained them, take

delight in riding them, and show their skill and dexterity in races; others put them to chariots of mother-of-pearl, adorned with an infinite number of shells of all sorts, of the brightest colours. These chariots are open; and in the middle there is a throne upon which the king sits, and shows himself to his subjects. The horses are trained up to draw by themselves; so that there is no occasion for a charioteer to guide them. I pass over a thousand other curious particulars relating to these marine countries, which would be very entertaining to your majesty; but you must permit me to defer it to a future leisure, to speak of something of much greater consequence. I should like to send for my mother and my cousins, and at the same time to desire the king my brother's company, to whom I have a great desire to be reconciled. They will be very glad to see me again, after I have related my story to them, and when they understand I am wife to the mighty king of Persia. I beseech your majesty to give me leave to send for them: I am sure they will be happy to pay their respects to you; and I venture to say you will be extremely pleased to see them."

"Madam," replied the King of Persia, "you are mistress; do whatever you please; I will endeavour to receive them with all the honours they deserve. But I would fain know how you would acquaint them with what you desire, and when they will arrive, that I may give orders to make preparation for their reception, and go myself in person to meet them."

"Sire," replied the Queen Gulnare, "there is no need of these ceremonies; they will be here in a moment; and if your majesty will but look through the lattice, you shall see the manner of their arrival."

Queen Gulnare then ordered one of her women to bring her a brazier with a little fire. After that she bade her retire, and shut the door. When she was alone, she took a piece of aloes out of a box, and put it into the brazier. As soon as she saw the smoke rise, she repeated some words unknown to the King of Persia, who from a recess observed with great attention all that she did. She had no sooner ended, than the sea began to be disturbed. At length the sea opened at some distance; and presently there rose out of it a tall, handsome young man, with moustaches of a sea-green colour; a little behind him, a lady, advanced in years, but of a majestic air, attended by five young ladies, nowise inferior in beauty to the Queen Gulnare.

Queen Gulnare immediately went to one of the windows, and saw the king her brother, the queen her mother, and the rest of her relations, who at the same time perceived her also. The company came forward, borne, as it were, upon the surface of the waves. When they came to the edge, they nimbly, one after another, sprang up to the window, from whence Queen Gulnare had retired to make room for them. King Saleh, the queen her mother, and the rest of her relations, embraced her tenderly, with tears in their eyes, on their first entrance.

After Queen Gulnare had received them with all imaginable honour, and made them sit down upon a sofa, the queen her mother addressed herself to her: "Daughter," said she, "I am over-joyed to see you again after so long an absence; and I am confident that your brother and your relations are no less so. Your leaving us without acquainting anybody with it involved us in inexpressible concern; and it is impossible to tell you how many tears we have shed upon that account. We know of no other reason that could induce you to take such a surprising step, but what your brother told us of the conversation that passed between him and you. The advice he gave you seemed to him at that time very advantageous for settling you handsomely in the world, and very suitable to the then posture of our affairs. If you had not approved of his proposal,

you ought not to have been so much alarmed; and, give me leave to tell you, you took the thing in a quite different light from what you ought to have done. But no more of this; we and you ought now to bury it for ever in oblivion: give us an account of all that has happened to you since we saw you last, and of your present situation; but especially let us know if you are satisfied."

Queen Gulnare immediately threw herself at her mother's feet; and after rising and kissing her hand, "I own," said she, "I have been guilty of a very great fault, and I am indebted to your goodness for the pardon which you are pleased to grant me." She then related the whole of what had befallen her since she quitted the sea.

As soon as she had acquainted them with her having been sold to the King of Persia, in whose palace she was at present; "Sister," said the king her brother, "you now have it in your power to free yourself. Rise, and return with us into my kingdom, that I have reconquered from the proud usurper who had made himself master of it."

The King of Persia, who heard these words from the recess where he was concealed, was in the utmost alarm. "Ah!" said he to himself, "I am ruined; and if my queen, my Gulnare, hearkens to this advice, and leaves me, I shall surely die." But Queen Gulnare soon put him out of his fears.

"Brother," said she, smiling, "I can scarce forbear being angry with you for advising me to break the engagement I have made with the most puissant and most renowned monarch in the world. I do not speak here of an engagement between a slave and her master; it would be easy to return the ten thousand pieces of gold that I cost him; but I speak now of a contract between a wife and a husband, and a wife who has not the least reason to complain. He is a religious, wise, and temperate king. I am his wife, and he has declared me Queen of Persia, to share with him in his councils. Besides, I have a child, the little Prince Beder. I hope then neither my mother, nor you, nor any of my cousins, will disapprove of the resolution or the alliance I have made, which will be an equal honour to the kings of the sea and the earth. Excuse me for giving you the trouble of coming hither from the bottom of the deep, to communicate it to you, and for the pleasure of seeing you after so long a separation."

"Sister," replied King Saleh, "the proposal I made you of going back with us into my kingdom was only to let you see how much we all love you, and how much I in particular honour you, and that nothing in the world is so dear to me as your happiness."

The queen confirmed what her son had just spoken, and addressing herself to Queen Gulnare, said, "I am very glad to hear you are pleased; and I have nothing else to add to what your brother has just said to you. I should have been the first to have condemned you, if you had not expressed all the gratitude you owe to a monarch that loves you so passionately, and has done such great things for you."

When the King of Persia, who was still in the recess, heard this he began to love her more than ever, and resolved to express his gratitude in every possible way.

Presently Queen Gulnare clapped her hands, and in came some of her slaves, whom she had ordered to bring in a meal: as soon as it was served up, she invited the queen her mother, the king her brother, and her cousins, to sit down and take part of it. They began to reflect, that without asking leave, they had got into the palace of a mighty king, who had never seen nor heard of them, and that it would be a great piece of rudeness to eat at his table without him. This reflection raised a blush in their faces; in their emotion their eyes glowed like fire, and they breathed flames at their mouths and nostrils.

This unexpected sight put the King of Persia, who was totally ignorant of the cause of it, into a dreadful consternation. Queen Gulnare suspecting this, and understanding the intention of her relations, rose from her seat, and told them she would be back in a moment. She went directly to the recess, and recovered the King of Persia from his surprise.

"Sir," said she, "give me leave to assure you of the sincere friendship that the queen my mother and the king my brother are pleased to honour you with: they earnestly desire to see you, and tell you so themselves: I intended to have some conversation with him by ordering a banquet for them, before I introduced them to your majesty, but they are very impatient to pay their respects to you: and therefore I desire your majesty would be pleased to walk in, and honour them with your presence."

"Madam," said the King of Persia, "I should be very glad to salute persons that have the honour to be so nearly related to you, but I am afraid of the flames that they breathe at their mouths and nostrils."

"Sir," replied the queen, laughing, "you need not in the least be afraid of those flames, which are nothing but a sign of their unwillingness to eat in your palace, without your honouring them with your presence, and eating with them."

The King of Persia, encouraged by these words, rose up, and came out into the room with his Queen Gulnare. She presented him to the queen her mother, to the king her brother, and to her other relations, who instantly threw themselves at his feet, with their faces to the ground. The King of Persia ran to them, and lifting them up, embraced them one after another. After they were all seated, King Saleh began: "Sir," said he to the King of Persia, "we are at a loss for words to express our joy to think that the queen my sister should have the happiness of falling under the protection of so powerful a monarch. We can assure you she is not unworthy of the high rank you have been pleased to raise her to; and we have always had so much love and tenderness for her, that we could never think of parting with her to any of the puissant princes of the sea, who often demanded her in marriage before she came of age. Heaven has reserved her for you, Sir, and we have no better way of returning thanks to it for the favour it has done her, than by beseeching it to grant your majesty a long and happy life with her, and to crown you with prosperity and satisfaction."

"Certainly," replied the King of Persia, "I cannot sufficiently thank either the queen her mother, or you, Prince, or your whole family, for the generosity with which you have consented to receive me into an alliance so glorious to me as yours." So saying, he invited them to take part of the luncheon, and he and his queen sat down at the table with them. After it was over, the King of Persia conversed with them till it was very late; and when they thought it time to retire, he waited upon them himself to the several rooms he had ordered to be prepared for them.

Next day, as the King of Persia, Queen Gulnare, the queen her mother, King Saleh her brother, and the princesses their relations, were discoursing together in her majesty's room, the nurse came in with the young Prince Beder in her arms. King Saleh no sooner saw him, than he ran to embrace him; and taking him in his arms, fell to kissing and caressing him with the greatest demonstration of tenderness. He took several turns with him about the room, dancing and tossing him about, when all of a sudden, through a transport of joy, the window being open, he sprang out, and plunged with him into the sea.

The King of Persia, who expected no such sight, set up a hideous cry, verily believing that he should either see the dear prince his son no more, or else that he should see him drowned; and he nearly died of grief and affliction. "Sir," said Queen Gulnare (with a quiet and undisturbed countenance, the better to comfort him), "let your majesty fear nothing; the young prince is my son as well as yours, and I do not love him less than you do. You see I am not alarmed; neither in truth ought I to be so. He runs no risk, and you will soon see the king his uncle appear with him again, and bring him back safe and sound. For he will have the same advantage his uncle and I have, of living equally in the sea and upon the land." The queen his mother and the princesses his relations confirmed the same thing; yet all they said had no effect on the king's fright, from which he could not recover till he saw Prince Beder appear again before him.

The sea at length became troubled, when immediately King Saleh arose with the young prince in his arms, and holding him up in the air, he re-entered at the same window he went out at. The King of Persia being overjoyed to see Prince Beder again, and astonished that he was as calm as before he lost sight of him, King Saleh said, "Sir, was not your majesty in a great fright, when you first saw me plunge into the sea with the prince my nephew?"

"Alas! Prince," answered the King of Persia, "I cannot express my concern. I thought him lost from that very moment, and you now restore life to me by bringing him again."

"I thought as much," replied King Saleh, "though you had not the least reason to apprehend any danger; for, before I plunged into the sea with him I pronounced over him certain mysterious words, which were engraven on the seal of the great Solomon, the son of David. We do the same to all those children that are born in the regions at the bottom of the sea, by virtue of which they receive the same privileges that we have over those people who inhabit the earth. From what your majesty has observed, you may easily see what advantage your son Prince Beder has acquired by his birth, for as long as he lives, and as often as he pleases, he will be at liberty to plunge into the sea, and traverse the vast empires it contains in its bosom."

Having so spoken, King Saleh, who had restored Prince Beder to his nurse's arms, opened a box he had fetched from his palace in the little time he had disappeared. It was filled with three hundred diamonds, as large as pigeons' eggs, a like number of rubies of extraordinary size, as many emerald wands, each half a foot long, and thirty strings or necklaces of pearl, consisting each of ten feet. "Sir," said he to the King of Persia, presenting him with this box, "when I was first summoned by the queen my sister, I knew not what part of the earth she was in, or that she had the honour to be married to so great a monarch. This made us come empty-handed. As we cannot express how much we have been obliged to your majesty, I beg you to accept this small token of gratitude, in acknowledgement of the many particular favours you have been pleased to show her."

It is impossible to express how greatly the King of Persia was surprised at the sight of so much riches, enclosed in so little compass. "What! Prince," cried he, "do you call so inestimable a present a small token of your gratitude? I declare once more, you have never been in the least obliged to me, neither the queen your mother nor you. Madam," continued he, turning to Gulnare, "the king your brother has put me into the greatest confusion; and I would beg of him to permit me to refuse his present, were I not afraid of disobliging him; do you therefore endeavour to obtain his leave that I may be excused accepting it."

"Sir," replied King Saleh, "I am not at all surprised that your majesty thinks this present so extraordinary. I know you are not accustomed upon earth to see precious stones of this quality and quantity: but if you knew, as I do, the mines whence these jewels were taken, and that it is in my power to form a treasure greater than those of all the kings of the earth, you would wonder we should have the boldness to make you a present of so small a value. I beseech you, therefore, not to regard it in that light, but on account of the sincere friendship which obliges us to offer it to you not to give us the mortification of refusing it." This obliged the King of Persia to accept the present, for which he returned many thanks both to King Saleh and the queen his mother.

A few days after, King Saleh gave the King of Persia to understand that the queen his mother, the princesses his relations and himself, could have no greater pleasure than to spend their whole lives at his court; but that having been so long absent from their own kingdom, where their presence was absolutely necessary, they begged of him not to take it ill if they took leave of him and Queen Gulnare. The King of Persia assured them he was very sorry that it was not in his power to return their visit in their own dominions; but he added, "As I am verily persuaded you will not forget Queen Gulnare, but come and see her now and then, I hope I shall have the honour to see you again more than once."

Many tears were shed on both sides upon their separation. King Saleh departed first; but the queen his mother, and the princesses his relations, were fain to force themselves in a manner from the embraces of Queen Gulnare, who could not prevail upon herself to let them go. This royal company were no sooner out of sight than the King of Persia said to Queen Gulnare, "Madam, I should have looked with suspicion upon the person that had pretended to pass those off upon me for true wonders, of which I myself have been an eye-witness from the time I have been honoured with your illustrious family at my court. But I cannot refuse to believe my own eyes; and shall remember it as long as I live, and never cease to bless Heaven for sending you to me, instead of to any other prince."

PRINCE CAMARALZAMAN AND
THE PRINCESS OF CHINA

ABOUT twenty days' sail from the coast of Persia, in the Islands of the Children of Khaledan, there lived a king who had an only son, Prince Camaralzaman. He was brought up with all imaginable care; and when he came to a proper age, his father appointed him an experienced governor and able tutors. As he grew up he learned all the knowledge which a prince ought to possess, and acquitted himself so well that he charmed all that saw him, and particularly the sultan his father.

When the prince had attained the age of fifteen years, the sultan, who loved him tenderly, and gave him every day new marks of his affection, had thoughts of giving him a still greater one, by resigning to him his throne, and he acquainted his grand vizier with his intentions. "I fear," said he, "lest my son should lose in the inactivity of youth those advantages which nature and education have given him; therefore, since I am advanced in age, and ought to think of retirement, I have thoughts of resigning the government to him, and passing the remainder of my days in the satisfaction of seeing him reign. I have undergone the fatigue of a crown a long while, and think it is now proper for me to retire."

The grand vizier did not wholly dissuade the sultan from such a proceeding, but sought to modify his intentions. "Sir," replied he, "the prince is yet but young, and it would not be, in my humble opinion, advisable to burden him with the weight of a crown so soon. Your majesty fears, with great reason, his youth may be corrupted in indolence, but to remedy that do not you think it would be proper to marry him? Your majesty might then admit him to your council, where he would learn by degrees the art of reigning, and so be prepared to receive your authority whenever in your discernment you shall think him qualified."

The sultan found this advice of his prime minister highly reasonable, therefore he summoned the prince to appear before him at the same time that he dismissed the grand vizier.

The prince, who had been accustomed to see his father only at certain times, without being sent for, was a little startled at this summons; when, therefore, he came before him, he saluted him with great respect, and stood with his eyes fixed on the ground.

The sultan perceiving his constraint, said to him in a mild way, "Do you know, son, for what reason I have sent for you?"

The prince modestly replied, "God alone knows the heart; I shall hear it from your majesty with pleasure."

"I sent for you," said the sultan, "to inform you that I have an intention of providing a proper marriage for you; what do you think of it?"

Prince Camaralzaman heard this with great uneasiness; it so

surprised him, that he paused and knew not what answer to make. After a few moments' silence, he replied, "Sir, I beseech you to pardon me if I seem surprised at the declaration you have made to me. I did not expect such proposals to one so young as I am. It requires time to determine on what your majesty requires of me."

Prince Camaralzaman's answer extremely afflicted his father. He was not a little grieved to see what an aversion he had to marriage, yet would not charge him with disobedience, nor exert his paternal authority. He contented himself with telling him he would not force his inclinations, but give him time to consider the proposal.

The sultan said no more to the prince: he admitted him into his council, and gave him every reason to be satisfied. At the end of the year he took him aside, and said to him, "My son, have you thoroughly considered what I proposed to you last year about marrying? Will you still refuse me that pleasure I expect from your obedience, and suffer me to die without it?"

The prince seemed less disconcerted than before, and was not long answering his father to this effect: "Sir, I have not neglected to consider your proposal, but after the maturest reflection find myself more confirmed in my resolution to continue as I am, so that I hope your majesty will pardon me if I presume to tell you it will be in vain to speak to me any further about marriage." He stopped here, and went out without staying to hear what the sultan would answer.

Any other monarch would have been very angry at such freedom in a son, and would have made him repent it, but the sultan loved him, and preferred gentle methods before he proceeded to compulsion. He communicated this new cause of discontent to his prime minister. "I have followed your advice," said he, "but Camaralzaman is further than ever from complying with my desires. He delivered his resolution in such free terms that it required all my reason and moderation to keep my temper. Tell me, I beseech you, how I shall reclaim a disposition so rebellious to my will?"

"Sir," answered the grand vizier, "patience brings many things about that before seemed impracticable, but it may be this affair is of a nature not likely to succeed in that way. Your majesty would have no cause to reproach yourself if you gave the prince another year to consider the matter. If, in this interval he returns to his duty, you will have the greater satisfaction, and if he still continues averse to your proposal when this is expired, your majesty may propose to him in full council that it is highly necessary for the good of the state that he should marry, and it is not likely he will refuse to comply before so grave an assembly, which you honour with your presence."

The year expired, and, to the great regret of the sultan, Prince Camaralzaman gave not the least proof of having changed his mind. One day, therefore, when there was a great council held, the prime vizier, the other viziers, the principal officers of the crown, and the generals of the army being present, the sultan began to speak thus to the prince: "My son, it is now a long while since I have expressed to you my earnest desire to see you married; and I imagined you would have had more consideration for a father, who required nothing unreasonable of you, than to oppose him so long. But after so long a resistance on your part, which has almost worn out my patience, I have thought fit to propose the same thing once more to you in the presence of my council. I would have you consider that you ought not to have refused this, not merely to oblige a parent; the well-being of my dominions requires it; and the assembly here present joins with me to require it of you. Declare yourself, then; that, according to your answer, I may take the proper measures."

The prince answered with so little reserve, or rather with so much warmth, that the sultan, enraged to see himself thwarted in full council, cried out, "Unnatural son! have you the insolence to talk thus to your father and sultan?" He ordered the guards to take him away, and carry him to an old tower that had been unoccupied for a long while, where he was shut up, with only a bed, a little furniture, some books, and one slave to attend him.

Camaralzaman, thus deprived of liberty, was nevertheless pleased that he had the freedom to converse with his books, and that made him look on his imprisonment with indifference. In the evening he bathed and said his prayers; and after having read some chapters in the Koran, with the same tranquillity of mind as if he had been in the sultan's palace, he undressed himself and went to bed, leaving his lamp burning by him all the while he slept.

In this tower was a well, which served in the daytime for a retreat to a certain fairy, named Maimoune, daughter of Damriat, king or head of a legion of genies. It was about midnight when Maimoune sprang lightly to the mouth of the well, to wander

about the world after her wonted custom, where her curiosity led her. She was surprised to see a light in Prince Camaralzaman's chamber, and entered, without stopping, over the slave who lay at the door.

Prince Camaralzaman had but half-covered his face with the bed-clothes, and Maimoune perceived the finest young man she had seen in all her rambles through the world. "What crime can he have committed," said she to herself, "that a man of his high rank can deserve to be treated thus severely?" for she had already heard his story, and could hardly believe it.

She could not forbear admiring the prince, till at length, having kissed him gently on both cheeks and in the middle of the forehead without waking him, she took her flight into the air. As she mounted high to the middle region, she heard a great flapping of wings, which made her fly that way; and when she approached, she knew it was a genie who made the noise, but it was one of those that are rebellious. As for Maimoune, she belonged to that class whom the great Solomon compelled to acknowledge him.

This genie, whose name was Danhasch, knew Maimoune, and was seized with fear, being sensible how much power she had over him by her submission to the Almighty. He would fain have avoided her, but she was so near him that he must either fight or yield. He therefore broke silence first.

"Brave Maimoune," said he, in the tone of a suppliant, "swear to me that you will not hurt me; and I swear also on my part not to do you any harm."

"Cursed genie," replied Maimoune, "what hurt canst thou do me? I fear thee not; but I will grant thee this favour; I will swear not to do thee any harm. Tell me then, wandering spirit, whence thou comest, what thou hast seen, and what thou hast done this night."

"Fair lady," answered Danhasch, "you meet me at a good time to hear something very wonderful. I come from the utmost limits of China, which look on the last islands of this hemisphere. But, charming Maimoune," said Danhasch, who so trembled with fear at the sight of this fairy that he could hardly speak, "promise me at least that you will forgive me, and let me go on after I have satisfied your demands."

"Go on, go on, cursed spirit," replied Maimoune; "go on and fear nothing. Dost thou think I am as perfidious an elf as thyself, and capable of breaking the solemn oath I have made? Be sure you tell nothing but what is true, or I shall clip thy wings, and treat thee as thou deservest."

Danhasch, a little heartened at the words of Maimoune, said, "My dear lady, I will tell you nothing but what is strictly true, if you will but have the goodness to hear me. The country of China, from whence I come, is one of the largest and most powerful kingdoms of the earth. The king of this country is at present Gaiour, who has an only daughter, the finest maiden that ever was seen in the world since it was a world. Neither you nor I, nor your class nor mine, nor all our respective genies, have expressions strong enough, nor eloquence sufficient to describe this brilliant lady. Any one that did not know the king, father of this incomparable princess, would scarcely be able to imagine the great respect and kindness he shows her. No one has ever dreamed of such care as his to keep her from every one but the man who is to marry her; and, that the retreat which he has resolved to place her in may not seem irksome to her, he has built for her seven palaces, the most extraordinary and magnificent that ever were known.

"The first palace is of rock crystal, the second of copper, the third of fine steel, the fourth of brass, the fifth of touchstone, the sixth of silver, and the seventh of massy gold. He has furnished these palaces most sumptuously, each in a manner suited to the materials that they are built of. He has filled the gardens with grass and flowers, intermixed with pieces of water, water-works, fountains, canals, cascades, and several great groves of trees, where the eye is lost in the prospect, and where the sun never enters, and all differently arranged. King Gaiour, in a word, has shown that he has spared no expense.

"Upon the fame of this incomparable princess's beauty, the most powerful neighbouring kings sent ambassadors to request her in marriage. The King of China received them all in the same obliging manner; but as he resolved not to compel his daughter to marry without her consent, and as she did not like any of the suitors, the ambassadors were forced to return as they came: they were perfectly satisfied with the great honours and civilities they had received.

" 'Sir,' said the princess to the king her father, 'you have an inclination to see me married, and think to oblige me by it; but where shall I find such stately palaces and delicious gardens as I have with your majesty? Through your good pleasure I am under no constraint, and have the same honours shown to me as are paid

this means it will be easy for us to compare them together and determine the dispute."

Danhasch consented to what Maimoune had proposed, and determined to set out immediately for China upon that errand. But Maimoune told him she must first show him the tower whither he was to bring the princess. They flew together to the tower, and when Maimoune had shown it to Danhasch, she cried, "Go, fetch your princess, and do it quickly, for you shall find me here: but listen, you shall pay the wager if my prince is more beautiful than your princess, and I will pay it if your princess is more beautiful than my prince."

Danhasch left Maimoune, and flew towards China, whence he soon returned with incredible speed, bringing the fair princess along with him, asleep. Maimoune received him, and introduced him into the tower of Prince Camaralzaman, where they placed the princess still asleep.

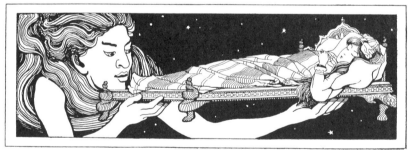

At once there arose a great contest between the genie and the fairy about their respective beauty. They were some time admiring and comparing them without speaking: at length Danhasch broke silence, and said to Maimoune, "You see, as I have already told you, my princess is handsomer than your prince; now, I hope, you are convinced of it."

"Convinced of it!" replied Maimoune; "I am not convinced of it, and you must be blind if you cannot see that my prince is far handsomer. The princess is fair, I do not deny; but if you compare them together without prejudice, you will quickly see the difference."

"Though I should compare them ever so often," said Danhasch, "I could never change my opinion. I saw at first sight what I see now, and time will not make me see differently: however, this shall not hinder my yielding to you, charming Maimoune, if you desire it."

"Yield to me as a favour? I scorn it," said Maimoune: "I would not receive a favour at the hand of such a wicked genie; I refer the matter to an umpire, and if you will not consent I shall win by your refusal."

Danhasch no sooner gave his consent than Maimoune stamped with her foot; the earth opened, and out came a hideous, humpbacked, squinting, and lame genie, with six horns on his head, and claws on his hands and feet. As soon as he had come forth, and the earth had closed up, he, perceiving Maimoune, cast himself at her feet, and then rising up on one knee asked her what she would please to do with him.

"Rise, Caschcasch," said Maimoune, "I brought you hither to determine a difference between me and Danhasch. Look there, and tell me, without partiality, which is the handsomest of those two that lie asleep, the young man or the young lady."

Caschcasch looked at the prince and princess with great attention, admiration and surprise; and after he had considered them a good while, without being able to determine which was the handsomer, he turned to Maimoune, and said, "Madam, I must confess I should deceive you and betray myself, if I pretended to say that one was a whit handsomer than the other: the more I examine them, the more it seems to me that each possesses, in a sovereign degree, the beauty which is betwixt them. But if there be any difference, the best way to determine it is to awaken them one after the other, and by their conduct to decide which ought to be deemed the most beautiful."

This proposal of Caschcasch's pleased equally both Maimoune and Danhasch. Maimoune then changed herself into a gnat, and leaping on the prince's neck stung him so smartly that he awoke, and put up his hand to the place; but Maimoune skipped away, and resumed her own form, which, like those of the two genies, was invisible, the better to observe what he would do.

In drawing back his hand, the prince chanced to let it fall on that of the Princess of China, and on opening his eyes, was exceedingly surprised to perceive a lady of the greatest beauty. He raised his head and leaned on his elbow, the better to consider her. She was so beautiful that he could not help crying out, "What beauty! my heart! my soul!" In saying which he kissed her with so little caution that she would certainly have been awaked by it, had she not slept sounder than ordinary, through the enchantment of Danhasch.

He was going to awaken her at that instant, but suddenly refrained himself. "Is not this she," said he, "that the sultan my father would have had me marry? He was in the wrong not to let me see her sooner. I should not have offended him by my disobedience and passionate language to him in public, and he would have spared himself the confusion which I have occasioned him."

The prince began to repent sincerely of the fault he had committed, and was once more upon the point of waking the Princess of China. "It may be," said he, recollecting himself, "that the sultan my father has a mind to surprise me with this young lady. Who knows but he has brought her himself, and is hidden behind the curtains to make me ashamed of myself. I will content myself with this ring, as a remembrance of her."

He then gently drew off a fine ring which the princess had on her finger, and immediately put on one of his own in its place.

After this he fell into a more profound sleep than before through the enchantment of the genies.

As soon as Prince Camaralzaman was in a sound sleep, Danhasch transformed himself, and went and bit the princess so rudely on the lip that she forthwith awoke, started up, and opening her eyes, was not a little surprised to see a beautiful young prince. From surprise she proceeded to admiration, and from admiration to a transport of joy.

"What," cried she, "is it you the king my father has designed me for a husband? I am indeed most unfortunate for not knowing it before, for then I should not have made him so angry with me. Wake then, wake!"

So saying, she took Prince Camaralzaman by the arm and shook him so that he would have awaked, had not Maimoune increased his sleep by enchantment. She shook him several times, and finding he did not wake, she seized his hand, and kissing it eagerly, perceived he had a ring upon his finger which greatly resembled hers, and which she was convinced was her own, by seeing she had

another on her finger instead of it. She could not comprehend how this exchange could have been made. Tired with her fruitless endeavours to awaken the prince, she soon fell asleep.

When Maimoune saw that she could now speak without fear of awaking the princess, she cried to Danhasch, "Ah, cursed genie, dost thou not now see what thy contest has come to? Art thou not now convinced how much thy princess is inferior to my prince? But I par-

don thee thy wager. Another time believe me when I assert anything." Then turning to Caschcasch, "As for you," said she, "I thank
you for your trouble; take the princess, you and Danhasch, and convey her back whence he has taken her." Danhasch and Caschcasch
did as they were commanded, and Maimoune retired to her well.

Prince Camaralzaman on waking next morning looked to see if
the lady whom he had seen the night before were there. When he
found she was gone, he cried out, "I thought indeed this was a
trick the king my father designed to play me. I am glad I was aware
of it." Then he waked the slave, who was still asleep, and bade
him come and dress him, without saying anything. The slave
brought a basin and water, and after he had washed and said his
prayers, he took a book and read for some time.

After this, he called the slave, and said to him, "Come hither,
and look you, do not tell me a lie. How came that lady hither, and
who brought her?"

"My lord," answered the slave with great astonishment, "I
know not what lady your highness speaks of."

"I speak," said the prince, "of her that came, or rather, that was
brought hither."

"My lord," replied the slave, "I swear I know of no such lady;
and how should she come in without my knowledge, since I lay at
the door?"

"You are a lying rascal," replied the prince, "and in the plot to
vex and provoke me the more." So saying, he gave him a box on the
ear which knocked him down; and after having stamped upon him
for some time, he at length tied the well-rope under his arms, and
plunged him several times into the water, neck and heels. "I will
drown thee," cried he, "if thou dost not tell me speedily who this
lady was, and who brought her."

The slave, perplexed and half-dead, said within himself, "The
prince must have lost his senses through grief." "My lord, then,"

cried he, in a suppliant tone, "I beseech your highness to spare my life, and I will tell you the truth."

The prince drew the slave up, and pressed him to tell him. As soon as he was out of the well, "My lord," said he, trembling, "your highness must perceive that it is impossible for me to satisfy you in my present condition; I beg you to give me leave to go and change my clothes first."

"I permit you, but do it quickly," said the prince, "and be sure you conceal nothing."

The slave went out, and having locked the door upon the prince, ran to the palace just as he was. The king was at that time in discourse with his prime vizier, to whom he had just related the grief in which he had passed the night on account of his son's disobedience and opposition to his will. The minister endeavoured to comfort his master by telling him that the prince himself had given him good cause to be angry. "Sir," said he, "your majesty need not repent of having treated your son after this sort. Have but patience to let him continue a while in prison, and assure yourself his temper will abate, and he will submit to all you require."

The grand vizier had just made an end of speaking when the slave came in and cast himself at the king's feet. "My lord," said he, "I am very sorry to be the messenger of ill news to your majesty, which I know must create you fresh affliction. The prince is distracted, my lord; and his treatment to me, as you may see, too plainly proves it." Then he proceeded to tell all the particulars of what Prince Camaralzaman had said to him, and the violence with which he had been treated.

The king, who did not expect to hear anything of this afflictive kind, said to the prime minister, "This is very melancholy, very different from the hopes you gave me just now: go immediately, without loss of time, see what is the matter, and come and give me an account."

The grand vizier obeyed instantly; and coming into the prince's chamber, he found him sitting on his bed in good temper, and with a book in his hand, which he was reading.

After mutual salutations, the vizier sat down by him, and said, "My lord, I wish that a slave of yours were punished for coming to frighten the king your father."

"What," replied the prince, "could give my father alarm? I have much greater cause to complain of that slave."

"Prince," answered the vizier, "God forbid that the news which he has told your father concerning you should be true; indeed, I myself find it to be false, by the good temper I observe you in."

"It may be," replied the prince, "that he did not make himself well understood; but since you are come, who ought to know something of the matter, give me leave to ask you who was that lady who was here last night?"

The grand vizier was thunderstruck at this question; however, he recovered himself and said, "My lord, be not surprised at my astonishment at your question. Is it possible that a lady, or any other person in the world, should penetrate by night into this place, without entering at the door and walking over the body of your slave? I beseech you, recollect yourself, and you will find it is only a dream which has made this impression on you."

"I give no ear to what you say," said the prince, raising his voice; "I must know of you absolutely what is become of the lady; and if you hesitate to obey me, I shall soon be able to force you to obey me."

At these stern words the grand vizier began to be in greater confusion than before, and was thinking how to extricate himself. He endeavoured to pacify the prince by good words, and begged of him, in the most humble and guarded manner, to tell him if he had seen this lady.

"Yes, yes," answered the prince, "I have seen her, and am very well satisfied you sent her. She played the part you had given her admirably well, for I could not get a word out of her. She pretended to be asleep, but I was no sooner fallen into a slumber than she arose and left me. You know all this; for I doubt not she has been to make her report to you."

"My lord," replied the vizier, "nothing of this has been done which you seem to reproach me with; neither your father nor I have sent this lady you speak of; permit me therefore to remind your highness once more that you have only seen this lady in a dream."

"Do you come to affront and contradict me," said the prince in a great rage, "and to tell me to my face that what I have told you is a dream?" At the same time he took him by the beard, and loaded him with blows as long as he could stand.

The poor grand vizier endured with respectful patience all the violence of his lord's indignation, and could not help saying within himself, "Now am I in as bad a condition as the slave, and shall think myself happy if I can, like him, escape from any further danger." In the midst of repeated blows he cried out for but a moment's audience, which the prince, after he had nearly tired himself with beating him, consented to give.

"I own, my prince," said the grand vizier, dissembling, "there is something in what your highness suspects; but you cannot be ignorant of the necessity a minister is under to obey his royal master's orders; yet, if you will but be pleased to set me at liberty, I will go and tell him anything on your part that you shall think fit to command me."

"Go, then," said the prince, "and tell him from me that if he pleases I will marry the lady he sent me. Do this quickly, and bring me a speedy answer." The grand vizier made a profound reverence, and went away, not thinking himself altogether safe till he had got out of the tower, and shut the door upon the prince.

He came and presented himself before the king, with a coun-tenance that sufficiently showed he had been ill-used, which the king could not behold without concern. "Well," said the king, "in what condition did you find my son?"

"Sir," answered the vizier, "what the slave reported to your majesty is but too true." He then began to relate his interview with Camaralzaman, how he flew into a passion upon his endeav-ouring to persuade him it was impossible that the lady he spoke of should have got in; the ill-treatment he had received from him; how he had been used, and by what means he made his escape.

The king, the more concerned as he loved the prince with excessive tenderness, resolved to find out the truth of this matter, and therefore proposed himself to go and see his son in the tower, accompanied by the grand vizier.

Prince Camaralzaman received the king his father in the tower with great respect. The king sat down, and, after he had made his son the prince sit down by him, put several questions to him, which he answered with great good sense. The king every now and then looked at the grand vizier, as intimating that he did not find his son had lost his wits, but rather thought he had lost *his*.

The king at length spoke of the lady to the prince. "My son," said he, "I desire you to tell me what lady it was that came here, as I have been told."

"Sir," answered Camaralzaman, "I beg of your majesty not to give me more vexation on that head, but rather to oblige me by letting me have her in marriage: this young lady has charmed me. I am ready to receive her at your hands with the deepest gratitude."

The king was surprised at this answer of the prince, so remote, as he thought, from the good sense he had shown before. "My son," said he to him, "you fill me with the greatest astonishment imaginable by what you now say to me; I declare to you by my crown, that is to devolve upon you after me, I know not one word of the lady you mention; and if any such has come to you, it was altogether without my knowledge. But how could she get into this tower without my consent? For whatever my grand vizier told you, it was only to appease you: it must therefore be a mere dream; and I beg of you not to believe otherwise, but to recover your senses."

"Sir," replied the prince, "I should be for ever unworthy of your majesty's favour, if I did not give entire credit to what you are pleased to say; but I humbly beseech you at the same time to give a patient hearing to what I shall say to you, and then to judge whether what I have the honour to tell you be a dream or not."

Then Prince Camaralzaman related to the king his father after what manner he had been awakened, and the pains he took to awaken the lady without effect, and how he had made the exchange of his ring with that of the lady: showing the king the ring, he added, "Sir, your majesty must needs know my ring very well, you have seen it so often. After this, I hope you will be convinced that I have not lost my senses, as you have been almost made to believe."

The king was so perfectly convinced of the truth of what his son had been telling him, that he had not a word to say, remaining astonished for some time, and not being able to utter a syllable.

"Son," at length replied the king, "after what I have just heard, and what I see by the ring on your finger, I cannot doubt but that you have seen this lady. Would I knew who she was, and I would make you happy from this moment, and I should be the happiest father in the world! But where shall I find her, and how seek for her? How could she get in here without my consent? Why did she come? These things, I must confess, are past my finding out." So saying, and taking the prince by the hand, "Come then, my son," he said, "let us go and be miserable together."

The king then led his son out of the tower, and conveyed him to the palace, where he no sooner arrived than in despair he fell ill, and took to his bed; the king shut himself up with him, and spent many a day in weeping, without attending to the affairs of his kingdom.

The prime minister, who was the only person that had admittance to him, came one day and told him that the whole court, and even the people, began to murmur at not seeing him, and that he did not administer justice every day as he was wont to do. "I humbly beg your majesty, therefore," proceeded he, "to pay them some attention; I am aware your majesty's company is a great comfort to the prince, but then you must not run the risk of letting all be lost. Permit me to propose to your majesty to remove with the prince to the castle in a little island near the port, where you may give audience to your subjects twice a week only; during these absences the prince will be so agreeably diverted with the beauty, prospect, and good air of the place, that he will bear them with the less uneasiness."

The king approved this proposal; and after the castle, where he had not resided for some time, had been furnished, he removed thither with the prince; and, excepting the times that he gave audience, as aforesaid, he never left him, but passed all his time by his son's pillow, endeavouring to comfort him in sharing his grief.

Whilst matters passed thus, the two genies, Danhasch and Caschcasch, had carried the Princess of China back to the palace where the king her father had shut her up.

When she awoke the next morning, and found by looking to the right and left that Prince Camaralzaman was not by, she cried out with a loud voice to her women. Her nurse, who presented herself first, desired to be informed what she would please to have, and if anything disagreeable had happened to her.

"Tell me," said the princess, "what is become of the young man whom I love with all my soul?"

"Madam," replied the nurse, "we cannot understand your highness, unless you will be pleased to explain yourself."

"A young man, the best and most amiable," said the princess, "whom I could not awake; I ask you where he is."

"Madam," answered the nurse, "your highness asks these questions to jest with us. I beseech you to rise."

"I am in earnest," said the princess, "and I must know where this young man is."

"Madam," insisted the nurse, "how any man could come without our knowledge we cannot imagine, for we all slept about the door of your chamber, which was locked, and I had the key in my pocket."

At this the princess lost all patience, and catching her nurse by the hair of her head, and giving her two or three sound cuffs, she cried, "You shall tell me where this young man is, old sorceress, or I will beat your brains out."

The nurse struggled to get from her, and at last succeeded; when she went immediately, with tears in her eyes, to complain to the queen her mother, who was not a little surprised to see her in this condition, and asked who had done this.

"Madam," began the nurse, "you see how the princess has treated me; she would certainly have murdered me, if I had not had the good fortune to escape out of her hands." She then began to tell what had been the cause of all that violent passion in the princess. The queen was surprised to hear it, and could not guess how she came to be so senseless as to take that for a reality which could be no other than a dream. "Your Majesty must conclude from all this, madam," continued the nurse, "that the princess is out of her senses. You will think so yourself if you go and see her."

The queen ordered the nurse to follow her; and they went together to the princess's palace that very moment.

The Queen of China sat down by her daughter's bed-side,

immediately upon her arrival in her apartment; and after she had informed herself about her health, she began to ask what had made her so angry with her nurse, that she should have treated her in the manner she had done. "Daughter," said she, "this is not right; and a great princess like you should not suffer herself to be so transported by passion."

"Madam," replied the princess, "I plainly perceive your majesty is come to mock me; but I declare I will never let you rest till you consent I shall marry the young man. You must know where he is, and therefore I beg of your majesty to let him come to me again."

"Daughter," answered the queen, "you surprise me; I know nothing of what you talk of." Then the princess lost all respect for the queen: "Madam," replied she, "the king my father and you persecuted me about marrying, when I had no inclination; I now have an inclination, and I will marry this young man I told you of, or I will kill myself."

Here the queen endeavoured to calm the princess by soft words. "Daughter," said she, "how could any man come to you?" But instead of hearing her, the princess interrupted her, and flew out into such violence as obliged the queen to leave her, and retire in great affliction to inform the king of all that had passed.

The king hearing it had a mind likewise to be satisfied in person; and coming to his daughter's apartment, asked her if what he had just heard was true. "Sir," replied the princess, "let us talk no more of that; I only beseech your majesty to grant me the favour that I may marry the young man. He was the finest and best made youth the sun ever saw. I entreat you, do not refuse me. But that your majesty may no longer doubt whether I have seen this young man, whether I did not do my utmost to awake him, without succeeding, see, if you please, this ring." She then reached forth her hand, and showed the king a man's ring on her finger. The king did not know what to make of all this; but as he had shut her up as mad, he began to think her more mad than ever: therefore, without saying anything more to her, for fear she might do violence to herself or somebody about her, he had her chained, and shut up more closely than before, allowing her only the nurse to wait on her, with a good guard at the door.

The king, exceedingly concerned at this indisposition of his daughter, sought all possible means to get her cured. He assembled his council, and after having acquainted them with the condition she was in, "If any of you," said he, "is capable of undertaking her cure, and succeeds, I will give her to him in marriage, and make him heir to my dominions and crown after my decease."

The desire of marrying a handsome young princess, and the hopes of one day governing so powerful a kingdom as that of China, had a strange effect on an emir, already advanced in age, who was present at this council. As he was well skilled in magic, he offered to cure the king's daughter, and flattered himself he should succeed.

"I consent," said the king, "but I forgot to tell you one thing, and that is, that if you do not succeed you shall lose your head. It would not be reasonable that you should have so great a reward, and yet run no risk on your part; and what I say to you," continued the king, "I say to all others that shall come after you, that they may consider beforehand what they undertake."

The emir, however, accepted the condition, and the king conducted him to where the princess was. She covered her face as soon as she saw them come in, and cried out, "Your majesty surprises me by bringing with you a man whom I do not know, and by whom my religion forbids me to let myself be seen."

"Daughter," replied the king, "you need not be scandalised, it is only one of my emirs who is come to demand you in marriage."

"It is not, I perceive, the person that you have already given me, and whose faith is plighted by the ring I wear," replied the princess; "be not offended that I will never marry any other."

The emir expected the princess would have said or done some extravagant thing, and was not a little disappointed when he heard her talk so calmly and rationally; for then he understood what was really the matter. He dared not explain himself to the king, who would not have suffered the princess to give her hand to any other than the person to whom he wished to give her with his own hand. He therefore threw himself at his majesty's feet, and said, "After what I have heard and observed, sir, it will be to no purpose for me to think of curing the princess, since I have no remedies suited to her malady, for which reason I humbly submit my life to your majesty's pleasure." The king, enraged at his incapacity and the trouble he had given him, caused him immediately to be beheaded.

Some days afterwards, his majesty, unwilling to have it said that he had neglected his daughter's cure, put forth a proclamation in his capital, to the effect that if there were any physician, astrologer, or magician, who would undertake to restore the princess to her senses, he need only come, and he should be employed, on condition of losing his head if he miscarried. He had the same published in the other principal cities and towns of his dominions, and in the courts of the princes his neighbours.

The first that presented himself was an astrologer and magician, whom the king caused to be conducted to the princess's prison. The astrologer drew forth out of a bag he carried under his arm an astrolabe, a small sphere, a chafing dish, several sorts of drugs for fumigations, a brass pot, with many other things, and desired he might have a fire lighted.

The princess demanded what all these preparations were for.

"Madam," answered the astrologer, "they are to exorcise the

evil spirit that possesses you, to shut him up in this pot, and throw him into the sea."

"Foolish astrologer," replied the princess, "I have no occasion for any of your preparations, but am in my perfect senses, and you alone are mad. If your art can bring him I love to me, I shall be obliged to you; otherwise you may go about your business, for I have nothing to do with you."

"Madam," said the astrologer, "if your case be so, I shall desist from all endeavours, believing that only the king your father can remedy your disaster." So putting up his apparatus again, he marched away, very much concerned that he had so easily undertaken to cure an imaginary malady.

Coming to give an account to the king of what he had done, he began thus boldly: "According to what your majesty published in your proclamation, and what you were pleased to confirm to me yourself, I thought the princess was distracted, and depended on being able to recover her by the secrets I have long been acquainted with, but I soon found that your majesty alone is the physician who can cure her, by giving her in marriage the person whom she desires."

The king was very much enraged at the astrologer, and had his head cut off upon the spot. Not to make too long a story of it, a hundred and fifty astrologers, physicians, and magicians all underwent the same fate, and their heads were set up on poles on every gate of the city.

The Princess of China's nurse had a son whose name was Marzavan, and who had been foster-brother to the princess, and brought up with her. Their friendship was so great during their childhood, and all the time they had been together, that they treated each other as brother and sister as they grew up, even some time after their separation.

This Marzavan, among other studies, had from his youth been

much addicted to judicial astrology, geomancy, and the like secret arts, wherein he became exceedingly skilful. Not content with what he had learned from masters, he travelled as soon as he was able to bear the fatigue, and there was hardly any person of note in any science or art but he sought him in the most remote cities, and kept company with him long enough to obtain all the information he desired, so great was his thirst after knowledge.

After several years' absence in foreign parts on this account, he returned to the capital city of his native country, China, where seeing so many heads on the gate by which he entered, he was exceedingly surprised; and coming home he demanded for what reason they had been placed there, but more especially he inquired after the princess his foster-sister, whom he had not forgotten. As he could not receive an answer to one inquiry without the other, he heard at length a general account with much sorrow, waiting till he could learn more from his mother, the princess's nurse.

Although the nurse, mother to Marzavan, was very much taken up with the princess, she no sooner heard that her dear son had returned than she found time to come out, embrace him, and converse with him a little. Having told him, with tears in her eyes, what a sad condition the princess was in, and for what reason the king her father had shut her up, he desired to know of his mother if she could not procure him a private sight of her royal mistress, without the king knowing it. After some pause, she told him she could say nothing for the present, but if he would meet her the next day at the same hour, she would give him an answer.

The nurse knowing that none could approach the princess but herself without leave of the officer who commanded the guard at the gate, addressed herself to him, who she knew had been so lately appointed that he could know nothing of what had passed at the court of China. "You know," said she to him, "I have brought up the princess, and you may likewise have heard that I had a daughter whom I brought up along with her. This daughter has since been married; yet the princess still does her the honour to love her, and would fain see her, but without anybody's perceiving her coming in or out."

The nurse would have gone on, but the officer cried, "Say no more; I will with pleasure do anything to oblige the princess; go and fetch your daughter, or send for her about midnight, and the gate shall be open to you."

As soon as night came, the nurse went to look for her son Marzavan, and having found him, she dressed him so artificially in women's clothes that nobody could know he was a man. She carried him along with her, and the officer, verily believing it was her daughter, admitted them together.

The nurse, before she presented Marzavan, went to the princess, and said, "Madam, this is not a woman I have brought to you; it is my son Marzavan in disguise, newly arrived from his travels, and he having a great desire to kiss your hand, I hope your highness will admit him to that honour."

"What! my brother Marzavan," said the princess, with great joy: "come hither," cried she, "and take off that veil; for it is not unreasonable, surely, that a brother and a sister should see each other without covering their faces."

Marzavan saluted her with profound respect, when she, without giving him time to speak, cried out, "I am rejoiced to see you returned in good health, after so many years' absence without sending the least account all the while of your welfare, even to your good mother."

"Madam," replied Marzavan, "I am infinitely obliged to your highness for your goodness in rejoicing at my health: I hoped to have heard a better account of yours than what to my great affliction I am now witness of. Nevertheless, I cannot but rejoice that I am come seasonably enough to bring your highness that remedy of which you stand so much in need; and though I should reap no other fruit of my studies and long voyage, I should think myself fully recompensed."

Speaking these words, Marzavan drew forth out of his pocket a book and other things, which he judged necessary to be used, according to the account he had had from his mother of the princess's illness. The princess, seeing him make all these preparations, cried out, "What! brother, are you then one of those that believe me mad? Undeceive yourself and hear me."

The princess then began to relate to Marzavan all the particulars of her story, without omitting the least circumstance, even to the ring which was exchanged for hers, and which she showed him.

After the princess had done speaking, Marzavan, filled with wonder and astonishment, continued for some time with his eyes fixed on the ground, without speaking a word; but at length he lifted up his head and said, "If it be as your highness says, which I do not in the least doubt, I do not despair of procuring you the satisfaction you desire; but I must first entreat your highness to arm yourself with patience for some time longer, till I shall return after I have travelled over kingdoms which I have not yet visited; and when you hear of my return, be assured that the object of your wishes is not far off." So saying, Marzavan took leave of the princess, and set out next morning on his intended journey.

He travelled from city to city, from province to province, and from island to island, and in every place he passed through he could hear of nothing but the Princess Badoura (which was the Princess of China's name), and her history.

About four months afterwards, Marzavan arrived at Torf, a seaport town, great and populous, where he no more heard of the Princess Badoura, but where all the talk was of Prince

Camaralzaman, who was ill, and whose history very much resembled hers. Marzavan was extremely delighted to hear this, and informed himself of the place where the prince was to be found. There were two ways to it; one by land and sea, the other by sea only, which was the shortest way.

Marzavan chose the latter, and embarking on board a merchant ship, he arrived safe in sight of the capital; but, just before it entered the port, the ship struck against a rock through the unskilfulness of the pilot, and foundered. It went down in sight of Prince Camaralzaman's castle, where were at that time the king and his grand vizier.

Marzavan could swim very well, and immediately on the ship's sinking cast himself into the sea, and got safe to the shore under the castle, where he was soon relieved by the grand vizier's order. After he had changed his clothes and been well treated, and had recovered, he was introduced to the grand vizier, who had sent for him.

Marzavan being a young man of good air and address, this minister received him very civilly; and when he heard him give such just and fitting answers to what was asked of him, conceived a great esteem for him. He also gradually perceived that he possessed a great deal of knowledge, and therefore said to him, "From what I can understand, I perceive you are no common man; you have travelled a great way: would to God you had learned any secret for curing a certain sick person, who has greatly afflicted this court for a long while!"

Marzavan replied that if he knew what malady it was, he might perhaps find a remedy for it.

Then the grand vizier related to him the whole story of Prince Camaralzaman from its origin, and concealed nothing; his birth, his education, the inclination the king his father had to see him married early, his resistance and extraordinary aversion to marriage, his disobeying his father in full council, his imprisonment, his pretended extravagancies in prison, which were afterwards changed into a violent madness for a certain unknown lady, who, he pretended, had exchanged a ring with him; though, for his part, he verily believed there was no such person in the world.

Marzavan gave great attention to all the grand vizier said; and was infinitely rejoiced to find that, by means of his shipwreck, he had so fortunately lighted on the person he was looking after. He saw no reason to doubt that Prince Camaralzaman was the man, and the Princess of China the lady; therefore, without explaining himself further to the vizier, he desired to see him, that he might be better able to judge of his illness and its cure. "Follow me," said the grand vizier, "and you will find the king with him, who has already desired that I should introduce you."

The first thing that struck Marzavan on entering the prince's chamber was to find him upon his bed languishing, and with his eyes shut. Although he saw him in that condition, and although the king his father was sitting by him, he could not help crying out, "Was there ever a greater resemblance!" He meant to the Princess of China; for it seems the princess and prince were much alike.

The words of Marzavan excited the prince's curiosity so far that he opened his eyes and looked at him. Marzavan, who had a ready wit, laid hold of that opportunity, and made his compliment in verse extempore: but in such a disguised manner, that neither the king nor grand vizier understood anything of the matter. However, he represented so nicely what had happened to him with the Princess of China, that the prince had no reason to doubt that he knew her, and could him give tidings of her. This made him so joyful, that the effects of it showed themselves in his eyes and looks.

After Marzavan had finished his compliment in verse which surprised Prince Camaralzaman so agreeably, his highness took the liberty to make a sign to the king his father, to go from the place where he was, and let Marzavan sit by him.

The king, overjoyed at this alteration, which gave him hopes of his son's speedy recovery, quitted his place, and taking Marzavan by the hand, led him to it. Then his majesty demanded of him who he was, and whence he came. And upon Marzavan's answering that he was a subject of China and came from that kingdom, the king cried out, "Heaven grant that you may be able to cure my son of this profound melancholy, and I shall be eternally obliged to you; all the world shall see how handsomely I will reward you." Having said thus, he left the prince to converse at full liberty with the stranger, whilst he went and rejoiced with the grand vizier.

Marzavan leaning down to the prince, spoke low in his ear, thus: "Prince," said he, "it is time you should cease to grieve. The lady for whom you suffer is the Princess Badoura, daughter of Gaiour, King of China. This I can assure your highness from what she has told me of her adventure, and what I have learned of yours. She has suffered no less on your account than you have on hers." Here he began to relate all that he knew of the princess's story, from the night of their extraordinary interview.

He omitted not to acquaint him how the king had treated those who had failed in their pretensions to cure the princess of her indisposition. "But your highness is the only person," added he, "that can cure her effectually, and may present yourself without fear. However, before you undertake so great a voyage, I would have you perfectly recovered, and then we will take such measures as are necessary. Think then immediately of the recovery of your health."

This discourse had a marvellous effect on the prince. He found such great relief that he felt he had strength to rise, and begged leave of his father to dress himself, with such an air as gave the old king incredible pleasure.

The king could not refrain from embracing Marzavan, without inquiring into the means he had used to produce this wonderful effect, and soon after went out of the prince's chamber with the grand vizier, to publish this agreeable news. He ordered public rejoicings for several days together, and gave great largesses to his officers and the people, alms to the poor, and caused the prisoners to be set at liberty throughout his kingdom. The joy was soon general in the capital and every corner of his dominions.

Prince Camaralzaman, though extremely weakened by almost continual want of sleep and long abstinence from almost all food, soon recovered his health. When he found himself in a condition to undertake the voyage, he took Marzavan aside, and said, "Dear Marzavan, it is now time to perform the promise you have made me. I burn with impatience to see the charming princess, and if we do not set out on our journey immediately I shall soon relapse into my former condition. One thing still troubles me," continued he, "and that is the difficulty I shall meet with in getting leave of my father to go. This would be a cruel disappointment to me, if you do not contrive a way to prevent it. You see he scarcely ever leaves me."

At these words the prince fell to weeping: and Marzavan said, "I foresaw this difficulty; let not your highness be grieved at that, for I will undertake to prevent it. My principal design in this voyage was to deliver the Princess of China from her malady, and this from all the reasons of mutual affection which we have borne to each other from our birth, besides the zeal and affection I otherwise owe her; and I should be wanting in my duty to her, if I did not do my best endeavour to effect her cure and yours, and exert my utmost skill. This then is the means I have contrived to obtain your liberty. You have not stirred abroad for some time, therefore let the king your father understand you have a mind to take the air, and ask his leave to go out on a hunting party for two or three days with me. No doubt he will grant your request; when he has done so, order two good horses to be got ready, one to mount, the other to change, and leave the rest to me."

Next day Prince Camaralzaman took his opportunity. He told the king he was desirous to take the air, and, if he pleased, would go and hunt for two or three days with Marzavan. The king gave his consent, but bade him be sure not to stay out above one night, since too much exercise at first might impair his health, and a too long absence create his majesty uneasiness. He then ordered him to choose the best horses in his stable, and himself took particular care that nothing should be wanting. When all was ready, his majesty embraced the prince, and having recommended the care of him to Marzavan, he let him go. Prince Camaralzaman and Marzavan were soon mounted, when, to amuse the two grooms that led the fresh horses, they made as if they would hunt, and so got as far off the city and out of the road as was possible. When night began to approach, they alighted at a caravanserai or inn, where they supped, and slept till about midnight; then Marzavan awakened the prince without awakening the grooms, and desired his highness to let him have his suit, and to take another for himself, which was brought in his baggage. Thus equipped, they mounted the fresh horses, and after Marzavan had taken one of the groom's horses by the bridle, they set out as hard as their horses could go.

At daybreak they were in a forest, where, coming to the meeting of four roads, Marzavan desired the prince to wait for him a little, and went into the forest. He then killed the groom's horse, and after having torn the prince's suit, which he had put off, he besmeared it with blood and threw it into the highway.

The prince demanded his reason for what he had done. He told his highness he was sure the king his father would no sooner find that he did not return, and come to know that he had departed without the grooms, than he would suspect something, and immediately send people in quest of them. "They that come to this place," said he, "and find these blood-stained clothes, will conclude you are devoured by wild beasts, and that I have escaped to avoid the king's anger. The king, persuading himself that you are dead, will stop further pursuit, and we may have leisure to continue our journey without fear of being followed. I must confess," continued Marzavan, "that this is a violent way of proceeding, to alarm an old father with the death of his son, whom he loves so passionately; but his joy will be the greater when he hears you are alive and happy."

"Brave Marzavan," replied the prince, "I cannot but approve such an ingenious stratagem, or sufficiently admire your conduct: I am under fresh obligations to you for it."

The prince and Marzavan, well provided with cash for their expenses, continued their journey both by land and sea, and found no other obstacle but the length of time which it necessarily took up. They, however, arrived at length at the capital of China, where Marzavan, instead of going to his lodgings, carried the prince to a public inn. They tarried there *incognito* for three days to rest themselves after the fatigue of the voyage; during which time Marzavan caused an astrologer's dress to be made for the prince. The three days being expired, the prince put on his astrologer's habit; and Marzavan left him to go and acquaint his mother, the Princess Badoura's nurse, of his arrival, to the end that she might inform the Princess.

Prince Camaralzaman, instructed by Marzavan as to what he was to do, and provided with all he wanted as an astrologer, came next morning to the gate of the king's palace, before the guards and porters, and cried aloud, "I am an astrologer, and am come to effect a cure on the estimable Princess Badoura, daughter of the most high and mighty monarch Gaiour, King of China, on the conditions proposed by his majesty, to marry her if I succeed, or else to lose my life for my fruitless and presumptuous attempt."

Besides the guards and porters at the gate, this drew together a great number of people about Prince Camaralzaman. No physician, astrologer, nor magician had appeared for a long time, deterred by the many tragic examples of ill success that appeared before their eyes; it was therefore thought that there were no more men of these professions in the world, or that there were no more so mad as those that had gone before them.

The prince's good mien, noble air, and blooming youth made everybody that saw him pity him. "What mean you, sir," said some that were nearest to him, "thus to expose a life of such promising expectation to certain death? Cannot the heads you see on all the gates of this city deter you from such an undertaking? Consider what you do: abandon this rash attempt, and be gone."

The prince continued firm, notwithstanding all these remonstrances; and as he saw nobody come to introduce him, he repeated the same cry with a boldness that made everybody tremble. Then they all cried, "Let him alone, he is resolved to die; God have mercy upon his youth and his soul!" He then proceeded to

cry out a third time in the same manner, when the grand vizier
came in person, and introduced him to the King of China.

As soon as the prince came into the king's presence, he bowed
and kissed the ground. The king, who, of all that had hitherto pre-
sumptuously exposed their lives on this occasion, had not seen
one worthy to cast his eyes upon, felt real compassion for Prince
Camaralzaman on account of the danger he was about to undergo.
But as he thought him more deserving than ordinary, he showed
him more honour, and made him come and sit by him. "Young
man," said he, "I can hardly believe that you, at this age, can have
acquired experience enough to dare attempt the cure of my

daughter. I wish you may succeed; and would give her to you in marriage with all my heart, with the greatest joy, more willingly than I should have done to others that have offered themselves before you; but I must declare to you at the same time, with great concern, that if you do not succeed in your attempt, notwithstanding your noble appearance and your youth you must lose your head."

"Sir," replied the prince, "I am under infinite obligations to your majesty for the honour you design me, and the great goodness you show to a stranger; but I desire your majesty to believe that I would not have come from so remote a country as I have done, the name of which perhaps may be unknown in your dominions, if I had not been certain of the cure I propose. What would not the world say of my fickleness, if, after such great fatigues and dangers as I have undergone on this account, I should abandon the enterprise? Even your majesty would soon lose that esteem you have conceived for me. If I must die, sir, I shall die with the satisfaction of not having lost your esteem after I have merited it. I beseech your majesty therefore to keep me no longer impatient to display the certainty of my art."

Then the king commanded the officer who had the custody of the princess to introduce Prince Camaralzaman into her apartment: but before he would let him go, he reminded him once more that he was at liberty to renounce his design; yet the prince paid no heed, but, with astonishing resolution and eagerness, followed the officer.

When they came to a long gallery, at the end of which was the princess's apartment, the prince, who saw himself so near the object of the wishes which had occasioned him so many tears, pushed on, and got before the officer.

The officer, redoubling his pace, with much ado got up with him. "Whither away so fast?" cried he, taking him by the arm; "you cannot get in without me: and it would seem that you have a great desire for death thus to run to it headlong. Not one of all those many astrologers and magicians I have introduced before made such haste as yourself to a place whither I fear you will come but too soon."

"Friend," replied the prince, looking earnestly at the officer, and continuing his pace, "this was because none of the astrologers you speak of were so sure of their art as I am of mine: they were certain, indeed, that they would die if they did not succeed, but they had no certainty of their success. On this account they had reason to tremble on approaching the place whither I go, and where I am sure to find my happiness." He had just spoken these words as he was at the door. The officer opened it, and introduced him into a great hall, whence was an entrance into the princess's chamber, divided from it only by a piece of tapestry.

Prince Camaralzaman stopt before he entered, speaking softly to the officer for fear of being heard in the princess's chamber. "To convince you," said he, "that there is neither presumption, nor whim, nor youthful conceit in my undertaking, I leave it to your own desire whether I should cure the princess in your presence, or where we are, without going any further?"

The officer was amazed to hear the prince talk to him with such confidence: he left off insulting him, and said seriously, "It is no matter whether you do it here or there, provided the business is done: cure her how you will, you will get immortal honour by it, not only in this court, but over all the world."

The prince replied, "It will be best then to cure her without seeing her, that you may be witness of my skill: notwithstanding my impatience to see a princess of her rank, who is to be my wife, yet, out of respect to you, I will deprive myself of that pleasure for a little while." He was furnished with everything suitable for an astrologer to carry about him; and taking pen, ink, and paper out of his pocket, he wrote a letter to the princess.

When the prince had finished his letter, he folded it up, and enclosed in it the princess's ring, without letting the officer see what he did. When he had sealed it, he gave it to him: "There, friend," said he, "carry it to your mistress; if it does not cure her as soon as she reads it, and sees what is enclosed in it, I give you leave to tell everybody that I am the most ignorant and impudent astrologer that ever was, is, or shall be."

The officer, entering the Princess of China's chamber, gave her the packet he received from Prince Camaralzaman. "Madam," said he, "the boldest astrologer that ever lived, if I am not mistaken, has arrived here, and pretends that on reading this letter and seeing what is in it you will be cured; I wish he may prove neither a liar nor an impostor."

The Princess Badoura took the letter, and opened it with a great deal of indifference, but when she saw the ring, she had not patience to read it through: she rose hastily, broke the chain that held her, ran to the door and opened it. She

knew the prince as soon as she saw him, and he knew her; they at once embraced each other tenderly, without being able to speak for excess of joy: they looked on one another a long time, wondering how they met again after their first interview. The princess's nurse, who ran to the door with her, made them come into her chamber, where the Princess Badoura gave the prince her ring, saying, "Take it; I cannot keep it without restoring yours, which I will never part with; neither can it be in better hands."

The officer immediately went to tell

the King of China what had happened. "Sir," said he, "all the astrologers and doctors who have hitherto pretended to cure the princess were fools in comparison with the last. He made use neither of schemes nor spells or perfumes, or anything else, but cured her without seeing her." Then he told the king how he did it. The monarch was agreeably surprised at the news, and going forthwith to the princess's chamber embraced her: he afterwards embraced the prince, and, taking his hand, joined it to the princess's.

"Happy stranger," said the king, "whoever you are, I will keep my word, and give you my daughter to marry; though, from what I see in you, it is impossible for me to believe that you are really what you appear to be, and would have me believe you."

Prince Camaralzaman thanked the king in the most humble tones, that he might the better show his gratitude. "As for my person," said he, "I must own I am not an astrologer, as your majesty very judiciously guessed; I only put on the habit of one, that I might succeed more easily in my ambition to be allied to the most potent monarch in the world. I was born a prince, and the son of a king and queen; my name is Camaralzaman; my father is Schahzaman, who now reigns over the islands that are well known by the name of the Islands of the Children of Khaledan." He then told him his history.

When the prince had done speaking, the king said to him, "This history is so extraordinary that it deserves to be known to posterity; I will take care it shall be; and the original being deposited in my royal archives, I will spread copies of it abroad, that my own kingdoms and the kingdoms around me may know it."

The marriage was solemnised the same day, and the rejoicings for it were universal all over the empire of China. Nor was Marzavan forgotten: the king immediately gave him an honourable post in his court, and a promise of further advancement; and held continual feastings for several months, to show his joy.

THE LOSS OF THE TALISMAN

SOON after his marriage Prince Camaralzaman dreamt one night that he saw his father Schahzaman on his death-bed, and heard him speak thus to his attendants: "My son, my son, whom I so tenderly loved, has abandoned me." He awoke with a great sigh, which aroused the princess, who asked him the cause of it. Next morning the princess went to her own father, and finding him alone kissed his hand and thus addressed herself to him: "Sir, I have a favour to beg of your majesty; it is that you will give me leave to go with the prince my husband to see King Schahzaman, my father-in-law."

"Daughter," replied the king, "though I shall be very sorry to part with you for so long a time, your resolution is worthy of you: go, child, I give you leave, but on condition that you stay no longer than a year in King Schahzaman's court."

The princess communicated the King of China's consent to Prince Camaralzaman, who was transported with joy to hear it.

The King of China gave orders for preparations to be made for the journey; and when all things were ready, he accompanied the prince and princess several days' journey on their way. They parted at length with great weeping on all sides: the king embraced them, and having desired the prince to be kind to his daughter, and to love her always, he left them to proceed on their journey, and, to divert his thoughts, hunted all the way home.

Prince Camaralzaman and the Princess Badoura travelled for about a month, and at last came to a meadow of great extent, planted with tall trees, forming an agreeable shade. The day being unusually hot, Camaralzaman thought it best to encamp there. They alighted in one of the finest spots, and the prince ordered his servants to pitch their tents, and went himself to give directions. The princess, weary with the fatigue of the journey, bade her women untie her girdle, which they laid down by her, and when she fell asleep, her attendants left her by herself.

Prince Camaralzaman having seen all things in order came to the tent where the princess was sleeping; he entered, and sat down without making any noise, intending to take a nap himself; but observing the princess's girdle lying by her, he took it up, and looked at the diamonds and rubies one by one. In doing this, he saw a little purse hanging to it, sewed neatly on to the stuff, and tied fast with a ribbon; he felt it, and found there was something solid inside it. Desirous to know what it was, he opened the purse, and took out a cornelian, engraven with unknown figures and characters. "This cornelian," said the prince to himself, "must be something very valuable, or my princess would not carry it with so much care." It was Badoura's talisman, which the Queen of China had given her daughter as a charm, to keep her, as she said, from any harm as long as she had it about her.

The prince, the better to look at the talisman, took it out to the light, the tent being dark; and while he was holding it up in his hand, a bird darted down from the air and snatched it away from him.

Imagine the concern and grief of Prince Camaralzaman when he saw the bird fly away with the talisman. He was more troubled at it than words can express, and cursed his unseasonable curiosity, by which his dear princess had lost a treasure that was so precious and so much valued by her.

The bird having got her prize settled on the ground not far off, with the talisman in her mouth. The prince drew near, in hopes she would drop it; but, as he approached, the bird took wing, and settled again on the ground further off. Camaralzaman followed, and the bird, having swallowed the talisman, took a further flight: the prince still followed; the further she flew, the more eager he grew in pursuing her. Thus the bird drew him along from hill to valley, and valley to hill all day, every step leading him further away from the field where he had left his camp and the Princess Badoura; and instead of perching at night on a bush where he might probably have taken her, she roosted on a high tree, safe from pursuit. The prince, vexed to the heart for taking so much pains to no purpose, thought of returning to the camp; "but," said he to himself, "which way shall I return? Shall I go down the hills and valleys which I passed over? Shall I wander in darkness? and will my strength bear me out? How dare I appear before my princess without her talisman?" Overwhelmed with such thoughts, and tired with the pursuit, he lay down under a tree, where he passed the night.

He awoke the next morning before the bird had left the tree, and, as soon as he saw her on the wing, followed her again that whole day, with no better success, eating nothing but herbs and fruits all the way. He did the same for ten days together, pursuing the bird, and keeping his eye upon her from morning to night, always lying under the tree where she roosted. On the eleventh day the bird continued flying, and came near a great city. When the bird came to the walls, she flew over them, and the prince saw no more of her; so he despaired of ever recovering the Princess Badoura's talisman.

Camaralzaman, whose grief was beyond expression, went into the city, which was built by the seaside, and had a fine port; he walked up and down the streets without knowing where he was, or where to stop. At last he came to the port, in as great uncertainty as ever what he should do. Walking along the river-side, he perceived the gate of a garden open, and an old gardener at work. The good man looked up and saw that he was a stranger and a Mussulman, so he asked him to come in, and to shut the door after him.

Camaralzaman entered, and, as the gardener bade him shut the door, demanded of the gardener why he was so cautious.

"Because," replied the old man, "I see you are a stranger newly arrived, and a Mussulman, and this city is inhabited for the most part by idolaters, who have a mortal aversion to us Mussulmans,

and treat those few of us that are here with great barbarity. I suppose you did not know this, and it is a miracle that you have escaped as you have thus far, these idolaters being very apt to fall upon the Mussulmans that are strangers, or to draw them into a snare, unless those strangers know how to beware of them."

Camaralzaman thanked the honest gardener for his advice, and the safety he offered him in his house: he would have said more, but the good man interrupted him, saying, "You are weary, and must want to refresh yourself. Come in and rest." He conducted him into his little hut, and after the prince had eaten heartily of what he set before him, he requested him to relate how he came there.

Camaralzaman complied with his request, and when he had ended his story, he asked him which was the nearest way to the king his father's territories; "for it is in vain," said he, "for me to think of finding my princess where I left her, after wandering eleven days from the spot. Ah!" continued he, "how do I know she is alive?" and so saying, he burst into tears.

The gardener replied that there was no possibility of his going thither by land, the roads were so difficult and the journey so long; besides, he must necessarily pass through the countries of so many barbarous nations that he would never reach his father's. It was a year's journey from the city where he was to any country inhabited only by Mussulmans; the quickest passage for him would be to go to the Isle of Ebony, whence he might easily transport himself to the Isles of the Children of Khaledan: a ship sailed from the port every year to Ebony, and he might take that opportunity of returning to those islands. "The ship departed," said the gardener, "but a few days ago: if you had come a little sooner you might have taken your passage in it. If you will wait the year round until it makes the voyage again, and will stay with me in my house, such as it is, you will be as welcome to it as to your own."

Prince Camaralzaman was glad he had met with such a place of refuge, in a place where he had no acquaintances. He accepted the offer, and lived with the gardener till the time came that the ship was to sail to the Isle of Ebony. He spent his time in working all day in the garden, and all night in sighs, tears and complaints, thinking of his dear Princess Badoura.

We must leave him in this place, to return to the princess, whom we left asleep in her tent.

The princess slept a long time, and, when she awoke, wondered that Prince Camaralzaman was not with her; she called her women, and asked them if they knew where he was. They told her they saw him enter the tent, but did not see him go out again. While they were talking to her, she took up her girdle, found the little purse open, and the talisman gone. She did not doubt but that Camaralzaman had taken it to see what it was, and that he would bring it back with him. She waited for him impatiently till night, and could not imagine what made him stay away from her so long.

When it was quite dark, and she could hear no news of him, she fell into violent grief; she cursed the talisman, and the man that made it. She could not imagine how her talisman should have caused the prince's separation from her: she did not however lose her judgment, and came to a courageous decision as to what she should do.

She only and her women knew of the prince's being gone; for his men were asleep in their tents. The princess, fearing they would betray her if they had any knowledge of it, moderated her grief, and forbade her women to say or do anything that might create the least suspicion. She then laid aside her robe, and put on one of Prince Camaralzaman's, being so like him that next day, when she came out, his men took her for him.

She commanded them to pack up their baggage and begin

their march; and when all things were ready, she ordered one of
her women to go into her litter, she herself mounting on horseback, and riding by her side.

They travelled for several months by land
and sea; the princess continuing the journey
under the name of Camaralzaman. They took
the Isle of Ebony on their way to the Isles of the
Children of Khaledan. They went to the capital
of the Isle of Ebony, where a king reigned whose
name was Armanos. The persons who first
landed gave out that the ship carried Prince
Camaralzaman, who was returning from a long
voyage and was driven in there by a storm, and
the news of his arrival was presently carried to
the court.

King Armanos, accompanied by most of his
courtiers, went immediately to meet the
prince, and met the princess just as she was
landing, and going to the lodging that had been
taken for her. He received her as the son of a king who was his
friend, and conducted her to the palace, where an apartment was
prepared for her and all her attendants, though she would fain
have excused herself, and have lodged in a private house. He
showed her all possible honour, and entertained her for three days
with extraordinary magnificence. At the end of this time, King
Armanos, understanding that the princess, whom he still took for
Prince Camaralzaman, talked of going on board again to proceed
on her voyage, charmed with the air and qualities of such an
accomplished prince as he took her to be, seized an opportunity
when she was alone, and spoke to her in this manner: "You see,
prince, that I am old, and cannot hope to live long; and, to my
great mortification, I have not a son to whom I may leave my

crown. Heaven has only blest me with one daughter, the Princess Haïatalnefous whose beauty cannot be better matched than with a prince of your rank and accomplishments. Instead of going home, stay and marry her from my hand, with my crown, which I resign in your favour. It is time for me to rest, and nothing could be a greater pleasure to me in my retirement than to see my people ruled by so worthy a successor to my throne."

The King of the Isle of Ebony's generous offer to bestow his only daughter in marriage, and with her his kingdom, on the Princess Badoura, put her into unexpected perplexity. She thought it would not become a princess of her rank to undeceive the king, and to own that she was not Prince Camaralzaman, but his wife, when she had assured him that she was he himself, whose part she had hitherto acted so well. She was also afraid to refuse the honour he offered her, lest, as he was much bent upon the marriage, his kindness might turn to aversion and hatred, and he might attempt something even against her life. Besides, she was not sure whether she might not find Prince Camaralzaman in the court of King Schahzaman his father.

These considerations, added to the prospect of obtaining a kingdom for the prince her husband, in case she found him again, determined her to accept the proposal of King Armanos, and marry his daughter; so after having stood silent for some minutes, she with blushes, which the king took for a sign of modesty, answered, "Sir, I am infinitely obliged to your majesty for your good opinion of me, for the honour you do me, and the great favour you offer me, which I cannot pretend to merit, and dare not refuse.

"But, sir," continued she, "I cannot accept this great alliance on any other condition than that your majesty will assist me with your counsel, and that I do nothing without first having your approbation."

The marriage treaty being thus concluded and agreed on, the ceremony was put off till next day. In the mean time Princess Badoura gave notice to her officers, who still took her for Prince Camaralzaman, of what she was going to do so that they might not be surprised at it, assuring them that the Princess Badoura consented. She talked also to her women, and charged them to continue to keep the secret.

The King of the Isle of Ebony, rejoicing that he had got a son-in-law so much to his satisfaction, next morning summoned his council, and acquainted them with his design of marrying his daughter to Prince Camaralzaman, whom he introduced to them; and having made him sit down by his side, told them he resigned the crown to the prince, and required them to acknowledge him for king, and swear fealty to him. Having said this, he descended from his throne, and the Princess Badoura, by his order, ascended it. As soon as the council broke up, the new king was proclaimed through the city, rejoicings were appointed for several days, and couriers despatched all over the kingdom to see the same ceremonies observed with the same demonstrations of joy.

As soon as they were alone, the Princess Badoura told the Princess Haïatalnefous the secret, and begged her to keep it, which she promised faithfully to do.

"Princess," said Haïatalnefous, "your fortune is indeed strange, that a marriage, so happy as yours was, should be shortened by so unaccountable an accident. Pray heaven you may meet with your husband again soon, and be sure that I will religiously keep the secret committed to me. It will be to me the greatest pleasure in the world to be the only person in the great kingdom of the Isle of Ebony who knows what and who you are, while you go on governing the people as happily as you have begun. I only ask of you at present to be your friend." Then the two princesses tenderly embraced each other, and after a thousand expressions of

mutual friendship lay down to rest.

While these things were taking place in the court of the Isle of Ebony, Prince Camaralzaman stayed in the city of idolaters with the gardener, who had offered him his house till the ship sailed.

One morning when the prince was up early, and, as he used to do, was preparing to work in the garden, the gardener prevented him, saying, "This day is a great festival among the idolaters, and because they abstain from all work themselves, so as to spend the time in their assemblies and public rejoicings, they will not let the Mussulmans work. Their shows are worth seeing. You will have nothing to do to-day: I leave you here. As the time approaches in which the ship is accustomed to sail for the Isle of Ebony, I will go and see some of my friends, and secure you a passage in it." The gardener put on his best clothes, and went out.

When Prince Camaralzaman was alone, instead of going out to take part in the public joy of the city, the solitude he was in brought to his mind, with more than usual violence, the loss of his dear princess. He walked up and down the garden sighing and groaning, till the noise which two birds made on a neighbouring tree tempted him to lift up his head, and stop to see what was the matter.

Camaralzaman was surprised to behold a furious battle between these two birds, fighting one another with their beaks. In a very little while one of them fell down dead at the foot of a tree; the bird that was victorious took wing again, and flew away.

In an instant, two other large birds, that had seen the fight at a distance, came from the other side of the garden, and pitched on the ground, one at the feet and the other at the head of the dead bird: they looked at it some time, shaking their heads in token of grief; after which they dug a grave with their talons, and buried it.

When they had filled up the grave with the earth they flew away, and returned in a few minutes, bringing with them the bird that had committed the murder, the one holding one of its wings in its beak, and the other one of its legs; the criminal all the while crying out in a doleful manner, and struggling to escape. They carried it to the grave of the bird which it had lately sacrificed to its rage, and there sacrificed it in just revenge for the murder it had committed. They killed the murderer with their beaks. They then opened it, tore out the entrails, left the body on the spot unburied, and flew away.

Camaralzaman remained in great astonishment all the time that he stood beholding this sight. He drew near the tree, and casting his eyes on the scattered entrails of the bird that was last killed, he spied something red hanging out of its body. He took it up, and found it was his beloved Princess Badoura's talisman, which had cost him so much pain and sorrow and so many sighs since the bird snatched it out of his hand. "Ah, cruel monster!" said he to himself, still looking at the bird, "thou tookest delight in doing mischief, so I have the less reason to complain of that which thou didst to me: but the greater it was, the more do I wish well to those that revenged my quarrel on thee, in punishing thee for the murder of one of their own kind."

It is impossible to express Prince Camaralzaman's joy: "Dear princess," continued he to himself, "this happy minute, which restores to me a treasure so precious to thee, is without doubt a presage of our meeting again, perhaps even sooner than I think."

So saying, he kissed the talisman, wrapped it up in a ribbon, and tied it carefully about his arm. Till now he had been almost every night a stranger to rest, his trouble always keeping him awake, but the next night he slept soundly: he rose somewhat later the next morning than he was accustomed to, put on his working clothes, and went to the gardener for orders. The good man made him root up an old tree which bore no fruit.

Camaralzaman took an axe and began his work. In cutting off a branch of the root, he found that his axe struck against something that resisted the blow and made a great noise. He removed the earth, and discovered a broad plate of brass, under which was a staircase of ten steps. He went down, and at the bottom saw a cavity about six yards square, with fifty brass urns placed in order around it, each with a cover over it. He opened them all, one after another, and there was not one of them which was not full of gold-dust. He came out of the cave, rejoicing that he had found such a vast treasure: he put the brass plate over the staircase, and rooted up the tree against the gardener's return.

The gardener had learned the day before that the ship which was bound for the Isle of Ebony would sail in a few days, but the exact time was not yet fixed. His friend promised to let him know the day, if he called upon him on the morrow; and while Camaralzaman was rooting up the tree, he went to get his answer. He returned with a joyful countenance, by which the prince guessed that he brought him good news. "Son," said the old man (so he always called him, on account of the difference of age between him and the prince), "be joyful, and prepare to embark in three days, for the ship will then certainly set sail: I have arranged with the captain for your passage."

"In my present situation," replied Camaralzaman, "you could not bring me more agreeable news; and in return, I have also tidings that will be as welcome to you; come along with me, and you shall see what good fortune heaven has in store for you."

The prince led the gardener to the place where he had rooted up the tree, made him go down into the cave, and when he was there showed him what a treasure he had discovered, and thanked Providence for rewarding his virtue, and the labour he had done for so many years.

"What do you mean?" replied the gardener: "do you imagine I will take these riches as mine? They are yours: I have no right to them. For fourscore years, since my father's death, I have done nothing but dig in this garden, and could not discover this treasure, which is a sign that it was destined for you, since you have been permitted to find it. It suits a prince like you, rather than me: I have one foot in the grave, and am in no want of anything. Providence has bestowed it upon you, just when you are returning to that country which will one day be your own, where you will make a good use of it."

Prince Camaralzaman would not be outdone in generosity by the gardener. They had a long dispute about it. At last the prince solemnly protested that he would have none of it, unless the gardener would divide it with him and take half. The good man, to please the prince, consented; so they parted it between them, and each had twenty-five urns.

Having thus divided it, "Son," said the gardener to the prince, "it is not enough that you have got this treasure; we must now contrive how to carry it so privately on board the ship that nobody may know anything of the matter, otherwise you will run the risk of losing it. There are no olives in the Isle of Ebony, and those that are exported hence are wanted there; you know I have plenty of them; take what you will; fill fifty pots, half with the gold-dust, and half with olives, and I will get them carried to the ship when you embark."

Camaralzaman followed this good advice, and spent the rest of the day in packing up the gold and the olives in the fifty pots, and fearing lest the talisman, which he wore on his arm, might be lost again, he carefully put it into one of the pots, marking it with a particular mark, to distinguish it from the rest. When they were all ready to be shipped, the prince retired with the gardener, and talking together, he related to him the battle of the birds, and how he had found the Princess Badoura's talisman again. The gardener was equally surprised and joyful to hear it for his sake.

Whether the old man was quite worn out with age, or had exhausted himself too much that day, he had a very bad night; he grew worse the next day, and on the third day, when the prince was to embark, was so ill that it was plain he was near his end. As soon as day broke, the captain of the ship came in person with several seamen to the gardener's; they knocked at the garden-door, and Camaralzaman opened it to them. They asked him where the passenger was that was to go with them. The prince answered, "I am he; the gardener who arranged with you for my passage is ill, and cannot be spoken with: come in, and let your men carry those pots of olives and my baggage aboard. I will only take leave of the gardener, and follow you."

The seamen took up the pots and the baggage, and the captain bade the prince make haste, for the wind being fair they were waiting for nothing but him.

When the captain and his men were gone, Camaralzaman went to the gardener, to take leave of him, and thank him for all his good offices: but he found him in the agonies of death, and had scarcely time to bid him rehearse the articles of his faith, which all good Mussulmans do before they die, when the gardener expired in his presence.

The prince, being under the necessity of embarking immediately, hastened to pay the last duty to the deceased. He washed his body, buried him in his own garden (for the Mahometans had no cemetery in the city of the idolaters, where they were only tolerated), and as he had nobody to assist him it was almost evening before he had put him in the ground. As soon as he had done it he ran to the waterside, carrying with him the key of the garden, intending, if he had time, to give it to the landlord; otherwise to deposit it in some trusty person's hand before a witness, that he might leave it when he was gone. When he came to the port, he was told the ship had sailed several hours before he came and was already out of sight. It had waited three hours for him, and the wind standing fair, the captain dared not stay any longer.

It is easy to imagine that Prince Camaralzaman was exceedingly grieved to be forced to stay longer in a country where he neither had nor wished to have any acquaintance: to think that he must wait another twelvemonth for the opportunity he had lost. But the greatest affliction of all was his having let go the Princess Badoura's talisman, which he now gave over for lost. The only course that was left for him to take was to return to the garden to rent it of the landlord, and to continue to cultivate it by himself, deploring his misery and misfortunes. He hired a boy to help him to do some part of the drudgery; and that he might not lose the other half of the treasure, which came to him by the death of the gardener, who died without heirs, he put the gold-dust into fifty other pots, which he filled up with olives, to be ready against the time of the ship's return.

While Prince Camaralzaman began another year of labour, sorrow and impatience, the ship, having a fair wind, continued her voyage to the Isle of Ebony, and happily arrived at the capital.

The palace being by the sea-side, the new king, or rather the Princess Badoura, espying the ship as she was entering the port, with all her flags flying, asked what vessel it was; she was told that it came annually from the city of the idolaters, and was generally richly laden.

The princess, who always had Prince Camaralzaman in her mind amidst the glories which surrounded her, imagined that the prince might be on board, and resolved to go down to the ship and meet him. Under pretence of inquiring what merchandise was on board, and having the first sight of the goods, and choosing the most valuable, she commanded a horse to be brought, which she mounted, and rode to the port, accompanied by several officers in waiting, and arrived at the port just as the captain came ashore. She ordered him to be brought before her, and asked whence he came, how long he had been on his voyage, and what good or bad fortune he had met with: if he had any stranger of quality on board, and particularly with what his ship was laden.

The captain gave a satisfactory answer to all her demands; and as to passengers, assured her that there were none but merchants in his ship, who were used to come every year and bring rich stuffs from several parts of the world to trade with, the finest linens painted and plain, diamonds, musk, ambergris, camphor, civet, spices, drugs, olives, and many other articles.

The Princess Badoura loved olives extremely: when she heard the captain speak of them, she said, "Land them, I will take them off your hands: as to the other goods, tell the merchants to bring them to me, and let me see them before they dispose of them, or show them to any one else."

The captain, taking her for the King of the Isle of Ebony, replied, "Sire, there are fifty great pots of olives, but they belong to a merchant whom I was forced to leave behind. I gave him notice myself that I was waiting for him, and waited a long time; but as he did not come, and the wind was good, I was afraid of losing it, and so set sail."

The princess answered, "No matter; bring them ashore; we will make a bargain for them."

The captain sent his boat aboard, and in a little time it returned with the pots of olives. The princess demanded how much the fifty pots might be worth in the Isle of Ebony. "Sir," said the captain, "the merchant is very poor, and your majesty will do him a singular favour if you give him a thousand pieces of silver."

"To satisfy him," replied the princess, "and because you tell me he is poor, I will order you a thousand pieces of gold for him, which do you take care to give him." The money was accordingly paid, and the pots carried to the palace in her presence.

Night was drawing on when the princess withdrew into the inner palace, and went to the Princess Haïatalnefous' apartment, ordering the fifty pots of olives to be brought thither. She opened one, to let the Princess Haïatalnefous taste them, and poured them into a dish. Great was her astonishment when she found the olives mingled with gold-dust. "What can this mean?" said she, "it is wonderful beyond comprehension." Her curiosity increasing, she ordered Haïatalnefous' women to open and empty all the pots in her presence; and her wonder was still greater, when she saw that the olives in all of them were mixed with gold-dust; but when she saw her talisman drop out of that into which the prince had put it, she was so surprised that she fainted away. The Princess Haïatalnefous and her women restored the Princess Badoura by throwing cold water on her face. When she recovered her senses, she took the talisman and kissed it again and again; but not being willing that the Princess Haïatalnefous' women, who were ignorant of her disguise, should hear what she said, she dismissed them.

"Princess," said she to Haïatalnefous, as soon as they were gone, "you, who have heard my story, surely guessed that it was at the sight of the talisman that I fainted. This is the talisman, the fatal cause of my losing my dear husband Prince Camaralzaman; but as it was that which caused our separation, so I foresee it will be the means of our meeting again soon."

The next day, as soon as it was light, she sent for the captain of the ship; and when he came she spoke to him thus: "I want to know something more of the merchant to whom the olives belong, that I bought of you yesterday. I think you told me you had left him behind you in the city of the idolaters: can you tell me what he is doing there?"

"Yes, sire," replied the captain, "I can speak on my own knowledge. I arranged for his passage with a very old gardener, who told me I should find him in his garden, where he worked under him. He showed me the place, and for that reason I told your majesty he was poor. I went there to call him. I told him what haste I was in, spoke to him myself in the garden, and cannot be mistaken in the man."

"If what you say is true," replied the Princess Badoura, "you must set sail this very day for the city of idolaters, and fetch me that gardener's man, who is my debtor; else I will not only confiscate all your goods and those of your merchants, but your and their lives shall answer for his. I have ordered my seal to be put on the warehouses where they are, which shall not be taken off till you bring me that man. This is all I have to say to you; go, and do as I command you."

The captain could make no reply to this order, the disobeying of which would be a very great loss to him and his merchants. He told them about it, and they hastened him away as fast as they could after he had laid in a stock of provisions and fresh water for his voyage. They were so diligent, that he set sail the same day. He had a prosperous voyage to the city of the idolaters, where he arrived in the night. When he was as near to the city as he thought convenient, he would not cast anchor, but let the ship ride off the shore; and going into his boat, with six of his stoutest seamen, he landed a little way off the port, whence he went directly to Camaralzaman's garden.

Though it was about midnight when he arrived there, the prince was not asleep. His separation from the fair Princess of China his wife afflicted him as usual. He cursed the minute in which his curiosity tempted him to touch the fatal girdle.

Thus did he pass those hours which are devoted to rest, when he heard somebody knock at the garden door. He ran hastily to it, half-dressed as he was; but he had no sooner opened it, than the captain and his seamen took hold of him, and carried him by force on board the boat, and so to the ship, and as soon as he was safely lodged, they set sail immediately, and made the best of their way to the Isle of Ebony.

Hitherto Camaralzaman, the captain, and his men had not said a word to one another; at last the prince broke silence, and asked

the captain, whom he recognised, why they had taken him away by force. The captain in his turn demanded of the prince whether he was not a debtor of the King of Ebony.

"I the King of Ebony's debtor!" replied Camaralza- man in amazement; "I do not know him, I never had anything to do with him in my life, and never set foot in his king- dom."

The captain answered, "You should know that better than I; you will talk to him yourself in a little while: till then, stay here and have patience."

Though it was night when he cast anchor in the port, the cap- tain landed immediately, and taking Prince Camaralzaman with him hastened to the palace, where he demanded to be introduced to the king.

The Princess Badoura had withdrawn into the inner palace; however, as soon as she had heard of the captain's return and Camaralzaman's arrival, she came out to speak to him. As soon as she set her eyes on the prince, for whom she had shed so many tears, she knew him in his gardener's clothes. As for the prince, who trembled in the presence of a king, as he thought her, to whom he was to answer for an imaginary debt, it did not enter into his head that the person whom he so earnestly desired to see stood before him. If the princess had followed the dictates of her inclination, she would have run to him and embraced him, but she put a constraint on herself, believing that it was for the interest of both that she should act the part of a king a little longer before she made herself known. She contented herself for the present with putting him into the hands of an officer, who was then in waiting, with a charge to take care of him till the next day.

When the Princess Badoura had provided for Prince Camaralzaman, she turned to the captain, whom she was now to reward for the important service he had done her. She commanded another officer to go immediately and take the seal off the warehouse where his and his merchants' goods were, and gave him a rich diamond, worth much more than the expense of both his voyages. She bade him besides keep the thousand pieces of gold she had given him for the pots of olives, telling him she would make up the account with the merchant herself.

This done, she retired to the Princess of the Isle of Ebony's apartment, to whom she communicated her joy, praying her to keep the secret still. She told her how she intended to manage to reveal herself to Prince Camaralzaman, and to give him the kingdom.

The Princess of the Isle of Ebony was so far from betraying her, that she rejoiced and entered fully into the plan.

The next morning the Princess of China ordered Prince Camaralzaman to be apparelled in the robes of an emir or governor of a province. She commanded him to be introduced into the council, where his fine person and majestic air drew all the eyes of the lords there present upon him.

The Princess Badoura herself was charmed to see him again, as handsome as she had often seen him, and her pleasure inspired her to speak the more warmly in his praise. When she addressed herself to the council, having ordered the prince to take his seat among the emirs, she spoke to them thus: "My lords, this emir whom I have advanced to the same dignity with you is not unworthy the place assigned him. I have known enough of him in my travels to answer for him, and I can assure you he will make his merit known to all of you."

Camaralzaman was extremely amazed to hear the King of the Isle of Ebony, whom he was far from taking for a woman, much less for his dear princess, name him, and declare that he knew him, while he thought himself certain that he had never seen him before in his life. He was much more surprised when he heard him praise him so excessively. Those praises, however, did not disconcert him, though he received them with such modesty as showed that he did not grow vain. He prostrated himself before the throne of the king, and rising again, "Sire," said he, "I want words to express my gratitude to your majesty for the honour you have done me: I shall do all in my power to render myself worthy of your royal favour."

From the council-board the prince was conducted to a palace, which the Princess Badoura had ordered to be fitted up for him; where he found officers and domestics ready to obey his commands, a stable full of fine horses, and everything suitable to the rank of an emir. Then the steward of his household brought him a strong box full of gold for his expenses.

The less he understood whence came his great good fortune, the more he admired it, but never once imagined that he owed it to the Princess of China.

Two or three days after, the Princess Badoura, that he might be nearer to her, and in a more distinguished post, made him high treasurer, which office had lately become vacant. He behaved himself in his new charge with so much integrity, yet obliging everybody, that he not only gained the friendship of the great but also the affections of the people, by his uprightness and bounty.

Camaralzaman would have been the happiest man in the world, if he had had his princess with him. In the midst of his good fortune he never ceased lamenting her, and grieved that he could hear no tidings of her, especially in a country where she must necessarily have come on her way to his father's court after their separation. He would have suspected something had the Princess Badoura still gone by the name of Camaralzaman, but on her accession to the throne she changed it, and took that of Armanos, in honour of the old king her father-in-law. She was now known only by the name of the young King Armanos. There were very few courtiers who knew that she had ever been called Camaralzaman, which name she assumed when she arrived at the court of the Isle of Ebony, nor had Camaralzaman so much acquaintance with any of them yet as to learn more of her history.

The princess fearing he might do so in time, and desiring that he should owe the discovery to herself only, resolved to put an end to her own torment and his; for she had observed that as often as she discoursed with him about the affairs of his office, he fetched such deep sighs as could be addressed to nobody but her. She herself also lived under such constraint that she could endure it no longer.

The Princess Badoura had no sooner made this decision with the Princess Haïatalnefous, than she took Prince Camaralzaman aside, saying, "I must talk with you about an affair, Camaralzaman, which requires much consideration, and on which I want your advice. Come hither in the evening, and leave word at home that you will not return; I will take care to provide you a bed."

Camaralzaman came punctually to the palace at the hour appointed by the princess; she took him with her into the inner apartment, and having told the chief chamberlain, who was preparing to follow her, that she had no occasion for his service, and that he should only keep the door shut, she took him into a different apartment.

When the prince and princess entered the chamber she shut the door, and, taking the talisman out of a little box, gave it to Camaralzaman, saying, "It is not long since an astrologer presented me with this talisman; you being skilful in all things, may perhaps tell me its use."

Camaralzaman took the talisman, and drew near a lamp to look at it. As soon as he recollected it, with an astonishment which gave the princess great pleasure, "Sire," said he to the princess, "your majesty asked me what this talisman is good for. Alas! it is only good to kill me with grief and despair, if I do not quickly find the most charming and lovely princess in the world to whom it belonged, whose loss it occasioned by a strange adventure, the very recital of which will move your majesty to pity such an unfortunate husband and lover, if you would have patience to hear it."

"You shall tell me that another time," replied the princess; "I am very glad to tell you I know something of it already; stay here a little, and I will return to you in a moment."

At these words she went into her dressing-room, put off her royal turban, and in a few minutes dressed herself like a woman; and having the girdle round her which she wore on the day of their separation, she entered the chamber.

Prince Camaralzaman immediately knew his dear princess, ran to her, and tenderly embraced her, crying out, "How much I am obliged to the king, who has so agreeably surprised me!"

"Do not expect to see the king any more," replied the princess, embracing him in her turn, with tears in her eyes; "you see him in me: sit down, and I will explain this enigma to you."

They sat down, and the princess told the prince the resolution she came to, in the field where they encamped the last time they were together, as soon as she perceived that she waited for him to no purpose; how she went through with it till she arrived at the Isle of Ebony, where she had been obliged to marry the Princess Haïatalnefous, and accept the crown which King Armanos offered her as a condition of the marriage: how the princess, whose merit she highly extolled, had kept the secret, and how she found the talisman in the pots of olives mingled with the gold-dust, and how the finding it was the cause of her sending for him to the city of the idolaters.

The Princess Badoura and Prince Camaralzaman rose next morning as soon as it was light, but the princess would no more put on her royal robes as king; she dressed herself in the dress of a woman, and then sent the chief chamberlain to King Armanos, her father-in-law, to desire he would be so good as to come to her apartment.

When the king entered the chamber, he was amazed to see there a lady who was unknown to him, and the high treasurer with her, who was not permitted to come within the inner palace. He sat down and asked where the king was.

The princess answered, "Yesterday I was king, sir, and today I am the Princess of China, wife of the true Prince Camaralzaman, the true son of King Schahzaman. If your majesty will have the patience to hear both our stories, I hope you will not condemn me for putting an innocent deceit upon you." The king bade her go on, and heard her discourse from the beginning to the end with astonishment. The princess on finishing it said to him, "Sir, in our religion men may have several wives; if your majesty will consent to give your daughter the Princess Haïatalnefous in marriage to Prince Camaralzaman, I will with all my heart yield up to her the rank and quality of queen, which of right belongs to her, and content myself with the second place. If this precedence was not her due, I would, however, give it her, after she has kept my secret so generously."

King Armanos listened to the princess with astonishment, and when she had done, turned to Prince Camaralzaman, saying, "Son, since the Princess Badoura your wife, whom I have all along thought to be my son-in-law, through a deceit of which I cannot complain, assures me that she is willing, I have nothing more to do but to ask you if you are willing to marry my daughter and accept the crown, which the Princess Badoura would deservedly wear as long as she lived, if she did not quit it out of love to you."

"Sir," replied Prince Camaralzaman, "though I desire nothing so earnestly as to see the king my father, yet the obligation I am under to your majesty and the Princess Haïatalnefous is so weighty, I can refuse her nothing." Camaralzaman was proclaimed king, and married the same day with all possible demonstrations of joy.

Not long afterwards they all resumed the long interrupted journey to the Isles of the Children of Khaledan, where they were fortunate enough to find the old King Schahzaman still alive and overjoyed to see his son once more; and after several months' rejoicing, King Camaralzaman and the two queens returned to the Island of Ebony, where they lived in great happiness for the remainder of their lives.

THE FIRST VOYAGE OF
SINBAD THE SAILOR

MY father left me a considerable estate, the best part of which I spent in riotous living during my youth; but I perceived my error, and reflected that riches were perishable, and quickly consumed by such ill managers as myself. I further considered that by my irregular way of living I had wretchedly misspent my time, which is the most valuable thing in the world. Struck with those reflections, I collected the remains of my furniture, and sold all my patrimony by public auction to the highest bidder. Then I entered into a contract with some merchants, who traded by sea: I took the advice of such as I thought most capable to give it me; and resolving to improve what money I had, I went to Balsora, and embarked with several merchants on board a ship which we jointly fitted out.

We set sail, and steered our course towards the East Indies, through the Persian Gulf, which is formed by the coasts of Arabia Felix on the right, and by those of Persia on the left, and, according to common opinion, is seventy leagues across at the broadest part. The eastern sea, as well as that of the Indies, is very spacious: it is bounded on one side by the coasts of Abyssinia, and is 4,500 leagues in length to the isles of Vakvak. At first I was troubled with sea-sickness, but speedily recovered my health, and was not afterwards troubled with that disease.

In our voyage we touched at several islands, where we sold or exchanged our goods. One day, whilst under sail, we were becalmed near a little island, almost even with the surface of the water, which resembled a green meadow. The captain ordered his sails to be furled, and permitted such persons as had a mind to do so to land upon the island, amongst whom I was one.

But while we were diverting ourselves with eating and drinking, and recovering ourselves from the fatigue of the sea, the
island on a sudden trembled, and shook us terribly.

They perceived the trembling of the island on board the ship,
and called us to re-embark speedily, or we should all be lost, for
what we took for an island was only the back of a whale. The nim-
blest got into the sloop, others betook themselves to swimming;
but for my part I was still upon the back of the whale when he dived
into the sea, and had time only to catch hold of a piece of wood that
we had brought out of the ship to make a fire. Meanwhile, the captain, having received those on board who were in the sloop, and taking up some of those that swam, resolved to use the favourable gale
that had just risen, and hoisting his sails, pursued his voyage, so
that it was impossible for me to regain the ship.

Thus was I exposed to the mercy of the waves, and struggled
for my life all the rest of the day and the following night. Next
morning I found my strength gone, and despaired of saving my
life, when happily a wave threw me against an island. The bank
was high and rugged, so that I could scarcely have got up had it not
been for some roots of trees, which fortune seemed to have preserved in this place for my safety. Being got up, I lay down upon
the ground half dead until the sun appeared; then, though I was
very feeble, both by reason of my hard labour and want of food, I
crept along to look for some herbs fit to eat, and had the good luck

not only to find some, but likewise a spring of excellent water, which contributed much to restore me. After this I advanced farther into the island, and came at last into a fine plain, where I perceived a horse feeding at a great distance. I went towards him, between hope and fear, not knowing whether I was going to lose my life or save it. Presently I heard the voice of a man from under ground, who immediately appeared to me, and asked who I was. I gave him an account of my adventure; after which, taking me by the hand, he led me into a cave, where there were several other people, no less amazed to see me than I was to see them.

I ate some victuals which they offered me, and then asked them what they did in such a desert place. They answered that they were grooms belonging to King Mihrage, sovereign of the island, and that every year they brought thither the king's horses. They added that they were to get home to-morrow, and had I been one day later I must have perished, because the inhabited part of the island was at a great distance, and it would have been impossible for me to have got thither without a guide.

Next morning they returned with their horses to the capital of the island, took me with them, and presented me to King Mihrage. He asked me who I was, and by what adventure I came into his dominions. And, after I had satisfied him, he told me he was much concerned for my misfortune, and at the same time ordered that I should want for nothing, which his officers were so generous and careful as to see exactly fulfilled.

Being a merchant, I frequented the society of men of my own profession, and particularly inquired for those who were strangers, if perhaps I might hear any news from Bagdad, or find an opportunity to return thither, for King Mihrage's capital was situated on the edge of the sea, and had a fine harbour, where ships arrived daily from the different quarters of the world. I frequented also the society of the learned Indians, and took delight in hearing

them discourse; but withal I took care to make my court regularly
to the king, and conversed with the governors and petty kings, his
tributaries, that were about him. They asked me a thousand questions about my country, and I, being willing to inform myself as to

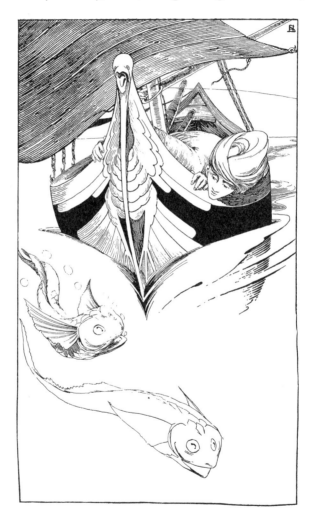

their laws and customs, asked them everything which I thought worth knowing.

There belonged to this king an island named Cassel. They assured me that every night a noise of drums was heard there, whence the mariners fancied that it was the residence of Degial. I had a great mind to see this wonderful place, and on my way thither saw fishes of one hundred and two hundred cubits long, that occasion more fear than hurt, for they are so timid that they will fly at the rattling of two sticks or boards. I saw likewise other fishes, about a cubit in length, that had heads like owls.

As I was one day at the port after my return, a ship arrived, and as soon as she cast anchor, they begun to unload her, and the merchants on board ordered their goods to be carried into the warehouse. As I cast my eye upon some bales, and looked at the name, I found my own, and perceived the bales to be the same that I had embarked at Balsora. I also knew the captain; but being persuaded that he believed me to be drowned, I went and asked him whose bales they were. He replied: "They belonged to a merchant of Bagdad, called Sinbad, who came to sea with us; but one day, being near an island, as we thought, he went ashore with several other passengers upon this supposed island, which was only a monstrous whale that lay asleep upon the surface of the water; but as soon as he felt the heat of the fire they had kindled on his back to dress some victuals he began to move, and dived under water: most of the persons who were upon him perished, and among them unfortunate Sinbad. Those bales belonged to him, and I am resolved to trade with them until I meet with some of his family, to whom I may return the profit."

"Captain," said I, "I am that Sinbad whom you thought to be dead, and those bales are mine."

When the captain heard me speak thus, "O heaven," said he, "whom can we ever trust now-a-days? There is no faith left among

men. I saw Sinbad perish with my own eyes, and the passengers on board saw it as well as I, and yet you tell me you are that Sinbad. What impudence is this! To look at you, one would take you to be a man of honesty, and yet you tell a horrible falsehood, in order to possess yourself of what does not belong to you."

"Have patience, captain," replied I; "do me the favour to hear what I have to say."

"Very well," said he, "speak; I am ready to hear you." Then I told him how I escaped, and by what adventure I met with the grooms of King Mihrage, who brought me to his court.

He was soon persuaded that I was no cheat, for there came people from his ship who knew me, paid me great compliments, and expressed much joy to see me alive. At last he knew me himself, and embracing me, "Heaven be praised," said he, "for your happy escape; I cannot enough express my joy for it: there are your goods; take and do with them what you will." I thanked him, acknowledged his honesty, and in return offered him part of my goods as a present, which he generously refused.

I took out what was most valuable in my bales, and presented it to King Mihrage, who, knowing my misfortune, asked me how I came by such rarities. I acquainted him with the whole story. He was mightily pleased at my good luck, accepted my present, and gave me one much more considerable in return. Upon this I took leave of him, and went aboard the same ship, after I had exchanged my goods for the commodities of that country. I carried with me wood of aloes, sandal, camphor, nutmegs, cloves, pepper, and ginger. We passed by several islands, and at last arrived at Balsora, from whence I came to this city, with the value of one hundred thousand sequins. My family and I received one another with transports of sincere friendship. I bought slaves and fine lands, and built me a great house. And thus I settled myself, resolving to forget the miseries I had suffered, and to enjoy the pleasures of life.

THE SECOND VOYAGE OF
SINBAD THE SAILOR

I DESIGNED, after my first voyage, to spend the rest of my days at Bagdad; but it was not long ere I grew weary of a quiet life. My inclination to trade revived. I bought goods suited to the commerce I intended, and put to sea a second time, with merchants of known probity. We embarked on board a good ship, and after recommending ourselves to God, set sail. We traded from island to island, and exchanged commodities with great profit. One day we landed on an island covered with several sorts of fruit trees, but so unpeopled, that we could see neither man nor beast upon it. We went to take a little fresh air in the meadows, and along the streams that watered them. Whilst some diverted themselves with gathering flowers, and others with gathering fruits, I took my wine and provisions, and sat down by a stream betwixt two great trees, which formed a curious shape. I made a very good meal, and afterwards fell asleep. I cannot tell how long I slept, but when I awoke the ship was gone.

I was very much surprised to find the ship gone. I got up and looked about everywhere, and could not see one of the merchants who landed with me. At last I perceived the ship under sail, but at such a distance that I lost sight of her in a very little time.

I leave you to guess at my melancholy reflections in this sad condition. I was ready to die with grief: I cried out sadly, beat my head and breast, and threw myself down upon the ground, where I lay some time in a terrible agony. I upbraided myself a hundred times for not being content with the produce of my first voyage, that might well have served me all my life. But all this was in vain, and my repentance out of season.

At last I resigned myself to the will of God; and not knowing what to do, I climbed up to the top of a great tree, from whence I looked about on all sides to see if there was anything that could give me hope. When I looked towards the sea, I could see nothing but sky and water, but looking towards the land I saw something white; and, coming down from the tree, I took up what provision I had left and went towards it, the distance being so great that I could not distinguish what it was.

When I came nearer, I thought it to be a white bowl of a prodigious height and bigness; and when I came up to it I touched it, and found it to be very smooth. I went round to see if it was open on any side, but saw it was not, and that there was no climbing up to the top of it, it was so smooth. It was at least fifty paces round.

By this time the sun was ready to set, and all of a sudden the sky became as dark as if it had been covered with a thick cloud. I was much astonished at this sudden darkness, but much more when I found it was occasioned by a bird, of a monstrous size, that came flying towards me. I remembered a fowl, called *roc*, that I had often heard mariners speak of, and conceived that the great bowl, which I so much admired, must needs be its egg. In short, the bird lighted, and sat over the egg to hatch it. As I perceived her coming, I crept close to the egg, so that I had before me one of the legs of the bird, which was as big as the trunk of a tree. I tied myself strongly to it with the cloth that went round my turban, in hopes that when the roc flew away next morning she would carry me with her out of this desert island. And after having passed the night in this condition, the bird really flew away next morning, as soon as it was day, and carried me so high that I could not see the earth. Then she descended all of a sudden, with so much rapidity that I lost my senses; but when the roc was settled,

and I found myself upon the ground, I speedily untied the knot, and had scarcely done so when the bird, having taken up a serpent of a monstrous length in her bill, flew away.

The place where she left me was a very deep valley, encompassed on all sides with mountains, so high that they seemed to reach above the clouds, and so full of steep rocks that there was no possibility of getting out of the valley. This was a new perplexity, so that when I compared this place with the desert island from which the roc brought me, I found that I had gained nothing by the change.

As I walked through this valley I perceived it was strewn with diamonds, some of which were of surprising bigness. I took a great deal of pleasure in looking at them; but speedily I saw at a distance such objects as very much diminished my satisfaction, and which I could not look upon without terror; they were a great number of serpents, so big and so long that the least of them was capable of swallowing an elephant. They retired in the day-time to their dens, where they hid themselves from the roc, their enemy, and did not come out but in the night-time.

I spent the day in walking about the valley, resting myself at times in such places as I thought most suitable. When night came on I went into a cave, where I thought I might be in safety. I stopped the mouth of it, which was low and straight, with a great stone, to preserve me from the serpents, but not so exactly fitted as to hinder light from coming in. I supped on part of my provisions, but the serpents, which began to appear, hissing about in the meantime, put me into such extreme fear that you may easily imagine I did not sleep. When day appeared the serpents retired, and I came out of the cave trembling. I can justly say that I walked a long time upon diamonds without feeling an inclination to touch any of them. At last I sat down, and notwithstanding my uneasiness, not having shut my eyes during the night, I fell asleep, after having eaten a little more of my provisions; but I had scarcely shut my eyes, when something that fell by me with great noise awakened me. This was a great piece of fresh meat, and at the same time I saw several others fall down from the rocks in different places.

I had always looked upon it as a fable when I heard mariners and others discourse of the valley of diamonds, and of the stratagems made use of by some merchants to get jewels from thence; but now I found it to be true. For, in reality, those merchants come to the neighbourhood of this valley when the eagles have young ones, and throwing great joints of meat into the valley, the diamonds, upon whose points they fall, stick to them; the eagles, which are stronger in this country than anywhere else, pounce with great force upon those pieces of meat, and carry them to their nests upon the top of the rocks to feed their young with, at which time the merchants, running to their nests, frighten the eagles by their noise, and take away the diamonds that stick to the meat. And this stratagem they make use of to get the diamonds out of the valley, which is surrounded with such precipices that nobody can enter it.

I believed till then that it was not possible for me to get out of this abyss, which I looked upon as my grave; but now I changed my mind, for the falling in of those pieces of meat put me in hopes of a way of saving my life.

I began to gather together the largest diamonds that I could see, and put them into the leathern bag in which I used to carry my provisions. I afterwards took the largest piece of meat I could find, tied it close round me with the cloth of my turban, and then laid myself upon the ground, with my face downwards, the bag of diamonds being tied fast to my girdle, so that it could not possibly drop off.

I had scarcely laid me down before the eagles came. Each of them seized a piece of meat, and one of the strongest having taken me up, with a piece of meat on my back, carried me to his nest on the top of the mountain. The merchants fell straightway to shouting, to frighten the eagles; and when they had obliged them to quit their prey, one of them came to the nest where I was. He was very much afraid when he saw me, but recovering himself, instead of inquiring how I came thither, he began to quarrel with me, and asked why I stole his goods. "You will treat me," replied I, "with more civility when you know me better. Do not trouble yourself; I have diamonds enough for you and myself too, more than all the other merchants together. If they have any, it is by

chance; but I chose myself in the bottom of the valley all those
which you see in this bag"; and having spoken those words, I
showed them to him. I had scarcely done speaking, when the
other merchants came trooping about us, much astonished to see
me; but they were much more surprised when I told them my
story. Yet they did not so much admire my stratagem to save
myself as my courage to attempt it.

They took me to the place where they were staying all

together, and there having opened my bag, they were surprised at the largeness of my diamonds, and confessed that in all the courts where they had been they had never seen any that came near them. I prayed the merchant to whom the nest belonged (for every merchant had his own), to take as many for his share as he pleased. He contented himself with one, and that too the least of them; and when I pressed him to take more, without fear of doing me any injury, "No," said he, "I am very well satisfied with this, which is valuable enough to save me the trouble of making any more voyages to raise as great a fortune as I desire."

I spent the night with those merchants, to whom I told my story a second time, for the satisfaction of those who had not heard it. I could not moderate my joy when I found myself delivered from the danger I have mentioned. I thought I was in a dream, and could scarcely believe myself to be out of danger.

The merchants had thrown their pieces of meat into the valley for several days, and each of them being satisfied with the diamonds that had fallen to his lot, we left the place next morning all together, and travelled near high mountains, where there were serpents of a prodigous length, which we had the good fortune to escape. We took ship at the nearest port and came to the Isle of Roha, where the trees grow that yield camphor. This tree is so large, and its branches so thick, that a hundred men may easily sit under its shade. The juice of which the camphor is made runs out from a hole bored in the upper part of the tree, is received in a vessel, where it grows thick, and becomes what we call camphor; and the juice thus drawn out the tree withers and dies.

There is in this island the rhinoceros, a creature less than the elephant, but greater than the buffalo; it has a horn upon its nose about a cubit long; this horn is solid, and cleft in the middle from one end to the other, and there are upon it white lines, representing the figure of a man. The rhinoceros fights with the elephant, runs his horn into him, and carries him off upon his head; but the blood of the elephant running into his eyes and making him blind, he falls to the ground, and then, strange to relate, the roc comes and carries them both away in her claws to be food for her young ones.

Here I exchanged some of my diamonds for good merchandise. From thence we went to other isles, and at last, having touched at several trading towns of the main land, we landed at Balsora, from whence I went to Bagdad. There I immediately gave great alms to the poor, and lived honourably upon the vast riches I had gained with so much fatigue.

THE THIRD VOYAGE OF
SINBAD THE SAILOR

THE pleasures of the life which I then led soon made me forget the risks I had run in my two former voyages; but, being then in the flower of my age, I grew weary of living without business; and hardening myself against the thought of any danger I might incur, I went from Bagdad, with the richest commodities of the country, to Balsora: there I embarked again with the merchants. We made a long voyage, and touched at several ports, where we drove a considerable trade. One day, being out in the main ocean, we were attacked by a horrible tempest, which made us lose our course. The tempest continued several days, and brought us before the port of an island, where the captain was very unwilling to enter; but we were obliged to cast anchor there. When we had furled our sails the captain told us that this and some other neighbouring islands were inhabited by hairy savages, who would speedily attack us; and though they were but dwarfs, yet our misfortune was that we must make no resistance, for they

were more in number than the locusts; and if we happened to kill one of them they would all fall upon us and destroy us.

This discourse of the captain put the whole company into a great consternation; and we found very soon, to our cost, that what he had told us was but too true; an innumerable multitude of frightful savages, covered all over with red hair, and about two feet high, came swimming towards us, and in a little time encompassed our ship. They spoke to us as they came near, but we understood not their language; they climbed up the sides of the ship with an agility that surprised us. We beheld all this with mortal fear, without daring to offer to defend ourselves, or to speak one word to divert them from their mischievous design. In short, they took down our sails, cut the cable, and, hauling to the shore, made us all get out, and afterwards carried the ship into another island, from whence they had come. All travellers carefully avoided that island where they left us, it being very dangerous to stay there, for a reason you shall hear anon; but we were forced to bear our affliction with patience.

We went forward into the island, where we found some fruits and herbs to prolong our lives as long as we could; but we expected nothing but death. As we went on we perceived at a distance a

great pile of building, and made towards it. We found it to be a
palace, well built, and very lofty, with a gate of ebony with double
doors, which we thrust open. We entered the court, where we saw
before us a vast apartment with a porch, having on one side a heap
of men's bones, and on the other a vast number of roasting spits.
We trembled at this spectacle, and, being weary with travelling,

our legs failed under us: we fell to the ground, seized with deadly fear, and lay a long time motionless.

The sun had set, and whilst we were in the lamentable condition just mentioned, the gate of the apartment opened with a great noise, and there came out the horrible figure of a black man, as high as a tall palm tree. He had but one eye, and that in the middle of his forehead, where it looked as red as a burning coal. His fore-teeth were very long and sharp, and stood out of his mouth, which was as deep as that of a horse; his upper lip hung down upon his breast; his ears resembled those of an elephant, and covered his shoulders; and his nails were as long and crooked as the talons of the greatest birds. At the sight of so frightful a giant we lost all our senses, and lay like men dead.

At last we came to ourselves, and saw him sitting in the porch, looking at us. When he had considered us well, he advanced towards us, and laying his hand upon me, he took me up by the nape of my neck, and turned me round as a butcher would do a sheep's head. After having viewed me well, and perceiving me to be so lean that I had nothing but skin and bone, he let me go. He took up all the rest, one by one, and viewed them in the same manner; and the captain being the fattest, he held him with one hand, as I might a sparrow, and thrusting a spit through him, kindled a great fire, roasted, and ate him in his apartment for his supper. This being done, he returned to his porch, where he lay and fell asleep, snoring louder than thunder. He slept thus till morning. For our parts, it was not possible for us to enjoy any rest; so that we passed the night in the most cruel fear that can be imagined. Day being come, the giant awoke, got up, went out, and left us in the palace.

When we thought him at a distance, we broke the melancholy silence we had kept all night, and every one grieving more than another, we made the palace resound with our complaints and groans. Though there were a great many of us, and we had but one enemy, we had not at first the presence of mind to think of delivering ourselves from him by his death.

We thought of several other things, but determined nothing; so that, submitting to what it should please God to order concerning us, we spent the day in running about the island for fruit and herbs to sustain our lives. When evening came, we sought for a place to lie down in, but found none; so that we were forced, whether we would or not, to return to the palace.

The giant failed not to come back, and supped once more upon one of our companions; after which he slept, and snored till day, and then went out and left us as formerly. Our condition was so very terrible that several of my comrades designed to throw themselves into the sea, rather than die so strange a death. Those who were of this mind argued with the rest to follow their example; upon which one of the company answered that we were forbidden to destroy ourselves; but even if it were lawful, it was more reasonable to think of a way to rid ourselves of the barbarous tyrant who designed so cruel a death for us.

Having thought of a project for that end, I communicated the same to my comrades, who approved it. "Brethren," said I, "you know there is a great deal of timber floating upon the coast; if you will be advised by me, let us make several rafts that may carry us, and when they are done, leave them there till we think fit to make use of them. In the meantime we will execute the design to deliver ourselves from the giant, and if it succeed, we may stay here with patience till some ship pass by to carry us out of this fatal island; but if it happen to miscarry, we will speedily get to our rafts, and put to sea. I confess, that by exposing ourselves to the fury of the waves, we run a risk of losing our lives; but if we do, is it not better to be buried in the sea than in the entrails of this monster, who has already devoured two of us?" My advice was relished,

and we made rafts capable of
carrying three persons each.

We returned to the palace
towards evening, and the giant
arrived a little while after. We
were forced to see another of our comrades roasted. But at last we
revenged ourselves on the brutish giant thus. After he had made
an end of his cursed supper, he lay down on his back, and fell
asleep. As soon as we heard him snore, according to his custom,
nine of the boldest among us, and myself, took each of us a spit,
and putting the points of them into the fire till they were burning
hot, we thrust them into his eye all at once, and blinded him. The
pain occasioned him to make a frightful cry, and to get up and
stretch out his hands in order to sacrifice some of us to his rage,
but we ran to places where he could not find us; and after having
sought for us in vain, he groped for the gate, and went out, howling dreadfully.

We went out of the palace after the giant, and came to the
shore, where we had left our rafts, and put them immediately into
the sea. We waited till day in order to get upon them, in case the
giant came towards us with any guide of his own species; but we

hoped that if he did not appear by sunrise, and gave over his howling, which we
still heard, he would die; and if that happened to be the case, we resolved to stay
in the island, and not to risk our lives
upon the rafts. But day had scarcely
appeared when we perceived our cruel
enemy, accompanied by two others
almost of the same size leading him, and
a great number more coming before him
with a very quick pace.

When we saw this, we made no delay,
but got immediately upon our rafts, and
rowed off from the shore. The giants,
who perceived this, took up great stones,
and running to the shore entered the
water up to their waists, and threw so
exactly that they sank all the rafts but
that I was upon, and all my companions,
except the two with me, were drowned.
We rowed with all our might, and got out
of the reach of the giants; but when we
got out to sea, we were exposed to the
mercy of the waves and winds, and
tossed about, sometimes on one side,
and sometimes on another, and spent
that night and the following day under a
cruel uncertainty as to our fate; but next morning we had the good
luck to be thrown upon an island, where we landed with much joy.
We found excellent fruit there, that gave us great relief, so that we
pretty well recovered our strength.

In the evening we fell asleep on the bank of the sea, but were awakened by the noise of a serpent as long as a palm tree, whose scales made a rustling as he crept along. He swallowed up one of my comrades, notwithstanding his loud cries and the efforts he made to rid himself from the serpent, which shook him several times against the ground, and crushed him; and we could hear him gnaw and tear the poor wretch's bones, when we had fled a great distance from him. Next day we saw the serpent again, to our great terror, and I cried out, "O heaven, to what dangers are we exposed! We rejoiced yesterday at having escaped from the cruelty of a giant and the rage of the waves, and now are we fallen into another danger altogether as terrible."

As we walked about we saw a large tall tree, upon which we designed to pass the following night, for our security; and having satisfied our hunger with fruit, we mounted it accordingly. A little while after, the serpent came hissing to the root of the tree, raised itself up against the trunk of it, and meeting with my comrade, who sat lower than I, swallowed him at once, and went off.

I staid upon the tree till it was day, and then came down, more like a dead man than one alive, expecting the same fate as my two companions. This filled me with horror, so that I was going to throw myself into the sea; but nature prompting us to a desire to live as long as we can, I withstood this temptation to despair, and submitted myself to the will of God, who disposes of our lives at His pleasure.

In the meantime I gathered together a great quantity of small wood, brambles, and dry thorns, and making them up into faggots made a great circle with them round the tree, and also tied some of them to the branches over my head. Having done thus, when the evening came I shut myself up within this circle, with this melancholy piece of satisfaction, that I had neglected nothing which could preserve me from the cruel destiny with which I was threatened. The serpent failed not to come at the usual hour, and went round the tree, seeking for an opportunity to devour me, but was prevented by the rampart I had made, so that he lay till day, like a cat watching in vain for a mouse that has retreated to a place of safety. When day appeared he retired, but I dared not to leave my fort until the sun arose.

I was fatigued with the toil he had put me to, and suffered so much from his poisonous breath that, death seeming preferable to me than the horror of such a condition, I came down from the tree, and not thinking on the resignation I had made to the will of God the preceding day, I ran towards the sea, with a design to throw myself into it headlong.

God took compassion on my desperate state, for just as I was going to throw myself into the sea, I perceived a ship at a considerable distance. I called as loud as I could, and taking the linen from my turban, displayed it that they might observe me. This had the desired effect; all the crew perceived me, and the captain sent his boat for me. As soon as I came aboard, the merchants and seamen flocked about me to know how I came to that desert island; and after I had told them of all that befell me, the oldest among them said they had several times heard of the giants that dwelt in that island, that they were cannibals and ate men raw as well as roasted; and as to the serpents, he added, there were abundance in the isle that hid themselves by day and came abroad by night. After having testified their joy at my escaping so many dangers, they brought me the best of what they had to eat; and the captain, seeing that I was all in rags, was so generous as to give me one of his own suits.

We were at sea for some time, touched at several islands, and at last landed at that of Salabat, where there grows sanders, a wood of great use in physic. We entered the port, and came to anchor. The merchants began to unload their goods, in order to sell or exchange them. In the meantime the captain came to me, and said, "Brother,

I have here a parcel of goods that belonged to a merchant who sailed some time on board this ship; and he being dead, I intend to dispose of them for the benefit of his heirs, when I know them." The bales he spoke of lay on the deck, and showing them to me, he said, "There are the goods; I hope you will take care to sell them, and you shall have a commission." I thanked him that he gave me an opportunity to employ myself, because I hated to be idle.

The clerk of the ship took an account of all the bales, with the names of the merchants to whom they belonged; and when he asked the captain in whose name he should enter those he gave me the charge of, "Enter them" said the captain, "in the name of Sinbad the sailor." I could not hear myself named without some emotion, and looking steadfastly on the captain, I knew him to be the person who, in my second voyage, had left me in the island where I fell asleep by a brook, and set sail without me, and without sending to look for me. But I could not remember him at first, he was so much altered since I saw him.

And as for him, who believed me to be dead, I could not wonder at his not knowing me. "But, captain," said I, "was the merchant's name to whom those goods belonged Sinbad?"

"Yes," replied he, "that was his name; he came from Bagdad, and embarked on board my ship at Balsora. One day, when we landed at an island to take in water and other refreshments, I know not by what mistake I set sail without observing that he did not re-embark with us; neither I nor the merchants perceived it till four hours after. We had the wind in our stern and so fresh a gale that it was not then possible for us to tack about for him."

"You believe him then to be dead?" said I.

"Certainly," answered he.

"No, captain," said I; "look upon me, and you may know that I am Sinbad, whom you left in that desert island. I fell asleep by a brook, and when I awoke I found all the company gone."

The captain, having considered me attentively, knew me at last, embraced me, and said, "God be praised that fortune has supplied my defect. There are your goods, which I always took care to preserve and to make the best of at every port where I touched. I restore them to you, with the profit I have made on them." I took them from him, and at the same time acknowledged how much I owed to him.

From the Isle of Salabat we went to another, where I furnished myself with cloves, cinnamon, and other spices. As we sailed from that island we saw a tortoise that was twenty cubits in length and breadth. We observed also a fish which looked like a cow, and gave milk, and its skin is so hard that they usually make bucklers of it. I saw another which had the shape and colour of a camel. In short, after a long voyage, I arrived at Balsora, and from thence returned to this city of Bagdad, with so much riches that I knew not what I had. I gave a great deal to the poor, and bought another great estate in addition to what I had already.

THE FOURTH VOYAGE OF
SINBAD THE SAILOR

THE pleasures I took after my third voyage had not charms enough to divert me from another. I was again prevailed upon by my passion for traffic and curiosity to see new things. I therefore settled my affairs, and having provided a stock of goods fit for the places where I designed to trade, I set out on my journey. I took the way of Persia, of which I travelled over several provinces, and then arrived at a port, where I embarked. We set sail, and having touched at several ports of the mainland and some of the eastern islands, we put out to sea, and were overtaken by a sudden gust of wind that obliged the captain to furl his sails, and to take all other necessary precautions to prevent the danger that threatened us. But all was in vain; our endeavours had no effect, the sails were torn into a thousand pieces, and the ship was stranded; so that a great many of the merchants and seamen were drowned, and the cargo lost.

I had the good fortune, with several of the merchants and mariners, to get a plank, and we were carried by the current to an island which lay before us: there we found fruit and spring water, which preserved our lives. We stayed all night near the place where the sea cast us ashore, without consulting what we should do, our misfortune had dispirited us so much.

Next morning, as soon as the sun was up, we walked from the shore, and advancing into the island, saw some houses, to which we went; and as soon as we came thither we were encompassed by a great number of black men, who seized us, shared us among them, and carried us to their respective habitations.

I and five of my comrades were carried to one place; they made us sit down immediately, and gave us a certain herb, which they made signs to us to eat. My comrades, not taking notice that the black men ate none of it themselves, consulted only the satisfying of their own hunger, and fell to eating with greediness: but I, suspecting some trick, would not so much as taste it, which happened well for me; for in a little time I perceived my companions had lost their senses, and that when they

spoke to me they knew not what
they said.

The black men fed us afterwards with rice, prepared with oil
of cocoanuts, and my comrades,
who had lost their reason, ate of it
greedily. I ate of it also, but very
sparingly. The black men gave us
that herb at first on purpose to
deprive us of our senses, that we
might not be aware of the sad destiny prepared for us; and they gave
us rice on purpose to fatten us, for,
being cannibals, their design was to eat us as soon as we grew fat.
They did accordingly eat my comrades, who were not aware of
their condition; but my senses being entire, you may easily guess
that instead of growing fat, as the rest did, I grew leaner every day.
The fear of death under which I laboured turned all my food into
poison. I fell into a languishing illness which proved my safety, for
the black men having killed and eaten up my companions, seeing
me to be withered, lean, and sick, deferred my death till another
time.

Meanwhile, I had a great deal of liberty, so that there was
scarcely any notice taken of what I did, and this gave me an opportunity one day to get at a distance from the houses, and to make
my escape. An old man who saw me, and suspected my design,
called to me as loud as he could to return, but instead of obeying
him, I redoubled my pace, and quickly got out of sight. At that
time there was none but the old man about the houses, the rest
being away, and not to come home till night, which was pretty
usual with them; therefore, being sure that they could not come
in time to pursue me, I went on till night, when I stopped to rest a

little, and to eat some of the provisions I had taken care to bring;
but I speedily set forward again, and travelled seven days, avoid-
ing those places which seemed to be inhabited, and living for the
most part upon cocoanuts, which served me for both meat and
drink. On the eighth day I came near the sea, and all of a sudden
saw white people like myself, gathering pepper, of which there
was great plenty in that place. This I took to be a good omen, and
went to them without any scruple.

The people who gathered pepper came to meet me as soon as
they saw me, and asked me in Arabic who I was, and whence I
came. I was overjoyed to hear them speak in my own language, and
satisfied their curiosity by giving them an account of my shipwreck, and how I fell into the hands of the black men. "Those
black men," replied they, "are cannibals, and by what miracle did
you escape their cruelty?" I told them the same story I now tell
you, at which they were wonderfully surprised.

I stayed with them till they had gathered their quantity of pepper, and then sailed with them to the island from whence they
came. They presented me to their king, who was a good prince.
He had the patience to hear the relation of my adventures, which
surprised him, and he afterwards gave me clothes, and commanded care to be taken of me.

The island was very well peopled, plentiful in everything, and
the capital was a place of great trade. This agreeable retreat was
very comfortable to me after my misfortune, and the kindness of
this generous prince towards me completed my satisfaction. In a
word, there was not a person more in favour with him than myself;
and, in consequence, every man in court and city sought to oblige
me, so that in a very little time I was looked upon rather as a native
than a stranger.

I observed one thing which to me appeared very extraordinary.
All the people, the king himself not excepted, rode their horses

without bridle or stirrups. This made me one day take the liberty
to ask the king how that came to pass. His majesty answered, that
I talked to him of things which nobody knew the use of in his
dominions. I went immediately to a workman, and gave him a
model for making the stock of a saddle. When that was done, I
covered it myself with velvet and leather, and embroidered it
with gold. I afterwards went to a locksmith, who made me a bridle according to the pattern I showed him, and then he made me
also some stirrups. When I had all things completed, I presented
them to the king, and put them upon one of his horses. His
majesty mounted immediately, and was so pleased with them,
that he testified his satisfaction by large presents to me. I could
not avoid making several others for his ministers and the principal officers of his household, who all of them made me presents
that enriched me in a little time. I also made some for the people
of best quality in the city, which gained me great reputation and
regard.

As I paid court very constantly to the king, he said to me one
day, "Sinbad, I love thee; and all my subjects who know thee treat
thee according to my example. I have one thing to demand of
thee, which thou must grant."

"Sir," answered I, "there is nothing but I will do, as a mark of my obedience to your majesty, whose power over me is absolute."

"I have a mind thou shouldst marry," replied he, "that so thou mayst stay in my dominion, and think no more of thy own country."

I dared not resist the prince's will, and so he gave me one of the ladies of his court, a noble, beautiful, and rich lady. The ceremonies of marriage being over, I went and dwelt with the lady, and for some time we lived together in perfect harmony. I was not, however, very well satisfied with my condition, and therefore designed to make my escape on the first occasion, and to return to Bagdad, which my present settlement, how advantageous soever, could not make me forget.

While I was thinking on this, the wife of one of my neighbours, with whom I had contracted a very close friendship, fell sick and died. I went to see and comfort him in his affliction, and finding him swallowed up with sorrow, I said to him as soon as I saw him, "God preserve you and grant you a long life."

"Alas!" replied he, "how do you think I should obtain that favour you wish me? I have not above an hour to live."

"Pray," said I, "do not entertain such a melancholy thought; I hope it will not be so, but that I shall enjoy your company for many years."

"I wish you," said he, "a long life; but for me my days are at an end, for I must be buried this day with my wife. This is a law which our ancestors established in this island, and always observed inviolably. The living husband is interred with the dead wife, and the living wife with the dead husband. Nothing can save me; every one must submit to this law."

While he was entertaining me with an account of this barbarous custom, the very hearing of which frightened me cruelly, his kindred, friends and neighbours came in a body to assist at the

funerals. They put on the corpse the woman's richest apparel, as if
it had been her wedding-day, and dressed her with all her jewels;
then they put her into an open coffin, and lifting it up, began their
march to the place of burial. The husband walked at the head
of the company, and followed the corpse. They went up to a
high mountain, and when they came thither, took up a great
stone, which covered the mouth of a very deep pit, and let down
the corpse, with all its apparel and jewels. Then the husband,

embracing his kindred and friends, suffered himself to be put into another open coffin without resistance, with a pot of water, and seven little loaves, and was let down in the same manner as they let down his wife. The mountain was pretty long, and reached to the sea. The ceremony being over, they covered the hole again with the stone, and returned.

It is needless to say that I was the only melancholy spectator of this funeral, whereas the rest were scarcely moved at it, the practice was so customary to them. I could not forbear speaking my thoughts of this matter to the king. "Sir," said I, "I cannot but wonder at the strange custom in this country of burying the living with the dead. I have been a great traveller, and seen many countries, but never heard of so cruel a law."

"What do you mean, Sinbad?" said the king; "it is a common law. I shall be interred with the queen, my wife, if she die first."

"But, sir," said I, "may I presume to ask your majesty if strangers be obliged to observe this law?"

"Without doubt," replied the king, smiling at my question; "they are not exempted, if they are married in this island."

I went home very melancholy at this answer, for the fear of my wife dying first, and my being interred alive with her, occasioned me very mortifying reflections. But there was no remedy: I must have patience, and submit to the will of God. I trembled, however, at every little indisposition of my wife; but alas! in a little time my fears came upon me all at once, for she fell ill, and died in a few days.

You may judge of my sorrow; to be interred alive seemed to me as deplorable an end as to be devoured by cannibals. But I must submit; the king and all his court would honour the funeral with their presence, and the most considerable people of the city would do the like. When all was ready for the ceremony, the corpse was put into a coffin, with all her jewels and magnificent apparel.

The cavalcade began, and, as second actor in this doleful tragedy, I went next to the corpse, with my eyes full of tears, bewailing my deplorable fate. Before I came to the mountain, I addressed myself to the king, in the first place, and then to all those who were round me, and bowing before them to the earth to kiss the border of their garments, I prayed them to have compassion upon me. "Consider," said I, "that I am a stranger, and ought not to be subject to this rigorous law, and that I have another wife and child in my own country." It was to no purpose for me to speak thus, no soul was moved at it; on the contrary, they made haste to let down my wife's corpse into the pit, and put me down the next moment in an open coffin, with a vessel full of water and seven loaves. In short, the fatal ceremony being performed, they covered up the mouth of the pit, notwithstanding the excess of my grief and my lamentable cries.

As I came near the bottom, I discovered, by help of the little light that came from above, the nature of this subterranean place; it was a vast long cave, and might be about fifty fathoms deep. I immediately smelt an insufferable stench proceeding from the multitude of corpses which I saw on the right and left; nay, I fancied that I heard some of them sigh out their last. However, when I got down, I immediately left my coffin, and, getting at a distance from the corpses, lay down upon the ground, where I stayed a long time, bathed in tears. Then reflecting on my sad lot, "It is true," said I, "that God disposes all things according to the decrees of His providence; but, poor Sinbad, art not thou thyself the cause of thy being brought to die so strange a death? Would to God thou hadst perished in some of those tempests which thou hast escaped! Then thy death had not been so lingering and terrible in all its circumstances. But thou hast drawn all this upon thyself by thy cursed avarice. Ah! unfortunate wretch, shouldst thou not rather have stayed at home, and quietly enjoyed the fruits of thy labour?"

Such were the vain com-
plaints with which I made the
cave echo, beating my head and
breast out of rage and despair,
and abandoning myself to the
most afflicting thoughts.
Nevertheless, I must tell you
that, instead of calling death to
my assistance in that miserable
condition, I felt still an inclination to live, and to do all I could
to prolong my days. I went groping about, with my nose

stopped, for the bread and water that was in my coffin, and took
some of it. Though the darkness of the cave was so great that I
could not distinguish day and night, yet I always found my coffin
again, and the cave seemed to be more spacious and fuller of
corpses than it appeared to me at first. I lived for some days upon
my bread and water, which being all used up at last I prepared for
death.

As I was thinking of death, I heard something walking, and
blowing or panting as it walked. I advanced towards that side from
whence I heard the noise, and upon my approach the thing puffed
and blew harder, as if it had been running away from me. I
followed the noise, and the thing seemed to stop sometimes, but
always fled and blew as I approached. I followed it so long and so
far that at last I perceived a light resembling a star; I went on
towards that light, and sometimes lost sight of it, but always
found it again, and at last discovered that it came through a hole in
the rock large enough for a man to get out at.

Upon this I stopped some time to rest myself, being much
fatigued with pursuing this discovery so fast. Afterwards coming

up to the hole I went out
at it, and found myself
upon the shore of the sea. I leave you to guess
the excess of my joy; it was such that I could
scarce persuade myself of its being real.

But when I had recovered from my surprise,
and was convinced of the truth of the matter, I
found that the thing which I had followed and
heard puff and blow was a creature which came
out of the sea, and was accustomed to enter at
that hole to feed upon the dead carcasses.

I examined the mountain, and perceived it
to be situated betwixt the sea and the town, but
without any passage or way to communicate
with the latter, the rocks on the side of the sea
were so rugged and steep. I fell down upon the
shore to thank God for this mercy, and afterwards entered the cave again to fetch bread and
water, which I did by daylight, with a better
appetite than I had done since my interment in the dark hole.

I returned thither again, and groped about among the biers for
all the diamonds, rubies, pearls, gold bracelets, and rich stuffs I
could find. These I brought to the shore, and, tying them up
neatly into bales with the cords that let down the coffins, I laid
them together upon the bank to wait till some ship passed by,
without fear of rain, for it was not then the season.

After two or three days I perceived a ship that had but just
come out of the harbour and passed near the place where I was. I
made a sign with the linen of my turban, and called to them as
loud as I could. They heard me, and sent a boat to bring me on
board, when the mariners asked by what misfortune I came
thither. I told them that I had suffered shipwreck two days ago,

and made shift to get ashore with the goods they saw. It was happy for me that those people did not consider the place where I was, nor inquire into the probability of what I told them; but without any more ado took me on board with my goods. When I came to the ship, the captain was so well pleased to have saved me, and so much taken up with his own affairs, that he also took the story of my pretended shipwreck upon trust, and generously refused some jewels which I offered him.

We passed with a regular wind by several islands, among others the one called the Isle of Bells, about ten days' sail from Serendib, and six from that of Kela, where we landed. This island produces lead from its mines, Indian canes, and excellent camphor.

The king of the Isle of Kela is very rich and potent, and the Isle of Bells, which is about two days' journey in extent, is also subject to him. The inhabitants are so barbarous that they still eat human flesh. After we had finished our commerce in that island we put to sea again, and touched at several other ports. At last I arrived happily at Bagdad with infinite riches of which it is needless to trouble you with the detail. Out of thankfulness to God for His mercies, I gave great alms for the support of several mosques, and for the subsistence of the poor, and employed myself wholly in enjoying the society of my kindred and friends, and in making merry with them.

THE FIFTH VOYAGE OF
SINBAD THE SAILOR

THE pleasures I enjoyed again had charm enough to make me forget all the troubles and calamities I had undergone, without curing me of my inclination to make new voyages. Therefore I bought goods, ordered them to be packed up and loaded, and set out with them for the best seaport; and there, that I might not be obliged to depend upon a captain, but have a ship at my own command, I waited till one was built on purpose at my own expense. When the ship was ready, I went on board with my goods; but not having enough to load her, I took on board with me several merchants of different nations, with their merchandise.

We sailed with the first fair wind, and after a long voyage, the first place we touched at was a desert island, where we found an egg of a roc, equal in size to that I formerly mentioned. There was a young roc in it just ready to be hatched, and the bill of it began to appear.

The merchants whom I had taken on board my ship, and who landed with me, broke the egg with hatchets, and made a hole in it, from whence they pulled out the young roc piece by piece, and roasted it. I had earnestly persuaded them not to meddle with the egg, but they would not listen to me.

Scarcely had they made an end of their feast, when there appeared in the air, at a considerable distance from us, two great clouds. The captain whom I hired to manage my ship, knowing by experience what it meant, cried that it was the cock and hen roc

that belonged to the young one, and pressed us to re-embark with all speed, to prevent the misfortune which he saw would otherwise befall us. We made haste to do so, and set sail with all possible diligence.

In the meantime the two rocs approached with a frightful noise, which they redoubled when they saw the egg broken, and their young one gone. But having a mind to avenge themselves, they flew back towards the place from whence they came, and disappeared for some time, while we made all the sail we could to prevent that which unhappily befell us.

They returned, and we observed that each of them carried between their talons stones, or rather rocks, of a monstrous size. When they came directly over my ship, they hovered, and one of them let fall a stone; but by the dexterity of the steersman, who turned the ship with the rudder, it missed us, and falling by the side of the ship into the sea, divided the water so that we could see almost to the bottom. The other roc, to our misfortune, threw the stone so exactly upon the middle of the ship that it split into a thousand pieces. The mariners and passengers were all killed by the stone, or sunk. I myself had the last fate; but as I came up again I fortunately caught hold of a piece of the wreck, and swimming sometimes with one hand and sometimes with the other, but always holding fast to my board, the wind and the tide favouring me, I came to an island, where the beach was very steep. I overcame that difficulty however, and got ashore.

I sat down upon the grass, to recover myself a little from my fatigue, after which I got up, and went into the island to view it. It seemed to be a delicious garden. I found trees everywhere, some of them bearing green and others ripe fruits, and streams of fresh pure water, with pleasant windings and turnings. I ate of the fruits, which I found excellent, and drank of the water, which was very pleasant.

Night being come, I lay down upon the grass in a convenient place enough, but I could not sleep for an hour at a time, my mind was so disturbed with the fear of being alone in so desert a place. Thus I spent the best part of the night in fretting, and reproached myself for my imprudence in not staying at home, rather than undertaking this last voyage. These reflections carried me so far, that I began to form a design against my own life, but daylight dispersed these melancholy thoughts, and I got up, and walked among the trees, but not without apprehensions of danger.

When I was a little advanced into the island, I saw an old man who appeared very weak and feeble. He sat upon the bank of a stream, and at first I took him to be one who had been shipwrecked like myself. I went towards him and saluted him, but he only bowed his head a little. I asked him what he did there, but instead of answering he made a sign for me to take him upon my

back and carry him over the brook, signifying that it was to gather fruit.

I believed him really to stand in need of my help, so took him upon my back, and having carried him over, bade him get down, and for that end stooped that he might get off with ease: but instead of that (which I laugh at every time I think of it), the old man, who to me had appeared very decrepit, clasped his legs nimbly about my neck, and then I perceived his skin to resemble that of a cow. He sat astride upon my shoulders, and held my throat so tight that I thought he would have strangled me, the fright of which made me faint away and fall down.

Notwithstanding my fainting, the ill-natured old fellow kept fast about my neck, but opened his legs a little to give me time to recover my breath. When I had done so, he thrust one of his feet against my stomach, and struck me so rudely on the side with the other, that he forced me to rise up against my will. Having got up, he made me walk under the trees, and forced me now and then to stop, to gather and eat fruit such as we found. He never left me all day, and when I lay down to rest by night, he laid himself down with me, always holding fast about my neck. Every morn- ing he pushed me to make me wake, and afterwards obliged me to get up and walk, and pressed me with his feet. You may judge then what trouble I was in, to be loaded with such a burden as I could by no means rid myself of.

One day I found in my way several dry calabashes that had fallen from a tree; I took a large one, and, after cleaning it, pressed into it some juice of grapes, which abounded in the island. Having filled the cal- abash, I set it in a conve- nient place; and coming hither again some days after, I took up my cal- abash, and setting it to my mouth found the wine to be so good that it presently made me not only forget my sorrow, but grow vigorous, and so light-hearted that I began to sing and dance as I walked along.

The old man, perceiving the effect which this drink had upon me, and that I carried him with more ease than I did before, made a sign for me to give him some of it. I gave him the calabash, and the liquor pleasing his palate, he drank it all off. He became drunk immediately, and the fumes getting up into his head he began to sing after his manner, and to dance upon my shoulders. His jolting about made him sick, and he loosened his legs from about me by degrees; so finding that he did not press me as before, I threw him upon the ground, where he lay without motion, and then I took up a great stone, with which I crushed his head to pieces.

I was extremely rejoiced to be freed thus for ever from this cursed old fellow, and walked along the shore of the sea, where I met the crew of a ship that had cast anchor to take in water to refresh themselves. They were extremely surprised to see me, and to hear the particulars of my adventures. "You fell," said they, "into the hands of the old man of the sea, and are the first that has ever escaped strangling by him. He never left those he had once made himself master of till he destroyed them, and he has made this island famous for the number of men he has slain; so that the merchants and mariners who landed upon it dared not advance into the island but in numbers together."

After having informed me of these things they carried me with them to the ship; the captain received me with great satisfaction when they told him what had befallen me. He put out again to sea, and after some days' sail we arrived at the harbour of a great city, where the houses were built of good stone.

One of the merchants of the ship, who had taken me into his friendship, asked me to go along with him, and took me to a place appointed as a retreat for foreign merchants. He gave me a great bag, and having recommended me to some people of the town, who were used to gather cocoanuts, he desired them to take me with them to do the like: "Go," said he, "follow them, and do as you see them do, and do not separate from them, otherwise you endanger your life." Having thus spoken, he gave me provisions for the journey, and I went with them.

We came to a great forest of trees, extremely straight and tall, their trunks so smooth that it was not possible for any man to climb up to the branches that bore the fruit. All the trees were cocoanut trees, and when we entered the forest we saw a great number of apes of all sizes, that fled as soon as they perceived us, and climbed up to the top of the trees with surprising swiftness.

The merchants with whom I was gathered stones, and threw them at the apes on the top of the trees. I did the same, and the apes, out of revenge, threw cocoanuts at us as fast and with such gestures as sufficiently testified their anger and resentment: we gathered up the cocoanuts, and from time to time threw stones to provoke the apes: so that by this stratagem we filled our bags with cocoanuts, which it had been impossible for us to do otherwise.

When we had gathered our number, we returned to the city, where the merchant who sent me to the forest gave me the value of the cocoanuts I had brought; "Go on," said he, "and do the like every day, until you have money enough to carry you home." I thanked him for his good advice, and gathered together as many cocoanuts as amounted to a considerable sum.

The vessel in which I came sailed with merchants who loaded her with cocoanuts. I expected the arrival of another, whose merchants landed speedily for the like loading. I embarked on board the same all the cocoanuts that belonged to me, and when she was ready to sail I went and took leave of the merchant who had been so kind to me; but he could not embark with me because he had not finished his business.

We set sail towards the islands where pepper grows in great plenty. From thence we went to the Isle of Comari, where the best sort of wood of aloes grows, and whose inhabitants have made it an inviolable law to drink no wine themselves, nor to suffer any kind of improper conduct. I exchanged my cocoanuts in those two islands for pepper and wood of aloes, and went with other merchants pearl-fishing. I hired divers, who fetched me up those that were very large and pure. Then I embarked joyfully in a vessel that happily arrived at Balsora; from thence I returned to Bagdad, where I made vast sums by my pepper, wood aloes, and pearls. I gave the tenth of my gains in alms, as I had done upon my return from other voyages, and endeavoured to ease myself from my fatigue by diversions of all sorts.

THE SIXTH VOYAGE OF
SINBAD THE SAILOR

AFTER being shipwrecked five times, and escaping so many dangers, could I resolve again to try my fortune, and expose myself to new hardships? I am astonished at it myself when I think of it, and must certainly have been induced to it by my stars. But be that as it will, after a year's rest I prepared for a sixth voyage, notwithstanding the entreaties of my kindred and friends, who did all that was possible to prevent me. Instead of taking my way by the Persian Gulf, I travelled once more through several provinces of Persia and the Indies, and arrived at a sea-port, where I embarked on board a ship, the captain of which was resolved on a long voyage.

It was very long indeed, but at the same time so unfortunate that the captain and pilot lost their course, and knew not where they were. They found it at last, but we had no reason to rejoice at it. We were all seized with extraordinary fear when we saw the captain quit his post, and cry out. He threw off his turban, pulled his beard, and beat his head like a madman. We asked him the reason, and he answered that he was in the most dangerous place in all the sea. "A rapid current carries the ship along with it," he said, "and we shall all of us perish in less than a quarter of an hour. Pray to God to deliver us from this danger; we cannot escape it if He does not take pity on us." At these words he ordered the sails to be changed; but all the ropes broke, and the ship, without its being possible to help it, was carried by the current to the foot of an inaccessible mountain, where she ran ashore, and was broken to pieces, yet so that we saved our lives, our provisions, and the best of our goods.

This being over, the captain said to us, "God has done what pleased Him; we may every man dig our grave here, and bid the world adieu, for we are all in so fatal a place that none shipwrecked here have ever returned to their homes again." His discourse afflicted us sorely, and we embraced each other with tears in our eyes, bewailing our deplorable lot.

The mountain at the foot of which we were cast was the coast of a very long and large island. This coast was covered all over with wrecks, and from the vast number of men's bones we saw everywhere, and which filled us with horror, we concluded that abundance of people had died there. It is also impossible to tell what a quantity of goods and riches we found cast ashore there. All these objects served only to augment our grief. Whereas in all other places rivers run from their channels into the sea, here a great river of fresh water runs out of the sea into a dark cave, whose entrance is very high and large. What is most remarkable in this place is that the stones of the mountain are of crystal, rubies, or other precious stones. Here is also a sort of fountain of pitch or bitumen, that runs into the sea, which the fishes swallow, and then vomit up again, turned into ambergris; and this the waves throw up on the beach in great quantities. Here also grow trees, most of which are wood of aloes, equal in goodness to those of Comari.

To finish the description of this place, which may well be called a gulf, since nothing ever returns from it – it is not possible for ships to get away again when once they come near it. If they are driven thither by a wind from the sea, the wind and the current ruin them; and if they come into it when a land-wind blows, which might seem to favour their getting out again, the height of the mountain stops the wind, and occasions a calm, so that the force of the current runs them ashore, where they are broken to pieces, as ours was; and that which completes the misfortune is that there is no possibility to get to the top of the mountain, or to get out any manner of way.

We continued upon the shore, like men out of their senses, and expected death every day. At first we divided our provisions as equally as we could, and thus everyone lived a longer or shorter time, according to their temperance, and the use they made of their provisions.

Those who died first were interred by the rest; and, for my part, I paid the last duty to all my companions. Nor are you to wonder at this; for besides that I husbanded the provision that fell to my share better than they, I had provision of my own, which I did not share with my comrades; yet when I buried the last, I had so little remaining that I thought I could not hold out long: so I dug a grave, resolving to lie down in it, because there was none left to inter me. I must confess to you at the same time that while I was thus employed I could not but reflect upon myself as the cause of my own ruin, and repented that I had ever undertaken this last voyage; nor did I stop at reflections only, but had well nigh hastened my own death, and began to tear my hands with my teeth.

But it pleased God once more to take compassion on me, and put it in my mind to go to the bank of the river which ran into the great cave; where, considering the river with great attention, I said to myself, "This river, which runs thus under ground, must come out somewhere or other. If I make a raft, and leave myself to the current, it will bring me to some inhabited country, or drown me. If I be drowned I lose nothing, but only change one kind of death for another; and if I get out of this fatal place, I shall not only

avoid the sad fate of my comrades, but perhaps find some new occasion of enriching myself. Who knows but fortune waits, upon my getting off this dangerous shelf, to compensate my shipwreck with interest?"

I immediately went to work on a raft. I made it of large pieces of timber and cables, for I had choice of them, and tied them together so strongly that I had made a very solid little raft. When I had finished it I loaded it with some bales of rubies, emeralds, ambergris, rock-crystal, and rich stuffs. Having balanced all my cargo exactly and fastened it well to the raft, I went on board it with two little oars that I had made, and, leaving it to the course of the river, I resigned myself to the will of God.

As soon as I came into the cave I lost all light, and the stream carried me I knew not whither. Thus I floated for some days in perfect darkness, and once found the arch so low that it well nigh broke my head, which made me very cautious afterwards to avoid the like danger. All this while I ate nothing but what was just necessary to support nature; yet, notwithstanding this frugality, all my provisions were spent. Then a pleasing sleep fell upon me. I cannot tell how long it continued; but when I awoke, I was surprised to find myself in the middle of a vast country, at the bank of a river, where my raft was tied, amidst a great number of negroes. I got up as soon as I saw them and saluted them. They spoke to me, but I did not understand their language. I was so transported with joy that I knew not whether I was asleep or awake; but being persuaded that I was not asleep, I recited the following words in Arabic aloud: "Call upon the Almighty, he will help thee; thou needest not perplex thyself about anything else; shut thy eyes, and while thou art asleep, God will change thy bad fortune into good."

One of the blacks, who understood Arabic, hearing me speak thus, came towards me and said, "Brother, be not surprised to see us; we are inhabitants of this country, and came hither to-day to water our fields, by digging little canals from this river, which comes out of the neighbouring mountain. We saw something floating upon the water, went speedily to find out what it was, and perceiving your raft, one of us swam into the river, and brought it hither, where we fastened it, as you see, until you should awake. Pray tell us your history, for it must be extraordinary; how did you venture into this river, and whence did you come?"

I begged of them first to give me something to eat, and then I would satisfy their curiosity. They gave me several sorts of food; and when I had satisfied my hunger, I gave them a true account of all that had befallen me, which they listened to with wonder. As soon as I had finished my discourse, they told me, by the person who spoke Arabic and interpreted to them what I said, that it was one of the most surprising stories they ever heard, and that I must go along with them, and tell it to their king myself; the story was too extraordinary to be told by any other than the person to whom it happened. I told them

I was ready to do whatever they pleased.

They immediately sent for a horse, which was brought in a little time; and having made me get upon him, some of them walked before me to show me the way, and the rest took my raft and cargo, and followed me.

We marched thus altogether, till we came to the city of Serendib, for it was in that island I landed. The blacks presented me to their king; I approached his throne, and saluted him as I used to do the kings of the Indies, that is to say, I prostrated myself at his feet, and kissed the earth. The prince ordered me to rise up, received me with an obliging air, and made me come up, and sit down near him. He first asked me my name, and I answered, "They call me Sinbad the sailor, because of the many voyages I have undertaken, and I am a citizen of Bagdad."

"But," replied he, "how came you into my dominions, and from whence came you last?"

I concealed nothing from the king; I told him all that I have now told you, and his majesty was so surprised and charmed with it, that he commanded my adventure to be written in letters of gold, and laid up in the archives of his kingdom. At last my raft was brought in, and the bales opened in his presence: he admired the quantity of wood of aloes and ambergris; but, above all, the rubies and emeralds, for he had none in his treasury that came near them.

Observing that he looked on my jewels with pleasure, and viewed the most remarkable among them one after another, I fell prostrate at his feet, and took the liberty to say to him, "Sir, not only my person is at your majesty's service, but the cargo of the raft, and I would beg of you to dispose of it as your own."

He answered me with a smile, "Sinbad, I will take care not to covet anything of yours, nor to take anything from you that God has given you; far from lessening your wealth, I design to augment it, and will not let you go out of my dominions without marks of my liberality."

All the answer I returned was prayers for the prosperity of this prince, and commendations of his generosity and bounty. He charged one of his officers to take care of me, and ordered people to serve me at his own charge. The officer was very faithful in the execution of his orders, and caused all the goods to be carried to the lodgings provided for me. I went every day at a set hour to pay court to the king, and spent the rest of my time in seeing the city, and what was most worthy of notice.

The Isle of Serendib is situated just under the equinoctial line, so that the days and nights there are always of twelve hours each, and the island is eighty parasangs in length, and as many in breadth.

The capital city stands at the end of a fine valley formed by a mountain in the middle of the island, which is the highest in the world. I made, by way of devotion, a pilgrimage to the place where Adam was confined after his banishment from Paradise, and had the curiosity to go to the top of it.

When I came back to the city, I prayed the king to allow me to return to my country, which he granted me in the most obliging and honourable manner. He would needs force a rich present upon me, and when I went to take my leave of him, he gave me one much more valuable, and at the same time charged me with a letter for the Commander of the Faithful, our sovereign, saying to me, "I pray you give this present from me and this letter to Caliph Haroun Alraschid, and assure him of my friendship." I took the present and letter in a very respectful manner, and promised his majesty punctually to execute the commission with which he was pleased to honour me. Before I embarked, this prince sent for the captain and the merchants who were to go with me, and ordered them to treat me with all possible respect.

The letter from the King of Serendib was written on the skin of a certain animal of great value, because of its being so scarce, and of a yellowish colour. The writing was azure, and the contents as follows:-

"The king of the Indies, before whom march a hundred elephants, who lives in a palace that shines with a hundred thousand rubies, and who has in his treasury twenty thousand crowns enriched with diamonds, to Caliph Haroun Alraschid:

"Though the present we send you be inconsiderable, receive it as a brother and a friend, in consideration of the hearty friendship which we bear to you, and of which we are willing to give you proof. We desire the same part in your friendship, considering that we believe it to be our merit, being of the same dignity with yourself. We conjure you this in the rank of a brother. Farewell."

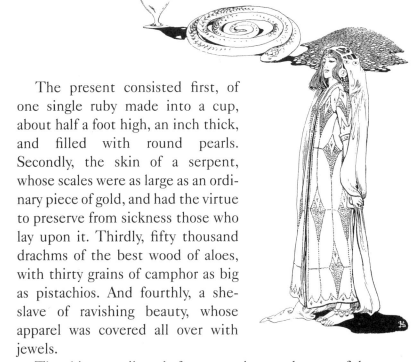

The present consisted first, of one single ruby made into a cup, about half a foot high, an inch thick, and filled with round pearls. Secondly, the skin of a serpent, whose scales were as large as an ordinary piece of gold, and had the virtue to preserve from sickness those who lay upon it. Thirdly, fifty thousand drachms of the best wood of aloes, with thirty grains of camphor as big as pistachios. And fourthly, a she-slave of ravishing beauty, whose apparel was covered all over with jewels.

The ship set sail, and after a very long and successful voyage, we landed at Balsora; from thence I went to Bagdad, where the first thing I did was to acquit myself of my commission.

I took the King of Serendib's letter, and went to present myself at the gate of the Commander of the Faithful, followed by the beautiful slave and such of my own family as carried the presents. I gave an account of the reason of my coming, and was immediately conducted to the throne of the caliph. I made my reverence, and after a short speech gave him the letter and present. When he had read what the King of Serendib wrote to him, he asked me if that prince were really so rich and potent as he had said in this letter. I prostrated myself a second time, and rising again, "Commander of the Faithful," said I, "I can assure your majesty he doth not exceed the truth on that head: I am witness of it. There is nothing more capable of raising a man's admiration than the magnificence of his palace. When the prince appears in public, he has a throne fixed on the back of an elephant, and marches betwixt two ranks of his ministers, favourites, and other people of his court; before him, upon the same elephant, an officer carries a golden lance in his hand, and behind the throne there is another, who stands upright with a column of gold, on the top of which there is an emerald half a foot long and an inch thick; before him march a guard of a thousand men, clad in cloth of gold and silk, and mounted on elephants richly caparisoned.

"While the king is on his march, the officer who is before him on the same elephant cries from time to time, with a loud voice, 'Behold the great monarch, the potent and redoubtable Sultan of the Indies, whose palace is covered with a hundred thousand rubies, and who possesses twenty thousand crowns of diamonds.' After he has pronounced these words, the officer behind the throne cries in his turn, 'This monarch so great and so powerful, must die, must die, must die.' And the officer in front replies, 'Praise be to Him who lives for ever.'

"Further, the King of Serendib is so just that there are no judges in his dominions. His people have no need of them. They understand and observe justice of themselves."

The caliph was much pleased with my discourse. "The wisdom of this king," said he, "appears in his letter, and after what you tell me I must confess that his wisdom is worthy of his people, and his people deserve so wise a prince." Having spoken thus he dismissed me, and sent me home with a rich present.

THE SEVENTH AND LAST VOYAGE
OF SINBAD THE SAILOR

B EING returned from my sixth voyage, I absolutely laid aside all thoughts of travelling any farther; for, besides that my years now required rest, I was resolved no more to expose myself to such risk as I had run; so that I thought of nothing but to pass the rest of my days in quiet. One day, as I was treating some of my friends, one of my servants came and told me that an officer of the caliph asked for me. I rose from the table, and went to him. "The caliph," said he, "has sent me to tell you that he must speak with you." I followed the officer to the palace, where, being presented to the caliph, I saluted him by prostrating myself at his feet. "Sinbad," said he to me, "I stand in need of you; you must do me the service to carry my answer and present to the King of Serendib. It is but just I should return his civility."

This command of the caliph to me was like a clap of thunder. "Commander of the Faithful," replied I, "I am ready to do whatever your majesty shall think fit to command me; but I beseech you most humbly to consider what I have undergone. I have also made a vow never to go out of Bagdad." Here I took occasion to give him a large and particular account of all my adventures, which he had the patience to hear out.

As soon as I had finished, "I confess," said he, "that the things you tell me are very extraordinary, yet you must for my sake undertake this voyage which I propose to you. You have nothing to do but to go to the Isle of Serendib, and deliver the commission which I give you. After that you are at liberty to return. But you must go; for you know it would be indecent, and not suitable to my dignity, to be indebted to the king of that island." Perceiving that the caliph insisted upon it, I submitted, and told him that I was willing to obey. He was very well pleased at it, and ordered me a thousand sequins for the expense of my journey.

I prepared for my departure in a few days, and as soon as the caliph's letter and present were delivered to me, I went to Balsora, where I embarked, and had a very happy voyage. I arrived at the Isle of Serendib, where I acquainted the king's ministers with my commission, and prayed them to get me speedy audience. They did so, and I was conducted to the palace in an honourable manner, where I saluted the king by prostration, according to custom. That prince knew me immediately, and testified very great joy to see me. "O Sinbad," said he, "you are welcome; I swear to you I have many times thought of you since you went hence; I bless the day upon which we see one another once more." I made my compliment to him, and after having thanked him for his kindness to me, I delivered the caliph's letter and present, which he received with all imaginable satisfaction.

The caliph's present was a complete set of cloth of gold, valued at one thousand sequins; fifty robes of rich stuff, a hundred others of white cloth, the finest of Cairo, Suez, Cusa, and Alexandria; a royal crimson bed, and a second of another fashion; a vessel of agate broader than deep, an inch thick, and half a foot wide, the bottom of which represented in bas-relief a man with one knee on the ground, who held a bow and an arrow, ready to let fly at a lion.

He sent him also a rich table, which, according to tradition, belonged to the great Solomon. The caliph's letter was as follows:

"Greeting in the name of the Sovereign Guide of the Right Way, to the potent and happy Sultan, from Abdallah Haroun Alraschid, whom God hath set in the place of honour, after his ancestors of happy memory:

"We received your letter with joy, and send you this from the council of our port, the garden of superior wits. We hope, when you look upon it, you will find our good intention, and be pleased with it. Farewell."

The King of Serendib was highly pleased that the caliph returned his friendship. A little time after this audience, I solicited leave to depart, and had much difficulty to obtain it. I obtained it, however, at last, and the king, when he dismissed me, made me a very considerable present. I embarked immediately to return to Bagdad, but had not the good fortune to arrive there as I hoped. God ordered it otherwise.

Three or four days after my departure, we were attacked by pirates, who easily seized upon our ship. Some of the crew offered resistance, which cost them their lives. But as for me and the rest, who were not so imprudent, the pirates saved us on purpose to make slaves of us.

We were all stripped, and instead of our own clothes they gave us sorry rags, and carried us into a remote island, where they sold us.

I fell into the hands of a rich merchant, who, as soon as he bought me, carried me to his house, treated me well, and clad me handsomely for a slave. Some days after, not knowing who I was, he asked me if I understood any trade. I answered that I was no mechanic, but a merchant, and that the pirates who sold me had robbed me of all I had.

"But tell me," replied he, "can you shoot with a bow?"

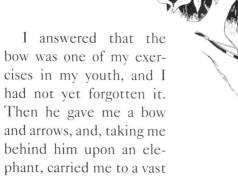

I answered that the bow was one of my exercises in my youth, and I had not yet forgotten it. Then he gave me a bow and arrows, and, taking me behind him upon an elephant, carried me to a vast forest some leagues from the town. We went a great way into the forest, and when he thought fit to stop he bade me alight; then showing me a great tree, "Climb up that tree," said he, "and shoot at the elephants as you see them pass by, for there is a prodigious number of them in this forest, and, if any of them fall, come and give me notice of it." Having spoken thus, he left me victuals, and returned to the town, and I continued upon the tree all night.

I saw no elephant during that time, but next morning, as soon as the sun was up, I saw a great number: I shot several arrows among them, and at last one of the elephants fell; the rest retired immediately, and left me at liberty to go and acquaint my patron with my booty. When I had told him the news, he gave me a good meal, commended my dexterity, and caressed me highly. We afterwards went together to the forest, where we dug a hole for the elephant; my patron intending to return when it was rotten, and to take the teeth, etc., to trade with.

I continued this game for two months, and killed an elephant every day, getting sometimes upon one tree, and sometimes upon

another. One morning, as I looked for the elephants, I perceived with an extreme amazement that, instead of passing by me across the forest as usual, they stopped, and came to me with a horrible noise, in such a number that the earth was covered with them, and shook under them. They encompassed the tree where I was with their trunks extended and their eyes all fixed upon me. At this frightful spectacle I remained immoveable, and was so much frightened that my bow and arrows fell out of my hand.

My fears were not in vain; for after the elephants had stared upon me for some time, one of the largest of them put his trunk round the root of the tree, and pulled so strong that he plucked it up and threw it on the ground; I fell with the tree, and the elephant taking me up with his trunk, laid me on his back, where I sat more like one dead than alive, with my quiver on my shoulder: then he put himself at the head of the rest, who followed him in troops, and carried me to a place where he laid me down on the ground, and retired with all his companions. Conceive, if you can, the condition I was in: I thought myself to be in a dream; at last,

after having lain some time, and seeing the elephants gone, I got up, and found I was upon a long and broad hill, covered all over with the bones and teeth of elephants. I confess to you that this furnished me with abundance of reflections. I admired the instinct of those animals; I doubted not

but that this was their burying place, and that they carried me thither on purpose to tell me that I should forbear to persecute them, since I did it only for their teeth. I did not stay on the hill, but turned towards the city, and, after having travelled a day and a night, I came to my patron; I met no elephant on my way, which made me think they had retired farther into the forest, to leave me at liberty to come back to the hill without any hindrance.

As soon as my patron saw me: "Ah, poor Sinbad," said he, "I was in great trouble to know what had become of you. I have been at the forest, where I found a tree newly pulled up, and a bow and arrows on the ground, and after having sought for you in vain I despaired of ever seeing you more. Pray tell me what befell you, and by what good hap you are still alive."

I satisfied his curiosity, and going both of us next morning to the hill, he found to his great joy that what I had told him was true. We loaded the elephant upon which we came with as many teeth as he could carry; and when we had returned, "Brother," said my patron – "for I will treat you no more as my slave – after having made such a discovery as will enrich me, God bless you with all happiness and prosperity. I declare before Him that I give you your liberty. I concealed from you what I am now going to tell you.

"The elephants of our forest have every year killed a great many slaves, whom we sent to seek ivory. Notwithstanding all the cautions we could give them, those crafty animals killed them one time or other. God has delivered you from their fury, and has bestowed that favour upon you only. It is a sign that He loves you, and has use for your service in the world. You have procured me incredible gain. We could not have ivory formerly but by exposing the lives of our slaves, and now our whole city is enriched by your means. Do not think I pretend to have rewarded you by giving you your liberty; I will also give you considerable riches. I could engage all our city to contribute towards making your fortune, but I will have the glory of doing it myself."

To this obliging discourse I replied, "Patron, God preserve you. Your giving me my liberty is enough to discharge what you owe me, and I desire no other reward for the service I had the good fortune to do to you and your city, than leave to return to my own country."

"Very well," said he, "the monsoon will in a little time bring ships for ivory. I will send you home then, and give you wherewith to pay your expenses." I thanked him again for my liberty, and his good intentions towards me. I stayed with him until the monsoon; and during that time we made so many journeys to the hill that we filled all our warehouses with ivory. The other merchants who traded in it did the same thing, for it could not be long concealed from them.

The ships arrived at last, and my patron himself having made choice of the ship wherein I was to embark, he loaded half of it with ivory on my account, laid in provisions in abundance for my passage, and obliged me besides to accept as a present, curiosities of the country of great value. After I had returned him a thousand thanks for all his favours, I went on board. We set sail, and as the adventure which procured me this liberty was very extraordinary, I had it continually in my thoughts.

We stopped at some islands to take in fresh provisions. Our vessel being come to a port on the main land in the Indies, we touched there, and not being willing to venture by sea to Balsora, I landed my proportion of the ivory, resolving to proceed on my journey by land. I made vast sums by my ivory, I bought several rarities, which I intended for presents, and when my equipage was ready, I set out in the company of a large caravan of merchants. I was a long time on the way, and suffered very much, but endured all with patience, when I considered that I had nothing to fear from the seas, from pirates, from serpents, nor from the other perils I had undergone.

All these fatigues ended at last, and I came safe to Bagdad. I went immediately to wait upon the caliph, and gave him an account of my embassy. That prince told me he had been uneasy, by reason that I was so long in returning, but that he always hoped God would preserve me. When I told him the adventure of the elephants, he seemed to be much surprised at it, and would never have given any credit to it had he not known my sincerity. He reckoned this story, and the other narratives I had given him, to be so curious that he ordered one of his secretaries to write them in characters of gold, and lay them up in his treasury. I retired very well satisfied with the honours I received and the presents which he gave me; and after that I gave myself up wholly to my family, kindred and friends.

THE STORY OF ALI BABA AND THE FORTY THIEVES

PART I

IN a town in Persia, there lived two brothers, one named Cassim, the other Ali Baba. Their father left them no great property; though as he had divided it equally between them, their fortune should have been equal; but it was otherwise.

Cassim married a widow, who, soon after their marriage, became heiress to a large estate, and a good shop and warehouse full of rich merchandise; so that all at once he became one of the richest merchants, and lived at his ease.

Ali Baba, on the other hand, who married a woman as poor as himself, lived in a very mean dwelling, and had no other means of maintaining his wife and children than his daily labour in cutting wood in a forest near the town, and bringing it upon three asses to town to sell.

One day, when Ali Baba was in the forest, and had just cut wood enough to load his asses, he saw at a distance a great cloud of dust, which seemed to approach towards him: he observed it very attentively, and distinguished a large body of horse coming briskly on; and though they did not fear robbers in that country, Ali Baba began to think that they might prove such, and, without considering what might become of his asses, he resolved to save himself. He climbed up a large tree, whose branches, at a little distance from the ground, divided in a circular form so close to one another that there was but little space between them. He placed himself in the middle, from whence he could see all that passed without being seen. This tree stood at the bottom of a single rock, which was very high, and so steep and craggy that nobody could climb it.

The troop, who were all well mounted and well armed, came to the foot of this rock, and there dismounted. Ali Baba counted forty of them, and 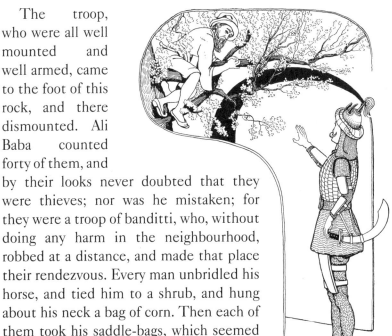 by their looks never doubted that they were thieves; nor was he mistaken; for they were a troop of banditti, who, without doing any harm in the neighbourhood, robbed at a distance, and made that place their rendezvous. Every man unbridled his horse, and tied him to a shrub, and hung about his neck a bag of corn. Then each of them took his saddle-bags, which seemed to Ali Baba to be full of gold and silver by the weight. One, whom he took to be their captain, came with his saddle-bags on his back under the tree in which Ali Baba was hidden, and, making his way through some shrubs, pronounced these words, "Open, Sesame," so distinctly, that Ali Baba heard him. As soon as the captain of the robbers uttered these words, a door opened; and after he had made all his troop go in before him, he followed them, and the door shut again of itself.

The robbers stayed some time within the rock, and Ali Baba, who feared that some or all of them together might come out and catch him if he endeavoured to make his escape, was obliged to sit patiently in the tree. He was nevertheless tempted once or twice to get down and mount one of their horses, and, leading another,

to drive his asses before him to the town
with all the haste he could; but uncertainty
made him choose the safest way.

At last the door opened again, and the
forty robbers came out. As the captain went
in last, so he came out first, and stood to see
them all pass by; and then Ali Baba heard
him make the door fast by pronouncing the
words, "Shut, Sesame." Every man went
and bridled his horse, fastened his saddle-
bags, and mounted again; and when the
captain saw them all ready, he put himself
at their head, and they returned the way
they came.

Ali Baba did not immediately quit his
tree; "for," said he to himself, "they may
have forgotten something and come back again, and then I shall
be caught." He followed them with his eyes as far as he could see
them; and after that waited some time before he came down.
Remembering the words the captain of the robbers had made use
of to cause the door to open and shut, he had the curiosity to try
whether his pronouncing them would have the same effect.
Accordingly, he went among the shrubs, and perceiving the door
concealed behind them, he stood before it, and said, "Open,
Sesame." The door instantly flew open.

Ali Baba, who expected a dark dismal place, was very much surprised to see it well lighted and spacious, cut out by men's hands
in the form of a vault, which received the light from an opening at
the top of the rock. He saw all sorts of provisions, and rich bales of
merchandise, of silk, stuff, brocade, and valuable carpeting, piled
one upon another; and, above all, gold and silver in great heaps,
and money in great leather purses. The sight of all these riches

made him believe that the cave had been occupied for ages by robbers, who succeeded one another.

Ali Baba did not stand long to consider what to do, but went
immediately into the cave, and as soon as he was in, the door shut.
But this did not disturb him, because he knew the secret of opening it again. He disregarded the silver, but made the best use of his
time in carrying out as much of the gold coin, which was in bags, as
he thought his three asses could carry. When he had done, he
fetched his asses which had strayed, and, when he had loaded
them with the bags, laid the wood on them in such a manner that
the bags could not be seen. When he had done, he stood before
the door, and pronouncing the words, "Shut, Sesame," the door
closed after him; for it had shut of itself while he was within, and
remained open while he was out. He then made the best of his
way to the town.

When Ali Baba got home, he drove his asses into a little yard,
and shut the gates very carefully, threw off the wood that covered
the bags, carried them into his house, and ranged them in order
before his wife, who sat on a sofa.

His wife handled the bags, and finding them full of money, suspected that her husband had been stealing, insomuch that when
he had brought them all in, she could not help saying, "Ali Baba,
have you been so unhappy as to—"

"Be quiet, wife," interrupted Ali Baba; "do not frighten yourself: I am no robber, unless he can be one who steals from robbers.
You will no longer have a bad opinion of me, when I tell you my
good fortune." Then he emptied the bags, which raised such a
great heap of gold as dazzled his wife's eyes; and when he had
done, he told her the whole adventure from beginning to end;
and, above all, recommended her to keep it secret.

The wife recovered, and, cured of her fears, rejoiced with her
husband at their good luck, and wanted to count all the gold,

piece by piece. "Wife," replied Ali Baba, "you do not know what you are undertaking when you try to count the money; you will never have done. I will go and dig a hole, and bury it; there is no time to be lost."

"You are in the right, husband," replied the wife; "but let us know, as nearly as possible, how much we have. I will go and borrow a small measure in the neighbourhood, and measure it, while you dig the hole."

"What you are going to do is to no purpose, wife," said Ali Baba; "if you take my advice, you had better let it alone; but be sure to keep the secret, and do what you please."

Away the wife ran to her brother-in-law Cassim, who lived close by, but was not then at home; and addressing herself to his wife, asked her to lend her a measure for a little while. Her sister-in-law asked her whether she would have a large or a small one. "A small one," said she. Cassim's wife bade her wait a little, and she would readily fetch one.

The sister-in-law did so, but as she knew very well Ali Baba's poverty, she was curious to know what sort of grain his wife wanted to measure, and bethought herself of artfully putting some suet at the bottom of the measure; then she brought it to her with the excuse that she was sorry that she had made her wait so long, but that she could not find it sooner.

Ali Baba's wife went home, set the measure upon the heap of gold, and filled it and emptied it, at a small distance upon the sofa, till she had done: and she was very well satisfied to find that the number of measures

amounted to so many as they did, and went to tell her husband, who had almost finished digging the hole. While Ali Baba was burying the gold, his wife, to show her punctuality to her sister-in-law, carried the measure back again, without noticing that a piece of gold stuck at the bottom. "Sister," said she, giving it back to her again, "you see that I have not kept your measure long: I am much obliged to you, and return it with thanks."

As soon as Ali Baba's wife's back was turned, Cassim's wife looked at the bottom of the measure, and was inexpressibly surprised to find a piece of gold sticking to it. Envy immediately possessed her heart. "What!" said she, "has Ali Baba gold so plentifully as to measure it? Where has that poor wretch got all this gold?" Cassim, her husband, was at his shop, which he left always in the evening. His wife waited for him, and thought the time an age; so great was her impatience to tell him the news, at which he would be so much surprised.

When Cassim came home, his wife said to him, "Cassim, you

think yourself rich, but you are much mistaken; Ali Baba is infinitely richer than you; he does not count his money, but measures it." Cassim desired her to explain the riddle, which she did, telling him the stratagem by which she had made the discovery, and showing him the piece of money, which was so old a coin that they could not tell in what prince's reign it was coined.

Cassim, instead of being pleased at his brother's prosperity, could not sleep all that night for jealousy, but went to him in the morning before sunrise. Now Cassim, after he had married the rich widow, never treated Ali Baba as a brother, but forgot him. "Ali Baba," said he, "you are very reserved in your affairs; you pretend to be miserably poor, and yet you measure gold!"

"What, brother?" replied Ali Baba; "I do not know what you mean: explain yourself."

"Do not pretend ignorance," replied Cassim, showing him the piece of gold his wife had given him. "How many of these pieces have you? My wife found this at the bottom of the measure you borrowed yesterday."

By this Ali Baba perceived that Cassim and his wife, through his own wife's folly, knew what they had such good reason to keep secret; but what was done could not be recalled; therefore without showing the least surprise or vexation, he confessed all, and told his brother by what chance he had discovered this retreat of the thieves, and where it was; and offered him part of his treasure to keep the secret. "I expected as much," replied Cassim haughtily; "but I will know exactly where this treasure is, and the signs and tokens by which I may go to it myself when I have a mind; otherwise I will go and inform against you, and then you will not only get no more, but will lose all you have got, and I shall have my share for my information."

Ali Baba, more out of his natural good temper than frightened by the insulting threats of a barbarous brother, told him all he desired, and even the very words he was to make use of to go into the cave and to come out again.

Cassim, who wanted no more of Ali Baba, left him, resolving to be beforehand with him, and hoping to get all the treasure to himself. He rose early the next morning, a long time before sunrise, and set out with ten mules laden with great chests, which he designed to fill: intending to carry many more the next time, according to the riches he found; and followed the road which Ali Baba had told him. It was not long before he came to the rock, and found out the place by the tree. When he came to the door, he pronounced the words, "Open, Sesame," and it opened; and when he was in, shut again. In examining the cave, he was astonished to find much more riches than he had supposed from Ali Baba's story. He was so covetous and fond of riches that he could have spent the whole day in feasting his eyes with so much treasure, if the thought that he came to carry some away with him had not hindered him. He laid as many bags of gold as he could carry away by the entrance, and, coming at last to open the door, his thoughts were so full of the great riches he should possess that he could not think of the necessary word; but instead of "Open, Sesame," said, "Open, Barley," and was very much amazed to find that the door did not open, but remained fast shut. He named several sorts of grain, – all but the right one, – and the door would not open.

Cassim had never expected such an accident, and was so frightened at the danger he was in that the more he endeavoured to remember the word "Sesame," the more his memory failed, and he had as much forgotten it as if he had never heard it in his life. He threw down the bags with which he had laden himself, and walked hastily up and down the cave, without the least attention to all the riches that were around him. In this miserable condition we will leave him, bewailing his fate, and undeserving of pity.

About noon the robbers returned to their cave, and from some distance saw Cassim's mules straggling about the rock with great chests on their backs. Alarmed at this unexpected sight, they galloped full speed to the cave. They drove away the mules, which Cassim had neglected to fasten, and which strayed away through the forest so far that they were soon out of sight. The robbers never gave themselves the trouble of pursuing the mules: they were more concerned to know to whom they belonged. And while some of them searched about the rock, the captain and the rest went straight to the door, with naked sabres in their hands, and on their pronouncing the words, it opened.

Cassim, who heard the noise of the horses' feet from the middle of the cave, never doubted the coming of the robbers, and his approaching death; but he was resolved to make one effort to escape. To this end he stood ready at the door, and no sooner heard the word "Sesame," which he had forgotten, and saw the door open, than he jumped briskly out, and threw the captain down, but could not escape the other robbers, who with their sabres soon deprived him of life.

The first care of the robbers after this was to go into the cave. They found all the bags which Cassim had brought to the door, and carried them all back again to their place, without perceiving what Ali Baba had taken away before. Then holding a council, and deliberating upon the matter, they guessed that Cassim, when he was in, could not get out again; but they could not imagine how he had got in. It came into their heads that he might have got down by the top of the cave; but the opening by which it received light was so high, and the top of the rock so inaccessible without – besides that, nothing showed that he had done so – that they believed it hopeless for them to find out. That he came in at the door they could not feel sure, unless he had the secret of making it open. In short, none of them could imagine which way he entered; for they were all persuaded that nobody knew their secret, little imagining that Ali Baba had watched them. But, however it had happened, it was a matter of the greatest importance to them to secure their riches. They agreed, therefore, to cut Cassim's body into four quarters, and to hang two on one side, and two on the other, inside the door of the cave, to terrify any person who might attempt the same thing. They had no sooner taken this resolution than they executed it; and when they had nothing more to detain them, they left the place of their retreat well closed. They mounted their horses, and went to range the roads again, and to attack the caravans they might meet.

In the meantime Cassim's wife was very uneasy when night came, and her husband had not returned. She ran to Ali Baba in a terrible fright, and said, "I believe, brother-in-law, you know that Cassim, your brother, has gone to the forest, and why; it is now night, and he has not returned; I am afraid some misfortune has befallen him." Ali Baba, who never doubted that his brother, after what he had said, would go to the forest, told her, without any reflection upon her husband's unhandsome behaviour, that she need not alarm herself, for that certainly Cassim would not think it proper to come into the town till the night was pretty far advanced.

Cassim's wife, considering how much it behoved her husband to keep this thing secret, was the more easily persuaded to believe him. She went home again, and waited patiently till midnight. Then her fear redoubled, and she repented of her foolish curiosity, and cursed her desire to penetrate into the affairs of her brother- and sister-in-law. She spent all that night in weeping; and as soon as it was light, went to them, showing by her tears the reason of her coming.

Ali Baba did not wait for his sister-in-law to ask him to go and see what had become of Cassim, but went immediately with his three asses, begging her first to moderate her grief. He went to the forest, and when he came near the rock, having seen neither his brother nor his mules on the way, he was very much surprised to see some blood spilt by the door. This he took for an ill omen, but when he had pronounced the words, and the door opened, he was much more startled at the dismal sight of his brother in quarters. He was not long in  determining how he should pay the last dues to his brother, and without remembering how little brotherly friendship he had shown to him, went into the cave to find something to wrap the remains in, put them on one of his asses, and covered them over with wood. The other two asses he loaded with bags of gold, covering them with wood also as before. Then bidding the door shut, he came away; but was cautious enough to stop some time at the end of the forest, that he might not go into the town before nightfall. When he came home, he drove the two asses laden with gold into his little yard, and left the care of unloading them to his wife, while he led the other to his sister-in-law's.

Ali Baba knocked at the door, which was opened by Morgiana, an intelligent slave, clever in inventing plans for the most difficult undertakings: and Ali Baba knew she was. When he came into the court, he unloaded the ass, and taking Morgiana aside, said to her, "The first thing I ask of you is inviolable secrecy, which you will find is necessary both for your mistress' sake and mine. Your master's body is contained in these two bundles, and our business is to bury him as if he had died a natural death. Go and tell your mistress I want to speak to her, and mind what I say."

Morgiana went to her mistress, and Ali Baba followed. "Well, brother," said she, with great impatience, "what news do you bring me of my husband? I perceive no comfort in your face."

"Sister," answered Ali Baba, "I cannot tell you anything before you hear my story from the beginning to the end, without speaking a word; for it is of as great importance to you as to me to keep what has happened secret."

"Alas!" said she, "this tells me that my husband is dead; but as I know the necessity of the secrecy you require of me, I must contain myself: say on, I will hear you."

Then Ali Baba told his sister all about his journey, till he came to the finding of Cassim's body. "Now," said he, "sister, I have something to tell you which will distress you much more, because it is what you so little expect; but it cannot now be remedied. We must now think of acting so that my brother may appear to have died a natural death. I think you may leave the management of it to Morgiana, and I will contribute all that lies in my power."

What could Cassim's widow do better than accept this proposal? Ali Baba left the widow, and, recommending Morgiana to act her part well, then returned home with his ass.

Morgiana went out to an apothecary, and asked him for some lozenges which he prepared, and which were very efficacious in the most dangerous illnesses. The apothecary asked her who was ill at her master's. She replied, with a sigh, her good master Cassim himself: they knew not what his illness was, but he could neither eat nor speak. After these words, Morgiana carried the lozenges home with her, and the next morning went to the same apothecary's again, and, with tears in her eyes, asked for an essence which they used to give sick people only when at the last extremity. "Alas!" said she, taking it from the apothecary, "I am afraid that this remedy will have no better effect than the lozenges, and that I shall lose my good master."

On the other hand, as Ali Baba and his wife were often seen to go between Cassim's and their own house all that day, and to seem melancholy, nobody was surprised in the evening to hear the lamentable shrieks and cries of Cassim's wife and Morgiana, who told everyone that her master was dead.

Next morning, soon after daylight appeared, Morgiana, who knew a certain old cobbler who opened his stall early, before other people, went to him, and bidding him good-morning, put a piece of gold into his hand. "Well," said Baba Mustapha, which was his name, and who was a merry old fellow, looking at the gold, though it was hardly daylight, and seeing what it was, "this is good handling; what must I do for it? I am ready."

"Baba Mustapha," said Morgiana, "you must take with you your sewing tackle, and go with me; but I shall blindfold you when you come to a certain place."

Baba Mustapha seemed to hesitate a little at these words. "Oh, ho!" replied he, "you would have me do something against my conscience, or against my honour."

"Nay," said Morgiana, putting another piece of gold into his hand, "only come along with me, and fear nothing."

Baba Mustapha went with Morgiana, who, after she had bound his eyes with a handkerchief, at the place she told him of, took him to her deceased master's house, and never unbandaged his eyes till he came in. "Baba Mustapha," said she, "you must make haste and sew these pieces of my master together; and when you have done, I will give you another piece of gold."

After Baba Mustapha had done, she blindfolded him again, gave him the third piece of gold as she had promised, imposed secrecy on him, and led him back to the place where she first bound his eyes. Then she pulled off the bandage, and let him go home, but watched till he was quite out of sight, for fear he should have the curiosity to return and dodge her; and then went home.

Morgiana had scarcely got home before the iman and the other ministers of the mosque came. Four neighbours carried the coffin on their shoulders to the burying-ground, following the iman, who recited some prayers. Morgiana, as a slave of the deceased, followed, weeping, beating her breast, and tearing her hair; and Ali Baba came after with some neighbours.

Cassim's wife stayed at home mourning, uttering lamentable cries with the women of the neighbourhood, who came according to custom during the funeral, and, joining their lamentations with hers, filled the quarter far and near with sorrow.

In this manner Cassim's melancholy death was concealed and hushed up between Ali Baba, his wife, Cassim's widow, and Morgiana, so that nobody in the city had the least knowledge or suspicion of the reason of it.

Three or four days after the funeral, Ali Baba removed his few goods to his brother's widow's house; the money he had taken from the robbers he conveyed thither by night; and soon afterwards the marriage with his sister-in-law was published, and as these marriages are common in the Mussulman religion, nobody was surprised.

As for Cassim's shop, Ali Baba gave it to his own eldest son, who had been some time out of his apprenticeship to a great merchant, promising him withal that, if he managed well, he would soon give him a fortune to marry upon.

THE STORY OF ALI BABA

PART II

LET us now return to the forty robbers.

They came again at the appointed time to visit their retreat in the forest; but how great was their surprise to find Cassim's body taken away, and some of their bags of gold! "We are certainly discovered," said the captain, "and shall be undone, if we do not take care; otherwise we shall gradually lose all the riches which our ancestors have been so many years amassing together with so much pains and danger. All that we can think of is that the thief whom we surprised had the secret of opening the door, and we came luckily as he was coming out; but his body being removed, and with it some of our money, plainly shows that he had an accomplice. As it is likely that there were but two who had got the secret, and one has been caught, we must look narrowly after the other. What say you to it, my lads?"

All the robbers thought the captain's proposal so reasonable that they unanimously approved of it, and agreed that they must lay all other enterprises aside, to follow this closely, and not give it up till they had succeeded.

"I expected no less," said the captain, "from your courage and bravery: but, first of all, one of you who is bold, artful, and enterprising, must go into the town dressed like a traveller and stranger, and do all he can to see if he can hear any talk of the strange death of the man whom we killed, as he deserved, and to find out who he was, and where he lived. This is a matter of the first importance for us to know, that we may do nothing which we may have reason to repent of, by revealing ourselves in a country where we have lived so long unknown, and where we have so much reason to remain: but to warn the man who shall take upon himself this commission, and to prevent our being deceived by his giving us a false report, which might be the cause of our ruin, I ask you all, whether you do not think it fit that if he does he shall suffer death?"

Without waiting for his companions, one of the robbers started up, and said, "I submit to this law, and think it an honour to expose my life by taking such a commission upon me; but remember, at least, if I do not succeed, that I wanted neither courage nor good-will to serve the troop."

After this robber had received great commendation from the captain and his comrades, he disguised himself so that nobody would take him for what he was; and taking leave of the troop that night, went into the town just at daybreak; and walked up and down till he came to Baba Mustapha's stall, which was always open before any of the shops of the town.

Baba Mustapha was sitting on his seat with an awl in his hand, just going to work. The robber saluted him, and perceiving that he

was very old, he said, "Honest man, you begin to work very early: is it possible that any one of your age can see so well? I question whether you can see to stitch."

"Certainly," replied Baba Mustapha, "you must be a stranger, and not know me; for, old as I am, I have extraordinarily good eyes; and you will not doubt it when I tell you that I sewed the pieces of a dead man together in a place where I had not so much light as I have now."

The robber was overjoyed to think that he had addressed himself, at his first coming into the town, to a man who gave him the information he wanted, without being asked. "A dead man!" replied he with amazement. "What could you sew up a dead man for? You mean you sewed up his winding sheet."

"No, no," answered Baba Mustapha, "I know what I say; you want to have me speak out, but you shall know no more."

The robber needed no great insight to be persuaded that he had discovered what he came about. He pulled out a piece of gold, and putting it into Baba Mustapha's hand, said, "I do not want to know your secret, though I can assure you I would not divulge it, if you trusted me. The only thing which I request of you is to do me the favour to point out the house where you stitched up the dead man."

"If I wanted to do you that favour," replied Baba Mustapha, holding the money in his hand, ready to return it, "I assure you I cannot; on my word, I was taken to a certain place, where they first blindfolded me, and then led me to the house, and brought me back again after the same manner; therefore you see the impossibility of doing what you desire."

"Well," replied the robber, "you may remember a little of the way that you were led blindfold. Come, let me bind your eyes at the same place. We will walk together by the same way and turnings; perhaps you may remember some part; and as everybody ought to be paid for their trouble, there is another piece of gold for you: gratify me in what I ask you." So saying, he put another piece of gold into his hand.

The two pieces of gold were a great temptation to Baba Mustapha. He looked at them a long time in his hand, without saying a word, thinking what he should do; but at last he pulled

out his purse, and put them in. "I cannot assure you," said he to the robber, "that I remember the way exactly; but, since you desire it, I will try what I can do." At these words Baba Mustapha rose up, to the great satisfaction of the robber, and without shutting up his shop, where he had nothing valuable to lose, he led the robber to the place where Morgiana had bound his eyes. "It was here," said Baba Mustapha, "that I was blindfolded; and I turned as you see me." The robber, who had his handkerchief ready, tied it over his eyes, and walked by him till he stopped, partly leading him, and partly guided by him. "I think," said Baba Mustapha, "I went no further," and he had now stopped directly opposite Cassim's house, where Ali Baba lived then; upon which the thief, before he pulled off the handkerchief, marked the door with a piece of chalk, which he had ready in his hand; and when he had pulled it off, he asked him if he knew whose house that was: to which Baba Mustapha replied, that as he did not live in the neighbourhood, he could not tell.

The robber, finding he could discover no more from Baba Mustapha, thanked him for the trouble he had taken, and left him to go back to his stall, while he returned to the forest, persuaded that he would be very well received.

A little while after the robber and Baba Mustapha parted, Morgiana went out of Ali Baba's house for something, and coming home again, she saw the mark the robber had made, and stopped to observe it. "What is the meaning of this?" said she to herself:

"either somebody intends my master no good, or else some boy has been playing the rogue: with whatever intention it was done, it is good to guard against the worst." Accordingly she went and fetched a piece of chalk, and marked two or three doors on each side in the same manner, without saying a word to her master or mistress.

In the meantime the thief rejoined his troop again in the forest, and told then the success he had had, dwelling upon his good fortune in meeting so soon with the only person who could tell him what he wanted to know. All the robbers listened to him with the utmost satisfaction. Then the captain, after commending his diligence, addressed himself to them all and said, "Comrades, we have no time to lose: let us all set off well armed, without its appearing who we are; and that we may not give any suspicion, let one or two go privately into the town together, and appoint the rendezvous in the great square; and in the meantime our comrade, who brought us the good news, and myself will go and find out the house."

This speech and plan was approved by all, and they were soon ready. They filed off in small groups of two or three, at the proper distance from each other; and all got into the town without being in the least suspected. The captain and he that came in the morning as spy came in last of all. He led the captain into the street where he had marked Ali Baba's house, and when they came to one of the houses which Morgiana had marked, he pointed it out.

But going a little further, to avoid being noticed, the captain observed that the next door was chalked after the same manner, and in the same place; and showing it to his guide, asked him which house it was, that, or the first. The guide was so bewildered, that he knew not what answer to make; much less, when he and the captain saw five or six houses marked in the same manner. He assured the captain that he had marked but one, and could not tell who had chalked the rest; and owned, in his confusion, that he could not distinguish it.

The captain, finding that their design proved abortive, went at once to the place of rendezvous, and told the first of his troop that he met that they had lost their labour, and must return to their cave. He himself set them the example, and they all returned as they came.

When the troop was all together, the captain told them the reason for their returning; and presently the conductor was declared by all to be worthy of death. He condemned himself, acknowledging that he ought to have taken better precautions, and knelt down to receive the stroke from him that was appointed to cut off his head.

But as it was for the safety of the troop that an injury should not go unpunished, another of the gang, who promised that he would succeed better, presented himself; and his offer being accepted, he went and corrupted Baba Mustapha, as the other had done, and being shown the house, marked it, in a place more remote from sight, with red chalk.

Not long after, Morgiana, whose eyes nothing could escape, went out. She saw the red chalk, and, arguing after the same manner with herself, marked the neighbours' houses in the same place and manner.

The robber, on his return to his company, prided himself very much upon the precaution he had taken, which he looked upon as an infallible way of distinguishing Ali Baba's house from those of his neighbours, and the captain and all of them thought it must succeed. They conveyed themselves into the town in the same manner as before, and when the robber and his captain came to the street, they found the same difficulty, at which the captain was enraged, and the robber in as great confusion as his predecessor.

Thus the captain and his troop were forced to retire a second time, still more dissatisfied; and the robber, as the author of the mistake, underwent the same punishment, to which he willingly submitted.

The captain, having lost two brave fellows of his troop, was afraid of diminishing it too much by pursuing this plan to get information about Ali Baba's house. He found, by their example, that their heads were not so good as their hands on such occasions, and therefore resolved to take upon himself this important commission.

Accordingly, he went and addressed himself to Baba Mustapha who did him the same service as he had done to the former men. He did not amuse himself with setting any particular mark on the house, but examined and observed it so carefully, by passing and repassing, that it was impossible for him to mistake it.

The captain, very well satisfied with his journey, and informed of what he wanted to know, returned to the forest; and when he came into the cave, where the troops awaited him, he said: "Now, comrades, nothing can prevent our full revenge. I am certain of the house, and on my way hither I have thought how to act, and if any one knows a better plan, let him communicate it." Then he ordered them to go into the towns and villages round about, and buy nineteen mules, and thirty-eight large leather jars, one full, and the others all empty.

In two or three days' time the robbers purchased the mules and jars, and as the mouths of the jars were rather too narrow for his purpose, the captain caused them to be widened; and after having put one of his men into each, with the weapons which he thought suitable, and leaving open the seam which had been undone so as to leave them room to breathe, he rubbed the jars on the outside with oil from the full vessel.

Things being thus prepared, when the nineteen mules were loaded with thirty-seven robbers in jars and the jar of oil, the captain as their driver set out with them, and reached the town by the dusk of the evening, as he intended. He led them through the streets till he came to Ali Baba's, at whose door he had intended to knock. Ali Baba was sitting there, after supper, to take a little fresh air. The robber captain stopped his mules, and said, "I have brought some oil here a great way to sell at to-morrow's market, and it is now so late that I do not know where to lodge. If I should not be troublesome to you, do me the favour to let me pass the night here, and I shall be very much obliged to you."

Though Ali Baba had seen the captain of the robbers in the forest, and had heard him speak, it was impossible for him to know him in the disguise of an oil-merchant. He told him he would be welcome, and immediately opened his gates for the mules to go into the yard. At the same time he called to a slave, and ordered him, when the mules were unloaded, not only to put them into the stable, but to give them corn and hay, and then went to Morgiana, to bid her get a good hot supper for his guest, and make him a good bed.

To make his guest as welcome as possible, when he saw the captain had unloaded his mules, that they were put into the stables as he had ordered, and that he was looking for a place to pass the night out of doors, he brought him into the hall, telling him he could not suffer him to remain in the court. The captain excused himself, on pretence of not being troublesome, but really to have room to execute his design; and it was not until after the most pressing importunity that he yielded. Ali Baba, not content with showing hospitality to the man who had a design on his life,

continued talking with him till supper was ended, and repeated his offer of service.

The captain rose up at the same time, and went with him to the door, and, while Ali Baba went into the kitchen to speak to Morgiana, he went into the yard, under pretence of looking at his mules. Ali Baba, after charging Morgiana afresh to take great care of his guest, said to her, "To-morrow morning I intend to go to the baths before dawn. Take care that my bathing linen is ready, and give it to Abdalla," (which was the slave's name), "and make me some good broth by the time I come back." After this he went to bed.

In the meantime, the captain of the robbers went from the stable to give his people orders what to do, and beginning at the first jar, and so on to the last, said to each man, "As soon as I throw some stones out of my window, do not fail to cut open the jar with the knife you have about you, pointed and sharpened for the purpose, and come out, and I will be with you at once." After this he returned into the kitchen, and Morgiana, taking a light, conducted him to his chamber, where, after she had asked him if he wanted anything, she left him; and he, to avoid any suspicion, put the light out soon after, and laid himself down in his clothes, that he might be the more ready to get up again.

Morgiana, remembering Ali Baba's orders, got his bathing linen ready, and ordered Abdalla, who was not then gone to bed, to set on the pot for the broth; but while she scummed the pot the lamp went out, and there was no more oil in the house, nor any candles. What to do she did not know, for the broth must be made.

Abdalla, seeing her very uneasy, said, "Do not fret and tease yourself, but go into the yard and take some oil out of one of the jars."

Morgiana thanked Abdalla for his advice, and he went to bed, when she took the oil-pot and went into the yard, and as she came near the first jar, the robber within said softly, "Is it time?"

Though the robber spoke low, Morgiana was struck with the voice, the more because the captain, when he unloaded the mules opened this and all the other jars, to give air to his men, who were cramped and ill at ease.

Any other slave but Morgiana, surprised to find a man in a jar, instead of the oil she wanted, would have made such a noise as to have given an alarm, which would have been attended with evil consequences; whereas Morgiana, apprehending immediately the importance of keeping the secret, and the danger Ali Baba, his family, and she herself were in, and the necessity of taking quiet action at once, collected herself without showing the least alarm, and answered, "Not yet, but presently." She went in this manner to all the jars, giving the same answer, till she came to the jar of oil.

By this means Morgiana found out that her master, Ali Baba, who thought that he had entertained an oil-merchant, had admitted thirty-eight robbers into his house, with this pretended merchant as their captain. She made what haste she could to fill her oil-pot, and returned into her kitchen; where as soon as she had lighted the lamp, she took a great kettle, and went again to the oil-jar, filled the kettle, and set it on a great wood fire to boil. As soon

as it boiled, she went and poured enough into every jar to stifle
and destroy the robber within.

When this action, worthy of the courage of Morgiana, was executed without any noise, as she had intended, she returned to the
kitchen with an empty kettle, and shut the door; and having put
out the great fire she had made to boil the oil, and leaving just
enough to make the broth, put out also the lamp, and remained
silent; resolving not to go to bed till she had observed what was to
follow through a window of the kitchen, which opened into the
yard, so far as the darkness of the night permitted.

She had not waited a quarter of an hour before the captain of
the robbers got up, and opened the window; and finding no light,
and hearing no noise, or any one stirring in the house, he gave the
signal by throwing little stones, several of which hit the jars, as he
doubted not by the sound they made. Then he listened, and not
hearing or perceiving any thing whereby he could judge that his
companions stirred, he began to grow very uneasy, and threw
stones again a second and third time, and could not comprehend
the reason why none of them answered his signal. Much alarmed,

he went softly down into the yard, and going to the first jar, asked the robber, whom he thought alive, if he was asleep. Then he smelt the hot boiled oil, which sent forth a steam out of the jar, and knew thereby that his plot to murder Ali Baba and plunder his house was discovered. Examining all the jars one after another, he found that all his gang were dead; and by the oil he missed out of the last jar, he guessed at the means and manner of their death. Enraged to despair at having failed in his design, he forced the lock of a door that led from the yard to the garden, and, climbing over the walls of several gardens, at last made his escape.

When Morgiana heard no noise, and found, after waiting some time, that the captain did not return, she guessed that he chose to make his escape by the garden rather than by the street-door, which was double-locked. Satisfied and pleased to have succeeded so well, and to have saved the house, she went to bed and fell asleep.

Ali Baba rose before dawn, and, followed by his slave, went to the baths, entirely ignorant of the amazing event that had happened at home: for Morgiana did not think it right to wake him before for fear of losing her opportunity; and afterwards she thought it needless to disturb him.

When he returned from the baths, and the sun had risen, he was very much surprised to see the oil-jars, and that the merchant had not gone with the mules. He asked Morgiana, who opened the door, and had let all things stand as they were, that he might see them, the reason of it. "My good master," answered she, "you will be better informed of what you wish to know, when you have seen what I have to show you, if you will take the trouble to follow me."

As soon as Morgiana had shut the door, Ali Baba followed her; and when she brought him into the yard, she bade him look into the first jar, and see if there was any oil. Ali Baba did so, and seeing a man, started back frightened, and cried out. "Do not be afraid," said Morgiana; "the man you see there can do neither you nor any-body else any harm. He is dead."

"Ah, Morgiana!" said Ali Baba, "what is this you show me? Explain the meaning."

"I will," replied Morgiana; "do not excite the curiosity of your neighbours; for it is of great importance to keep this affair secret. Look in all the other jars."

Ali Baba examined all the other jars, one after another; and when he came to that which had the oil in it, he found it much sunk, and stood for some time motionless, sometimes looking at the jars, and sometimes at Morgiana, without saying a word, so great was his surprise. At last, when he had recovered himself, he said, "And what has become of the merchant?"

"Merchant!" answered she: "he is as much one as I am. I will tell you who he is, and what has become of him; but you had better hear the story in your own room; for it is time for your health that you had your broth after your bathing."

While Ali Baba went to his room, Morgiana went into the kitchen to fetch the broth, and carry it to him; but before he would drink it, he first bade her satisfy his curiosity, and tell him the whole story, and she obeyed him.

"This," said Morgiana, when she had finished, "is the account you asked for; and I am convinced it is the sequel of an observation which I had made two or three days before, but did not think it necessary to acquaint you with; for when I came in one morning, early, I found our street-door marked with white chalk, and the next morning with red; and both times, without knowing what was the meaning of those chalks, I marked two or three neigh-bours' doors on each side in the same manner. If you reflect on this, and on what has since happened, you will find it to be a plot of the robbers of the forest, of whose gang there are two missing, and now they are reduced to three. All this shows that they had sworn your destruction, and it is right that you should stand upon your guard, while there is one of them alive: for my part, I shall not neglect anything necessary to your preservation, as I am in duty bound."

When Morgiana left off speaking, Ali Baba was so impressed with a sense of the great service she had done him, that he said to her, "I will not die without rewarding you as you deserve. I owe my life to you, and I give you your liberty from this moment, till I can complete your recompense as I intend. I am persuaded, with you, that the forty robbers have laid all manner of snares for me. All that we have to do is to bury the bodies of these pests of mankind immediately, and with all the secrecy imaginable, that nobody may suspect what is become of them. But that Abdalla and I will undertake."

Ali Baba's garden was very long, and shaded at the further end by a great number of large trees. Under these trees he and the slave went and dug a trench, long and wide enough to hold all the robbers, and as the earth was light, they were not long doing it. Afterwards they lifted the robbers out of the jars, took away their weapons, carried them to the end of the garden, laid them in the trench, and levelled the ground again. When this was done, Ali Baba hid the jars and weapons; and as for the mules, as he had no occasion for them, he sent them at different times to be sold in the market by his slave.

While Ali Baba took these measures to prevent the public from knowing how he came by his riches in so short a time, the captain of the forty robbers returned to the forest, in the most inconceivable mortification. He entered the cave, not having been able, all the way from the town, to come to any resolution as to what to do to Ali Baba.

The loneliness of the dark place seemed frightful to him. "Where are you, my brave lads?" cried he, "old companions of my watchings, inroads, and labour! What can I do without you? Did I collect you to lose you by so base a fate, one so unworthy of your courage? Had you died with your sabres in your hands, like brave men, my regret had been less! When shall I get such a gallant troop again? And if I could, can I undertake it without exposing so much gold and treasure to him who has already enriched himself out of it? I cannot, I ought not to think of it, before I have taken away his life. I will undertake that myself which I could not accomplish with powerful assistance; and when I have taken care to secure this treasure from being pillaged, I will provide for it new masters and successors after me, who shall preserve and augment it to all posterity." This resolution being taken, he became easy in his mind, and, full of hope, he slept all that night very quietly.

When he woke early the next morning as he had proposed he dressed himself in accordance with the project he had in his head, went down to the town, and took a lodging in a khan. And as he expected that what had happened at Ali Baba's might make a great noise in the town, he asked his host, casually, what news there was in the city. Upon which the innkeeper told him a great many things which did not concern him in the least. He judged by this that the reason why Ali Baba kept the affair so secret was lest people should find out where the treasure lay, and the means of getting at it. And this urged him the more to neglect nothing which might rid himself of so dangerous a person.

The next thing that the captain had to do was to provide himself with a horse, and to convey a great many sorts of rich stuffs and fine linen to his lodging, which he did by a great many journeys to the forest, with all the precautions imaginable to conceal the place whence he brought them. In order to dispose of the merchandise when he had amassed it together, he took a furnished shop, which happened to be opposite to Cassim's, which Ali Baba's son had not long occupied.

He took upon him the name of Cogia Houssain, and, as a new comer, was, according to custom, extremely civil and complaisant to all the merchants his neighbours. And as Ali Baba's son was young

and handsome, and a man of good sense, and was often obliged to converse with Cogia Houssain, he soon introduced them to him. He strove to cultivate his friendship, more particularly when, two or three days after he was settled, he recognised Ali Baba, who came to see his son, and stopped to talk with him as he was accustomed to do; and when he was gone the robber captain learnt from his son who he was. He increased his attentions, made him some small presents, often asked him to dine and sup with him, and treated him very handsomely.

Ali Baba's son did not care to lie under such obligations to Cogia Houssain without making a like return; but he was so much straitened for want of room in his house that he could not entertain him so well as he wished. He therefore told his father Ali Baba that it did not look well for him to receive such favours from Cogia Houssain without inviting him again.

Ali Baba, with great pleasure, took the matter upon himself. "Son," said he, "to-morrow (Friday), which is a day that the shops of such great merchants as Cogia Houssain and yourself are shut, get him to take a walk with you after dinner, and as you come back, pass by my door, and call in. It will look better to have it happen accidentally than if you gave him a formal invitation. I will go and order Morgiana to provide a supper."

The next day, after dinner, Ali Baba's son and Cogia Houssain met by appointment, and took their walk, and, as they returned, Ali Baba's son led Cogia Houssain through the street where his father lived; and when they came to the house, he stopped and knocked at the door.

"This, sir," said he, "is my father's house; when I told him of your friendship, he charged me to gain him the honour of your acquaintance."

Though it was the sole aim of Cogia Houssain to introduce himself into Ali Baba's house, that he might kill him without hazarding his own life or making any noise, he excused himself, and offered to take leave. But a slave having opened the door, Ali Baba's son took him kindly by the hand, and in a manner forced him in.

Ali Baba received Cogia Houssain with a smiling countenance, and in the most obliging manner he could wish. He thanked him for all the favours he had done his son; adding that the obligation was the greater, as his son was a young man not very well acquainted with the world, and that he might learn much from him.

Cogia Houssain returned the compliment by assuring Ali Baba that, though his son might not have acquired the experience of older men, he had good sense equal to the experience of many others. After a little more conversation on different subjects, he offered again to take his leave; when Ali Baba, stopping him, said, "Where are you going, sir, in such haste? I beg you will do me the honour to sup with me, though what I have to give you is not worth your acceptance; but such as it is, I hope you will accept it as heartily as I give it."

"Sir," replied Cogia Houssain, "I am thoroughly persuaded of your good-will; and if I ask you not to take it ill that I do not accept your kind invitation, I beg you to believe that it does not proceed from any slight or intention to affront, but from a certain reason which you would approve of if you knew it."

"And what may that reason be, sir," replied Ali Baba, "if I may be so bold as to ask you?"

"It is," answered Cogia Houssain, "that I can eat no food that has any salt in it."

"If that is the only reason," said Ali Baba, "it ought not to deprive me of the honour of your company at supper; for, in the first place, there is no salt ever put into my bread, and, as for the meat we shall have to-night, I promise you there shall be none. I will go and take care of that. Therefore you must do me the favour to stay; I will come back immediately."

Ali Baba went into the kitchen, and ordered Morgiana to put no salt to the meat that was to be cooked that night; and to make quickly two or three ragoûts besides what he had ordered, but to be sure to put no salt in them.

Morgiana, who was always ready to obey her master, could not help, this time, seeming somewhat dissatisfied at his new order. "Who is this difficult man," said she, "who eats no salt with his meat? Your supper will be spoiled, if I keep it back so long."

"Do not be angry, Morgiana," replied Ali Baba, "he is an honest man; therefore do as I bid you."

Morgiana obeyed, though with no little reluctance; and was curious to see this man who ate no salt. So when she had done what she had to do in the kitchen, and Abdalla had

laid the cloth, she helped to carry up the dishes; and looking at
Cogia Houssain she knew him at first sight to be the captain of the
robbers, notwithstanding his disguise; and examining him very
carefully, she perceived that he had a dagger hidden under his garment. "I am not in the least amazed," said she to herself, "that
this wicked wretch, who is my master's greatest enemy, would eat
no salt with him, since he intends to assassinate him; but I will
prevent him."

When Morgiana had sent up the supper by Abdalla, while they
were eating, she made the necessary preparations for executing
one of the boldest acts which could be thought of, and had just
done, when Abdalla came again for the dessert. This she carried
up, and as soon as Abdalla had taken the meat away, she set it upon
the table; after that, she set a little table and three glasses by Ali
Baba, and going out, took Abdalla along with her to supper, and to
give Ali Baba the more freedom for conversation with his guest.

Then the pretended Cogia Houssain, or rather captain of the
robbers, thought he had a favourable opportunity to kill Ali Baba.
"I will," said he to himself, "make the father and son both drunk;
and then the son, whose life I intend to spare, will not be able to
prevent my stabbing his father to the heart; and while the slaves
are at supper, or asleep in the kitchen, I can make my escape over
the gardens as before."

Instead of going to supper, Morgiana, who penetrated into the
intention of the sham Cogia Houssain, dressed herself neatly with
a suitable head-dress like a dancer, girded her waist with a silver-
gilt girdle, to which there hung a poniard with a hilt and guard of
the same metal, and put a handsome mask on her face. When she
had thus disguised herself, she said to Abdalla, "Take your tabor,
and let us go and amuse our master and his son's guest, as we do
sometimes when he is alone."

Abdalla took his tabor and played before Morgiana all the way into the hall. When she came to the door, she made a low curtsy, with a deliberate air, by way of asking leave to show what she could do. Abdalla, seeing that his master wanted to say something, left off playing. "Come in, Morgiana," said Ali Baba, "and let Cogia Houssain see what you can do, that he may tell us what he thinks of you. But, sir," said he, turning towards Cogia Houssain, "do not think that I put myself to any expense to give you this entertainment, since these are my slave and my cook and housekeeper; and I hope you will not find it disagreeable."

Cogia Houssain, who did not expect this diversion after supper, began to fear that he should not have the opportunity that he thought he had found; but he hoped, if he missed it now, to have one another time, by keeping up a friendly correspondence with the father and son; therefore, though he could have wished Ali Baba to let it alone, he pretended to be much obliged to him for it, and had the good manners to express pleasure at what he saw pleased his host.

As soon as Abdalla saw that Ali Baba and Cogia Houssain had done talking, he began to play an air on the tabor, to which Morgiana, who was an excellent dancer, danced in such a manner as would have created admiration in any company.

After she had danced several dances with the same grace and strength, she drew the poniard, and holding it in her hand, danced a dance in which she outdid herself by the many different figures and light movements, and the surprising leaps and wonderful exertions with which she accompanied it. Sometimes she presented the poniard to one person's breast, sometimes to another's, and oftentimes seemed to strike her own. At last, as if she were out of breath, she snatched the tabor from Abdalla with her left hand, and, holding the dagger in her right, presented the other side of the tabor, after the manner of those who get a livelihood by dancing, for the liberality of the spectators.

Ali Baba put a piece of gold into the tabor, as did also his son; and Cogia Houssain, seeing that she was coming to him, pulled out his purse to make her a present; but while he was putting his hand into it, Morgiana, with a courage and resolution worthy of herself, plunged the poniard into his heart.

Ali Baba and his son, frightened at this action, cried out aloud.

"Unhappy wretch!" exclaimed Ali Baba, "what have you done to ruin me and my family?"

"It was to preserve you, not to ruin you," answered Morgiana; "for see here," said she (opening Cogia Houssain's garment, and showing the dagger), "what an enemy you had entertained! Look well at him, and you will find him to be both the pretended oil-merchant, and the captain of the gang of forty robbers. Remember, too, that he would eat no salt with you; and what more would you have to persuade you of his wicked design? I suspected him as soon as you told me you had such a guest. You now find that my suspicion was not groundless."

Ali Baba, who immediately felt the new obligation he was under to Morgiana for saving his life a second time, embraced her.

"Morgiana," said he, "I gave you your liberty, and then promised you that my gratitude should not stop there, but that I would soon complete it. The time is come for me to give you a proof of this, by making you my daughter-in-law." Then addressing himself to his son, he said to him: "I believe you, son, to be so dutiful, that you will not refuse Morgiana for your wife. You see that Cogia Houssain sought your friendship with a treacherous design to take away my life; and, if he had succeeded, there is no doubt but that he would also have sacrificed you to his revenge. Consider that by marrying Morgiana you marry the support of my family and your own."

The son, far from showing any dislike, readily consented to the marriage; not only because he would not disobey his father, but because he loved Morgiana for herself.

After this, they thought of burying the captain of the robbers with his comrades, and did it so privately that nobody knew anything of it till a great many years afterwards.

After a few days, Ali Baba celebrated the marriage of his son and Morgiana with great solemnity and a sumptuous feast, and the usual dancing and shows; and he had the satisfaction of seeing that his friends and neighbours, who were not unacquainted with Morgiana's good qualities, commended his generosity and goodness of heart.

Ali Baba forbore, for a long time after this marriage, to go again to the robbers' cave, for fear of finding them there and being surprised by them. He kept away after the death of the thirty-seven robbers and their captain, supposing that the other two robbers, of whom he could get no account, might be alive.

But at the year's end, when he found that they had not made any attempt to disturb him, he had the curiosity to make another journey, taking the necessary precautions for his safety. He mounted his horse and when he came to the cave, and saw no footsteps of men or horses, he looked upon it as a good sign. He alighted off his horse, and tied him to a tree; and on his presenting himself before the door, and pronouncing the words, "Open, Sesame," the door opened. He went in, and, by the condition that he found things in, he judged that nobody had been there since the false Cogia Houssain, when he fetched the goods for his shop, and that the gang of forty robbers was completely destroyed; and he never doubted that he was the only person in the world who had the secret of opening the cave, and that all the treasure was solely at his disposal. With as much gold as his horse would carry, he returned to town.

Afterwards Ali Baba took his son to the cave and told him the secret, which they handed down to their posterity; and using their good fortune with moderation, lived in great honour and splendour, and filled the highest offices of the city.

THE STORY OF THE ENCHANTED HORSE

THE Nevrouz, or New Year's Day, is an ancient and solemn feast, which has been continued from the time of idolatry throughout all Persia, and celebrated with extraordinary rejoicings not only in the great cities, but in every little town, village, and hamlet. But the rejoicings are the most extraordinary at the court, owing to the variety of new and surprising sights; insomuch that strangers are invited from the neighbouring states and the most remote parts, and by the liberality of the king rewards are given to those who most excel in their inventions.

On one of these feast days, after the most skilful inventors of the country had repaired to Schiraz, where the court then resided, had entertained the king and all the court with their shows, and had been bountifully and liberally rewarded according to their merit by the king, just as the assembly was breaking up, an Indian appeared at the foot of the throne, with an artificial horse richly bridled and saddled, and so well made that at first sight he looked like a living horse.

The Indian prostrated himself before the throne; and, pointing to the horse, said to the king, "Though, sir, I present myself last before your majesty, yet I can assure you that nothing that has been shown to-day is so wonderful as this horse, on which I beg your majesty will be pleased to cast your eyes."

"I see nothing more in the horse," said the king, "than the natural appearance the workman has given him; which the skill of another workman may do as well or better."

"Sir," replied the Indian, "it is not for his outward form and appearance that I recommend my horse to your majesty, but for the use I know how to make of him, and what any other person, when I have communicated the secret to him, may do as well. Whenever I mount him, be it where it will, if I wish to transport myself through the air to the most distant part of the world, I can do it in a very short time. This, sir, is the wonder of my horse; a wonder which nobody ever heard of, and which I offer to show your majesty, if you command me."

The King of Persia, who was fond of everything that was curious, and, after the many wonderful things he had seen and desired to see, had never seen or heard of anything that came up to this, told the Indian that nothing but personal experience should convince him; and that he was ready to see him perform what he promised.

The Indian immediately put his foot into the stirrup, and mounted his horse with activity; and when he had got the other foot into the stirrup, and had fixed himself in the saddle, he asked the King of Persia where he was pleased to send him.

About three leagues from Schiraz there was a high mountain visible from the large square before the palace, where the king and his court, and a great concourse of people, then were.

"Do you see that mountain?" said the king, pointing to the hill: "Go to it; it is not a great way off, but it is far enough for me to judge of the haste you can make in going and coming. But because it is not possible for the eye to follow you so far, for a certain sign that you have been there I expect you to bring me a branch of a palm tree that grows at the bottom of the hill."

The King of Persia had no sooner declared his will, than the Indian turned a peg which was in the hollow of the horse's neck just by the pummel of the saddle: and in an instant the horse rose off the ground and carried his rider into the air like lightning, to such a height that those who had the strongest sight could not discern him, to the wonder of the king and all the spectators. In less than a quarter of an hour they saw him come back with a palm branch in his hand: but, before he came quite down, he took two or three turns in the air, amid the acclamations of all the people: then descended upon the same spot of ground whence he had set off, without receiving the least shock from the horse to disorder him. He dismounted; and, going up to the throne, prostrated himself, and laid the branch of the palm tree at the king's feet.

The King of Persia, who was an eye-witness, with admiration and astonishment, of this unheard-of feat which the Indian had exhibited, conceived a great desire to have the horse, and persuaded himself that he should not find it a difficult matter to treat with the Indian for whatever sum of money he should value it at. "To judge of thy horse by his outward appearance," said he to the Indian, "I did not think him so much worth my consideration. As you have showed me his merits, I am obliged to you for undeceiving me; and, to show you how much I esteem him, I will buy him of you, if he is to be sold."

"Sir," replied the Indian, "I never doubted that your majesty, who has the character of being the most judicious prince on earth, would set a just value on my work as soon as I had shown you why he was worthy of your attention. I also foresaw that you would not only admire and commend him, but would desire to have him. For my part, sir, though I know the true value of him, and that my being master of him will render my name immortal in the world, yet I am not so fond of him that I could not resign him to gratify that noble desire of your majesty; but in making this declaration, I have a request to add, without which I cannot resolve to part with him, and perhaps you may not approve of it.

"Your majesty will not be displeased," continued the Indian, "if I tell you that I did not buy this horse, but obtained him of the inventor and maker by giving him my only daughter in marriage, and promising at the same time never to sell him; but, if I parted with him, to exchange him for something that I should like."

The Indian would have gone on; but at the word "exchange," the King of Persia interrupted him. "I am willing," said he, "to give you what you will ask in exchange. You know my kingdom is large, and contains many great, rich, and populous cities; I will give you the choice of whichever you like best, in full sovereignty for the rest of your life."

This exchange seemed royal and noble to the whole court, but was much below what the Indian proposed to himself. "I am infinitely obliged to your majesty for the offer you make me," answered he, "and cannot thank you enough for your generosity; yet I must beg of you not to be angry with me if I have the

boldness to tell you that I cannot resign to you my horse, except on receiving the hand of the princess, your daughter, as my wife; this is the only price at which I can give him up."

The courtiers could not forbear laughing aloud at this extravagant demand of the Indian; but Prince Firouz Schah, the king's eldest son and presumptive heir to the crown, could not hear it without indignation. The king was of a very different opinion, and thought he might sacrifice the princess of Persia to the Indian, to satisfy his curiosity. He remained, however, undetermined, considering what he should do.

Prince Firouz Schah, who saw his father hesitate as to what answer he should make, began to fear lest he should comply with the Indian's demand, and looked upon it as injurious not only to the royal dignity and to his sister, but also to himself; therefore, to anticipate his father, he said, "Sir, I hope your majesty will forgive me for daring to ask you if it is possible that your majesty should hesitate a moment about denying so insolent a demand from such an insignificant fellow and scandalous juggler, and that you should give him reason to flatter himself for a moment on being allied to one of the most powerful monarchs in the world? I beg of you to consider what you owe to yourself, and to your own flesh and blood, and the high rank of your ancestors."

"Son," replied the King of Persia, "I very much approve of your remonstrance, and your zeal for preserving the lustre of your noble birth, but you do not enough consider the excellence of the horse, nor that the Indian, if I should refuse him, may make the offer somewhere else, where this nice point of honour may be waived. I shall be in the utmost despair if another prince should boast of having exceeded me in generosity, and deprived me of the glory of possessing a horse which I esteem as the most singular and wonderful thing in the world. I will not say I consent to grant him what he asks. Perhaps he has not made up his mind about this exorbitant demand; and, putting my daughter the princess out of the question, I may make another agreement with him that will answer his purpose as well. But before I strike the bargain with him, I should be glad if you would examine the horse, try him yourself, and give me your opinion. I doubt not he will allow it."

As it is natural for us to flatter ourselves over what we desire, the Indian fancied, by what he heard the King of Persia say, that he was not entirely averse to the alliance by taking the horse at his price, and that the prince, instead of being against it, might become more favourable to him, and not oppose the desire the king seemed to have. So, to show that he consented to it with pleasure, he expressed much joy, ran before the prince to help him to mount, and showed him how to guide and manage the horse.

The prince mounted the horse with wonderful skill, without the Indian assisting him, and no sooner had he got his feet in both stirrups than, without waiting for the Indian's advice, he turned the peg he had seen him use, and mounted into the air as quick as an arrow shot out of a bow by the stoutest and most adroit archer, and in a few moments the king, court, and the numerous assembly lost sight of him. Neither horse nor prince was to be seen, and the King of Persia made vain efforts to discern them. The Indian, alarmed at what had happened, prostrated himself before the throne, and forced the king to pay attention to what he said. "Sir," said he, "your majesty yourself saw that the prince was so hasty that he would not permit me to give him the necessary instructions how to govern my horse. From what he saw me do, he would show that he wanted not my advice. He was too willing to show his cleverness, but knows not how to turn the horse round and bring him back again. Therefore, sir, the favour I ask of your majesty is not to make me accountable for whatever accidents may befall him."

This discourse of the Indian very much surprised and afflicted

the King of Persia, who saw the danger his son
was in if, as the Indian said, there was another
secret to bring him back again different from
that which carried him away, and asked, in a passion, why he did not call him back the moment
he went.

"Sir," answered the Indian, "your majesty saw
as well as I with what swiftness the
horse and the prince flew away. The
surprise in which I then was, and
still am, deprived me of the use of
my speech, and, if I could have spo-
ken, he had got too far to hear me. If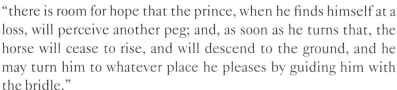
he had heard me, he knew not the secret to bring
him back, which, through his impatience, he
would not wait to learn. But, sir," added he,
"there is room for hope that the prince, when he finds himself at a
loss, will perceive another peg; and, as soon as he turns that, the
horse will cease to rise, and will descend to the ground, and he
may turn him to whatever place he pleases by guiding him with
the bridle."

Notwithstanding all these arguments of the Indian, the King
of Persia was terribly frightened at the evident danger of his son.
"I suppose," replied he, "it is very uncertain whether my son per-
ceives the other peg and makes a right use of it; may not the horse,
instead of lighting on the ground, fall upon some rock, or tumble
into the sea with him?"

"Sir," replied the Indian, "I can deliver your majesty from this
fear by assuring you that the horse crosses seas without ever
falling into them, and always carries his rider wherever he has a
mind to go. And your majesty may assure yourself that, if the
prince does but find out the other peg which I mention, the horse

will carry him where he pleases to go. It is not to be supposed that he will go anywhere but where he can find assistance, and make himself known."

"Be it as it will," replied the King of Persia, "as I cannot depend upon the assurance you give me, your head shall answer for my son's life, if he does not return safe and sound in three days' time, or I hear certainly that he is alive." Then he ordered his officers to secure the Indian, and keep him a close prisoner; after which he retired to his palace, extremely grieved that the feast of Nevrouz should afford him and his court so much sorrow.

In the meantime Prince Firouz Schah was carried through the air with prodigious swiftness, and in less than an hour's time he had got so high that he could not distinguish any thing on the earth; mountains and plains seemed confused together. It was then he began to think of returning from whence he came, and thought to do it by turning the same peg the contrary way, and pulling the bridle at the same time. But when he found that the horse still rose with the same swiftness, his astonishment was extreme. He turned the peg several times, one way and the other, but all in vain. It was then that he grew aware of his fault, in not taking the necessary precautions to guide the horse before he mounted him. He immediately apprehended the great danger he was in, but it did not deprive him of his reason. He examined the horse's head and neck with great attention, and perceived behind the horse's right ear another peg, smaller and less discernible than the other. He turned that peg, and immediately perceived that he descended in the same oblique manner as he mounted, but not so swiftly.

Night had overshadowed that part of the earth over which the prince then was for almost half an hour, when he found out and turned the small peg; and, as the horse descended, he lost sight of the sun by degrees, till it grew quite dark, insomuch that, instead of choosing what place he would go to, he was forced to let the bridle lie upon the horse's neck and wait patiently till he alighted, though not without dread lest it should be in the desert, a river, or the sea.

At last, after midnight, the horse alighted and stopped, and Prince Firouz Schah dismounted very faint and hungry, having eaten nothing since the morning, when he came out of the palace with his father to assist at the festival. The first thing he had to do in this darkness of the night was to endeavour to find out where he was. He found himself to be on the terrace of a magnificent palace, surrounded with a balustrade of white marble breast high, and groping about, found a flight of stairs, which led down into the palace, the door of which was half open.

None but Prince Firouz Schah would have ventured to go down those stairs, dark as it was, and exposed to danger from friends or foes. But no consideration could stop him. "I do not come," said he to himself, "to do anybody any harm, and certainly, whoever meets or sees me first, and finds that I have no arms in my hands, will not attempt anything against my life, before they hear what I have to say for myself." After this reflection, he opened the door wider, without making any noise, and went softly down the stairs, that he might not wake anybody, and, when he came to a landing place on the staircase, he found the door open of a great hall, that had a light in it.

The prince stopped at the door, and listening, heard no other noise than the snoring of some people who were fast asleep. He advanced a little into the room, and, by the light of a lantern, saw that the persons whom he heard snore were black chamberlains, with naked sabres laid by them, which was enough to inform him that this was the guardchamber of some queen or princess; which latter it proved to be.

In the next room to this was the princess, as appeared by the

light he saw, the door being open, and a thin silken curtain hanging before the doorway. Prince Firouz Schah advanced on tip-toe, without waking the chamberlains. He put by the curtain and looked in. The princess lay asleep on a sofa, and her women on the floor.

The prince immediately fell in love with her. He gently woke her, and the princess at once opened her eyes without fear. Seeing the prince on his knees as a suppliant, she asked him what was the matter.

The prince made use of this favourable moment, bowed his head down to the ground, and rising, said, "Most noble princess, by the most extraordinary and wonderful adventure imaginable you see here at your feet a suppliant prince, the son of the King of Persia, who was yesterday morning with his father at his court, at the celebration of a solemn feast, and is now in a strange country, in danger of his life, if you have not the goodness and generosity to give him your assistance and protection. These I implore, adorable princess, with confidence that you will not refuse me. So much beauty and majesty cannot entertain the least inhumanity."

This princess, to whom Prince Firouz Schah so fortunately addressed himself, was the Princess of Bengal, eldest daughter of the king of that kingdom, who had built this palace at a small distance from his capital, whither she went to enjoy the country. After she had heard the prince, she replied with kindness:

"Prince, you are not in a barbarous country; take courage; hospitality, humanity, and politeness are to be met with in the kingdom of Bengal, as well as in that of Persia. It is not I who grant you the protection you ask; you may find it not only in my palace, but throughout the whole kingdom; you may believe me, and depend upon what I say."

The Prince of Persia would have thanked the Princess of Bengal for her kindness, and the favour she did him, and had already bowed down his head, but she would not give him leave to speak. "Notwithstanding my desire," said she, "to know by what miracle you have come hither from the capital of Persia in so short a time, and by what enchantment you have been able to come to my apartment, and to have escaped the vigilance of my guards; as you must want some refreshment I will waive my curiosity, and give orders to my women to regale you, and show you to a room where you may rest after your fatigue."

The princess's women each took a wax candle, of which there were numbers in the room, and after the prince had taken leave very respectfully, they went before him, and conducted him into a handsome chamber, where, notwithstanding that it was so unseasonable an hour, they did not make Prince Firouz Schah wait long, but brought him all sorts of meat; and when he had eaten, they removed the table, and left him to repose.

In the meantime the Princess of Bengal was so struck with the intelligence, politeness, and other good qualities which she had discovered in that short conversation with the prince, that she could not sleep, but, when her women came into her room again, she asked them if they had taken care of him, and if he wanted anything, and particularly what they thought of him.

The women answered: "We do not know what you may think of him, but, for our part, we think you would be very happy if the king your father would marry you to so amiable a prince, for there is not a prince in all the kingdom of Bengal to be compared to him, nor can we hear that any of the neighbouring princes are worthy of you."

This flattering discourse was not displeasing to the Princess of Bengal, but she imposed silence upon them, telling them they talked without reflection.

Next day, the princess dressed herself very carefully, and sent to know if the Prince of Persia was awake, and charged the messenger to tell him she would pay him a visit.

The Prince of Persia by his night's rest had recovered from the fatigue he had undergone the day before, and when the lady-in-waiting had acquitted herself of her errand, he replied: "It shall be as the princess thinks fit; I came here to be solely at her pleasure."

As soon as the Princess of Bengal understood that the Prince of Persia waited for her, she immediately went to pay him a visit. After mutual compliments on both sides, the princess said: "Through my impatience to hear the surprising adventure which procures me the happiness of seeing you, I chose to come hither that we may not be interrupted; therefore, I beg of you to oblige me."

Prince Firouz Schah began his discourse with the solemn and

annual feast of the Nevrouz, relating all the sights worthy of her curiosity which had amazed the court of Persia and the whole town of Schiraz. Afterwards he came to the enchanted horse; the description of which, with the account of the wonders which the Indian had performed on him before so august an assembly, and of what had happened to himself, convinced the princess that nothing of the kind could be imagined more surprising in all the world.

For two whole months Prince Firouz Schah remained the guest of the Princess of Bengal, taking part in all the amusements she arranged for him, as if he had nothing else to do but to pass his whole life in this manner. But after that time he declared seriously that he could not stay any longer, and begged her to give him leave to return to his father; repeating a promise he had made her to return soon in a style worthy of her and of himself, and to demand her in marriage of the King of Bengal.

"And, princess," replied the Prince of Persia, "that you may not doubt the truth of what I say, and that you may not rank me among those false lovers who forget the object of their love as soon as they are absent from them; but to show that it is real, and that life cannot be pleasant to me when absent from so lovely a princess, I would presume, if I were not afraid you would be offended at my request, to ask the favour of taking you along with me to visit the king my father."

The Princess of Bengal consented. The only difficulty was that the prince knew not very well how to manage the horse, and she was apprehensive of being involved with him in the same kind of perilous adventure as when he made the experiment. But the prince soon removed her fear, by assuring her that she might trust herself with him, for after the experience he had had, he defied the Indian himself to manage him better.

The next morning, a little before daybreak, they went out on the terrace of the palace. The prince turned the horse towards

Persia, and placed him where the princess could easily get up behind him; which she had no sooner done, and was well settled with her arms round his waist, for better security, than he turned the peg, and the horse mounted into the air, and making his usual haste, under the guidance of the prince, in two hours' time the prince discovered the capital of Persia.

He would not alight at the great square from whence he had set out, nor in the sultan's palace, but directed his course towards a palace at a little distance from the town. He led the princess into a handsome apartment, where he told her that, to do her all the honour that was due, he would go and inform his father of their arrival, and return to her immediately. He ordered the house-keeper of the palace, who was then present, to provide the princess with whatever she had occasion for.

After the prince had taken his leave of the princess, he ordered a horse to be saddled, and after sending back the housekeeper to the princess with orders to provide her breakfast immediately, he set out for the palace. As he passed through the streets, he was received with acclamations by the people, who were overjoyed to see him again. The sultan his father was giving audience, when he appeared before him in the midst of his council, all of whom, as well as the sultan and the whole court, had been in mourning ever since he had been absent. The sultan received him, and embracing him with tears of joy and tenderness, asked him what had become of the Indian's horse.

This question gave the prince an opportunity to tell him of the embarrassment and danger he was in when the horse mounted into the air with him, and how he arrived at last at the Princess of Bengal's palace, and the kind reception he met with there: and how after promising to marry her, he had persuaded her to come with him to Persia. "But, sir," added the prince, "I have promised that you would not refuse your consent, and have brought her with me on the Indian's horse, to a palace where your majesty often goes; and have left her there, till I could return and assure her that my promise was not in vain."

After these words the prince prostrated himself before the sultan to gain his consent, but his father raised him up, embraced him a second time, and said: "Son, I not only consent to your marriage with the Princess of Bengal, but will go and meet her myself, and thank her for the obligation I am under to her, and will bring her to my palace, and celebrate your wedding this day."

Then the sultan gave orders for his court to go out of mourning, and make preparations for the princess's entry; that the rejoicings should begin with a grand concert of military music, and that the Indian should be fetched out of prison. When the Indian was brought before the sultan, he said to him, "I secured thy person, that thy life might answer for that of the prince my son, whom, thank Heaven! I have found again; go, take your horse, and never let me see your face more."

As the Indian had learned of those who fetched him out of prison that Prince Firouz Schah had returned, and had brought a princess behind him on his horse, and was also informed of the place where he had alighted and left her, and that the sultan was making preparations to go and bring her to his palace; as soon as he got out of the sultan's presence, he bethought himself of being beforehand with him and the prince, and, without losing any time, went direct to the palace, and addressing himself to the housekeeper told him that he came from the Sultan and Prince of Persia, to fetch the Princess of Bengal, and to carry her behind him through the air to the sultan, who waited in the great square of his palace to gratify the whole court and city of Schiraz with that wonderful sight.

The housekeeper, who knew the Indian, and knew that the sultan had imprisoned him, gave the more credit to what he said, because he saw that he was at liberty. He presented him to the Princess of Bengal, who no sooner understood that he came from the Prince of Persia, than she consented to what the prince, as she thought, desired of her.

The Indian, overjoyed at his success, and the ease with which he had accomplished his villainy, mounted his horse, took the princess behind him with the assistance of the housekeeper, turned the peg, and presently the horse mounted into the air with him and the princess.

At the same time the Sultan of Persia, followed by his court, was on the way from his own palace to the palace where the Princess of Bengal was left, and the Prince of Persia had ridden on before to prepare the Princess of Bengal to receive him, when the Indian, to defy them both and revenge himself for the ill-treatment he had received, passed over their heads with his prize.

When the Sultan of Persia saw this, he stopped. His surprise and affliction were the more keen because it was not in his power to make him repent of so outrageous an affront. He loaded him with a thousand imprecations, as also did all the courtiers, who were witnesses of so signal a piece of insolence and unparalleled villainy.

The Indian, little moved by their curses, which just reached his ears, continued his way, while the sultan, extremely mortified to find that he could not punish its author, returned to his palace.

But what was Prince Firouz Schah's grief to see the Indian carry away the Princess of Bengal, whom he loved so dearly that he could not live without her! At so unexpected a sight he was thunderstruck, and before he could make up his mind whether he should let fly all the reproaches his rage could invent against the Indian, or bewail the deplorable fate of the princess, or ask her pardon for not taking better care of her, the horse was out of sight. He could not resolve what to do, and so continued his way to the palace where he had left his princess.

When he came there, the housekeeper, who was by this time convinced that he had been deceived by the Indian, threw himself at his feet with tears in his eyes, and accused himself of the crime which he thought he had committed, and condemned himself to die.

"Rise up," said the prince to him, "I do not impute the loss of my princess to thee, but to my own folly. But do not lose time, fetch me a dervish's robe, and take care you do not give the least hint that it is for me."

Not far from this palace there stood a convent of dervishes, the sheik or superior of which was the palace-keeper's particular friend. He went to this sheik, and telling him that it was for an officer at court, a man to whom he had been much obliged and wished to favour by giving him an opportunity to withdraw from the sultan's rage, he easily got a complete dervish's suit of clothes, and carried it to Prince Firouz Schah. The prince immediately pulled off his own clothes, and put them on; and being so disguised, and provided with a box of jewels, which he had brought as a present to the princess, he left the palace in the evening, uncertain which way to go, but resolved not to return till he had found out his princess, and brought her back again.

But to return to the Indian: he managed his enchanted horse so well that day, that he arrived early in the evening at a wood near the capital of the kingdom of Cashmire. Being hungry, and inferring that the princess was hungry also, he alighted in an open part of the wood, and left the princess on a grassy spot, by a rivulet of clear fresh water.

During the Indian's absence, the Princess of Bengal, who knew that she was in the power of a base deceiver, whose violence she dreaded, thought of getting away from him, and seeking a sanctuary. But as she had eaten scarcely anything on her arrival at the palace in the morning, she was so faint that she was forced to abandon her plan, and to stay where she was, without any other resource than her courage, and a firm resolution to suffer death rather than be unfaithful to the Prince of Persia. When the Indian returned, she did not wait to be asked twice, but ate with him, and recovered herself enough to reply with courage to the insolent language he began to use to her when they had done. After a great many threats, as she saw that the Indian was preparing to use violence, she rose up to make resistance, and, by her cries and shrieks, drew about them a company of horsemen, who happened to be the Sultan of Cashmire and his attendants, returning from hunting.

The sultan addressed himself to the Indian, and asked him

who he was, and what he presumed to do to the lady. The Indian, with great impudence, replied that she was his wife; and what had anyone to do with his quarrel with her?

The princess, who knew neither the rank nor the quality of the person who came so seasonably to her relief, told the Indian he was a liar; and said to the sultan, "Sir, whoever you are that Heaven has sent to my assistance, have compassion on a princess, and give no credit to that impostor. Heaven forbid that I should be the wife of so vile and despicable an Indian! a wicked magician, who has taken me away from the Prince of Persia, to whom I was going to be married, and has brought me hither on the enchanted horse you see."

The Princess of Bengal had no occasion to say any more to persuade the Sultan of Cashmire that she told him the truth. Her beauty, majestic air, and tears spoke sufficiently for her. Justly enraged at the insolence of the Indian, the Sultan of Cashmire ordered his guards to surround him, and cut off his head: which sentence was immediately executed, as the Indian, just released

from prison, was unprovided with any weapon to defend himself.

The princess, thus delivered from the persecution of the Indian, fell into another no less afflicting to her. The sultan, after he had ordered her a horse, carried her with him to his palace, where he lodged her in the most magnificent apartment, next his own, and gave her a great number of women-slaves to attend her, and a guard. He showed her himself into the apartment he assigned her; where, without giving her time to thank him, he said, "As I am certain, princess, that you must want rest, I will here take my leave of you till to-morrow, when you will be better able to give me all the circumstances of this strange adventure;" and then left her.

The Princess of Bengal's joy was inexpressible, to find that she was so soon freed from the violence of a man she could not look upon without horror. She flattered herself that the Sultan of Cashmire would complete his generosity by sending her back to the Prince of Persia when she told him her story, and asked that favour of him; but she was very much deceived in these hopes, for the Sultan of Cashmire resolved to marry her the next day; and to that end had ordered rejoicings to be made by daybreak, by beating of drums and sounding of trumpets and other instruments; which echoed not only through the palace, but throughout the city.

The Princess of Bengal was awakened by these tumultuous concerts; but attributed them to a very different cause from the true one. When the Sultan of Cashmire, who had given orders that he should be informed when the princess was ready to receive a visit, came to enquire after her health, he told her that all those rejoicings were to render their wedding more solemn; and at the same time desired her to approve. This discourse put her into such consternation that she fainted away.

The women-slaves, who were present, ran to her assistance;

and the sultan did all he could to bring her to herself again, though it was a long time before they could. But when she recovered, rather than break the promise she had made to Prince Firouz Schah, by consenting to marry the Sultan of Cashmire, who had proclaimed their wedding before he had asked her consent, she resolved to feign madness. She began to say the most extravagant things before the sultan, and even rose off her seat to fly at him; insomuch that the sultan was very much surprised and afflicted that he should have made such a proposal so unseasonably.

When he found that her frenzy rather increased than abated, he left her with her women, charging them never to leave her alone, but to take great care of her. He sent often that day to know how she was; but received no other answer than that she was rather worse than better. In short, at night she seemed much worse than she had been all day.

The Princess of Bengal continued to talk wildly, and show other marks of a disordered mind, next day and the following ones; so that the sultan was obliged to send for all the physicians belonging to his court, to consult them about her disease, and to ask them if they could cure her.

The physicians all agreed that there were several sorts and degrees of this distemper, some curable and others not; and told the sultan that they could not judge of the Princess of Bengal's malady unless they saw her: upon which the sultan ordered the chamberlain to introduce them into the princess's chamber, one after another, according to their rank.

The princess, who foresaw what would happen, and feared that, if she let the physicians come near her to feel her pulse, the least experienced of them would soon know that she was in a good state of health, and that her madness was only feigned, flew into such a rage and passion that she was ready to tear out their eyes if they came near her; so none of them dared approach her.

Some of them, who pretended to be more skilful than the rest, and boasted of judging of diseases only by sight, ordered her some medicines, which she made less objection to take, well knowing she could be ill or well at pleasure, and that they could do her no harm.

When the Sultan of Cashmire saw that his court physicians could not cure her, he called in the most noted and experienced in the city, who had no better success. Afterwards he sent for the most famous in the kingdom, who met with no better reception than the others from the princess, and what they ordered had no better effect. Afterwards he despatched messengers to the courts of neighbouring princes, with a description of the princess's case, to be distributed among the most famous physicians, with a promise of a handsome reward, besides travelling expenses, to any who should come and cure the Princess of Bengal.

A great many physicians came from all parts, and undertook the cure; but none of them could boast of better success than their fellows, since it was a case that did not depend on their skill, but on the will of the princess herself.

During this interval, Prince Firouz Schah, disguised in the habit of a dervish, had travelled through a great many provinces and towns, full of grief, and having endured much fatigue, not knowing which way to direct his course, or whether he was not taking the very opposite road to the right one to hear the tidings he sought. He made diligent enquiry after her at every place he came to; till at last passing through a great town in India, he heard the people talk very much of a Princess of Bengal who went mad on the day of her marriage with the Sultan of Cashmire. At the name of the Princess of Bengal, and supposing that there was no other Princess of Bengal than she upon whose account he undertook his travels, he set out for the kingdom of Cashmire, and on his arrival at the capital he went and lodged at a khan, where the

same day he was told the story of the Princess of Bengal, and the unhappy fate of the Indian, which he richly deserved. By all the circumstances, the prince knew he could not be deceived, but that she was the princess he had sought after so long.

The Prince of Persia, being informed of all these particulars, provided himself with a physician's robe, and, having let his beard grow during his travels, he passed for a physician; and, through the greatness of his impatience to see his princess, went to the sultan's palace. Here, presenting himself to the chief of the officers, he told him that perhaps it might be looked upon as a very bold undertaking in him to offer to attempt the cure of the princess after so many had failed; but that he hoped some specifics, which he had had great experience of and success from, would effect the cure. The chief of the officers told him he was very welcome, that the sultan would receive him with pleasure, and that if he should have the good fortune to restore the princess to her former health, he might expect a liberal reward from the sultan his master. "Wait a moment," added he, "I will come to you again presently."

It was a long time since any physician had offered himself; and the Sultan of Cashmire, with great grief, had begun to lose all hope of ever seeing the Princess of Bengal restored to her former health, that he might marry her. He ordered the officer to bring in the physician he had announced.

The Prince of Persia was presented to the Sultan of Cashmire in the robe and disguise of a physician, and the sultan, without wasting time in superfluous discourse, after having told him that the Princess of Bengal could not bear the sight of a physician without falling into the most violent transports, which increased her illness, took him into a private room, from whence, through a window, he might see her without being seen.

There Prince Firouz Schah saw his lovely princess sitting carelessly, singing a song with tears in her eyes, deploring her unhappy fate, which deprived her, perhaps for ever, of the prince she loved so tenderly.

The prince was so much affected at the melancholy condition in which he found his dear princess, that he at once comprehended that her illness was feigned. When he came away he told the sultan that he had discovered the nature of the princess's illness, and that she was not incurable, but added that he must speak to her in private, and by himself; and, notwithstanding her

violent fits at the sight of physicians, he hoped she would hear and receive him favourably.

The sultan ordered the princess's door to be opened, and Prince Firouz Schah went in. As soon as the princess saw him (taking him by his appearance to be a physician), she rose up in a rage, threatening and giving way to the most abusive language. He made directly towards her, and when he was near enough for her to hear him, for he did not wish to be heard by anyone else, he said to her, in a low voice, and in a most respectful manner, to make her believe him, "Princess, I am not a physician, but the Prince of Persia, and am come to set you at liberty."

The princess, who immediately knew the sound of the voice, and the upper features of his face, notwithstanding his beard, grew calm at once, and a secret joy and pleasure overspread her face. Her agreeable surprise deprived her for some time of speech, and gave Prince Firouz Schah time to tell her as briefly as possible how despair seized him when he saw the Indian carry her away; the resolution he took afterwards to leave nothing undone to find out where she was, and never to return home till he had found her, and forced her out of the hands of the perfidious wretch; and by what good fortune at last, after a long and fatiguing journey, he had the satisfaction of finding her in the palace of the Sultan of Cashmire. He then desired the princess to inform him of all that happened to her from the time she was taken away till that moment, telling her that it was of the greatest importance to know this, that he might take the proper measures to deliver her from the tyranny of the Sultan of Cashmire.

The Princess of Bengal told the prince how she was delivered from the Indian's violence by the Sultan of Cashmire, as he was returning home from hunting; but how ill she was treated by his overhasty design to marry her that very day, without even asking her consent; that this violent and tyrannical conduct put her into a swoon, after which she thought she had no other way to save herself for a prince to whom she had given her heart and faith, and would rather die than marry the sultan, whom she neither loved, nor ever could.

Then the Prince of Persia asked her if she knew what had

become of the horse after the Indian's death. To which she answered that she knew not what orders the sultan had given about it, but believed he would take care of it.

As Prince Firouz Schah never doubted that the sultan had the horse, he communicated to the princess his design of making use of it to carry them both back to Persia, and after they had consulted together on the measures they were to take, they agreed that the princess should next day receive the sultan civilly, but without speaking to him.

The Sultan of Cashmire was overjoyed when the Prince of Persia told him the effect his first visit had had on the Princess of Bengal. And the next day, when the princess received him in such a manner as persuaded him that her cure was far advanced, he looked upon the prince as the greatest physician in the world, and contented himself with telling her how rejoiced he was to see her so likely to recover her health. He exhorted her to follow the directions of so thoughtful a physician, and to complete what he had so well begun, and then retired, without waiting for her answer.

The Prince of Persia, who went with the Sultan of Cashmire out of the princess's chamber, asked him if, without failing in due respect, he might enquire how the Princess of Bengal came into the dominions of Cashmire thus alone, since her own country lay so far off? This he said on purpose to introduce some remark about the enchanted horse, and to know what had become of it.

The Sultan of Cashmire, who could not penetrate the Prince of Persia's motive for asking this question, concealed nothing, but told him much the same story as the Princess of Bengal had done; adding that he had ordered the enchanted horse to be kept safe in his treasury as a great curiosity, though he knew not the use of it.

"Sir," replied the pretended physician, "the information which your majesty gives me affords me a means of curing the princess.

As she was brought hither on this horse, and the horse is enchanted, she has contracted somewhat of the enchantment, which can be dissipated only by certain incense which I am acquainted with. If your majesty would be pleased to entertain yourself, your court, and the people of your capital with the most surprising sight that ever was seen, let the horse be brought into the great square before the palace, and leave the rest to me. I promise to show you, and all that assembly in a few moments' time, the Princess of Bengal as well in body and mind as ever she was in her life. But, the better to effect what I propose, it would be best that the princess should be dressed as magnificently as possible, and adorned with the best jewels your majesty has." The sultan agreed.

Early the next day, the enchanted horse was, by his order, taken out of the treasury, and placed in the great square before the palace. A report was spread through the town that there was something extraordinary to be seen, and crowds of people flocked thither from all parts, insomuch that the sultan's guards were placed to prevent disorder, and to keep space enough round the horse.

The Sultan of Cashmire, surrounded by all his nobles and ministers of state, sat in state on a platform erected on purpose. The Princess of Bengal, attended by a vast number of ladies whom the sultan had assigned her, went up to the enchanted horse and the

women helped her to get upon its back. When she was fixed in the saddle, and had the bridle in her hand, the pretended physician placed round the horse a great many vessels full of fire, which he had ordered to be brought, and going round it, he cast a strong and pleasant perfume into these pots; then, collected in himself, with downcast eyes, and his hands upon his breast, he ran three times about the horse, pretending to pronounce certain words. The moment the pots sent forth a dark cloud of pleasant scent, which so surrounded the princess that neither she nor the horse was to be discerned, the prince, watching his opportunity, jumped nimbly up behind her, and stretching out his hand to the peg, turned it; and just as the horse rose with them into the air, he pronounced these words, which the sultan heard distinctly – "Sultan of Cashmire, when you would marry princesses who implore your protection, learn first to obtain their consent."

Thus the Prince of Persia recovered the Princess of Bengal, and

carried her that same day to the capital of Persia, where he
alighted in the midst of the palace, before the king his father's
window. The king deferred the marriage no longer than until he
could make the preparations necessary to render the ceremony
pompous and magnificent.

After the days appointed for the rejoicing were over, the King
of Persia's first care was to appoint an ambassador to go and give
the King of Bengal an account of what had happened, and to
demand his approval and ratification of the alliance. This the King
of Bengal took as an honour, and granted with great pleasure and
satisfaction.

THE STORY OF THE FISHERMAN
AND GENIE

PART I

THERE was once a very old fisherman, so poor, that he could scarcely earn enough to maintain himself, his wife, and three children. He went every day to fish betimes in the morning; and imposed it as a law upon himself not to cast his nets above four times a day. He went one morning by moonlight, and coming to the seaside, undressed himself, and cast in his nets. As he drew them towards the shore, he found them very heavy, and thought he had a good draught of fish, at which he rejoiced within himself; but perceiving a moment after that, instead of fish, there was nothing in his nets but the carcass of an ass, he was much vexed.

When the fisherman, vexed to have made such a sorry draught, had mended his nets, which the carcass of the ass had broken in several places, he threw them in a second time; and, when he drew them, found a great deal of resistance, which made him think he had taken abundance of fish; but he found nothing except a basket full of gravel and slime, which grieved him extremely. "O Fortune!" cried he in a lamentable tone, "be not angry with me, nor persecute a wretch who prays thee to spare him. I came hither from my house to seek for my livelihood, and thou pronouncest death against me. I have no trade but this to subsist by; and, notwithstanding all the care I take, I can scarcely provide what is absolutely necessary for my family."

Having finished this complaint, he threw away the basket in a fret, and washing his nets from the slime, cast them the third time; but brought up nothing except stones, shells, and mud. Nobody can express his dismay; he was almost beside himself.

However, when the dawn began to appear, he did not forget to say his prayers, like a good Mussulman, and afterwards added this petition: "Lord, thou knowest that I cast my nets only four times a day; I have already drawn them three times, without the least reward for my labour: I am only to cast them once more; I pray thee to render the sea favourable to me, as thou didst to Moses."

The fisherman, having finished his prayer, cast his nets the fourth time; and when he thought it was time, he drew them as before, with great difficulty; but, instead of fish, found nothing in them but a vessel of yellow copper, which by its weight seemed to be full of something; and he observed that it was shut up and sealed, with a leaden seal upon it. This rejoiced him: "I will sell it," said he, "at the foundry, and with the money arising from the produce buy a measure of corn." He examined the vessel on all sides, and shook it, to see if what was within made any noise, but heard  nothing. This, with the impression of the seal upon the leaden cover, made him think there was something precious in it. To try this, he took a knife, and opened it with very little trouble. He presently turned the mouth downward, but nothing came out, which surprised him extremely. He set it before him, and while he looked upon it attentively, there came out a very thick smoke which obliged him to retire two or three paces away.

The smoke ascended to the clouds, and extending itself along the sea and upon the shore, formed a great mist, which, we may well imagine, did mightily astonish the fisherman. When the smoke was all out of the vessel, it reunited itself, and became a solid body, of which there was formed a genie twice as high as the

greatest of giants. At the sight of a monster of such unwieldy bulk, the fisherman would fain have fled, but he was so frightened that he could not go one step.

"Solomon," cried the genie immediately, "Solomon, great prophet, pardon, pardon; I will never more oppose thy will, I will obey all thy commands."

When the fisherman heard these words of the genie, he

recovered his courage, and said to him, "Proud spirit, what is it that you say? It is above eighteen hundred years since the prophet Solomon died, and we are now at the end of time. Tell me your history, and how you came to be shut up in this vessel."

The genie, turning to the fisherman with a fierce look, said, "You must speak to me with more civility; you are very bold to call me a proud spirit."

"Very well," replied the fisherman, "shall I speak to you with more civility, and call you the owl of good luck?"

"I say," answered the genie, "speak to me more civilly, before I kill thee."

"Ah!" replied the fisherman, "why would you kill me? Did I not just now set you at liberty, and have you already forgotten it?"

"Yes, I remember it," said the genie, "but that shall not hinder me from killing thee: I have only one favour to grant thee."

"And what is that?" said the fisherman.

"It is," answered the genie, "to give thee thy choice, in what manner thou wouldst have me take thy life."

"But wherein have I offended you?" replied the fisherman. "Is that your reward for the good service I have done you?"

"I cannot treat you otherwise," said the genie; "and that you may be convinced of it, hearken to my story.

"I am one of those rebellious spirits that opposed the will of Heaven: all the other genii owned Solomon, the great prophet, and submitted to him. Sacar and I were the only genii that would never be guilty of a mean thing: and, to avenge himself, that great monarch sent Asaph, the son of Barakhia, his chief minister, to apprehend me. That was accordingly done. Asaph seized my person, and brought me by force before his master's throne.

"Solomon, the son of David, commanded me to quit my way of living, to acknowledge his power, and to submit myself to his commands: I bravely refused to obey, and told him I would rather expose myself to his resentment than swear fealty, and submit to him, as he required. To punish me, he shut me up in this copper vessel; and to make sure that I should not break prison, he himself stamped upon this leaden cover his seal, with the great name of God engraven upon it. Then he gave the vessel to one of the genii who submitted to him, with orders to throw me into the sea, which was done, to my sorrow.

"During the first hundred years' imprisonment, I swore that if anyone would deliver me before the hundred years expired, I would make him rich, even after his death: but that century ran out, and nobody did me the good office. During the second, I made an oath that I would open all the treasures of the earth to anyone that should set me at liberty; but with no better success. In the third, I promised to make my deliverer a potent monarch, to be always near him in spirit, and to grant him every day three requests, of what nature soever they might be: but this century ran out as well as the two former, and I continued in prison. At last, being angry, or rather mad, to find myself a prisoner so long, I swore that if afterwards anyone should deliver me, I would kill him without mercy, and grant him no other favour but to choose what kind of death he would die; and, therefore, since you have delivered me to-day, I give you that choice."

This tale afflicted the poor fisherman extremely: "I am very unfortunate," cried he, "to have done such a piece of good service to one that is so ungrateful. I beg you to consider your injustice and to revoke such an unreasonable oath; pardon me, and heaven will pardon you; if you grant me my life, heaven will protect you from all attempts against yours."

"No, thy death is resolved on," said the genie, "only choose how you will die."

The fisherman, perceiving the genie to be resolute, was terribly grieved, not so much for himself as for his three children, and the misery they must be reduced to by his death. He endeavoured still to appease the genie, and said, "Alas! be pleased to take pity on me, in consideration of the good service I have done you."

"I have told thee already," replied the genie, "it is for that very reason I must kill thee."

"That is very strange," said the fisherman, "are you resolved to reward good with evil? The proverb says, 'He who does good to one who deserves it not is always ill rewarded.' I must confess I thought it was false; for in reality there can be nothing more contrary to reason, or to the laws of society. Nevertheless, I find now by cruel experience that it is but too true."

"Do not lose time," replied the genie, "all thy reasonings shall not divert me from my purpose; make haste, and tell me which way you choose to die."

Necessity is the mother of invention. The fisherman bethought himself of a stratagem. "Since I must die then," said he to the genie, "I submit to the will of heaven; but, before I choose the manner of death, I conjure you by the great name which was engraven upon the seal of the prophet Solomon, the son of David, to answer me truly the question I am going to ask you."

The genie finding himself bound to a positive answer trembled, and replied to the fisherman, "Ask what thou wilt, but make haste."

The genie having thus promised to speak the truth, the fisherman said to him, "I wish to know if you were actually in this vessel. Dare you swear it by the Great Name?"

"Yes," replied the genie, "I do swear by that Great Name that I was; and it is a certain truth."

"In good faith," answered the fisherman, "I cannot believe you. The vessel is not capable of holding one of your feet, and how is it possible that your whole body could lie in it?"

"I swear to thee, notwithstanding," replied the genie, "that I

was there just as thou seest me here. Is it possible that thou dost not believe me after this great oath that I have taken?"

"Truly, I do not," said the fisherman; "nor will I believe you unless you show it me."

Upon which the body of the genie was dissolved, and changed itself into smoke, extending itself as formerly upon the sea and shore, and then at last, being gathered together, it began to re-enter the vessel, which it continued to do by a slow and equal motion in a smooth and exact way, till nothing was left out, and immediately a voice said to the fisherman, "Well, now, incredulous fellow, I am all in the vessel; do not you believe me now?"

The fisherman, instead of answering the genie, took the cover of lead, and speedily shut the vessel. "Genie," cried he, "now it is your turn to beg my favour, and to choose which way I shall put you to death; but it is better that I should throw you into the sea, whence I took you: and then I will build a house upon the bank, where I will dwell, to give notice to all fishermen who come to throw in their nets to beware of such a wicked genie as thou art, who hast made an oath to kill him that shall set thee at liberty."

The genie, enraged, did all he could to get out of the vessel again; but it was not possible for him to do it, for the impression of Solomon's seal prevented him. So, perceiving that the fisherman had got the advantage of him, he thought fit to dissemble his anger. "Fisherman," said he, in a pleasant tone, "take heed you do not do what you say, for what I spoke to you before was only by way of jest, and you are to take it no otherwise."

"Oh, genie!" replied the fisherman, "thou who wast but a moment ago the greatest of all genii, and now art the least of them, thy crafty discourse will avail thee nothing. Back to the sea thou shalt go. If thou hast been there already so long as thou hast told me, thou mayst very well stay there till the day of judgment. I begged of thee, in God's name, not to take away my life, and thou didst reject my prayers; I am obliged to treat thee in the same manner."

The genie omitted nothing that might prevail upon the fisherman. "Open the vessel," said he; "give me my liberty, I pray thee, and I promise to satisfy thee to thy heart's content."

"Thou art a mere traitor," replied the fisherman; "I should deserve to lose my life if I were such a fool as to trust thee. Notwithstanding the extreme obligation thou wast under to me for having set thee at liberty, thou didst persist in thy design to kill me; I am obliged in my turn, to be as hard-hearted to thee."

"My good friend fisherman," replied the genie, "I implore thee once more not to be guilty of such cruelty; consider that it is not good to avenge oneself, and that, on the other hand, it is commendable to return good for evil; do not treat me as Imama treated Ateca formerly."

"And what did Imama do to Ateca?" replied the fisherman.

"Ho!" said the genie, "if you have a mind to hear, open the vessel: do you think that I can be in a humour to tell stories in so strait a prison? I will tell you as many as you please when you let me out."

"No," said the fisherman, "I will not let you out; it is vain to talk of it. I am just going to throw you to the bottom of the sea."

"Hear me one word more," cried the genie. "I promise to do

thee no hurt; nay, far from that, I will show thee how thou mayest become exceedingly rich."

The hope of delivering himself from poverty prevailed with the fisherman.

"I might listen to you," said he, "were there any credit to be given to your word. Swear to me by the Great Name that you will faithfully perform what you promise, and I will open the vessel. I do not believe you will dare to break such an oath."

The genie swore to him, and the fisherman immediately took off the covering of the vessel. At that very instant the smoke came out, and the genie having resumed his form as before, the first thing he did was to kick the vessel into the sea. This action frightened the fisherman.

"Genie," said he, "what is the meaning of that? Will you not keep the oath you just now made?"

The genie laughed at the fisherman's fear, and answered: "No, fisherman, be not afraid; I only did it to please myself, and to see if thou wouldst be alarmed at it; but to persuade thee that I am in earnest, take thy nets and follow me." As he spoke these words, he walked before the fisherman, who took up his nets, and followed him, but with some distrust. They passed by the town, and came to the top of a mountain, from whence they descended into a vast plain, and presently to a great pond that lay betwixt four hills.

When they came to the side of the pond, the genie said to the fisherman, "Cast in thy nets and catch fish." The fisherman did not doubt of catching some, because he saw a great number in the pond; but he was extremely surprised when he found that they were of four colours – white, red, blue, and yellow. He threw in his nets, and brought out one of each colour. Having never seen the like, he could not but admire them, and, judging that he might get a considerable sum for them, he was very joyful.

"Carry those fish," said the genie, "and present them to the

sultan; he will give you more money for them than ever you had in your life. You may come every day to fish in this pond; and I give you warning not to throw in your nets above once a day, otherwise you will repent it. Take heed, and remember my advice." Having spoken thus, he struck his foot upon the ground, which opened and swallowed up the genie.

The fisherman, being resolved to follow the genie's advice

exactly, forebore casting in his nets a second time, and returned to
the town very well satisfied with his fish, and making a thousand
reflections upon his adventure. He went straight to the sultan's
palace.

The sultan was much surprised when he saw the four fishes.
He took them up one after another,
and looked at them with attention;
and, after having admired them a
long time, he said to his first vizier,
"Take those fishes to the handsome
cook-maid that the Emperor of the
Greeks has sent me. I cannot imagine
but that they must be as good as they
are fine."

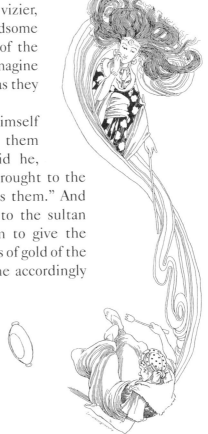

The vizier carried them himself
to the cook, and delivering them
into her hands, "Look," said he,
"here are four fishes newly brought to the
sultan; he orders you to dress them." And
having so said, he returned to the sultan
his master, who ordered him to give the
fisherman four hundred pieces of gold of the
coin of that country, which he accordingly
did.

The   fisherman,
who had never seen so
much cash in his life-
time, could scarcely
believe his own good
fortune. He thought it
must be a dream, until
he found it to be real,

when he provided necessaries for his family with it.

As soon as the sultan's cook had cleaned the fishes, she put them upon the fire in a frying-pan with oil; and when she thought them fried enough on one side, she turned them upon the other; but scarcely were they turned when the wall of the kitchen opened, and in came a young lady of wonderful beauty and comely size. She was clad in flowered satin, after the Egyptian manner, with pendants in her ears, a necklace of large pearls, bracelets of gold garnished with rubies, and a rod of myrtle in her hand. She came towards the frying-pan, to the great amazement of the cook, who stood stock-still at the sight, and, striking one of the fishes with the end of the rod, said, "Fish, fish, art thou in thy duty?"

The fish having answered nothing, she repeated these words, and then the four fishes lifted up their heads all together, and said to her, "Yes, yes; if you reckon, we reckon; if you pay your debts, we pay ours; if you fly, we overcome, and are content." As soon as they had finished these words, the lady overturned the frying-pan, and entered again into the open part of the wall, which shut immediately, and became as it was before.

The cook was greatly frightened at this, and, on coming a little to herself, went to take up the fishes that had fallen upon the hearth, but found them blacker than coal, and not fit to be carried to the sultan. She was grievously troubled at it, and began to weep most bitterly. "Alas!" said she, "what will become of me? If I tell the sultan what I have seen, I am sure he will not believe me, but will be enraged."

While she was thus bewailing herself, in came the grand vizier, and asked her if the fishes were ready. She told him all that had happened, which we may easily imagine astonished him; but, without speaking a word of it to the sultan, he invented an excuse that satisfied him, and sending immediately for the fisherman, bade him bring four more such fish, for a misfortune had befallen the other ones. The fisherman, without saying anything of what the genie had told him, but in order to excuse himself from bringing them that very day, told the vizier that he had a long way to go for them, but would certainly bring them to-morrow.

Accordingly the fisherman went away by night, and, coming to the pond, threw in his nets betimes next morning, took four such fishes as before, and brought them to the vizier at the hour appointed. The minister took them himself, carried them to the kitchen, and shut himself up all alone with the cook: she cleaned them and put them on the fire, as she had done the four others the day before. When they were fried on one side, and she had turned them upon the other, the kitchen wall opened, and the same lady came in with the rod in her hand, struck one of the fishes, spoke to it as before, and all four gave her the same answer.

After the four fishes had answered the young lady, she overturned the frying-pan with her rod, and retired into the same place of the wall from whence she had come out. The grand vizier being witness to what had passed said, "This is too surprising and extraordinary to be concealed from the sultan; I will inform him." Which he accordingly did, and gave him a very faithful account of all that had happened.

The sultan, being much surprised, was impatient to see it for himself. He immediately sent for the fisherman, and said to him, "Friend, cannot you bring me four more such fishes?"

The fisherman replied, "If your majesty will be pleased to allow me three days' time, I will do it." Having obtained his time, he went to the pond immediately, and at the first throwing in of his net, he caught four fishes, and brought them at once to the sultan. The sultan rejoiced at it, as he did not expect them so soon, and ordered him four hundred pieces of gold. As soon as the sultan had received the fish, he ordered them to be carried into his room, with all that was necessary for frying them; and having shut himself up there with the vizier, the minister cleaned them, put them in the pan upon the fire, and when they were fried on one side, turned them upon the other; then the wall of the room opened, but instead of the young lady there came out a black man, in the dress of a slave, and of gigantic stature, with a great green staff in his hand. He advanced towards the pan, and touching one of the fishes with his staff, said to it in a terrific voice, "Fish, art thou in thy duty?"

At these words the fishes raised up their heads, and answered, "Yes, yes; we are; if you reckon, we reckon; if you pay your debts, we pay ours; if you fly, we overcome, and are content."

The fishes had no sooner finished these words than the black man threw the pan into the middle of the room, and reduced the fishes to a coal. Having done this, he retired fiercely, and entering again into the hole of the wall, it shut, and appeared just as it did before.

"After what I have seen," said the sultan to the vizier, "it will not be possible for me to be easy in my mind. These fish without doubt signify something extraordinary." He sent for the fisherman, and said to him, "Fisherman, the fishes you have brought us make me very uneasy; where did you catch them?"

"Sir," answered he, "I fished for them in a pond situated between four hills, beyond the mountain that we see from here."

"Know'st thou that pond?" said the sultan to the vizier.

"No, sir," replied the vizier, "I never so much as heard of it: and yet it is not sixty years since I hunted beyond that mountain and thereabouts."

The sultan asked the fisherman how far was the pond from the palace.

The fisherman answered that it was not above three hours' journey.

Upon this, there being daylight enough beforehand, the sultan commanded all his court to take horse, and the fisherman served them for a guide. They all ascended the mountain, and at the foot of it they saw, to their great surprise, a vast plain, that nobody had observed till then, and at last they came to the pond which they found really to be situated between four hills, as the fisherman had said. The water of it was so transparent that they observed all the fishes to be like those which the fisherman had brought to the palace.

The sultan stood upon the bank of the pond, and after beholding the fishes with admiration, he demanded of his emirs and all his courtiers if it was possible that they had never seen this pond, which was within so little a way of the town. They all answered that they had never so much as heard of it.

"Since you all agree," said he, "that you never heard of it, and as I am no less astonished than you are, I am resolved not to return to my palace till I know how this pond came here, and why all the fish in it are of four colours." Having spoken thus he ordered his court to encamp; and immediately his pavilion and the tents of his household were pitched upon the banks of the pond.

THE STORY OF THE FISHERMAN AND GENIE
PART II

WHEN night came, the sultan retired to his pavilion and spoke to the grand vizier by himself.

"Vizier, my mind is very uneasy; this pond transported hither;

the black man that appeared to us in my room, and the fishes that we heard speak; all this does so much excite my curiosity that I cannot resist the impatient desire I have to satisfy it. To this end I am resolved to withdraw alone from the camp, and I order you to keep my absence secret."

The grand vizier said much to turn the sultan from this design. But it was to no purpose; the sultan was resolved on it, and would go. He put on a suit fit for walking, and took his scimitar; and as soon as he saw that all was quiet in the camp, he went out alone, and went over one of the hills without much difficulty. He found the descent still more easy, and, when he came to the plain, walked on till the sun rose, and then he saw before him, at a considerable distance, a great building. He rejoiced at the sight, and hoped to learn there what he wanted to know. When he came near, he found it was a magnificent palace, or rather a very strong castle, of fine black polished marble, and covered with fine steel, as smooth as a looking-glass. Being highly pleased that he had so speedily met with something worthy of his curiosity, he stopped before the front of the castle, and considered it attentively.

The gate had two doors, one of them open; and though he might have entered, he yet thought it best to knock. He knocked at first softly, and waited for some time. Seeing nobody, and supposing they had not heard him, he knocked harder the second time, and then neither seeing nor hearing anybody, he knocked again and again. But nobody appeared, and it surprised him extremely; for he could not think that a castle in such good repair was without inhabitants. "If there is nobody in it," said he to himself, "I have nothing to fear; and if there is, I have wherewith to defend myself."

At last he entered, and when he came within the porch, he called out, "Is there nobody here to receive a stranger, who comes in for some refreshment as he passes by?" He repeated the same two or three times; but though he shouted, nobody answered. The silence increased his astonishment: he came into a very spacious court, and looked on every side, to see if he could perceive anybody; but he saw no living thing.

Perceiving nobody in the court, the sultan entered the great halls, which were hung with silk tapestry; the alcoves and sofas were covered with stuffs of Mecca, and the porches with the richest stuffs of India, mixed with gold and silver. He came afterwards into a magnificent court, in the middle of which was a great

fountain, with a lion of massive gold at each corner; water issued from the mouths of the four lions, and this water, as it fell, formed diamonds and pearls, while a jet of water, springing from the middle of the fountain, rose almost as high as a cupola painted after the Arabian manner.

On three sides the castle was surrounded by a garden, with flower-pots, fountains, groves, and a thousand other fine things; and to complete the beauty of the place, an infinite number of birds filled the air with their harmonious songs, and always stayed there, nets being spread over the trees, and fastened to the palace to keep them in. The sultan walked a long time from apartment to apartment, where he found everything very grand and magnificent. Being tired with walking, he sat down in a room which had a view over the garden, and there reflected upon what he had already seen, when all of a sudden he heard lamentable cries. He listened with attention, and distinctly heard these sad words: "O Fate! thou who wouldst not suffer me longer to enjoy a happy lot, and hast made me the most unfortunate man in the world, forbear to persecute me, and by a speedy death put an end to my sorrows. Alas! is it possible that I am still alive, after so many torments as I have suffered?"

The sultan, touched at these pitiful complaints, rose up, and made toward the place whence he heard the voice; and when he came to the gate of a great hall, he opened it, and saw a handsome young man, richly dressed, seated upon a throne raised a little above the ground. Melancholy was painted on his looks. The sultan drew near, and saluted him; the young man returned him his salute, by a low bow with his head; but not being able to rise up, he said to the sultan, "My lord, I am very sure you deserve that I should rise up to receive you, and do you all possible honour; but I am hindered from doing so by a very sad reason, and therefore hope you will not take it ill."

"My lord," replied the sultan, "I am very much obliged to you for having so good an opinion of me: as to your not rising, whatever your excuse may be, I heartily accept it. Being drawn hither by your complaints, and distressed by your grief, I come to offer you my help. I flatter myself that you would willingly tell me the history of your misfortunes; but pray tell me first the meaning of the pond near the palace, where the fishes are of four colours. What is this castle? how came you to be here? and why are you alone?"

Instead of answering these questions, the young man began to weep bitterly. "How inconstant is fortune;" cried he: "she takes pleasure in pulling down those she had raised up. Where are they who enjoy quietly their happiness, and whose day is always clear and serene?"

The sultan, moved with compassion, prayed him forthwith to tell him the cause of his excessive grief. "Alas! my lord," replied the young man, "how can I but grieve, and my eyes be inexhaustible fountains of tears?" At these words he lifted up his gown, and showed the sultan that he was a man only from the head to the waist, and that the other half of his body was black marble.

The sultan was strangely surprised when he saw the deplorable condition of the young man. "That which you show me," said he, "while it fills me with horror, so excites my curiosity that I am impatient to hear your history, which, no doubt, is very extraordinary, and I am persuaded that the pond and the fishes have some part of it; therefore I beg you to tell it me. You will find some comfort in doing so, since it is certain that unfortunate people obtain some sort of ease in telling their misfortunes."

"I will not refuse you this satisfaction," replied the young man, "though I cannot do it without renewing my grief. But I give you notice beforehand, to prepare your ears, your mind, and even your eyes, for things which surpass all that the most extraordinary imagination can conceive.

"You must know, my lord," he began, "that my father Mahmoud was king of this country. This is the kingdom of the Black Isles, which takes its name from the four little neighbouring mountains; for those mountains were formerly islands: the capital, where the king, my father, had his residence, was where that pond now is.

"The king, my father, died when he was seventy years of age; I had no sooner succeeded him than I married, and the lady I chose to share the royal dignity with me was my cousin. Nothing was comparable to the good understanding between us, which lasted for five years. At the end of that time I perceived that the queen, my cousin, took no more delight in me.

"One day I was inclined to sleep after dinner, and lay down upon the sofa. Two of her ladies came and sat down, one at my head, and the other at my feet, with fans in their hands to moderate the heat, and to hinder the flies from troubling me. They thought I was fast asleep, and spoke very low; but I only shut my eyes, and heard every word they said.

"One of them said to the other, 'Is not the queen much in the wrong not to love such an amiable prince as this?'

" 'Certainly,' replied the other; 'for my part, I do not understand it. Is it possible that he does not perceive it?'

" 'Alas!' said the first, 'how would you have him perceive it? She mixes every evening in his drink the juice of a certain herb, which makes him sleep so soundly that she has time to go where she pleases; then she wakes him by the smell of something she puts under his nose.'

"You may guess, my lord, how much I was surprised at this conversation; yet, whatever emotion it excited in me, I had command enough over myself to dissemble, and pretended to awake without having heard one word of it.

"The queen returned, and with her own hand presented me with a cup full of such water as I was accustomed to drink; but instead of putting it into my mouth, I went to a window that was open, and threw out the water so quickly that she did not notice it, and I put the cup again into her hands, to persuade her that I had drunk it.

"Soon after, believing that I was asleep, though I was not, she got up with little precaution, and said, so loudly, that I could hear it distinctly, 'Sleep, and may you never wake again!'

"As soon as the queen, my wife, went out, I got up in haste, took my scimitar, and followed her so quickly, that I soon heard the sound of her feet before me, and then walked softly after her, for fear of being heard. She passed through several gates, which opened on her pronouncing some magical words; and the last she opened was that of the garden, which she entered. I stopped there that she might not perceive me, and looking after her as far as the darkness permitted, I perceived that she entered a little wood, whose walks were guarded by thick palisades. I went thither by another way, and slipping behind the palisades of a long walk, I saw her walking there with a man.

"I listened carefully, and heard her say, 'I do not deserve to be upbraided by you for want of diligence; you need but command me, you know my power. I will, if you desire it, before sunrise, change this great city, and this fine palace, into frightful ruins, which shall be inhabited by nothing but wolves, owls, and ravens. If you wish me to transport all the stones of those walls, so solidly built, beyond the Caucasus, and out of the bounds of the habitable world, speak but the word, and all shall undergo a change.'

"As the queen finished these words, the man and she came to the end of the walk, turned to enter another, and passed before me. I had already drawn my scimitar, and the man being nearest to me, I struck him on the neck, and made him fall to the ground. I thought I had killed him, and therefore retired speedily, without making myself known to the queen, whom I chose to spare, because she was my kinswoman.

"The blow I had given was mortal; but she preserved his life by the force of her enchantments; in such a manner, however, that he could not be said to be either dead or alive. As I crossed the garden, to return to the palace, I heard the queen cry out lamentably.

"When I returned home, being satisfied with having punished the villain, I went to sleep; and, when I awoke next morning, found the queen there too.

"Whether she slept or not I cannot tell, but I got up and went out without making any noise. I held my council, and at my return the queen, clad in mourning, her hair hanging about her eyes, and part of it torn off, presented herself before me, and said: 'Sir, I come to beg your majesty not to be surprised to see me in this condition. I have just now received, all at once, three afflicting pieces of news.'

" 'Alas! what is the news, madam?' said I.

" 'The death of the queen my dear mother,' answered she; 'that of the king my father, killed in battle; and that of one of my brothers, who has fallen down a precipice.'

"I was not ill-pleased that she made use of this pretext to hide the true cause of her grief. 'Madam,' said I, 'I am so far from blaming your grief that I assure you I share it. I should very much wonder if you were insensible of so great a loss. Mourn on, your tears are so many proofs of your good nature. I hope, however, that time and reason will moderate your grief.'

"She retired into her apartment, and gave herself wholly up to sorrow, spending a whole year in mourning and afflicting herself. At the end of that time she begged leave of me to build a burying-place for herself, within the bounds of the palace, where she would remain, she told me, to the end of her days. I agreed, and she built a stately palace, with a cupola, that may be seen from hence, and she called it the Palace of Tears. When it was finished she caused the wounded ruffian to be brought thither from the place where she had caused him to be carried the same night, for she had hindered his dying by a drink she gave him. This she carried to him herself every day after he came to the Palace of Tears.

"Yet with all her enchantments she could not cure the wretch. He was not only unable to walk and to help himself, but had also lost the use of his speech, and gave no sign of life but by his looks. Every day she made him two long visits. I was very well informed of all this, but pretended to know nothing of it.

"One day I went out of curiosity to the Palace of Tears to see how the queen employed herself, and going to a place where she could not see me, I heard her speak thus to the scoundrel: 'I am distressed to the highest degree to see you in this condition. I am as sensible as yourself of the tormenting pain you endure, but, dear soul, I constantly speak to you, and you do not answer me; how long will you be silent? Speak only one word. I would prefer the pleasure of always seeing you to the empire of the universe.'

"At these words, which were several times interrupted by her sighs and sobs, I lost all patience, and, showing myself, came up to her, and said, 'Madam, you have mourned enough. It is time to give over this sorrow, which dishonours us both. You have too much forgotten what you owe to me and to yourself.'

" 'Sir,' said she, 'if you have any kindness left for me, I beseech you to put no restraint upon me. Allow me to give myself up to mortal grief, which it is impossible for time to lessen.'

"When I saw that what I said, instead of bringing her to her duty, served only to increase her rage, I gave over, and retired. She continued for two whole years to give herself up to excessive grief.

"I went a second time to the Palace of Tears while she was there. I hid myself again, and heard her speak thus: 'It is now three years since you spoke one word to me. Is it from insensibility or contempt? No, no, I believe nothing of it. O tomb! tell me by what miracle thou becamest the depositary of the rarest treasure that ever was in the world.'

"I must confess I was enraged at these words, for, in short, this creature so much doted upon, this adored mortal, was not such an one as you might imagine him to have been. He was a black Indian, a native of that country. I say I was so enraged that I appeared all of a sudden, and addressing the tomb in my turn, cried, 'O tomb! why dost not thou swallow up this pair of monsters?'

"I had scarcely finished these words when the queen, who sat by the Indian, rose up like a fury. 'Cruel man!' said she, 'thou art the cause of my grief. I have dissembled it but too long; it is thy barbarous hand which hath brought him into this lamentable condition, and thou art so hard-hearted as to come and insult me.'

" 'Yes,' said I, in a rage, 'it was I who chastised that monster according to his deserts. I ought to have treated thee in the same manner. I repent now that I did not do it. Thou hast abused my goodness too long.'

"As I spoke these words I drew out my scimitar, and lifted up my hand to punish her; but she, steadfastly beholding me, said, with a jeering smile, 'Moderate thy anger.' At the same time she pronounced words I did not understand, and added, 'By virtue of my enchantments, I command thee immediately to become half marble and half man.' Immediately I became such as you see me now, a dead man among the living, and a living man among the dead.

"After this cruel magician, unworthy of the name of a queen, had metamorphosed me thus, and brought me into this hall, by another enchantment she destroyed my capital, which was very flourishing and full of people; she abolished the houses, the public places and markets, and reduced it to a pond and desert field, which you may have seen; the fishes of four colours in the pond are the four sorts of people, of different religions, who inhabited the place. The white are the Mussulmans; the red, the Persians, who worship fire; the blue, the Christians; and the yellow, the Jews. The four little hills were the four islands that gave the name to this kingdom. I learned all this from the magician, who, to add to my distress, told me with her own mouth these effects of her rage. But this is not all; her revenge was not satisfied with the destruction of my dominions and the metamorphosis of my person; she comes every day, and gives me over my naked shoulders an hundred blows with an ox-goad, which makes me all over gore; and, when she has done, she covers me with a coarse stuff of goat's-hair, and throws over it this robe of brocade that you see, not to do me honour, but to mock me."

After this, the young king could not restrain his tears; and the sultan's heart was so pierced with the story, that he could not speak one word to comfort him. Presently he said: "Tell me whither this perfidious magician retires, and where may be the unworthy wretch who is buried before his death."

"My lord," replied the prince, "the man, as I have already told you, is in the Palace of Tears, in a handsome tomb in form of a dome, and that palace joins the castle on the side of the gate. As to the magician, I cannot tell precisely whither she retires, but every day at sunrise she goes to see him, after having executed her vengeance upon me, as I have told you; and you see I am not in a condition to defend myself against such great cruelty. She carries him the drink with which she has hitherto prevented his dying, and always complains of his never speaking to her since he was wounded."

"Unfortunate prince," said the sultan, "never did such an extraordinary misfortune befall any man, and those who write your history will be able to relate something that surpasses all that has ever yet been written."

While the sultan discoursed with the young prince, he told him who he was, and for what end he had entered the castle; and thought of a plan to release him and punish the enchantress, which he communicated to him. In the meantime, the night being far spent, the sultan took some rest; but the poor young prince passed the night without sleep, as usual, having never slept since he was enchanted; but he had now some hope of being speedily delivered from his misery.

Next morning the sultan got up before dawn, and, in order to execute his design, he hid in a corner his upper garment, which would have encumbered him, and went to the Palace of Tears. He found it lit up with an infinite number of tapers of white wax, and a delicious scent issued from several boxes of fine gold, of admirable workmanship, all ranged in excellent order. As soon as he saw the bed where the Indian lay, he drew his scimitar, killed the wretch without resistance, dragged his corpse into the court of the castle, and threw it into a well. After this, he went and lay down in the wretch's bed, took his scimitar with him under the counterpane, and waited there to execute his plan.

The magician arrived after a little time. She first went into the chamber where her husband the King of the Black Islands was, stripped him, and beat him with the ox-goad in a most barbarous manner. The poor prince filled the palace with his lamentations to no purpose, and implored her in the most touching manner to have pity on him; but the cruel woman would not give over till she had given him an hundred blows.

"*You* had no compassion," said she, "and you are to expect none from me."

After the enchantress had given the king, her husband, an hundred blows with the ox-goad, she put on again his covering of goat's-hair, and his brocade gown over all; then she went to the Palace of Tears, and, as she entered, she renewed her tears and lamentations; then approaching the bed, where she thought the Indian was: "Alas!" cried she, addressing herself unawares to the sultan; "my sun, my life, will you always be silent? Are you resolved to let me die, without giving me one word of comfort? My soul, speak one word to me at least, I implore you."

The sultan, as if he had waked out of a deep sleep, and counterfeiting the language of the Indians, answered the queen in a grave tone, "There is no strength or power but in God alone, who is almighty."

At these words the enchantress, who did not expect them, gave a great shout, to signify her excessive joy. "My dear lord," cried she, "do I deceive myself? Is it certain that I hear you, and that you speak to me?"

"Unhappy wretch," said the sultan, "art thou worthy that I should answer thee?"

"Alas!" replied the queen, "why do you reproach me thus?"

"The cries," replied he, "the groans and tears of thy husband, whom thou treatest every day with so much indignity and barbarity, hinder me from sleeping night and day. I should have been cured long ago, and have recovered the use of my speech, hadst thou disenchanted him. That is the cause of the silence which you complain of."

"Very well," said the enchantress; "to pacify you, I am ready to do whatever you command me. Would you have me restore him as he was?"

"Yes," replied the sultan, "make haste and set him at liberty, that I be no more disturbed with his cries."

The enchantress went immediately out of the Palace of Tears; she took a cup of water, and pronounced words over it, which caused it to boil, as if it had been on the fire. Then she went into the hall, to the young king her husband, and threw the water upon him, saying, "If the Creator of all things did form thee so as thou art at present, or if He be angry with thee, do not change. But if thou art in that condition merely by virtue of my enchantments, resume thy natural shape, and become what thou wast before."

She had scarcely spoken these words, when the prince, finding himself restored to his former condition, rose up freely, with all imaginable joy, and returned thanks to God.

Then the enchantress said to him, "Get thee gone from this castle, and never return here on pain of death!"

The young king, yielding to necessity, went away from the enchantress, without replying a word, and retired to a remote place, where he patiently awaited the success of the plan which the sultan had so happily begun.

Meanwhile the enchantress returned to the Palace of Tears, and, supposing that she still spoke to the black man, said, "Dearest, I have done what you ordered."

The sultan continued to counterfeit the language of the blacks. "That which you have just now done," said he, "is not sufficient for my cure. You have only eased me of part of my disease; you must cut it up by the roots."

"My lovely black man," replied she, "what do you mean by the roots?"

"Unfortunate woman," replied the sultan, "do you not understand that I mean the town, and its inhabitants, and the four islands, which thou hast destroyed by thy enchantments? The fishes every night at midnight raise their heads out of the pond, and cry for vengeance against thee and me. This is the root cause of the delay of my cure. Go speedily, restore things as they were, and at thy return I will give thee my hand, and thou shalt help me to rise."

The enchantress, filled with hope from these words, cried out in a transport of joy, "My heart, my soul, you shall soon be restored to health, for I will immediately do what you command me." Accordingly she went that moment, and when she came to the brink of the pond, she took a little water in her hand, and sprinkling it, she pronounced some words over the fishes and the pond, and the city was immediately restored. The fishes became men, women, and children; Mahometans, Christians, Persians, or Jews; freemen or slaves, as they were before; every one having recovered his natural form. The houses and shops were immediately filled with their inhabitants, who found all things as they were before the enchantment. The sultan's numerous retinue, who had encamped in the largest square, were astonished to see themselves in an instant in the middle of a large, handsome, and well-peopled city.

To return to the enchantress. As soon as she had effected this wonderful change, she returned with all diligence to the Palace of Tears. "My dear," she cried, as she entered, "I come to rejoice with you for the return of your health: I have done all that you required of me; then pray rise, and give me your hand."

"Come near," said the sultan, still counterfeiting the language of the blacks. She did so. "You are not near enough," said he, "come nearer." She obeyed. Then he rose up, and seized her by the arm so suddenly, that she had not time to discover who it was, and with a blow of his scimitar cut her in two, so that one half fell one way, and the other another. This done, he left the carcass at the place, and going out of the Palace of Tears, he went to look for the young King of the Black Isles, who was waiting for him with great impatience. "Prince," said he, embracing him, "rejoice; you have nothing to fear now; your cruel enemy is dead."

The young prince returned thanks to the sultan in such a manner as showed that he was thoroughly sensible of the kindness that he had done him, and in return, wished him a long life and all happiness. "You may henceforward," said the sultan, "dwell peaceably in your capital, unless you will go to mine, where you shall be very welcome, and have as much honour and respect shown you as if you were at home."

"Potent monarch, to whom I am so much indebted," replied the king, "you think, then, that you are very near your capital?"

"Yes," said the sultan, "I know it; it is not above four or five hours' journey."

"It will take you a whole year," said the prince. "I do believe, indeed, that you came hither from your capital in the time you speak of, because mine was enchanted; but since the enchantment is taken off, things are changed. However, this shall not prevent my following you, were it to the utmost corners of the earth. You are my deliverer, and that I may show you that I shall acknowledge this during my whole life, I am willing to accompany you, and to leave my kingdom without regret."

The sultan was extremely surprised to learn that he was so far from his dominions, and could not imagine how it could be. But the young King of the Black Islands convinced him beyond a possibility of doubt. Then the sultan replied, "It is no matter: the trouble of returning to my own country is sufficiently recompensed by the satisfaction of having obliged you, and by acquiring you for a son; for since you will do me the honour to accompany me, as I have no child, I look upon you as such, and from this moment I appoint you my heir and successor."

The conversation between the sultan and the King of the Black Islands concluded with the most affectionate embraces; after which the young prince was totally taken up in making preparations for his journey, which were finished in three weeks' time, to the great regret of his court and subjects, who agreed to receive at his hands one of his nearest kindred for their king.

At last the sultan and the young prince began their journey, with an hundred camels laden with inestimable riches from the treasury of the young king, followed by fifty handsome gentlemen on horseback, well mounted and dressed. They had a very happy journey; and when the sultan, who had sent couriers to give notice of his delay, and of the adventure which had occasioned it, came near his capital, the principal officers he had left there came to receive him, and to assure him that his long absence had occasioned no alteration in his empire. The inhabitants came out also in great crowds, received him with acclamations, and made public rejoicings for several days.

On the day after his arrival, the sultan gave all his courtiers a very ample account of the events which, contrary to his expectation, had detained him so long. He told them he had adopted the King of the Four Black Islands, who was willing to leave a great kingdom to accompany and live with him; and as a reward for their loyalty, he made each of them presents according to their rank.

As for the fisherman, since he was the first cause of the deliverance of the young prince, the sultan gave him a plentiful fortune, which made him and his family happy for the rest of their days.

THE   END

The vast collection of folk tales from India and the Middle East known as *The Arabian Nights Entertainments* is also called *The Thousand and One Nights* because of the framework in which the tales are set. They are said to be told by Shahrazad (Scheherazade), who beguiles her husband night after night into putting off his plan to kill her until finally he abandons it altogether. Many of the tales were told orally for centuries before being written down, and some are still told by public story-tellers in the Middle East today. They were first introduced into Europe in the early eighteenth century by the French traveller and orientalist, Antoine Galland, who, in translating the stories from a Syrian text, both bowdlerized and adapted them to suit contemporary taste. The first English version, by an unknown writer, was translated from Galland's *Mille et une Nuits* in 1706–8, and it was not until the nineteenth century that a number of translations from the Arabic appeared, of which the best known is that of Sir Richard Burton.

Since the late eighteenth century a number of selections and adaptations of the tales have been made for children. The fourteen stories in this edition include 'Aladdin' and 'Ali Baba', which have become special favourites of children throughout the world.

WILLIAM HEATH ROBINSON (1872–1944) was the youngest of the three artist sons of a wood engraver. Born in Hornsey Rise, north London, he studied at Islington School of Art and briefly at the Royal Academy Schools. His grandfather, Thomas Robinson, had been a book-binder working in Newcastle for the famous wood engraver, Thomas Bewick, and subsequently took up engraving and illustrating himself. It is not surprising, therefore, that all three brothers – Thomas, Charles and William – became book and magazine illustrators. William was still in his twenties when he was commissioned, with other young artists – Helen Stratton, A. D. McCormick, A. L. Davis and A. E. Norbury – to illustrate a collection of stories from *The Arabian Nights*, published in 1899. William's contribution was by far the largest and the best, demonstrating the beauty of line and composition that characterized his illustrations for other literary classics. But now he is chiefly remembered for his humorous draw-ings and the weird contraptions that gave his name to the English language for any mechanical device 'absurdly complicated in design and having a simple function'. At the Memorial Exhibition after his death, one of his few peers in comic drawing, Nicolas Bentley, compared him to Leonardo da Vinci, claiming that Heath Robinson 'had the advantage of Leonardo, in that some of his inventions did at least *look* as if they might have worked'.

ROGER LANCELYN GREEN *The Adventures of Robin Hood*
Illustrated by Walter Crane

King Arthur and his Knights
of the Round Table
Illustrated by Aubrey Beardsley

THE BROTHERS GRIMM *Fairy Tales*
Illustrated by Arthur Rackham

NATHANIEL HAWTHORNE *A Wonder-Book*
Illustrated by Arthur Rackham

JOSEPH JACOBS *English Fairy Tales*
Illustrated by John Batten

WALTER JERROLD *Mother Goose's Nursery Rhymes*
Illustrated by Charles Robinson

RUDYARD KIPLING *The Jungle Book*
Illustrated by Kurt Wiese

Just So Stories
Illustrated by the Author

JEAN DE LA FONTAINE *Fables*
Illustrated by R. de la Nézière

EDWARD LEAR *A Book of Nonsense*
Illustrated by the Author

GEORGE MACDONALD *At the Back of the North Wind*
Illustrated by Arthur Hughes

The Princess and the Goblin
Illustrated by Arthur Hughes

L. M. MONTGOMERY *Anne of Green Gables*
Illustrated by Sybil Tawse

E. NESBIT *The Railway Children*
Illustrated by C. E. Brock

BARONESS ORCZY *The Scarlet Pimpernel*